T0113222

ST. FAMOUS

ST. FAMOUS

A NOVEL

JONATHAN DEE

DOUBLEDAY   New York   London   Toronto   Sydney   Auckland

PUBLISHED BY DOUBLEDAY
a division of Bantam Doubleday Dell Publishing Group, Inc.
1540 Broadway, New York, New York 10036

DOUBLEDAY and the portrayal of an anchor with a dolphin are
trademarks of Doubleday, a division of Bantam Doubleday Dell
Publishing Group, Inc.

Designed by Bonni Leon-Berman

Library of Congress Cataloging-in-Publication Data
  Dee, Jonathan.
    St. Famous / Jonathan Dee.
        p.   cm.
      I. Title.
    PS3554.E355S7   1996   95–8363
    813'.54—dc20   CIP
    ISBN 978-0-385-50750-9

146484122

In memory of John Hersey

A man does not talk to himself quite truly—not even to himself: the happiness or misery that he secretly feels proceeds from causes that he cannot quite explain, because as soon as he raises them to the level of the explicable they lose their native quality. The novelist has a real pull here. He can show the subconscious short-circuiting straight into action (the dramatist can do this too); he can also show it in its relation to soliloquy. He commands all the secret life, and he must not be robbed of this privilege.

—E. M. Forster

1927

ST. FAMOUS

PART ONE

VICTIM'S RIGHTS

SOMEONE—A DISAFFECTED NURSE, PERHAPS, OR AN ORderly, tired of being snapped at and looking to supplement his meager income—must have tipped off one of the journalists that Paul Soloway was leaving the hospital that day; and since media people never manifested singly, a pack of them had been waiting just outside the doors of the Lenox Hill lobby, and now there was a different pack standing in the slush and dim sunshine as the cab pulled up to Paul and Renata's apartment building. Or perhaps it was the same pack in both places, and with their inestimable cunning they had discovered a shortcut between Lenox Hill and West 107th Street that neither the Soloways nor their Slavic cab driver knew anything about. The cabby, anyway, was impressed. "Hey," he said, as the eager men and women huddled around his cab with their cumbersome cameras and portable lights. He looked in his rearview mirror with an effort of memory. "Who are you?"

"If you gotta ask," Paul said, turning to look uneasily at the faces against the windows all around him frozen in a rictus of friendliness. Even as he was speaking, Renata—who was more accustomed to these situations—heedlessly kicked open the door on her side, scattering the journalists like a cloud of bugs. She got out, slammed the door before they could stick their heads in, and—not in anger so much as in a spiteful effort not to give them anything they could print or put on the air—swore like a dock worker as she made her way around the cab to Paul's side. He gave the cabby an extra fifty cents—not a celebrity tip—and slowly swung himself around on the seat. He opened the door, to a new frenzy of shouting; grimacing with pain, he put his good leg and his cane on the wet sidewalk, took Renata's arm, and lifted himself to his feet.

The questions they were shouting signified pity and caring; yet they themselves made no effort to get out of his path as he negotiated his way toward home. In fact, the collective if not the individual will seemed to be to stop him in his tracks, to force him to stare into the lights and answer them. How are you feeling? Are you happy? Are you angry? Have you seen your children yet? How are you feeling?

Paul did not look at them; his focus was on the sidewalk, looking for anything that might trip him, that might lie waiting to break his hip or his knee again and send him back to the awful hospital bed. He didn't even think to enjoy the day, which, gray though it was, represented his first exposure to the outdoors in almost eight weeks. He felt humiliated by his infirmity, a private humiliation that had nothing to do with the cameras. And it was possible to be both grateful for and a little embarrassed by his wife's firm command of the whole ridiculous situation. With one hand on his arm and the other swinging his bag of books and toiletries from the hospital like a machete through jungle growth, she cleared them a path to the front door. "Later!" she yelled. "Later, you cocksuckers, you scumbags!" They shied away from her, with exclamations of what sounded to Paul like genuine surprise.

At last they were in the dingy lobby, the door locked behind them, the voices choked off, though a muffled note or two of frustration still reached them. Renata breathed deeply and shook her wrists to calm herself as they waited for the elevator; she glanced over at Paul and saw him turning his head to take it all in, the chipped paint, the water-stained ceiling, the cracked floor tiles, the mailboxes with their broken locks, the building directory with its mismatched or missing letters. He was smiling. The vision of neglect, the smell of decay, were pleasures not only because they were familiar, but because they were so gloriously not the hospital—the tiny room with its changing cast of roommates behind the heavy curtain, the electric bed, the plastic water jug, the antiseptic corridor it had taken him five painful, maddening weeks just to learn to reach its featureless end.

In the elevator, out of sight, they kissed. "Welcome home," she said, appending an ironic smile as a hedge against her own sudden swell of emotion; then she added, solicitously, "Tired?" "No, no," he lied. "I'm okay." He stepped out at the third floor; Renata had to go up to seven to collect the kids, whom she had decided to spare the media assault, from Mrs. Perez, their babysitter. "See you in a minute," she said as the door closed again.

So Paul had the first few moments of homecoming to himself. He hadn't used his keys in eight weeks: yet another measure of strangeness. After the door swung open, he stood still for a few seconds, as if waiting for permission to enter. Taped to the edge of the low bookcase in the front hallway was a hand-lettered sign that said, "Welcome Home Daddy!!!" It hurt him to bend over, so he pulled the sign off the shelf and looked at it up close; as a little flourish to go beside the uneven lettering was a sticker of Donatello, one of the Ninja Turtles. Paul was surprised to notice himself moving the little sign back and forth in front of his eyes, trying to make it come into focus, as an old man might do. His vision was not going to be the same.

The signs, it turned out, were all over the apartment, on the old TV, on the bathroom mirror, taped to the chain that turned on the overhead light in the kitchen, everywhere. Each welcomed him home, and each was enlivened, at least to a four-year-old's eye, by a single illustration—one of the Turtles, or Thomas the Tank Engine, or, somewhat alarmingly, a crude drawing of Paul himself in bed with a thermometer in his mouth. He was able to collect five of them before all the walking began to get to him, and he stopped in the center of the book-lined living room to catch his breath.

And then, with his older son's messages in one hand and

a metal cane in the other, the thing that he was able to
forget now for longer and longer periods came back to
him with such force that his mouth formed a soundless *o*:
that there had been a time not so long ago when he had
had very good reason to expect that he was never going to
see any of this, not his home, not his wife, not his two
sons, ever again. . . . He caught his breath when he heard
Renata's keys in the door.

"Easy," Renata cautioned, "easy!" but the boys had
slipped around her legs and were running toward their un-
stable father as fast as they could. Peter, the older, had
enough presence of mind to slow up a bit, but Leo was just
barely three and had only two gears of locomotion, walking and a full sprint which tested his balance. Paul threw
down his cane and quickly picked them both up, one in
each arm, because he could not yet kneel down as he liked
to do and because he did not want them to hug his legs, as
they liked to do.

"Did you see the signs?" Peter asked.

"I sure did. They're beautiful. I don't know if I found
them all yet, though."

"I made them," Leo lied, and if they had been out of
their father's arms Peter would have punched him for this
selfishness; but Paul said, "Well, I know you're happy to
have me home too," and gave Peter a knowing, grown-up
look, and the slight was forgotten that quickly.

"Daddy, Mrs. Perez has Super Nintendo?" Peter said.
"Or her son has it and he's in grade seven. And he let me
try it once and this—"

"Paul?" Renata said, in one of those mysterious tones of
voice that passed over Peter's head like a high-tension
wire. He looked up at his father's face, and sure enough,
there was that little smile that told him he had missed
something, that something was going on outside of his understanding.

"Okay," Renata said briskly, "come on, kids," and she

walked over and took them one by one off their father. Peter was still studying Paul's face, and Paul knew it, but he still couldn't keep the pain out of his smile as he searched for the cane again. So that's what it was, Peter said to himself. His mother had given the boys a warning about being very careful with Daddy as she collected them from Mrs. Perez (indeed, she had given them that warning at least once a day for the last three days), but he hadn't really been able to connect this idea of being careful with anything in his bank of imagination and experience until now. There was something dislocating about it, even though he knew his father's fragility was only supposed to last for a few weeks, something strange, and he could tell that it was strange, as opposed to simply being new, because of that inauthentic expression on his father's face. He was trying to keep something from them. Leo, of course, lived at a level beneath all of this. His father was nature itself; he might be funny, or frightening, or even boring, but there was no way he could be not himself. When Leo's feet were placed on the floor, he ran over to the window.

"Want to go lie down?" Renata said. Paul nodded, feeling defeated and angry, but also filled with a sudden sweet longing for their own bed. "Can you get the Vicodin out of my bag?" he said as he walked slowly into the hall.

"Whoa!" Peter said. Renata turned and saw both boys with their faces pressed to the window. Peter began trying to open it, and even though there was no way he could do so without a key, she came over and gently pulled them back. As she did, she saw the upturned faces and cameras of half a dozen reporters, still camped out by the front door. She rolled her eyes.

By the time she got to the bedroom with the Vicodin and a glass of water, Paul's eyes were closed, though he still panted with the effort of getting himself into bed. She woke him to take the pill, knowing that his pain was always worsened by the involuntary movements of his sleep. She left the door open an inch or two, just in case he called out.

The boys were a little hard to control at first, but she knew they were just coming down from the natural excitement of having their father back. They were really very good kids, she said to herself; within half an hour, Leo was asleep in his own bed and Peter, who usually played quietly in any case, was absorbed in a book, mumbling the words to himself in the same fairy-tale cadences his parents used, as if that were the way the words themselves were written. Renata, while she thought of it, went into the kitchen, opened the silverware drawer, and pulled out everything—the letters, the bills, and the four full answering machine tapes—that she had hidden in there, not wanting Paul to lay eyes on them in his first hours home.

At six, she poured herself a glass of wine and, hoping against hope, sat down to watch the local news. They didn't lead with it; but then, about ten minutes into the broadcast, there she was on the screen, guiding her frail-looking husband, her face in a contortion she couldn't believe—snarling, her nostrils flaring, protective, dangerous.

"Later," she heard herself yell. "Later, you scumbags!"

"Oh, fantastic," she muttered, and thought of Paul's mother watching the news out in Connecticut. She would have to make a mental note to cross "scumbag" off her list of untransmittable epithets. She had a sip of wine. "New frontiers in television," she said.

His office was near the bathroom, which meant that there was a good chance of someone walking past his door every three or four minutes; so Edward Garland, when his pacing brought him to that end of the small square room, gently pushed the door shut. Let everyone think he was on an important call. He stood and leaned back against it for a while, arms folded across his stomach, looking without seeing through the ungenerous, begrimed window. It was not an office made for pacing—it was only twelve feet from end to end, and to go even that far you had to detour around the desk—but somehow he had picked up the habit anyway, in his five years there, whereas before he had considered himself insusceptible to stress.

He was having an ethical crisis, one well beyond the point at which he might have asked any one of his colleagues at the agency for advice—advice that, given the nature of the problem, could not have been untouched by jealousy or competitiveness. Nor, though the temptation was much stronger, did he want to go to his boss, Andrea Bayley. Andy rarely paused even a moment before coming to any business decision; and on the few occasions when she did, when confronted with the kind of quandary that would have left Garland insomniac, the pause would last just long enough for her to look down thoughtfully into her lap and twist her wedding ring once or twice around her long finger before giving an invariably sage answer. This one, Garland felt sure, would have been a ring-twister; and, impressed as he was by her every move, he was terribly curious to know what she would recommend. But no, he had to fight that down. The whole idea was to handle it himself from beginning to end, to present it to her as a *fait accompli* which would bring the agency a five-figure commission, to set himself apart from his coworkers who ran to her for counsel on every puny negotiation—in short, to impress her, as Garland lived to do in a way that sometimes went beyond mere concern for his career. By any measure a mogul in the world of publishing, Andy had turned her own maternal good nature into a formidable weapon—calling everyone, for instance, from Garland to Rupert Murdoch, "sweetie" without ever giving offense; the remarkable thing about her considerable power was how lightly she wielded it. Garland, who, in part because he was slightly overweight, tended to sweat when things

cause Paul was demanding—far from it, he was downright uncommunicative—but because his seriousness turned out to be an almost insuperable obstacle to his own success. From the day Paul signed on, Garland had bent over backwards—knowing, from their lunch, that the Soloways were nearly broke—to get him magazine assignments, interviews with authors or actors, even an anonymous horoscope job. He turned them all down, sometimes with a note of disgust in his voice which he fought unsuccessfully to disguise, as if his agent had suggested whoring or volunteering for medical experiments. Nothing appealed to him. It was especially embarrassing for Garland to have to go back to the magazine editors whom he had sold so hard on this complete unknown and try to explain why the proposal they had spent so much time hammering out wouldn't be right after all. The only thing that seemed sufficient to hold Paul's attention was his own novel, which he worked on constantly, which grew and grew in uncertain directions but never seemed discernibly closer to being finished. In their twenty months as agent and client, Garland had yet to make back in commissions the cost of that initial lunch.

But now. Now, like some fairy-tale prince, like someone from a business school textbook, his heroic patience, his astounding foresight in picking this obscure author from the vast forest of obscure authors, was going to be rewarded. Now he and Paul Soloway, in a way that was too extraordinary to be pure chance, were sitting on a book proposal that, though born of misfortune, was going to make Paul rich, that was going to engrave Garland's name with one lightning-stroke on the New York literary map, that was going to rocket him ahead of those meek losers in their offices on either side of his, and maybe even set him up in the inevitable retirement arrangements of his approving boss and mentor.

The problem was, he didn't think Paul was going to want to do it.

At least, he told himself, not right off the bat. He knew Paul would reject the idea, though he didn't know exactly why; he couldn't hear the precise words Paul would say, but he could hear clearly that tone of voice, at once apologetic and revolted, anxious to get off the phone. But this was no five-hundred-dollar magazine assignment. Soloway had a family; he had his children to think about. Once he heard what kind of money they were discussing, Garland felt, there was just no way he could turn it down.

Still, the fact was that Soloway's own touchy earnestness, and the sexiness of this imaginary book, meant that the usual order of business was going to have to be reversed: the publisher wouldn't need any convincing at all; it was the author to whom Garland was going to have to give the hard sell. This one was different, Garland had been repeating to himself all morning; this was a unique negotiation. And on the basis of its uniqueness, he was going to get an offer on the book before even proposing to Paul that he write it.

What sent him pacing through his cage of an office, though, what had him checking under his new black cardigan for excessive sweat stains, was not the notion that there was anything wrong, in a moral sense, with this strategy. He hated the nineteenth-century atmosphere of most book deals, the patronage and gentility which usually wound up costing the poor underconfident writer the money he deserved. No other business he could think of had rules that weren't there to be broken, or at any rate meant to evolve. Those rules were for timid thumbsuckers like his colleagues at Bayley. No, what brought him, if he thought about it too hard, to the point of hyperventilation was the enormous practical downside for him, personally, if this whole scheme didn't come off. Imagine if Bob Spain at Copeland made a six-figure offer for a book, getting approval from his own board, and then discovered that the property did not exist outside the imagination of some junior agent he'd never heard of. It wouldn't be beyond him, at least judging from stories of uncertain provenance that Garland had heard, to come over to the Bayley office unannounced and ream him out right there in front of his open-mouthed coworkers and amazed boss. It could conceivably cost him his job.

The walls of his office were lined with cheap particle-board bookshelves from Conran's on Lexington Avenue. The shelves were half filled with books and magazines, but Garland had not fooled himself with them. They were there just to take up space; they were remainder copies of books by Bayley's less successful clients, or obscure new novels that junior editors had brought to lunch dates with him as unconvincing evidence that their own careers were on the rise, or even books he had brought from home. Not one of them was a book that he himself had been instrumental in bringing into the world. He thought of Andy Bayley, whose office at the other end of the hall was four times the size of his but whose every inch of shelf space, floor to ceiling, was crammed with copies of some of the best-selling and most important books of the last thirty years, books that were quite often adoringly dedicated to her by their authors, books, some of them, that had made Garland, as a college student, understand that literature was not a preserved corpse but a vital enterprise, worth an ambitious young man's labor if anything was. He thought about how many years lay between his tiny, infertile work space and that glorious den, just thirty feet away, where his boss sat with her hands behind her head, smiling the beatific smile of one whose life has furthered her love.

Bob, he said to himself yet again, we met once at a *Paris Review* party for Julian Barnes. You might remember we talked about my beginning to take on some of my own clients. Well, by sheer coincidence really—and you're the only one I'm going to with this—one of my oldest clients happens to be Paul Soloway. Right, the same guy. Did you know he was a writer? I think it was in some of the early press accounts. Quite a good one, too. How about that?

He wiped his hands on the slick armrests of his chair, took a deep breath, and dialed Copeland Simonds. Spain's assistant put him right through.

"Bob?" he said. "It's Ned Garland, at Andy Bayley." Always go with the nickname. It's a sign of real power, to feel comfortable going with the nickname.

It seemed to Paul, in his first few days home, that he could feel himself recovering almost from moment to moment, not speedily but inexorably, whereas in the hospital, with nothing to do but inventory his healing body for progress, he had been able to detect in himself only the same torpor day after day. Now, his head hurt less, he ate more, he moved from bed to chair or from chair to bathroom in a new personal-best time every few hours. The one exception was his leg. The injury was so deep there, he supposed, that any mere improvement of his spirits was too remote, too modern in a way, to reach it. It was going to have to follow its own laws, speaking to him from time to time in an atavistic language of sharp, peremptory pain, and there was nothing he could do about it. In another week or so he would have to start returning to the hospital twice weekly for physical therapy. It was a depressing prospect, to say nothing of the cab fare which, for the Soloways, was not a budgeted expense; but Renata's insurance company had politely refused to pay for any in-home therapist.

His good spirits, he noticed, were not diminished even on that first Monday morning when he sat in his green flannel pajamas in the patched recliner by the living room window and watched, like an old home movie, the farce-paced preparations of Renata, Peter, and Leo for work and school. He wasn't concerned about being left alone. A surprising measure of his comfort, it seemed, was derived simply from being surrounded by his things—the hundreds of haphazardly shelved books, the small oak desk in the corner with his typewriter on it, the drawers full of his

now that you're back home, and I'm sorry to bother you, but we're of course busy putting together our case against Mr. Hartley and his cohorts, so when you do feel up to it, would you please call me. I have just a few questions for now. 555-7884. Thank you."

At the sound of the name Hartley, Paul felt a flash of anger and residual fear, but it passed quickly. He looked back at the manuscript in its box. The first two thirds of the top page were blank white space, a kind of affectation under the circumstances, something he had done only because it made the text look more like that of a printed book. Even the heavy, typewritten print was similarly thrilling. It made the words seem substantial. He read the opening paragraph, though he could easily have recited it from memory, having reworked it, both subtly and fundamentally, twenty times, or thirty, or maybe more.

I was eight years old when I understood for the first time the compulsion to remember; I recall it as a fall Saturday afternoon, in a house silenced by tragedy, that I wound up spending in a heroic, strained effort to think further and further backward, wombward even, and I would not accept that it couldn't be done. My birth was the moment of the birth of a consciousness, after all, and there in the privacy of my suburban bedroom, newly fatherless, having exhausted books and pictures and other models of escape and explanation, the idea that any moment of that consciousness might be permanently unrecoverable sent me into a panic—as it sends me still.

The sonority of words! He had not gone this long without looking at his work in progress since—well, he could not think of a time. He was always struggling, in these rereadings, to flush out his mind, to make himself a blank, to imitate his own projected readers and see this prose as it really was. After two months, this was still not a perfectly objective reading, but it was as close, perhaps, as he was ever going to come. The original rhythm was restored to those laboriously tinkered-with sentences. The horrible intrusion of the world on his work was, in this small way, also a blessing. A wave of anticipation rode through him, mingled, though, with a wave of great fatigue, brought on by the complex emotions of the morning and by the Vicodin he had taken with breakfast. It would be some time, he could see, before he could really get back to work.

Outside it was a brilliant day. The sun streamed in through the finger-printed windows, and he could hear the melting slush and ice running noisily off the roof. Maybe "taxing" is a better word than "strained," Paul thought, but his eyes were already closing.

The phone rang. "Paul, it's Ned. I hope you're doing well, I left a few messages for Renata but I'm sure she's been just swamped. Listen, call me as soon as you feel up to it, I've got something very important to tell you about. It's great to have you back at home, by the way. Talk to you soon."

At the sound of his agent's voice, his heartbeat quickened a bit, as it always did, but he did not open his eyes. That voice was the voice of his future, he always felt, the voice of public affairs, of the outside world about which his feelings were so clouded. In his dreamy state, he imagined Garland was talking about the novel. He listened to the tape rewind itself. Soon he was asleep in the bright room.

Renata spent the day in a state of distraction, concentrating not on her work but on every ringing phone within earshot, and on the sentence that followed each "Hello, Photo Archive." If that sentence was, "Just a second, I'll see if she's in," then she listened even harder, trying to expel the image of her husband back in the hospital or, worse, still sprawled helplessly in the apartment. He might have tripped on the rug, or he might have become dizzy from his strong medication and fallen and hit his head. Or it might have been something even less obvious and more sinister, something that had been hiding like a bomb since the blows to Paul's head, an aneurysm or embolism or whatever the hell it was. She had a phone at her own desk

chance to live like normal people. She had seen those tab-loid shows, and sincerely loathed them, and had wondered what could induce people to divest themselves of any shred of complexity or dignity, to lay themselves open in the most lascivious possible public forum. Now perhaps she knew. How bad could it be? she said to herself, even though she knew full well what her answer to Callahan would have to be. How bad? Paul of course would never do it. But Christ, at this point, for four thousand dollars I'd let this guy come over and do me right on the desk—

"Renata?"

"Yes, I'm here. Listen, I don't know how many times I have to say this. All of you people always have this expression on your face, or in your voice, like you've come to save us, like you've come to rescue us from our own private lives. But the fact is, you people have descended at the very hardest time of our entire lives, and you've made it many times harder. I don't know how other people are fooled, I really don't, but it's crystal clear to me that whatever you might say, you don't care about me at all. In fact, you could not possibly have any less regard for me than you do. I'm not interested in your offer. We're going to get our lives back together, and we're going to do it privately. You can't watch. Now please don't call here again."

"Well," Callahan said, completely unruffled, "if you do change your mind—"

She did not like hanging up on people, but she had learned to do it. Her face felt hot. She saw Rhonda was staring at her. She was thinking how the speech she had just delivered was delivered, in a sense, to Paul, or for him —to pacify him, somehow—even though he would never hear it. She was curious about this. It was as if he had, in some way, taken over the role of her own conscience.

At three, she had to go to her boss and explain that she had to leave early to pick up her older son at school.

"Usually Paul does it," she said, anguished and abject, "and he probably will be able to start again in a couple weeks, but he's too weak right now, and the sidewalks are still icy. . . ." She trailed off.

"All right," Anthony said, though it was clearly not all right; he was struggling not to show her his own panicked calculations of how he would get the day's work done without her, and the consideration that showed moved Renata so much that she felt like reaching out and hugging him. "All right. That's fine. Can I ask you, though, is there any way you could maybe get in early tomorrow morning?"

She knew the virtual impossibility of this but did not want to concede it. She was, by now, just as loath to worry him as she was to get herself into further trouble. "I will," she said. "I'll drop the kids off a little early at school. I'll get in as soon as I can."

He looked her over and smiled sadly.

In the elevator the worst possible thing happened. Even after all this time, she still looked involuntarily at the lights above the door as she approached, and passed, the fifteenth floor, feeling a kind of lightness when the rhythm of the bell announcing the passage of each floor remained unbroken. Sometimes, of course, her elevator did stop on fifteen; this time, though, when the doors opened, Brian himself was standing right there, all alone, wearing his overcoat and holding his briefcase. They looked at each other in awkward surprise for a moment, before he stepped in and leaned back in simulated relaxation against the rear wall of the car, two feet away from her. Renata hoped wildly that someone would come running to catch the elevator, but the door slid shut and they were the only two passengers.

Brian was five or so years younger than she, and the more dressed up he was, the younger he looked. He wore his black hair moussed straight back in an aggressive, disagreeable style that allowed you to see the track of the comb on his head. Renata wondered if it was too ridiculous to hope that the ride would pass in silence.

"I saw on the news the other day that Paul's back home," Brian said. "That's wonderful news."

"Yes, it is," she said. They spoke like spies, their eyes focused on something they did not really see.

"I haven't seen you," he said, "so I really never got to tell you how sorry I am about that, about what happened to him. It's, it's—"

"I know. Everybody's sorry. I know." Then, more softly, "Thank you."

The bell kept to its slow tempo.

"Although, maybe it's bad of me to say, but I think I feel sorrier for you, you know? Maybe just because I know you. But my thoughts are mostly about how hard it must have been for you."

The note of the invisible machinery's hum glided lower, and they touched down at last on the first floor. Renata took a step forward, then had to wait for two more embarrassing seconds before the door finally opened on the traffic and echo of the lobby.

"Listen—"

"Please don't," she said without turning. She walked quickly into the crowd. He stepped out just before the elevator closed; he had one sudden glimpse of her at the front door, struggling to tie her scarf, before he lost her again.

In Los Angeles, her back to the broad window just one floor above the storefronts on Santa Monica Boulevard, Amy Rubinstein sat at her overcrowded white Formica desk reading a novel. She read with a sense of guilt; not because she was worried that anyone seeing her would think she was goofing off—on the contrary, reading was her job—but because she had known more than an hour ago, along about page twenty, that this book was all wrong for their purposes, far too static and internal and memory-driven to get any sort of movie treatment out of, yet she had continued to read it for the surreptitious purpose of pleasure. It was a first novel, by a young man about Amy's own age, a kind of impressionistic account of growing up gay. The narrative moved dreamily back and forth in time, and similarly back and forth over some boundary of realism, with dead characters reappearing as if nothing had happened to them. More than anything, it was the writing that held her attention; each sentence was a kind of jewel, with that perfect sense of rhythm and resolution coming with each period, a resolution experienced physically, like music to a deaf person. Sitting in a carpeted downtown office reading books was too far removed from making movies—which is what she had come out here to do—for her liking; but she was not long out of college, her career goals were at the far end of a long road, and so she took her pleasures, as right now, where she could find them.

But she knew this stolen hour was about to end when she heard the voice of her boss—Frank Pickert, of Frank Pickert Productions—rise suddenly through the open door of his office. Pickert spent his entire working day either on the telephone or at lunch, and the sound of his voice was a constant drone, like the air conditioning, which one noticed only when it modulated. A moment ago it had gone up precipitously, both in pitch and in volume. Amy sighed, and turned to look out the window at the sun lying heavily on the vacant sidewalks. When she heard Pickert coming out of his office, she flipped quickly back to page five of the novel and started reading again.

Pickert came and sat on the edge of her desk, pretending to read over her shoulder. Young, balding, expensively fit, Pickert was a petulant, foul-mouthed boss, a slave—like his employees—to the winds of his own temper. One of the least appealing of his attributes was his belief in his own unpredictability, when in fact he was as easy to read as a road sign. Just now, Amy thought, Pickert believed he was concealing his anger from her, the better to surprise

itself off the desk and carried it under his arm as he went to shut his door. Once, months ago, he had come near to suggesting to Andy that the offices be updated with cordless phones; but he was afraid that his explanation of why he needed one when he worked in a space that was twelve feet across would make him appear too neurotic, so he had never gone through with it. He pulled open the window.

"What about?" he said pleasantly, as if it were the most natural question in the world. "Well, it would be a nonfiction book, dealing with your firsthand account of your, of your experiences."

"My experiences?"

"Your recent, near-tragic experiences."

Paul, finally understanding what was being asked of him, picked his cane up off the floor and began tapping it rhythmically against the side of the dusty chair. An instinctive fear was beginning to circulate through him. "From when to when?" he said.

Garland wondered now if Paul was still just being naive, or if he wasn't actively and uncharacteristically trying to make him uncomfortable. He was taken aback, and reflexively began to lose his hold on his temper. "Well, come on, Paul," he said, still friendly. "Beginning with the abduction, or the events immediately leading up to it, through your two days as a hostage, and through your liberation by the police. Ending with, I don't know, your reunion with your family, or your coming home from the hospital. However you'd want to do it."

Garland, as he looked down at the lights blinking erratically on his phone, had one quick ephemeral flash of terror —he was too far out on his professional limb already. Of course Paul had his standards, unusual but still predictable. The thing was to have him balance those standards against the benefits that were at stake for everybody. He was, after all, a family man.

"Why would I want to write a book like that?" he said.

"Why? Well, let's be frank, the big reason is for the money. But there's also—"

"But money—" He stopped. "Ned, I know I must be a big disappointment to you sometimes."

"Oh, no—"

"I know you really have my best interests at heart, and I feel like you must think I'm ungrateful. But money and writing . . . it's tricky. I mean I'm happy to do something frivolous to make some money so that I can afford to write for a while. But writing a book *in order* to make money—it just makes a joke out of wanting to write at all. I had to reconcile myself a long time ago to the idea that I'm never going to make a lot of money as a novelist." (This wasn't strictly true, he realized; he dreamed of being enriched by a large following nearly every day.) "I've got nothing against winning the lottery, you know what I mean; but getting rich just isn't a big motivator for me. Does that make any sense?"

"Well, no, not completely. That is, I understand why you wouldn't want to produce some piece of hack work just for the money. But why is something, by definition, a piece of hack work *just because* you get a lot of money for it?"

Garland listened, but he heard nothing except a fire engine passing somewhere near Paul's window.

"I mean I'm surprised," he went on. "I could understand your being hesitant about giving up any more of your privacy than you've already had to. But then I would think that you'd *want*, with your skills, to tell the story of what's happened to you. It's a great story—great in the sense that it has a lot of complicated elements to it. It's a story—I don't know, it's a story of bravery, of a man's character being tested by hardship and pain, a story of survival, a real modern urban nightmare for a lot of people that you not only lived out but survived. Good and evil, face to face. You're an ordinary person to whom an extraordinary thing has happened; is that not the basis for a good book—for any number of good books? And I would think that you'd be frustrated by the sight of this story, which *belongs* to you, being taken away from you by the newspapers and TV, and told in such a shabby, sensational, oversimplified manner. You're a fiction writer, and so I know it's only natural that you pride yourself on the power of your imagination. But life, *your* life, has handed you this great story to tell—you're the *only* one in a position to tell it. Are you really going to pass it up? Just because there's money involved?"

Though Paul chafed a bit at being described as an ordinary person, he was still surprised that Ned was able to make such a good case. Already he felt very much on the defensive in this fight that, as he now recalled, Renata had once jokingly predicted, but that he hadn't understood until now would actually come looking for him.

"The thing is," he said, "I don't agree. I don't agree that it's a great story, or a complicated one. It's very simple—so simple that I'm not really sure what more you think can be said about it, to tell the truth. And my privacy doesn't enter into it, actually, because this was something which played itself out in public in the first place. Which is why I don't have any desire to write about it. Which is why I also don't agree, even, that it's my story. I can't accept the idea that this chance occurrence constitutes what my story is, what the story of my life is. Events, randomness, do not get to make that decision for me—randomness and art are completely at odds. And randomness is *absolutely* the essence of what happened to me. The whole nature of it is that it could have happened to anyone. It's a cheesy story of random violence, and I couldn't make it into *Crime and Punishment* even if I wanted to. It's that arbitrariness that defines it, and so it *already* belongs to the public, you see? Some events just *are* shabby and sensational and uninteresting, and they get the treatment, the existence, they deserve. So don't say it's my story. I don't want it."

"You don't care that in six months some book called *The Paul Soloway Story* is going to show up in the stores, a book you've never been consulted about, a book that I'm a hundred percent sure would disgust and embarrass you?"

Paul's momentum was indeed halted by this image. "Can somebody do that?" he said.

"It's done all the time. They'd much rather do it with your participation, because it's easier for them and because it's a cinch to promote, but even without you they'll absolutely go ahead. They can use news accounts, anything in the public domain. Court transcripts especially—"

"There may well not be any court transcripts," Paul said. "I talked to the DA's office just yesterday, and they think they're going to get the guy to plead out. Which is fine with me."

Garland's attention was so diverted by this that he walked right into the corner of his desk. No court transcripts? Without a trial, Paul became virtually the sole source of information about the case. This one idle remark had just raised their price dramatically. But he had to concentrate.

"Well, then they'll do without," he said, rubbing his leg. "It'll mean that the book will be written as much by lawyers as by reporters, in order to protect themselves from being sued by you, but they're accustomed to that. If they feel there's money at stake, they won't hesitate. And once that book's in print, it becomes a legitimate property to sell to TV or the movies. You know how vulgar something like that's bound to be. That doesn't frighten you?"

Alone in his quiet apartment, wearing his pajamas and sitting in his piebald recliner, Paul felt suddenly besieged —a warrior whose only remaining option was a beautiful death. "Of course it bothers me," he said petulantly. "But if I have to go through that, I'll go through it. What is the life of a book like that? Two months, maybe? A couple of humiliating months, and everyone will be on to the next piece of true-crime garbage. Whereas if I *wrote* the book, that act would dog me forever. How could I ever publish another book after that and have any expectation that it would be taken seriously? It would end my life as a writer. I only hope it hasn't effectively done that anyway. My only chance of not becoming some punchline, some Trivial Pursuit answer, like Kitty Genovese or Son of Sam, is just to lie low and trust in the short memory of lowbrow culture."

"But what I don't get," Garland said, "is why you think that this book about your real-life trials would be bad even if it were written by you. Isn't there a strong chance it would be good? Wouldn't it be a challenge, in a way, to make it good? You talked about randomness as the essence of what happened to you; why wouldn't that belong in the book?" He cringed to think of Bob Spain overhearing him now. He felt his arguments were already becoming more desperate and arbitrary.

But the question of quality appealed to Paul's vanity, it seemed, and so he did not treat it as frivolous. "Well, but," he said, "no matter how good it was, any publisher would do its very best to make it look and sound like trash, right? The jacket, the advertising, all that. Wouldn't they?"

"We could negotiate some say in that for you," Garland said after a moment.

"But even aside from that. The point is," he said, closing his eyes tightly, trying to decide what the point was. "The point is, even if I wrote this book and wrote it well, that would be acknowledging it as *The Paul Soloway Story*. You see? It would be an elevation of the whole experience, which is one I frankly would love to forget. It would be to accept the sensibility not of history or of art, but of the *New York Post*, as my final judgment. And I don't accept it. I get to decide what record I leave. That's the whole impulse of art, and it's one which I intend to honor." Paul was warming to his topic. "I mean, you've read my novel. You know what I'm talking about."

The sensibilities of history and art? Garland suddenly felt close to nauseous with fear. He decided to play his last card, even though he already had a diminishing sense of its significance.

"Paul," he said. "In the interest of fairness, I have to tell you that Copeland has offered you an advance of one hundred and eighty-five thousand dollars to write this book."

Paul knew it was a lot of money, but only in the same vague way he knew that, say, a million francs was a lot of money. He did know enough, though, to feel the first stirring of fear that Renata was going to find out about this.

"Money's not the issue," he said.

"Yeah, I thought it might not be," Garland said.

"Listen, I hope you're not upset with me. It's just that these are important questions to me. I try to live my life a certain way, and—"

And Ned had a sudden brainstorm. Clearly, Soloway had not talked all this out yet; clearly, it was important to him on some level that his agent come around fully to his point of view. These aesthetic issues were wholly animate and essential to him—so essential he would have thought nothing of debating them for another hour. And the debate did indeed have to be prolonged, if there was to be any chance of changing his mind.

Garland held the phone a few inches away from his face. "What? Oh, okay, thanks," he said. "Listen, Paul, I'm sorry, but I have to run. I have another call. We'll talk more about this later, okay?"

"But I haven't told—"

"Bye-bye." He hung up. The sudden panic in Paul's voice told him that he had gotten what he wanted—a lack of resolution. He grabbed his jacket, patting it to be sure the cigarettes were in there, and headed for the elevators, to have a five-minute smoke outdoors in peace. His face was hot; but his spontaneous acumen, in the face of near disaster, had made him more optimistic somehow. You might just make it after all, he said wryly to himself.

Paul hung up the phone. He stood, went to the kitchen for some soda, then sat back in the easy chair. He worried that he hadn't really managed to say what he meant; his lips continued to move silently for some minutes, forming arguments with forces that were disinclined to engage him, or even to show themselves at all. Through the open window came remote sounds, radios, cars, children, arguing, street life. He got up again, fetched the box with his manuscript in it, and sat wearily for a while, staring into space, with the weight of the thing in his lap, unsure of his existence in this world.

They let Victor Hartley sit at the long scarred table without his ankles chained, which he appreciated. He had to have his hands cuffed, but they were cuffed in front of him, which made all the difference in the world; nothing in all of prison life made him feel more vulnerable than having his wrists bound behind him, knowing that anyone, friend, enemy, or stranger, who took a notion to punch him in the stomach or kick him in the balls could do it and there was absolutely no way in the world to stop it. They let Victor have these modest liberties not only because there was an armed guard standing casually by the door behind him, just a few feet away, while he waited. This blank room, where prisoners met at the long table with their attorneys, was so deep within the terrible entrails of the OBCC, in the Rikers Island complex, that it had not seen direct sunlight since the day the walls were put up; even if he could somehow contrive to get past the guard, there were doors and doors for probably a quarter mile in any direction. At any one of them another guard, knowing he was out of earshot of the other inmates, would shoot you right through the face even if you had a change of heart and dropped to your knees to ask for mercy. No one would ever know about it. It happened all the time.

The room had been painted lazily perhaps twenty times, or forty or sixty, in the same shade of sky blue, without ever being scraped down, so that the walls had a pocked, uneven, almost swollen look, like walls in a cartoon or a drug hallucination. Government work, it was—robotic and uncaring. Victor had worked for a summer as a painter, and he would have been fired on the spot for such a careless job. Of course he'd been fired anyway. He was only seventeen at the time, and not prone to keep his mind on what was in front of him for very long. He remembered the oddly illicit sensation of going into strangers' apartments, all over the city, and just setting up your shop. He would look quickly, furtively, at the unimaginably wide variety of stuff people had in their homes, ugly statues, gigantic plants, sofas that looked like they cost three thousand dollars, before his boss would bark at him and together they would throw the dropcloth over it all, the same spattered dropcloth covering all those private belongings, all over the city.

The guard was playing with the chain of keys looped through his belt. The lawyer was already ten minutes late, and they were both bored, but they didn't say anything to each other. That was all right. The guards gave you orders all day, but you could be pretty sure that any time any one of them made any small talk with you it was only because he was trying to trick you into saying something he could hit or otherwise punish you for. Victor's fury at his lawyer was mounting. Not that he was being inconvenienced, of course—in fact, if he could have thought calmly about it, he would have appreciated the lawyer's tardiness, because these ten minutes sitting in silence and near-solitude compared very favorably to the atmosphere back in the cell block. But Victor looked for any excuse to cultivate his anger, particularly these days, particularly where the snide, ignorant, bumbling court-appointed lawyer was concerned.

And the maddening thing was, he had not always had a

bad temper. His mother, his two sisters, his friends, his girlfriends, none of them would have said so—none of them were going to say so, he felt sure, on the witness stand. In retrospect, he guessed he would have to say it had been building, all his twenty-four years—twenty-four years of the minute-to-minute pressure that anyone who had grown up in East Harlem understood instinctively and that anyone who had grown up elsewhere would never, ever understand. All those years, he thought, he had been like a volcano, only dimly aware himself, at times, of what was going on within him. No, a volcano was wrong: it was a symbol of release, of power, of tension resolved. Whereas what had happened to him was that his one explosive act of rage had, by its very uselessness, only multiplied his fury, as well as the sense that nothing but his death, if that, was going to rid him of it.

The door opened and the lawyer rushed in, red-faced, sweat showing on his big forehead and a private frown on his face. Victor and the guard slowly lifted their gazes to him. "Sorry," he said. "I got hung up."

The guard, who had been leaning against the wall, straightened up languidly and found the key to the door on his own side of the room. "No sweat," he said. "We were just playing I Spy." He smiled; then, as he put the key in the lock, he turned back to the lawyer. "I'll be right outside the door," he said significantly. "If you need anything."

The lawyer nodded. Victor, the only one seated, looked back and forth in disbelief at the two white men exchanging this understanding over his head. They didn't even have to say what they meant. These two men, *strangers* to each other, understood each other perfectly when it came to protecting themselves from him. Like he was an animal, a circus animal. He couldn't stand it. The guard left the room and bolted the door. Victor turned back to his lawyer, who had sat down and was patting his pockets in the hope of finding something with which to dry off his shining forehead.

His name was Pinsky. The judge had appointed him shortly after Victor's arraignment, when he had had to stand up, his ankles connected by a chain and his hands locked to his sides, and, in answer to the old judge's casual question, had to say that he and his family were destitute— in front of the press and his own mother, who looked close to fainting. Slave days, he remembered thinking as the judge and the lawyers droned on, seemingly as bored as could be. I can see myself right now, and I'm an image from the slave days. Sure enough, the *Amsterdam News* had made that same connection on the next day's front page, under his picture, only with a long, scholarly analysis of white society in place of his own mere intuitive leap. But Victor couldn't bring himself to follow their arguments in any case—because he knew he had blown it, he had fucked up, he had brought the hell of incarceration down upon himself. White people may want the opportunity to treat you like a slave again, but that was all the more reason to be vigilant, to withhold from them any excuse. He had known that once and then he had forgotten it.

"You're late," he said to Pinsky, just to work off some frustration.

Pinsky looked up, without lifting his head, from Victor's case file. "I told you, I got hung up," he said. "You're not my only client."

It was obvious to Victor that Pinsky was not rude by nature—on the contrary; this brusqueness was something that the lawyer had somehow decided would win him over, earn his respect, make them into buddies. In what sort of experience could a decision like that be grounded? White people were often literally funny in just this way, but Victor never found Pinsky funny at all.

"So what about the bail?" he said. "Did you get the bail lowered?"

Pinsky put·down his pen. "I went to the DA in private," he said, "like we discussed, because in open court the press is there. He said he absolutely would not consider it. Just like I told you ten times he wouldn't. Remember, he asked the judge for no bail at all originally. I tried, but no go."

"Then try again!" Victor blurted out. "You don't understand what I'm talking about. My family can't survive me being in here like this. I'm fine, I can take care of myself—they're in more danger than me. I had the only income in that house, the only benefits. My sister works half time but that's it. I have two children, one of them's born premature. When I went in here, they came off my insurance. Without me, they'll all go down. Even if it was just until the trial, if I was out, I could make some kind of arrangements. My boss owes me some money—you think if my mother comes calling, he's gonna give the money to *her?*"

He looked at his lawyer, who at least had stopped writing and was paying attention. Pinsky looked genuinely troubled. It was all too degrading for Victor to have to lay out his hardships and his desperation to this contemptible child of privilege, who was probably about four years older but who acted like he was Victor's grandfather. But he had to do it; it was the first door between him and his family. He went on.

"I'm not talking about things will be tough for them without me, how they'll have to struggle to get by. You don't know. I'm all they have. I'm talking about losing their home, I'm talking about my mother or my daughter dying waiting in some emergency room. I have to straighten some things out right away."

He brought his chained hands up carefully so he could lean forward on the table. "Is there a trial date yet?" he said.

Pinsky leaned back in his chair, to restore the distance between them. "Well, I have been working hard," he said, "and I didn't come without *some* good news. I've been talking with the DA pretty much constantly, and I've gotten them to agree to plead it down. So there'd be no trial. No circus for your family to go through, no media crawling all over them."

"Or you," Victor said.

"Hey." He looked irritated for a second but let it go. "So here's the offer. They'll drop attempted murder and kidnaping in exchange for a guilty plea on first-degree assault."

"How much time?" Victor said nervously.

"They'll ask the judge for eight to sixteen, and I'm sure they'll get it. Parole is technically possible in as little as four years and change, but in a high-profile case like this, I wouldn't expect it."

Victor turned to look at the wall. He tried to imagine the passage of eight years. His mother, his sisters, his children, the mothers of those children, one of whom might be okay but one of whom was capable of anything. Eight years. They wouldn't make it eight months. What had he done to them?

"It is my recommendation," he heard Pinsky say stiffly, warily, "that you accept this offer."

The grating note of his advocate's voice helped Victor focus again. Helpless in all but this man-to-man confrontation, he fixed his eyes on Pinsky until Pinsky looked away. "Your recommendation? Well, that's nice," he said. "But listen here. You're not understanding me. People are depending on me. You look at me and you think, There's another stupid nigger who tried to kill a white man, but no. Things are more complicated than that. I need to get out of here."

He had gotten to Pinsky, he saw, with the word "nigger." The lawyer angrily pulled at his lapels. Victor had broken through the condescending veneer, the overly patient air of professionalism, and had touched him where he really lived. Now, Victor thought, this guy is close to showing his true hatred of me; and when he does, finally we're going to have some basis for discussion.

"Yes, but," Pinsky said, "you're not telling me you expect to walk. I mean," and here he almost smiled, "just between us of course, you did commit a serious crime."

Victor looked at him with no expression, while thinking, with equal parts admiration and offense, that these were not the kinds of questions lawyers were supposed to ask. On the other hand, Pinsky had been careful not to phrase it as a question. "I don't *expect* to walk, no. If I have time to do, I will do it. You come in here like the idea of guilt is something you've got to explain to me, like a child, you pasty fucking racist." He closed his eyes and regrouped. "I'm telling you that as long as I can get out, make some arrangements, until the trial, six weeks or two or three months or whatever it is, then I'll come back and serve my time. Hell, you can plead me down the day the trial starts if you want. I'm not asking to be made the fucking governor, I'm asking that my lawyer get me out on bail. Even the sorriest fucking lawyer should be able to pull that off. It happens every damn day."

"It doesn't happen every damn day in a case that's been in the papers and on TV nationwide," Pinsky said. "In a case where the judge and the prosecutors know they're being watched like fucking hawks."

The word "fucking" was a ridiculous affront coming out of that thin mouth.

"So you're saying there's no chance of getting bail reduced?"

"That's not going to happen," Pinsky said. "You have to start being realistic. Of course, another way to go is to try to raise the bail that's been set."

Victor sat back in disbelief. "One hundred fifty thousand dollars," he said.

Pinsky cocked his head, as if to say it was rather a lot.

"I told you I have nothing," Victor said bitterly. "I said it in court. If I had a dime, then I wouldn't have a broken-down sweaty useless pale dick-pulling lawyer like yourself."

Pinsky had apparently stopped listening to these epithets. "You must know," he said, "even in here, that you have some new friends high up in the black community. They've decided that you're a political prisoner. Have you thought about hitting them up for bail money?"

He had been contacted indirectly by some of these leaders—newspaper editors, clergymen, self-appointed community spokesmen; he felt some complicated resentment of them, but he was certainly not going to show that to Pinsky. He had no desire to be their poster boy for oppression. They were a lot less interested in his real-life problems than in getting their big solemn faces in front of the cameras. It was as if he had been nobody, to them, all those years he was struggling to hold his family together by honest means; but when, in the single most selfish, unthinking moment of his life, he had undone all that good work, he had become a figure of nobility somehow. It was insulting. When he heard about them trying to drag his poor, dazed, unhealthy mother out of the apartment to some press conference they'd decided they needed to stage on his behalf, what he most wanted to do was get ahold of them and tell them to stay away from him and his family, to forget they'd ever heard of him. But such things weren't done; besides, he was helpless to enforce any desire like that in prison. They'd just do what they wanted anyway.

"I've thought of that," was all he said to Pinsky. "Just cause you see them on TV doesn't mean they have a lot of money at their disposal. They could help out with maybe fifty thousand. Even if it was twice that, it wouldn't help a damn bit."

Pinsky rubbed his eyes. He appeared bored with the whole subject. "How about TV?" he said.

"What TV?"

"Plenty of people from the tabloid shows have been in contact with me. 'Current Affair,' 'Hard Copy,' 'Inside Edition,' pretty much all of them. They'd pay for interviews with you."

"I hate those shows," Victor said sullenly, but he kept his eye on Pinsky. "How much?"

"Ten thousand. Of course, once you give the first interview to one of them, the price would go down on the others. They all want exclusives."

Victor tried to slam one manacled hand down on the table. "So this is your advice?" he shouted. "All this degrading myself, degrading my family, might net me like a hundred thousand, tops? You think that's a *help?* It might as well be nothing. Another fifty thousand dollars is a fortune to me, you could probably get it from your motherfucking daddy—"

He saw that Pinsky's gaze was leveled over his head. The lawyer tried to make a surreptitious circle out of his thumb and forefinger. Victor realized that his raised voice had summoned the guard to the safety-glass pane in the door, and that Pinsky had signaled to him that everything was fine, that he had it under control. Victor whipped around, but the guard's face was gone again. This was too much. He leaned forward until he was close to Pinsky's face and lowered his voice to a threatening whisper.

"Why are you wasting my time with this?" he said.

"Wasting *your* time?" Pinsky said. "I told you fifteen minutes ago bail wasn't an option for you, but you insist on it. Then if I try to play along with you, you accuse *me* of being unrealistic. I already told you what's far and away your best alternative. Cop the plea. Get out of jail while you're still a young man."

"I can't hear that," Victor said. "Now I did not say it was bail or nothing. I said I had to get out, at least temporarily. If bail's not an option, then we have to go to trial. You have to get me off."

Pinsky sat back and dropped his pen on top of the open file. "Get you off," he said. "How do you imagine I'd do that?"

"How the fuck should I know? If the DA wants to accept a plea, then he must think there's some chance of my walking, right? What are you, my judge or my lawyer?"

Pinsky sighed, and grabbed a handful of hair on either side of his head. "I'm your lawyer," he said. "Don't you think I'd recommend going to trial if I thought we had any chance of winning at all?"

"You just put me up on that stand, and—"

"Look at yourself. If you could, you'd climb over the table right now and smack me, wouldn't you? You can't control your anger in here. You think you can control it when the DA is going at you? You think the jury won't see what I see right now?"

"I can control it," Victor said.

"I don't think you can. And besides, what's our defense going to be? All they have to do is call that Soloway guy to the stand. The jury will watch him limp up there with his cane, they'll see his wife and two kids—"

"I have two kids too, you know!"

"His wife and two kids in the gallery. Then the DA will ask him about his injuries. Then he'll say, Do you see the man who held you captive for two days, who beat you nearly to death with a length of pipe, do you see that man in this courtroom today? And he's going to point at you. And you go to jail until you're middle-aged."

The two men stared angrily at each other for a long moment.

"You'd be better off if you'd killed him," Pinsky said.

A vein appeared on the left side of Victor's forehead.

"That's it," he said. "That's fucking it. You're out. I want a new lawyer."

Pinsky blew out a mouthful of air. Victor had the impression he was fighting not to look relieved. "There is a way to do that," Pinsky said. "We have to make a motion in court for new counsel."

"Then do it."

"It'll take a couple of weeks—"

"Do it. Don't drag your ass about it. I want it done now." He realized he wasn't going to have this Pinsky to vent his anger on for much longer; so he was trying to goad him, and it was working.

"Hey," Pinsky said, "don't you think I'll make that motion as fast as I possibly can? You think I like this? You think I like getting threatened over the phone and in the mail because I took this case? My wife has a police escort when she goes to work in the morning, because of you. You think I like *you?* Guard!" he suddenly shouted, and began throwing pens and paper back into his leather briefcase. Victor heard the guard enter the room behind him.

"We're through here," Pinsky said. He dropped a pen, and he stooped to pick it up. Victor turned his head and saw that the guard was watching the red-faced, awkward, discomposed lawyer with mild but undisguised amusement.

"I'll be in touch soon, Mr. Hartley," Pinsky muttered— trying belatedly to maintain a professional air in front of the third party.

"I want a black lawyer!" Victor shouted. He felt a little braver now, seeing that the guard was basically on his side.

"Well, I hope you get one then," Pinsky said. He locked his briefcase and headed for the door.

"I'll miss you!" Victor called, laughing, just before the door swung shut. But later, back in his cell, he reflected that that last joke might really have been on him. He felt the absence of Pinsky in his circumscribed life almost immediately; he felt it with surprising keenness. You could get right up in the man's face and voice your anger. Try that with a guard sometime, or even with a fellow prisoner.

The weather softened, and the bone-deep pains in his leg became less frequent, and so, by the end of April, Paul was able to assume more of his regular child-entertaining duties. In the mornings, he would sit on the bottom bunk in the boys' tiny, toy-strewn room and supervise their dressing, helping out with buttons or with heads stuck in armholes, while Renata made them breakfast; in the afternoons he could now walk all the way down to 100th Street —though he sometimes stopped to rest on the way—to pick Peter up after school. If it was Tuesday or Friday, he would have to take the boys upstairs to Mrs. Perez so he could go off to Lenox Hill for some grimly cheerful physical therapy, where he would be exhorted impersonally to keep up with the treadmill or lift weights with his mending knee; but on other days he could sit in his chair and oversee their play, not really able to join in physically, though the boys had learned to be very good about not jumping on Daddy's back or into Daddy's lap the way they once liked to, the way, he kept promising them, they would be allowed to do again sometime soon. If he needed a painkiller, he would try to wait until they were settled in front of the frail old Zenith TV, transfixed by some horrifying program like "Lamb Chop's Play-Along" or "Tiny Toon Adventures"; that way, if the pills made him fall asleep in the chair, no one would be put out.

And when the big playground in Riverside Park at 97th Street opened for the spring, he was able to take them there and sit on a bench with the mothers while Peter and Leo cavorted, with that little flatfooted run he loved so much, around the slides and jungle gyms and green plastic dinosaurs. There were three reasons he particularly liked going to the playground: it made him feel, even if he didn't move from the bench, like he was helping out poor Renata, who was tired all the time now; it saved money for them by cutting down on the need for the services of Mrs. Perez upstairs, so Paul could feel he was contributing to their financial survival at least in some roundabout way; and, most satisfying if also most guilt-inducing, it gave him a chance to see and talk with his best friend, Martin Rafferty. Martin wasn't entirely welcome at the Soloway home; he could be a bit abrasive, he drank and ate too much, and he was alarmingly cavalier with the boys, out of naiveté mostly—hanging them upside down by their ankles after dinner, for instance. For all these reasons, Renata didn't care for him, though Peter and Leo were crazy about him; and while Paul used to insist very gruffly that he had the right to have his best friend and literary foil visit the apartment any time he wanted, lately—with money so tight and with Renata stretched so thin, covering for him while he recuperated—it had seemed prudent not to ask him over. So they would meet at the playground, to talk idly or sometimes debate heatedly, as they loved to do, Martin raising his voice and staring intently at Paul while Paul's eyes flickered back and forth from Martin's face to the consternated faces of the other parents to the wayward boys, carried away in a roiling sea of toddlers.

Martin was a poet, with a few publications to his credit which, among the small circle who cared about such matters, would have been considered very fine credentials; but he had no prospects for a book as yet. Not that a book contract would have altered the circumstances of his life; advances for poetry collections, Paul had heard, were often less than a month's rent. It was, in fact, the very marginality and tenuousness of Martin's identity as a poet that held Paul's respect and attention. In other ways, Martin was a difficult friend: unreliable, self-centered, as likely to be surly and depressed as boisterous and supportive. They had met years earlier at a party given by one of Paul's friends from his brief stint as a cashier at Shakespeare & Co., and before the end of the evening Martin was shaking his head and pontificating about how Paul—who at that time had two part-time jobs and one published short story —had it easy, because he was a novelist. As if novelists were soap-opera actors or magazine illustrators, able to work at will if their standards were malleable enough. Of course it was offensive (particularly to Renata), but it was also attractive because no other stranger that Paul could remember meeting had taken him so seriously *as* a novelist when in fact there was no concrete evidence of his dedication or his talent. To most people, Paul was not what he might become but simply what he was—a twenty-six-year-old man who worked part time at the cash register of a bookstore.

And, indeed, Paul had to grant that, so far as imagining a future went, he did have it easier than Martin. So few people cared whether there were such things as living poets at all; and Martin seemed not to care much for those who did. He lived in a shockingly dark and messy studio east of Columbia, and took the train out to Long Island twice a week to teach poetry to undergraduates, an enterprise which he represented to Paul (and probably, knowing Martin, to his students as well) as a vast if not especially remunerative con game. The very first time they ran into each other on the street, a week or so after that party, he had practically hauled Paul up to his apartment, on one of the most dangerous-looking blocks Paul had ever seen, to give him some of his verses to look over, which was flattering, Paul supposed. The poems were, somewhat surprisingly, extremely good—lyric without seeming merely indulgent, unafraid of aphorism, neither imitative nor overly concerned with academic fashions in form. He was excellent, Paul thought, even if he was no Auden—a critical sentiment he knew enough to keep to himself, generous as it may have seemed. Martin would have been crushed to hear from someone he respected that he was no Auden—not because he thought he was, but because he honestly believed that, if you couldn't be as good as Auden, then what the hell was the point?

Characteristically, he had never visited Paul in the hospital. But once Paul had felt strong enough to reestablish phone contact (for there was no such thing as a casual chat with Martin), the poet had become exceedingly eager to get together, and would call a couple of times a day to see how Paul was feeling. Paul realized that Martin had missed him, in a touching if slightly selfish way. Overweight, oversensitive, ill at ease almost everywhere, alternately bored and outraged by the worldly trash that made up the cultural life of most people, he had very few friends to whom he could talk about the things that mattered most to him. When Paul asked if he'd like to accompany him and the boys to the 97th Street playground, Martin agreed immediately; playground, library, subway station, it clearly meant nothing to him where they went. The important thing was talk.

The sky was clear but the wind was cool and fitful. Paul and Martin settled on a park bench while the boys ran off to the military-style obstacle course that ended in a circular slide. Paul knew there would be an interval of ten or fifteen minutes here when he could afford to keep just one eye on them; they played well together, but only for a while, and at some point Peter would need to assert his eminence and Leo would either come running to complain or else just stand still and scream. Paul had mentioned the book proposal to Martin on the phone a few nights before —looking, really, for an echo of his own feelings of abhorrence, with which to blot out any lingering guilt over turning down all that money. But, distressingly, something different had happened; Martin was absolutely fascinated by the whole prospect. While he never went so far as to urge Paul to accept the offer and write the book, he couldn't stop talking about it either, examining the issue from every angle and pestering him with difficult questions. What was worse, Martin seemed most captivated by this as an aesthetic issue, touching not on Paul's own integrity but on the degraded state of the novel in their own generation, and though his thinking on this matter was rather labored, Paul could see it was also genuine. Of course, he thought, it might also have been the case that Martin knew that such a huge sum of money, even after all their debts were paid off, would surely contain some ultimate surplus, part of which might be lent to him.

As soon as the kids were out of earshot, Martin started in again, this time in an uncharacteristically practical vein.

"So what did Renata say when you told her?" he said.

"Renata" was surely the one word Paul wished he could keep out of this conversation. But it was a fair question. "She agreed with me," he said. "Or, rather, she didn't disagree with me. I told her about my conversation with Garland, and I told her why I turned the offer down, and she didn't raise any objection. She didn't say much at all, really."

There was a pause, filled with the mostly wordless shouts of the children.

"Of course," Paul said reluctantly, "I lied a little bit about the money. I told her it was eighty thousand."

Martin thought this was the funniest line he'd ever heard. He began to laugh so hard he drew the quizzical attention of a cluster of nearby children.

"What?" Paul said irritably. "Why is that so funny?"

"Oh, I don't know," Martin said. "Why did you lie about a thing like that?"

Paul frowned. "I have no idea, actually. It was pointless. It just came out of my mouth. I guess I thought it would soften the blow somehow."

"What blow?"

"What blow? Listen, money is money, and it's hard to pass it up when somebody lays it down right in front of you. It was hard for me too."

"A temptation from God."

Paul couldn't tell if this was meant sarcastically or not. "But there were principles involved," he went on. "So the dollar amount shouldn't have mattered. I should have just told her the truth."

"So you think she shares these principles?"

Paul sighed, and thought for a moment. "Not exactly," he said. "But she knows me, she knows what I believe in, and if I acted against that, I wouldn't be the same man she married and—and reproduced with. I don't think she would want or expect me to do anything other than what I did. Regardless of whether it's what she would have done."

Martin nodded vigorously. "So she's your audience," he said.

"What?"

"These acts of principle don't mean anything unless they have an audience. I mean, if it were enough for you to simply *have* beliefs, you wouldn't be a novelist, am I right? You'd just be an upstanding citizen. But you have to communicate these beliefs in order for them to mean something. In this case, you have to settle for an audience of one. But the audience principle is crucial. I mean that's why you're a novelist, right?"

"You mean as opposed to a poet?"

"Well, okay. As opposed to a poet."

Paul rolled his eyes. "The reason I am not a poet," he said, "is because the poems that I wrote when I was in college sucked."

Martin cocked his head. "Well, yeah, okay, good answer," he said finally. "But let me ask you this. This trial of your principles, the source of your unease, you said was turning down all the money that was laid in front of you."

"Right."

"But it wasn't laid in front of you, was it?" Paul looked confused. "The money was offered to you in exchange for the future labor of writing a book."

Paul shrugged impatiently. "So?"

"So explain to me this great contempt you have for the idea of being called upon to write something."

Martin stuck his hands under his arms. Though it was sunny, the wind was moving more briskly now across the broad playground, and he wore only a T-shirt. Paul, groping for his answer, gazed across the blacktop until he found Peter and Leo playing happily inside the long concrete wading pool, which stayed dry until around Memorial Day.

"What sort of life is it for a writer, to produce books whose subjects are a matter of popular vote?" he said finally. "What kind of artist could I hope to be if I jettisoned the book I wanted to write in favor of one that others wanted me to? If I chose my subjects based simply on which one would garner the most money?"

Martin smiled, and his eyes lifted up to the sky. His lips moved once, twice, three times in a series of false starts; his hands rose and then fell resignedly in his lap. "Okay," he said. "Okay, this is such rich stuff, I don't know where to begin, I don't want to forget anything you've just said. Okay, first of all, the money. The money does not proceed from the subject, the way some trees give better fruit than others. Right? The money represents something."

"Corruption."

"No, *not* corruption." He looked irritated now, and Paul noticed one woman, an attractive young mother in a Burberry raincoat, stop to stare frankly at them, as if they were a couple of old lunatics in a cafeteria. "The money represents popular taste. In a kind of convoluted, corporate way, all that money is a kind of offering to you, from your own people, a bounty offered in exchange for your story. It's all very tribal. It's beautiful in its way. And I don't think that, for a true storyteller, that kind of public need can be so lightly regarded. It's a burden, and you treat it like a nuisance."

Paul shook his head. "Well," he said, "that is really nuts. Leave it to you to confuse late capitalism with a big campfire. Besides, I don't want to fulfill my role in the tribe, God damn it. I want to outlive the tribe, I want to transcend it. What artists that you really respect wrote works on subjects that were dictated to them by strangers?"

"Bach, Haydn, Mozart—"

"Musicians don't count."

"Dryden, Wordsworth, Tennyson, Ted Hughes—"

"Oh, come on. Poets laureate? That's a totally different thing."

"Is it?"

"And even Haydn and Mozart were working for patrons, not the public."

"And so? Who are the patrons now? You're the one who raised the specter of late capitalism, not me."

Paul stared at him. "Do you really believe this, or are you just trying to provoke me? What are you, some kind of double agent?"

Martin laughed. "I don't know what I think, really. It's all another country to me. Is anyone ever going to offer me six figures for a book-length poem? I rather doubt it. The rules are all different for you prose people."

"See," Paul said, "but that's just it—"

Suddenly he cut himself off, as he saw, to his stupefaction, that the mother in the Burberry raincoat was approaching them. She had an odd, almost frightened look on her face. Were they scaring the children? Poet and novelist looked up at the raven-haired young woman as if she had awakened them from a dream.

"Excuse me," she said. "But aren't you Paul Soloway?"

Paul stared at her. No matter how married he was, he didn't think there was any way he could have forgotten meeting such an attractive woman. He took off his gray baseball cap and ran his hand through his hair. "Yes," he said slowly. "I'm sorry, have we met?"

The young woman looked mortified. "Oh, no, no," she said. "I'm just—I don't know what you'd call it—an admirer, I guess. I recognize your face from TV."

Martin's head began to move rapidly back and forth, trying to take in every aspect of the expressions on the faces of the two people, celebrity and fan. His mouth was open. Paul was worried that Martin might actually start clapping his hands with delight, like a child.

"Oh," Paul said awkwardly. "Well." He was trying to find some suitable alternative to thanking her, which would have been ridiculous.

But she rescued him. "You just showed such bravery,"

she said. "It was so awful what those people did to you. You were so strong, and so was your wife, I saw her too, and so—" Her lovely face was animated by a sudden idea. "Are your children here?" she said.

"Yes," he said immediately, grateful that the boys could provide some diversion. He began scanning the crowd for them. To his distress, he couldn't find them right away. "Where are they?" he said nervously, and promptly caught sight of them playing by the model dinosaurs. Peter was riding on the back of the Tyrannosaurus rex, and Leo was on the ground, wrestling fiercely with the immovable tip of its green tail. Paul pointed, and the woman squinted to see. "The dark-haired boy, on the dinosaur," he said. "In the green jacket, and the one lying on the ground there—"

"Oh," the woman said. Her hand went to her throat in a mysterious, upper-class gesture. "Oh, they're beautiful boys." She watched their uninspired play for a minute, then shook her head as if to clear it. "Well, I beg your pardon, I've bothered you long enough. It was wonderful to meet you, and, and—" She laughed nervously. "I don't know what to say. Congratulations?"

She held out her hand, and Paul, speechless, took it. Then she retreated back into the crowd of young families, to her own daughter, sleeping in a stroller, whose expression, Paul saw, was so angelic that she made his own sons look like delinquents.

"Okay," Martin said. His voice was trembling. "Okay, tell me that you hated that."

Paul turned to him. "I hated that," he said.

Martin threw up his hands in exasperation.

"Don't you get it?" Paul said. "Look, go back to what we were talking about before she came over here. You said this is all foreign to you, because it could never happen to you. That is *exactly* wrong. The precise nature of what has happened to me is that it could have happened to anyone. It was a chance event. Chance. That I happen to be a writer matters not at all in this context. If I hadn't stopped at the bakery that day on my way home with the car, that woman would have no idea who I was. Bravery. She doesn't know what she's talking about. It could as easily have happened to you. Or to her, for that matter. I exercised no will here. I made no judgment. Face it, there's no novel in it. If there's anything interesting about it"—and he realized with some surprise that he had not thought of this before—"it's all from the point of view of Victor Hartley. He's the violator of taboo, if you want to talk tribal. He's the one whose story should be of interest. But nobody wants that, because they have the convoluted idea that to pay attention to evil is to reward it. This is the culture of victimhood; this is the culture that is squeezing the life out of the novel. I should contribute to this process?"

He picked up his cane and tapped it against the soft synthetic blacktop.

"And anyway," Paul said more softly, "that woman already knows my kids' names, for Christ's sake. What is it exactly that I am supposed to have left to reveal? What is this fascination with autobiography?"

But Martin's attention, as often happened, had snagged on one thing in the middle of Paul's speech, and he seemed not to have heard the rest. "There's no novel," he said, "in an experience that could happen to anyone?"

"No decent novel," Paul said, aware that he was giving way to a perverse obstinacy.

"George Eliot," Martin said.

"Henry James."

"Jane Austen. Kafka. Joyce."

"Dostoyevsky. Proust. Nabokov." Then, after a pause, "Joyce."

"Dreiser."

"Dreiser's a hack," Paul said, and, grateful for the turn the conversation was taking, was about to explain why—when through the steady noise of children and wind and cars on the nearby West Side Highway cut one note that he recognized, the inevitable wail of Leo crying for redress for some injustice delivered by his big brother. Paul stood up and maneuvered through the hip-high throng, homing in on that unwavering note, until he spotted the boys. They were playing on a raised wooden platform which had, at either end, two mounted metal steering wheels. Leo was sitting on the platform near Peter's feet, red-faced and screaming, while Peter turned the steering wheel with a look of airy unconcern.

Paul tried to get down on one knee, then gave up and bent from the waist. "What's the problem?" he asked Leo. The boy choked out some disconnected phrases, which, to a parent, communicated that Peter had pushed him away from his steering wheel and taken it over. Paul looked up at Peter for a moment; the boy was conspicuously avoiding his eye. He looked back down at Leo and gently touched his wet cheek.

"Come here a minute, pal," he said. "I want to show you something." He picked him up, carried him to the opposite end of the platform, and, grimacing, set him down in front of the other, identical steering wheel.

"How's that?" he asked.

Leo shook his head. "I was using that one!" he wailed.

Paul's eyebrows went up in surprise. "Really?" he said in a lower, conspiratorial voice. "Why? Because, you know, I think this one's actually better."

Leo's tiny brows knitted, and he looked again critically at the wheel.

And in just another few seconds he was playing happily. Paul, thinking he would stay a minute more until he was sure everything was peaceful again, looked over to the benches to try to catch Martin's eye.

"Look out!" Leo yelled. "Get off the tracks!"

What he saw sent a small shiver through him. Martin was still on the bench, his eyes on the blacktop though he probably did not see it. His hands, and his lips, continued to move. He was lost in the aesthetic issues raised by their discussion, and, unable to let it go, was continuing the argument, probably on both sides. There beside the democratic boil of children, just on the margin of the activity of normal urban humanity, he was gone, he saw nothing. Four feet away from him, on the next bench, a woman with an empty stroller by her side was examining him with what appeared to be genuine fear.

Bob Spain checked his watch again, and he signaled for the waiter with the languid, minimal movements of a man who is accustomed to being attended to. But the waiter didn't respond. Surprised, Spain raised his hand higher, like an ordinary patron, like a child asking for a bathroom pass; then he remembered, vexedly, that he was not a regular here at Cafe Berne, that he had suggested it for today's lunch precisely because it was well outside the loop wherein publishing people—who might, if they saw him with today's lunch date, start wondering what exactly he was up to—could expect to be recognized. The waiter arrived at last, smiling expectantly, and Spain asked for a second glass of the house red.

He needed to contain his growing disbelief that the young man he was waiting for—a man he had never heard of until about two weeks ago, a man who normally couldn't have cracked Spain's lunch lineup if he'd held a gun to his assistant's head—was late. His lateness was moving beyond what could possibly be considered fashionable. It was insulting. If I were in his position, Spain said to himself, a junior agent making his very first serious business contact, I would have been here half an hour early, I would have dusted off the guy's chair and memorized the location of the men's room in case he needed to go. But that was the thing about agents; no matter how inconvenient they were—as an industry phenomenon or as individuals—they had something you needed, namely writers, and therefore you had to be kind to them. He had another mouthful of wine, opened the oversized menu, and closed it again.

He was mollified somewhat when he saw the young man burst into the restaurant, breathless, his eyes bright with fear, and stammer something to the maître d'. Though they had never met, Spain knew it was he even before the maître d' turned and pointed out the table to him. He looked every inch the part: faux-bohemian long hair, which his haste and the unusually humid day had given an electrified aspect; an overemphasis on clothes in spite of the appalling salary everyone his age in the publishing world received; a face unlined by experience or hardship. So young, Spain thought, to be so venal. He rose graciously as the young man made his way to the table, trying not to pant. His hand was damp.

"Ned Garland," he said, sitting down heavily. "I am so sorry to be late. My cab turned down 67th Street at Third Avenue, and there'd been an accident in the middle of the block. So the cabby tries to back up onto Third, and the guy behind him won't let him out. So they get out of their cars and start shoving each other. Finally I just got out of the cab and, uh, ran."

"Please, it's no problem," Spain said. "Really. I just got here myself."

"It's a great pleasure to meet you again," Garland said.

They chatted amiably for a while, Garland managing to secure a glass of ice water from the waiter which he drank in three gulps. Spain asked after his boss and mentioned, with perfect spontaneity, three or four landmark deals he and Andy had made together, one of which went on to win the Pulitzer Prize in 1970. Even as he was talking, Spain noticed Garland's brow furrow conspicuously as he looked over the menu. The cuisine at Cafe Berne ran to things like stuffed cabbage, schnitzel à la Holstein, and a twenty-two-dollar German meat loaf; but Garland didn't look much like the dieting kind, so that wouldn't account for the young man's evident shock. Then it dawned on him: a junior agent like this would customarily eat at his desk; so this whole lunch, arranged on Garland's own initiative, was a nerve-wracking, even slightly decadent novelty, a heady, illicit imitation of the life of the alpha dog. Spain was willing to bet that Bayley didn't even know the young man was here. Straight-faced, he opened his menu again.

He ordered rahmschnitzel with red cabbage and spaetzle, and a side of potato pancakes; Garland ordered a large Caesar salad. The young man wasn't drinking either, which made Spain feel old, and he silently reproached his bad manners. When the waiter departed, they looked at each other and smiled, each knowing that the other had been waiting for this moment through all the pleasantries, when the discussion of their real business could decorously begin.

"So," Spain said, and smiled. "Tell me what the snag is with our friend Mr. Soloway."

Ned took another sip of water and sat back. He had thought about nothing but his answer to this question ever since Spain's assistant Olivia had called to set up this lunch four days ago. How best to play it depended on his own reading of Paul—how deep his reservations went, how genuine was his disregard for the money, how much of what he said and did was only fooling himself—and these were things about which Garland changed his mind two or three times a day. But now, when he could hear that businesslike edge work its way through Spain's courtly demeanor almost in spite of himself, Garland's uncertainty over his client's ultimate wishes gave way to the immediacy of the deal, to the unmatched rush of negotiating, this time with one of the biggest, most predatory editors in the entire industry. The matter was between the two of them —the client was little more than a pretext, like the parameters of a war game; he would play it to test his nascent powers, to see what he was able to extract from a guy like Spain.

"The snag is, he's reluctant," he said. "Paul and his family have suffered a tremendous amount, not least from having had to surrender their private life completely. He's a very reluctant public figure. And, while he likes the idea of his family realizing some gain, to make up at least in some small part for what they've lost, he has to weigh that against the very attractive prospect of dropping out of the limelight entirely, and trying to resume a somewhat ordinary life."

Spain nodded pensively. Bullshit, he thought. "I can certainly understand that. He's been through a great deal. We don't want him to look at this book as another trial for him, but just the opposite. Just as you say—an opportunity to salvage something positive from such a horrible incident. We just want to give him an opportunity to tell his story."

"And it is a remarkable story, let's face it," Garland said.

Spain nodded respectfully. "It's got everything," he said.

"Of course, it would be painful for him to have to relive it."

"Oh, of course. Well, if that's a problem, if he has trouble getting going, I know several excellent ghosts we could set him up with. In fact, maybe we should have discussed that earlier—"

"Oh, no, that won't be necessary. Paul is actually a writer anyway, a very good one. A fiction writer, primarily. You might remember I mentioned that the first time we talked."

Spain was so sorry to hear this that, try as he might, he could not keep a look of deep disappointment from flashing across his face for just an instant. "Oh," he said, "really? I had no idea. What has he written?"

"Well," Garland said—making a mental note, in case the deal with Copeland Simonds fell through, to play down in future proposals the fact that Paul was a writer—"his stories have been published in *Ploughshares, Boulevard,* a few other places. Oh, and *Prairie Schooner.* But mostly he's working on a big novel. It's really magnificent, what I've seen of it."

"Mmm," Spain said. "Well, then a ghost is hardly the thing, is it? So tell me—the balance that you describe, between wanting to resume a normal life and wanting to get out his side of the story. What do you consider would be sufficient to tip that balance?"

Ned felt as though he was in complete contact with every nerve and muscle in his face. Drying his hands surreptitiously on the edge of the tablecloth in his lap, he said, with perfect confidence and equanimity, "Two-fifty."

Spain cocked his head slightly, as if he had heard someone calling his name out in the street. He broke a roll and began to butter it. "World?" he said.

"North American. And something in the contract spelling out his obligations as regards publicity."

"Hmm." He took a bite of the roll and, still chewing, said, "World English."

Ned pretended to think about it. "Fine. I mean fine with me. Of course I'll need to talk to Paul."

"Of course."

"But I don't anticipate a problem."

"Wonderful. Tell me. Is this proposal with anyone else?"

Garland shook his head. "It's exclusive to you," he said. "Right now."

Spain smiled. "Well, I'm extremely pleased this is working out," he said warmly, if somewhat patronizingly. "And I plan to tell Andy how well it's all gone. She'd better make sure to hang on to you."

"Thank you," he said. He waited a moment, then said, "Do you happen to know where the men's room is in here?"

Spain pointed to the sign, which was just a few feet away in plain sight. Garland, who did not need to use the men's room at all, walked stiffly toward the door, hoping he did not look as shaky as he felt. Two hundred and fifty thousand dollars, he thought. That's sixty-two fifty to me, almost 19K to the agency. At a minimum. That's most of my salary, earned back in one lunch. He thought of the look on Andy Bayley's face when he returned to the office with the news. No, better to wait until he'd talked to Soloway before springing it on Andy. You never know. Right now, he just needed to sit in the quiet stall and have a fast cigarette.

Spain watched him push through the door and disappear. He shook his head. In another minute the waiter came and set down the two plates. He pointed to Spain's wineglass, which was nearly empty. "Another?" he said.

"What else do you have by the glass?" Spain said.

"Reds? We have the Beaujolais, we have an '86 Château Margaux, we have a *very* nice '77 Pétrus—"

"And how much is that?"

The waiter inclined his head, as if forced to make an admission. "Fourteen dollars," he said. "Would you care to try it?"

"By all means," Spain said.

The waiter went off to get it. Spain picked up his glass and drained what little was left; he sighed, and held the glass up at eye level, looking absently at the glints of light in the cloudy, sedimented surface.

"By all means," he said.

Renata had met Paul when they were both undergraduates—she at Barnard, he at Columbia—in a lecture class on nineteenth-century American literature. She recognized him vaguely from a few other English Department courses; but he only really came alive for her when she heard a few of her friends discussing him, smirkingly, in the coffee station in the basement of the library, as part of the regular inventory of boys. He takes himself so seriously, they whispered; he's always disagreeing with his professors, for God's sake, about the meaning of Hawthorne or Whitman, in the middle of class, like anyone else cares what he thinks. So pretentious (the deadliest adjective in the college lexicon). Thinks he's God's gift—wants to be a writer himself. He has had some short stories in the undergrad literary magazine. And they weren't that bad, I heard. But still.

From then on Renata began to watch him. Such seriousness of purpose, about anything, was mysteriously compelling; it certainly stood out from its context. Renata found it hard even to imagine. She was an English major and loved to read, but the idea, at age twenty, of connecting this love to a whole way of living was something she had trouble fathoming. His permanent, private scowl, his disregard for social grace, his habit of talking urgently about literature with his other low-caste friends in the neighborhood diners—all this, had she met him five years later (and indeed he was little different five years later), might have come off as mere eccentricity. But at that age, in that careless milieu, it was not just a harbinger of talent but something like a talent itself. She watched him through the lectures on Poe, Twain, Henry Adams, watched his unconscious facial tics as he registered and evaluated every word from the bearded, endomorphic professor who seemed less interested in what he himself was saying than Paul was, the way he took one note for every five or six taken by the grade-oriented dullards around him, or the way he would sometimes slip into a kind of trance in the middle of the lecture, his brow furrowed, his pen hanging motionless above his notebook for minutes at a time. What was he thinking about that could call him away with such urgency from the here and now?

She watched him with such frankness that a couple of her friends noticed it even before Paul did; but, eventually, the force of her silent curiosity penetrated his private musings. She expected that he would be shy, that he would be the type who had been so absorbed with his own interests during adolescence that he had never really learned how to talk to girls; but he waited for her after class one morning just to introduce himself, and never mentioned what had led him to do so—rather suavely, she thought. He even suggested, a week or so later, that they meet for coffee late that afternoon.

But there things bogged down. They met for three or four weeks in a row at Tom's Diner, wonderful lazy afternoons full of talk and laughter of diminishing shyness. Nor did their conversation, as gossip would have led her to expect, focus entirely on art and artists—it began there and radiated quickly outward to topics at once more prosaic and more intimate, mostly about their families. Paul's father had died of a heart attack twelve years before; Renata's parents were unamicably divorced when she was in high school, and since then had done their unwitting best to ruin every one of her holidays, vacations, and even her high school graduation with their stinging competitiveness over her time and (if, to them, there was any difference) her love.

The strange thing was, they passed some point during their discussions after which Renata was acutely aware of the way Paul was staring at her. There was no mistaking what was in that look: it was desire, and of an unsettling intensity that had obviously overpowered any sort of self-awareness he had. It threw her, and not in an unpleasant way. Yet things went no further. They met for coffee, and they sat side by side in class, but he never suggested anything else, never indulged in the sort of supercharged, light, unspontaneous physical contact that guys who wanted you were always trying to get away with. For a short time she was confused. Then—and this talent for interpretation would remain the source of Paul's dependence on her—she saw this inaction for what it was. Not shyness, not sexual timidity or fear; he simply lived with a kind of tragic disconnection from his own wants, so that it was every bit as natural for him, upon experiencing this desire, simply to contemplate and be consumed by it as to act upon it. So she would have to take matters into her own hands. And—after inviting herself over to his apartment to read a short story he had mentioned recently finishing, about a psychiatrist's son who is home alone when a patient calls up threatening suicide—that's just what she did.

Out of their different backgrounds came a common contempt for the disregard of love's responsibilities, for half-measures and half-commitments; so, while they did live together for the last semester of college and for a year and a half after that, they were still the first people they knew of, at age twenty-four, to get married. Renata could have handled a big traditional wedding, but Paul would have felt smothered by it, and in any case neither family had the money for any such undertaking; so, after some deliberation, they went down to City Hall with Paul's mother as witness and were legally conjoined in just under sixty seconds. (Renata's mother's and father's disappointment at not being invited was canceled out by the happy news that the other had not been invited either.) It gave them a kind of temporary celebrity within their own circle of friends, and it made certain administrative corners of life, such as taxes and insurance, a bit easier. But the novelty wore off; and it was to be the end of novelty in their lives for quite a while.

Renata was working then as an editorial assistant at *Sports Illustrated*—which might as well have been *El Diario* for all she understood of what went into the magazine. But when she entered the Time Inc. personnel maze, that was where she had come out. The work week was problematic —the magazine came out on Wednesday, which meant she worked through the weekend and had Monday and Tuesday off—and the office was filled with an exotic boorishness at times, as the male editors spoke in a male language which made her feel like an amusement or a necessary evil; but the pay and benefits were excellent for such a job, and she was even able to spirit home the occasional box of pens or sheaf of typing paper for Paul, who had started work in earnest on his novel. The novel, which she had not yet seen and which produced nothing other than faith in its own promise, became nevertheless the center of the household. This was more than fine with Renata; she believed in Paul's talent wholeheartedly and was pleased to know that her belief was vital to him. Her occasional pangs of foreboding were directed not at him, nor at their marriage, but at herself entirely. Bright, literate, attractive, charming, she had no idea of how she wanted to make her mark in the world, no apparent preference among the multiplicity of paths open to her while her youth was still here. She had no doubt that, in creating a safe haven for Paul's talent, she was making a concrete if slow contribution to the betterment of things. Still, she felt guilty at times about her own happiness, as if happiness itself was indicative of some deficiency in her. She thought of the centuries of female obeisance to the male temperament, of the wasted Clara Schumann, of poor exasperated Louise Colet, of the unfortunate Mesdames Picasso, who suffered only for immortality in the form of cruel caricatures in their beloved's own hand.

Paul was a little self-absorbed, perhaps, but still more ingenuous than selfish; he agonized considerably over not doing his fair share to maintain the household, and looked earnestly for a job. But this only wound up reinforcing the idea of his unsuitability to the business world. He began with the best, broadest intentions, but the circle of jobs he was able to perform well and without disgust was quickly revealed to be quite small. He was not simply picky out of laziness—he would return from job interviews in publishing or paralegaling or even advertising and it would be clear to Renata that, through even this briefest of contacts with the brutal verities of commercial life, Paul had suffered actual injury. After the depressing gig as a bookstore clerk he landed a somewhat more substantial job, as an associate editor of a literary quarterly called *Conundrum.* Like all but a handful of such publications, this one operated on something less than a shoestring; its printers had taken to holding up each issue until the bill for the previous issue was paid in full, which would send the founder/ editor (a poet even Paul had never heard of) scavenging for a literary-minded angel with cash to keep the magazine afloat. He was able to hire Paul to read slush-pile fiction manuscripts, three days a week, for a yearly salary of nine thousand dollars. Nonetheless, Paul displayed a lot of pride about the job, and Renata was very pleased herself— at that point in their lives, an extra nine thousand was nothing to turn up one's nose at. Paul spent his working days in the *Conundrum* office (one room in the editor's father's apartment on West End) reading bad short stories and arguing about good short stories, which, though they stole him away from his own writing, Paul still found to be worthwhile ways to pass the time. He grew to treat the magazine—despite the fact that its total circulation was less than the population of the block he lived on—and its financial woes with the greatest seriousness. Within a year the editor had cut Paul down to two days a week, with a corresponding salary adjustment, in order to further trim costs. Nine months after that, *Conundrum* folded for good. Paul was upset, it was true, but Renata could see right away that he was upset more for her sake than his own. He took it, in truth, with great equanimity. Fun as it was, significant as it was to him in the battle to be one of the standard-bearers for what was valuable in art, he had never really considered it his job—more of a relatively painless compromise. His job was writing fiction.

Renata moved to a job at the Doleman Photo Archive, where the various benefits were not so generous but where, unlike *Sports Illustrated*, there was some sense that one might be, even want to be, promoted to a higher position. Here was an atmosphere at once vital and hurried and sometimes panicked with the demands of the day's news, yet fusty and relaxed as well, in the way of a library.

Sorting and filing and, when things were slow, just brows-
ing through all the cross-referenced people and places
waiting patiently to be rescued from oblivion by some
chance call, Renata felt something like a kinship to the
Paul she knew least, Paul in his working hours, wrestling
with the past and trying to keep a vein of history flowing,
working in solitude much more absolute than her own.
But this kinship was little to cling to. Their attraction to
each other never weakened, even as friends' loves came
and went, decaying awkwardly or flaming out in more
spectacular fashion; yet neither did it seem to be prosper-
ing in any way as the years slipped by. Life in their household changed barely at all; in fact, if anything it only became more circumscribed, as their rent went up and Paul's
attempts at income-producing kept to their level.

Naturally there was the occasional fray, when one or
both of them would give in to some small frustration; but
as they approached thirty, something more serious than
mere irritability began to set in. Paul worked hard every
day, knocking off only in the late afternoons to read Goethe or Wallace Stevens, yet was unable to say how much or
even if *Son of Mind* was closer to completion, and he made
it plain that he resented being asked. Renata had gotten
two good raises, enough for them both to live on if they
forswore certain pleasures like going to the movies (which
Paul denounced as a fetid swamp of corruption in any
case); they could have continued that way indefinitely—a
prospect which began to fill Renata with fear. One late
afternoon, unable to say it to him in person, she called
from her office and told him that she thought they ought
to have a child.

"I can't believe you're saying this," Paul said in a high
voice, completely off his guard. "Didn't we spend last
night figuring out which utility bill we could afford to skip
a payment on?"

"I know that," Renata said. "I know it better than you."

"I realize you do. That's why I can't understand this. You know I want to have a family, we've talked about this a hundred times. But now is not the right time."

"The right time is never going to come," she said.

There was a pause. "So what do you mean?" Paul said, panic edging into his voice. "What, you don't think I'm ever going to finish the book?"

"Of course I do," she said calmly. "I know you'll finish it, and I know it will be great. But it's also a literary book —you're never going to write a best-seller. Right?"

Paul did have a secret fantasy in which the world of readers was drawn to him by mysterious forces which he would do nothing to set in motion.

"So how much of a burden can we place on it?" Renata went on. "What do you think you'll get, fifteen, twenty thousand dollars? We have half that much in debts right now. Then you start a new book, and it's back to square one. I don't have anything against all that, but my question to you is this: when does real life begin for us?"

"This is real life," Paul said softly. "Writing and reading, working and sacrificing. That is the real life. To me, anyway. And I thought to you too."

"I love you," Renata said, "and I believe in you completely, and I'm unhappy. You have to figure out that those feelings are not incompatible."

So they conceived Peter, and, a year and a half later, Leo, because they had both been only children and were both set on a different environment for their own family. Paul became a little more conscientious about actively pulling in freelance work, and between that and child-care duties, the novel proceeded more slowly than ever. For all his seeming disorientation in the real world, Renata thought, he had turned out to be a very good father. In fact, he sometimes loved the boys too much, if such a thing was possible; he suffered exactly as they suffered, over the same rudimentary frustrations and with nearly the same intensity. He was all empathy, with too little of the detachment required to be a sane parent, with the result that Renata would sometimes have to grab his arm to keep him from getting out of bed every time he heard Peter fussing in the night, or suggest that, when one of the boys fell and bumped his head, he call her at work and describe the injury rather than proceed directly to the emergency room.

Though she couldn't imagine life without him, it was also true that life with him represented a kind of long-term sacrifice of possibility. The birth of the children was a victory of sorts for her, in her attempt to move them into the mainstream not of social but of natural life; and there was no doubt it had made their life together happier. Yet the sacrifices continued and were even multiplied. Of course, like any parent, she gave up most of her social life to child care; but beyond that were further sacrifices which had nothing to do with the children in any immediate way. To say that Paul had always been moody wouldn't really do, because he never had serious, confusing mood swings with which to contend; he was simply a dark person, a brooder, often depressed and contemptuous, always harder on himself than on others. It was part of what she had first found attractive in him and, indeed, a large part of what she still loved him for—that sense of rigor in a world of frivolity, that unself-conscious aspect of depth which some depth in her was roused to answer. (That and his shoulders.) But he would not—insofar as he could control it—show this side of himself to the boys. He was a different man, whether he admitted it or not, around them: energetic, optimistic, full of the boyish joy of discovery. The consequence of this was that the contemplation, the anxiety, above all the compulsion toward study and work which used to fill his days now filled only the hours when the boys were asleep or the three hours a day they could afford to send them upstairs to Mrs. Perez. Paul's days were now divided into the children's presence and the children's absence. Renata saw that she was not part of this reckoning.

He stayed up reading long after she had gone to bed; if she called during the day at an hour when she knew the boys would be upstairs, he wouldn't answer the phone, ostensibly because he was either writing or sleeping. True, she was often tired herself, but she missed talking to him. It could be a lot worse, she told herself—plenty of women she knew at work had husbands who considered child care to be something they might attend to when they were in a particularly generous mood. She knew that life was difficult for Paul, too, that between the kids and various freelance assignments work on the novel had slowed, even by his own patient standard, to a crawl. She couldn't bear to imagine herself as the kind of wife who buttonholed her husband and demanded that he talk to her; it was undignified, it signaled a lack of personal resources. She valued her marriage as much as anything, but she was not walled in by it; there were other sources of satisfaction. In fact, there was no shortage of precedent for that. When Paul decided he wouldn't go to any more Hollywood movies, she had found friends to go with; when he wouldn't go to the beach because it was a frighteningly bogus mass obeisance by people with no authentic remaining connection to nature, she took a book and some sunscreen and went by herself. Now, when she realized that she and her husband had not had sex in at least four months, she swore she would not turn into the kind of harpy who would nag about such things when he clearly had no sexual energy. She wasn't going to let that happen to her, for his sake and for her own.

So when she went outside the marriage for sex, she was not acting on some shameful impulse but with some measure of calculation. Of course, she did not deceive herself completely about it. She knew she was betraying him; but she was also, in a very real way, accommodating him. Because she was a young woman still, and she had certain irreducible needs in this area. She didn't go out and hunt down someone with whom to have an affair (if she had, she thought, it would have been someone her age or older, someone who wouldn't have to be disabused of ideas that this kind of dalliance might lead to anything else); but then, she told herself with some small pride, she didn't have to. Brian was a very good-looking lawyer who worked in the building, seven floors below the Doleman offices; he was only twenty-six, but already had the swagger, the obscene self-confidence she would have found surprising in anyone but a lawyer. They saw each other so frequently in the lobby and at lunch that she knew he was calculating it. She began meeting his stares and answering his forward questions with such candor that he was eventually put off his game, as it were. The truly surprising thing to her about infidelity was how easily it all came about, once you had opened yourself to it.

They met at his apartment on West 57th during lunch hours, one or two or three times a week, according to her inclination only, for his inclination was constant. At first she was awkward, then, when she saw that nothing disastrous was going to happen, relieved; then she entered into the sex as into another world, in large measure trying to block out the sunlight of guilt and self-accusation by descending into pleasure and wildness. In fact, she worried that it was beginning to get too wild; it was losing its connection to her real life of love and family—the maintenance of which life was presumably her excuse for being in this strange bed with this overbearing man to begin with—and to take on a powerful life of its own. And Brian, betraying his youth, was beginning to broach the subject of the state of Renata's marriage. She had no fear at all that she might say yes to him; but her fear that the matter was heading inexorably toward some damaging, ugly conclusion was mounting.

Then came the day of Paul's abduction.

Of course it happened while she and Brian were at one of their lunches. They came back separately; Brian, under-prepared for an afternoon conference call, had left her lying there in his large, undecorated bedroom, under the heavy comforter, and with the sudden silence and the whisper of the steam radiator she had very nearly fallen asleep, which would have been a logistical disaster. A car alarm somewhere beneath the window brought her completely awake; fifteen minutes later she had just exited the elevator on the twenty-second floor, unwinding her scarf, when the Doleman receptionist called out to her.

"Renata, you had a message from Riverside Preschool," Janine said. Peter's school. She froze instinctively despite the foolishness of having one glove in her teeth.

"Your husband didn't pick Peter up after school," she said. "They need someone to come get him."

Peter's class ended at twelve-thirty, and Paul went every day to escort him home. Her first thought, unavoidably, was that something had happened to Paul; she tried to dismiss that immediately, and almost succeeded, but not quite. "Did the school try home?" she asked, but the receptionist was already back on the phone and could only hold up one apologetic finger. Renata couldn't wait; she marched to her desk to call herself.

On the way, she passed an unusual gathering; six or seven colleagues were stooped or sitting in front of a small television. Text on the screen, as she passed it, indicated that the woman reporter was talking live outside the state Supreme Court building in lower Manhattan. Oh, Renata had time to think—the guilty verdict in the Fisk trial. She reached her desk and speed-dialed home. No answer. She called out past the answering machine: "Paul? Are you there? Are you asleep? Pick up!" She hung up, dialed Riverside Preschool, and said she would be there as soon as she was able.

It was the Friday before Presidents' Day, and they had planned to drive out to Pennsylvania after work, to spend the weekend with Renata's father in the country. The boys loved it so much out there, with the big backyard and the trails through the woods and the snow that (as Peter pointed out) stayed white its whole life, that Renata was reluctant to go simply because it broke her heart to bring them back to the apartment after each visit; but Mr. Hayes was so anxious to see his grandchildren that this time he had even offered to reimburse Paul and Renata for the rental car. Paul was supposed to drop Leo upstairs and then head over to East 85th Street, where the cheapest rental agency they knew of was located, to pick up the car around noon.

She took a cab—literally her first cab ride since she and Leo had come home from the hospital; but even apart from the expense she could hardly enjoy it. Her boss, normally a stickler, had been intent on the TV and had granted her permission to leave early with a wave of his hand. Then, as Renata was walking away, already pulling her gloves back on, he remembered where she lived and had a second thought: "Be careful up there," he said. It turned out that Wendell Fisk—a white man from Ozone Park who had fatally shot a black teenager in the back on his front stoop—had been acquitted, which seemed to defy all logic except the primitive logic of race prejudice; reporters, perhaps hysterically, were predicting riots not just in New York but in predominantly black neighborhoods all over the nation. Renata looked out the window as the cab sped north up Broadway, but she saw nothing out of the ordinary.

Peter wore a kind of dazed, withdrawn expression when Renata finally got to him. He was sitting on a bench outside the classroom with his teacher's aide beside him, talking to him, stroking the hair which had grown too long down his neck. He looked up at his mother with subdued interest.

"Honey, I'm very sorry you had to wait," she said. "Something came up and Daddy couldn't come today, so I had to come all the way from work. I'm sorry I'm so late. Are you okay?"

He nodded. He wasn't angry and he wasn't upset; he looked, in fact, just the way he looked when he had a fever, and Renata felt his forehead reflexively just in case. He had pulled back into himself just a bit; beginning with the first hushed phone call from his teacher to his mother's office, he had sensed that some sort of adult drama, with himself as its subject, was playing itself out above his head.

Renata thanked the teacher's aide and took Peter's hand. "You look so tired, sweetie," she said to him as they left the building. "Do you think you can walk home with me, like a big boy?"

He looked up at her.

"If you get tired," she said, "tell me, and I'll carry you for a while."

They walked up Broadway in the cold, holding hands. Renata thought about stopping to call home again. They passed a store whose owner was out front pulling down the metal security grate, and then another, and they were twenty feet farther on when it struck Renata that it was only two-thirty in the afternoon. She began to feel nervous in spite of herself. Peter, on the other hand, was beginning to come around to his normal self now that the scenario of abandonment at school was safely behind him. He started talking, in his nonsequential manner, about the day at school, specifically about the bucket of building blocks out of which he had made a real roundhouse with a ramp so a train could drive right in and out of it. Renata, still holding his hand, thought about asking him gently if he could walk a little faster; but no, he would pick up on her fright, he picked up instantly on anything like that.

When she pushed open the apartment door, she called out, "Paul?" but was answered by silence. Peter started into the living room; she hurried to get there ahead of him. It was empty and undisturbed. The answering machine showed only one message, which Renata knew would be her own. She didn't want to play it back in front of the boy.

"Where's Daddy?" he said.

"He went to get the car, so we can go see Grandpa," she said.

"When are we leaving?"

"As soon as he gets here. In the meantime, you want to come upstairs to Mrs. Perez's with me and get Leo?"

Since they would have to be good in the car for four hours, she let them watch TV for the rest of the afternoon. At least they weren't watching her, that way; she felt she had had the look of happy unconcern pasted on her face for as long as she could manage. Might he have had an accident in the rental car? Maybe she should call the hospitals just to check, the way people did on TV shows. But how did you go about checking the hospitals? She couldn't even remember all the names of the various hospitals on the East Side. She was making a mental list of them when there was a knock on the door, and there on the threshold she found the two silent policemen, shifting their feet, their faces red from the cold.

The next two days were a sustained knife-edge of panic which she could remember only as a kind of ghastly rondo of unfamiliar images—police stations, television lights, phone-tracing equipment, the intimate presence of men in uniform—always leading back in her mind to that primary visitation, the two cops in the doorway. She told herself at the time that she was keeping herself together for the sake of the boys, but in the aftermath she could see easily that the opposite was true, that she had refused to leave their side because she knew that, left alone even for a minute, she would fly apart. Peter was just old enough to be good and frightened by all the unhomely activity, the strange men and the long, long silences; Leo knew that his father had not been home for quite some time, but he could be coaxed away from this knowledge with relative ease. The first eight hours were the worst, when only the car itself had been found and they had no idea at all where Paul was or what had happened to him; and the hardest of those hours was when the amateur videotape surfaced on TV, the jumpy image of a shiny new car being surrounded and rocked and her own husband being pulled from the driver's seat and disappearing into a furious mill of black arms. Almost as vividly as that image on the local TV news, where it appeared in a seemingly endless loop for days, she remembered the young cop who had been assigned to sit in their apartment that night; when the expensively purchased videotape began to play, he rushed from the kitchen behind her (perhaps she had gasped or made some other involuntary noise to summon him), only to stop in confusion when he saw the incorporeal nature of the menace. Half a minute went by, enough time for the tape to play through twice more, before he had the presence of mind to take the remote from Renata's hand and switch off the set. He looked down at her abashedly, apologetically, as if he had failed to do his job, as if protecting her from the television were part of his duties at all. She remembered thinking that she did not want that young policeman ever to leave her and her children again.

Only when the standoff ended the next evening, when Paul was freed and had been rushed to the hospital and the threat of his death had passed, did she have the liberty to realize that at the very moment her husband was set upon she was giving herself to another man. The digital time was even there in the corner of the amateur videotape to help her make the connection. It was another reason to thank God Paul had not died. As it was, for a banality of the kind that her husband would loudly decry were he to come across it in a novel, it carried a ruthless punishment. Brian seemed to have some sense of that, too, for with an uncharacteristic sensitivity he had not tried to contact her at all, in person, by phone, or in writing, at work or at home, in the weeks following the attack. He understood that his condolences were no comfort, that the only imaginable comfort he could provide would be never to have existed at all, and so he simulated that as closely as he could. Even when, after three weeks, she returned to work —Doleman, naturally, had promised her an open, paid leave, but once the danger was past she asked to come back part time, needing something less taxing than anxiety and remorse to occupy her mind—there was no sign of him. It seemed a chapter in both their lives had been brought, through the agency of strangers, to an unimaginable end.

But we overestimate ourselves when it comes to our capacity to be changed by drama. And when, in the early days of May, Brian began to appear again in the elevators, in the lobby, to ask when they might get together and talk a bit since they had not talked for so long, she was frightened because in truth she had begun to think of him again even before he appeared, as if the shamefulness of her imagination commanded the power to call him back into being. She tried and usually managed to avoid conversation with him; but even in their most fleeting, public encounters she caught his expression, and each time his expression conveyed the same abysmal question: What has changed? An emergency had arisen, been dealt with, and was now past; what was different? And she worried that the answer was nothing: nothing was different, nothing had changed her, she was revealed as a despicably ordinary woman of pedestrian desires, a woman who needed to be saved from herself, and there was no one to do it.

Why was he doing this to her? He had a streak of cruelty in him, but she knew it was much more likely that he was simply in love with her, as he had begun claiming he was months before. Nor, she allowed herself to think, was Paul completely blameless in this matter. Already, already, she could see their life resuming its previous, customary path, the path it had worn smooth before the violence. His first few days at home had been full of the joy and the promise of renewal, but that had passed; in the end, she thought, Paul himself had not been changed by his ordeal so much as intensified—even more melancholy, even more withdrawn, even less communicative. And he hadn't yet gone back to work on the novel. They had both dared to count themselves extraordinary people, on a mission to better the sum of artistic achievement in a befogged culture—but here they were, too thick to be lastingly affected even by the most cataclysmic events, by the brutal world which had reached right into their home to awaken them. Nothing had changed; and what, therefore, might she look to that would ever change?

So when Paul told her that Copeland Simonds's offer for the book had now been raised to a quarter of a million dollars, she began to find his intractability somewhat harder to sanction. They were sitting in the kitchen, talking quietly while the boys watched TV in the next room. He had just finished telling her how he had tried to turn the offer down, again, but Ned Garland had made him promise to talk it over with her first.

"What?" Paul said quietly, worriedly, as Renata stood up from the table to put the boys' dishes in the sink, her expression blank. "What?"

She leaned against the counter and regarded him. "What do you mean, what? Nothing. It's your decision. It's your life, your book, your name."

He stared at her in confusion. She went back to straightening up the kitchen.

"You don't need to consult me at all," she went on, afraid to look at him, afraid of what her face would betray. "In fact, I sort of wish you wouldn't."

"What does that mean? Of course I'm going to consult you."

She sat down across from him. "No, I take it back," she said wearily. "The reason I wish you wouldn't tell me about it is that you *don't* consult with me, not really. You tell me what's happened, and then you tell me what you've decided about it. There's nothing for me to say. There's no role for me other than to back you up, to tell you that you've done exactly the right thing. And that's getting tougher for me to do."

Paul felt as if he were in a dream. He knew his mouth was literally hanging open in surprise, but he couldn't do anything about it.

"So you don't think I've been doing the right thing?" he said. "So you think I should take the money?"

She couldn't bring herself to say it. "Here's the way I see it. You tell me if this is wrong or unfair." She took a breath. "What has happened to you has been seized upon, by the media and also—let's face it—by a very large public, as emblematic of the dangers of modern life, as a story of random violence and of evil ultimately punished, a story of an innocent man who triumphs over blah blah blah. As a modern myth, in other words. And, as such, this story doesn't really belong to you. If you don't relinquish it, it could, so to speak, be taken from you by force—it could be made into some cheeseball TV movie without your cooperation, without your name even, which proves how little dependent the story itself is on you. Right?"

After a few moments Paul nodded. She'd never been someone who was concerned with getting rich; he was trying to think what he had done to upset her.

"So you have two choices. One, you can do nothing, in which case you and your family will be exploited on an even bigger scale than we have been already, and you get nothing in return. Two, you can insure that this same story will reach its inevitable, vast audience in an intelligent form, filtered not through some committee of anonymous hacks but through someone of real intellectual ability, someone who can make sense out of it—"

"There's no sense to be made out of it."

"All right, then, someone who can say *that*. It seems to

me that this kind of broad, attentive audience is exactly what you've spent your adult life dreaming about. And, not coincidentally, it would pull this family back from the edge of financial ruin. The thing is, you seem to want a third choice—to wish away the entire event, to wish away the great public interest in it, to wish away what you see as the banality of it. Well, I can understand your wishing for that, but that doesn't make it any more realistic. You've got to face the truth about what's happened to you."

Paul's heart was beating wildly. As in some horror movie, he felt, the forces which were pursuing him had now mysteriously seeped into his own home. Soon he would have nowhere to go except to retreat even further into himself. Worse, he felt himself buckling a bit—if no one, not even those closest to him, believed in his judgment, if he was an example to no one, then could he be truthfully called anything other than merely eccentric?

"Let me ask you this," he said. "If the offer for the book weren't so high—if it were, say, twenty thousand—would you be making the same argument?"

A burst of laughter from the television echoed through the apartment. "Turn it down, please," Renata called, then listened with her head cocked until the volume was lowered. She turned back to Paul, her voice just above a whisper again: "Well, first of all, it won't do for you to treat the money as arbitrary, or just as a temptation. The money represents in some way the publisher's expectation of how much money they'll make back—which in turn represents the popular desire for it. So to say it might as easily be twenty thousand misunderstands the very nature of the thing. I mean, we've both seen the reporters, we've both dealt with all the phone calls and mail from strangers. These people need something that you have."

"You don't think the media is really in the business of manufacturing that kind of need?"

"No, actually I think that's just the kind of grad-student-Marxist talk that you'd normally laugh at, but that's beside the point I wanted to make. Which is, yes, the money does make a difference to me. We need it. I'm—" She considered stopping herself—she could see the bewilderment, the undisguised hurt, in his face—but it was too late for that. "I'm tired of living like this. And lately it's begun to dawn on me that we're not living like this, where we can't buy the kids new clothes for school and we have to go downtown to get the phone turned back on—we're not living like this *for a while*, just until your book is done. This is the way we're going to live our whole lives. I'm not saying I couldn't do that, or even that there's anything wrong with it. But we have a chance right now to live differently. I'm not ashamed of being poor, except once in a while when it affects the boys. But I've been there, I've done that. I want to live in another way."

"I want, I want," Paul said, his voice a loud whisper that surprised him with its angry hiss. "Very easy for you to say. I'm the one who has to do the work."

Immediately he saw that he had said the wrong thing. Her nostrils flared, and her lip quivered; proximity to tears made her feel humiliated, and therefore angry. "You watch it," she said. "I cannot hack being taken for granted, I'll tell you that right now."

He took her hand. "I don't," he said, "I promise you I don't. I depend on you so much I don't think I could even survive anymore outside this family. That's why you're scaring me so much. I'm just so shocked. I want you to be proud of me, I really do, in everything, and it seems to me that if I took the money, and wrote that sort of book, I wouldn't even be the same man you married."

She finally gave his hand a squeeze. "You'd be the same man I married," she said, smiling, "except you'd have a quarter of a million dollars."

"The money's not the issue. I'm worried that stooping to that kind of work would change me. I'm worried that if

I relax those standards, all it'll mean is that I never really had any standards to begin with."

"Why? You don't like proofreading, but I've never heard you complain it was destroying you. I really think the money *is* the issue. For someone who claims to have such little regard for money, you have a terrible fetishism about it. Why are you so afraid of it?"

They were close to the uncomfortable truth of their marriage. In his secret heart, Paul's novel, his future as a novelist—as tenuous, even imaginary, as both things were—meant more to him than did his own wife. The test of this was his speculative knowledge that he would choose to live life without her before he would choose to live as anything other than a writer. But this choice was no longer possible in any case. Through his dependence on her he had grown into someone who would never be able to make his own way in the world. He had no skills for living. Thus, whatever he longed to do was now impossible without Renata's full participation. They gazed at each other, their kitchen now turned into unfamiliar turf, their love into an obstacle, their faces filled with resentment and tenderness and fear.

The phone rang.

Renata got up to answer it; Paul, who was shaking, sat back in his chair and crossed his legs. "Hello?" Renata said, and Paul saw her face cloud over. "Fine, thanks," she said. "One second." She let the hand holding the phone drop down to her waist. "Martin," she said.

"I'll get it in the living room," he said, and got up gratefully. The kids were sitting on the floor in front of the TV. "Could you turn it down a bit, please? I have a phone call," he said gently. Peter held up the remote control, turned the sound down, and, with practiced movements, the two of them scuttled a couple of feet closer to the screen. They were watching some sitcom which featured three single men taking care of several small children. Peter and Leo showed a distinct preference for any entertainment which featured small children, even if the jokes themselves were over their heads. The set stood on an old table just in front of the window, which was black with night. Paul sat down stiffly and picked up the phone.

"Hi, Martin. I left you a couple messages today, I don't know if you got them." Martin didn't always remember to check his own answering machine. Paul heard Renata hang up in the kitchen, and her footsteps falling away toward the bedroom.

"Oh, yeah, sorry," Martin said. "I was reading Blake all day, and I got kind of . . . But look, I've been looking for this quote all night, and I finally found it. Shit, where is it? Hold on."

The boys, with their backs to Paul, tensed ever so slightly, and he saw they were watching with great concentration an ad for the movie *The Little Mermaid*. Peter in particular had been talking about this movie, which he had not seen, for weeks. Paul knew what was coming. Peter turned around, still in his sitting position.

"Daddy? Will you take us to see *Little Mermaid*?"

He tried not to wince. "Later," he said. "Daddy's on the phone." Sixteen-fifty, plus popcorn, to line the pockets of the culture factory that had, among its other offenses, degraded forever some of the world's noblest fairy tales. Paul wondered how old Peter would have to be before he could lend him his copy of Ariel Dorfman's *How to Read Donald Duck*.

"You there?" Martin said suddenly.

"Yeah, yeah."

"Okay, good. Ready? 'An artist is a creature driven by demons. He is completely amoral in that he will rob, borrow, beg, or steal from anybody and everybody to get the work done. Everything goes by the board: honor, pride, decency, security, happiness, all, to get the book written. If a writer has to rob his mother, he will not hesitate; the "Ode on a Grecian Urn" is worth any number of old ladies.' "

He paused. Paul's living room was filled with the sound of canned laughter.

"William Faulkner," Martin said.

"So?"

"So? So William Faulkner! I mean, have you thought about this whole thing from that angle?"

"What thing?" Paul said, though he knew perfectly well.

"The money! Here you are struggling nobly to write this great novel. What is the chief obstacle to the completion of this project? Money! And now you have an opportunity to make so much money in one shot that you can do nothing but write fiction for years afterward, years. So this money comes from an unappealing source. So what? You think Faulkner would care?"

"Faulkner wouldn't prostitute his own talent," Paul said.

"He went to Hollywood, didn't he? Land of prostitution!"

Paul leaned on his elbow, so that he was supporting his face with the receiver. What a pass things have come to, he thought, when Martin and Renata find themselves in agreement about something. About me. He thought about reminding Martin that Tolstoy had advised an interval of fifty years before fictionalizing any historical event. But the evening had taken a lot out of him; he had little energy left for arguing. "True," he said.

"And do people hold that against him now? Does his reputation suffer because of it?"

Paul wasn't really listening; he was gazing at the backs of Leo and Peter, thin, poignantly boyish, the younger still with some of the roundness of infancy, the older growing all the time in strength and distinction. Leo was wearing clothes that Renata had bought for Peter in a discount store on Broadway two years ago. They broke his heart sometimes. He knew he ought to tell them that they'd watched enough TV. But cutting off their TV was only a punishment; it didn't seem constructive in any way. Their father understood so little about the real, fallen, forward-looking world, it was no wonder they looked to television to explain it to them. He had a vision of them growing up and away from him.

"I don't know," he said to Martin. "Maybe you're right. I don't know anymore."

This vulnerability seemed to take Martin by surprise. "Well, I'm just trying to look at the thing from all sides," he said defensively.

Then an image flickered on the screen that triggered Paul's attention again, and he looked up. "Do you have your TV on?" he said.

"No," Martin said.

"Turn on Channel 7." It was the ad for Levi's jeans which consisted of a staged poetry reading. The poem was a kind of indirect homage to the comfort of blue jeans. "Sky fits heaven, so ride it," Paul heard. "Child fits mother, so hold your baby tight."

"Ah, yes," Martin said uncomfortably when he had turned on the set.

"This guy lives right here in New York, right?" Paul said. "What's his name? Max Blagg."

Martin said nothing.

"I mean, what do you think when you see that?"

"Why do I have to think about it at all?" Martin said.

"Because this poem has bored its way into the minds of millions of people. Millions of people who have probably never read a poem in their entire adult life, now the single living American poet they can even recognize is Max Blagg."

"Is he American?" Martin asked.

"Whatever. Doesn't that make you angry, when you see that ad?"

"Why should it?"

"Because it's about nothing! It is completely divorced

from meaning. Advertising is art founded on the absence of conviction, right, and poetry is probably the last form left for it to take up and suck the blood right out of. Language in this culture is totally debased, and even poetry isn't safe from it."

"Uh-huh. So, if I understand this correctly, you are somehow worried that you're turning into Max Blagg?"

"Yes! Well, in a way. I mean this guy has forever forfeited his right to write a poem that anyone will take seriously, don't you agree?"

"I don't know that anyone ever took him seriously to begin with."

"He's as much as admitted that his own work means nothing to him, because its content is for sale. Isn't that just what I'd be doing? Does it matter that this money would help me finish my novel faster, when I'd be guaranteeing that nobody would take the novel seriously anyway?"

He had unknowingly raised his voice, and the kids had turned to look cautiously at him. He smiled reassuringly, feeling foolish.

"Look," Martin said. "I see your point. When the novel comes out, its immediate reception might be affected. But is that why you're writing it? For its immediate critical reception?"

He waited for an answer. "No," Paul said glumly.

"No. You have to put your trust in what lasts. How do you think I get the nerve to write poetry at all? All the other stuff will fall away; precisely what makes poetry poetry, what makes art art, is its capacity to outlive the cultural static. You and I are not so much at home in this world. Which is part of why we write: we write for, we write *to*, the next world. That's the only way to think of it."

Paul watched his sons watch TV. "And what if the next world is even less receptive?" he said. "What if there's no real home in it for written language, for the exaltation of language? You have to admit that's the direction the culture's moving in. Other forms have vanished, after all. What if we're living out the twilight of imaginative writing?"

"Then we're fucked," Martin said, "so we might as well take the money now."

Eight A.M. on another placid day in Los Angeles, and Amy was already on the phone. Her parents had spent her teenage years trying to wean her away from the telephone, and here it was turning out to be her most marketable skill. Like much of Hollywood's development community, she had to tailor her workday to account for the time difference in New York; she hadn't been able to adapt completely, though, unlike her boss, Frank, who was in every morning at six-thirty after a session with his trainer. Now there, thought Amy, was a guy who lived on the phone; according to his poor harried personal assistant, whose job prioritizing calls was akin to that of an air traffic controller in both its nature and its stress level, he took or made on average about a hundred and twenty calls per day, interrupting the flow only to have lunch with studio people or, on occasion, to scream at an unlucky underling. Made a millionaire by his acumen when it came to buying up properties for movies and TV, he no longer had the time or even the inclination to read what he was buying. Sometimes—Amy had been through it—he would order an employee to come with him when he drove to lunch and sit in the passenger seat reading treatments aloud to him; once they had reached the restaurant, the employee would have to catch a cab back to the office. What was annoying, though, was not how little Frank and his colleagues read, but how little they needed to. Any real mogul's feeling was that reading anything longer than a treatment only signified overcautiousness, a lack of gut instinct—a feeling that was in fact borne out nearly every day. Literacy, Amy thought, might eventually be bred out of the Hollywood civilization entirely, like a useless appendage.

She said an affectionate goodbye to her friend Olivia at Copeland Simonds and hung up the phone. Outside, a morning breeze blew through the evenly spaced trees on the empty sidewalk. She reminded herself that the day might end well if she got through it—she had a date with an aspiring screenwriter who was taking her to see the newly restored *Zéro de Conduite* at the New Beverly. Sighing, she picked up her notebook and walked through the open door of Pickert's office.

He was standing inches from his picture window, looking out, arms folded, nodding as someone spoke to him on his featherweight headset. He still wore the clothes from his morning workout, a *Home Alone 2* T-shirt and a pair of black spandex bike shorts; a freshly pressed suit hung in a dry cleaner's bag from a hook on the back of the door. "Whoa," he said. "Hold on. Hold on. There is nothing in there about script approval. You go back— You go back and check it. He signed the rights over and that's the end of it."

He turned to start pacing, saw Amy in the door, and halted with a frown. "Yes, but it *doesn't* contradict any facts," he said. "Right. Right. Well, look, I have a meeting now, but you tell him to go back and look at his contract. Poetic license isn't just for poets, you know." He laughed. "Right." He took off his expensive headset, threw it onto the desk, watched it skid off and fall to the floor, and said to Amy, "What have you got?"

She took a deep breath. "Paul Soloway," she said. "I talked to his agent, this Ned Garland—"

"Never heard of him."

"Well, nevertheless. He says they're close to finalizing a book deal, and that, according to the author's strict wishes, movie offers will be entertained for the book only, when it's done."

"Fuck me!" Pickert yelled. "That could take forever! Did he say—"

"He wouldn't come right out and say it, but it's pretty clear there's not even a proposal written down yet. And no ghost, so it'll take that much longer."

"Who does this guy think he is? What kind of shelf life does a story like this have, a couple of months? People are forgetting the name Paul Soloway even as we speak. We should be in production already with this. We should have had a script knocked out weeks ago. Every day that goes by, his price goes down, and this guy wants to dick around writing his own book?"

"Well, he's getting pretty good money for it. Three-ten, hard-soft. Maybe he figures any movie money is gravy after that."

Pickert's eyes narrowed. "The agent told you three-ten?"

"No." She smiled. "This is the good part. Remember I told you I had a mole at Copeland Simonds? Well, the book's going to Bob Spain, whose assistant was my sophomore-year roommate in college."

Pickert looked at her admiringly, as if she had brought this about by forethought rather than luck. "How soon can she get us pages?" he said.

Amy's eyes widened in alarm. "Come on, Frank," she said pleadingly. "She could get fired on the spot for that. She's a friend of mine."

"Well, work on her." He leaned back on the windowsill, fingertips pressed together, machinating. Black hair sprouted over the top of his T-shirt. In the silence Amy could hear the patient voice of his assistant putting people on hold. Pickert began shaking his head from side to side.

"No," he said. "No. It's not going to work. Even if we get some pirated pages, that helps us put together our bid ahead of time, but what's the soonest they could auction the book? Two, three months if the guy writes fast? It's too much time. The story's dead as a haddock by then. No network will want to touch it." He grimaced. "Besides, I hate auctions. They tend to level the playing field."

He walked to his desk and sat down behind it, putting his feet up, an odd sight in his tight shorts.

"But there's an opportunity here, God damn it, and I'm not letting it walk away," he said. "Three-ten is nice for him and his little agent, but for me it does jack." He turned and focused on Amy with his most unsettling intensity. "The thing is, this guy is maybe getting a little proprietary. After all, a story has many different angles. It can be seen from many different perspectives, at least as many as there were participants in the events of the story itself. It's that whole *Rashomon* thing. Do you follow me?"

Amy, caught in the beam of his bright eyes, was trying to think about *Zéro de Conduite*, about the end of the workday, which would surely come even if it seemed right now as remote as the millennium, about the dues that everyone who wanted to accomplish something worthwhile always had to pay.

"So I'm thinking," Pickert said, "that there's another way we could go."

To begin to defuse the situation in the apartment, Paul agreed to accompany the kids to the Metro to see *The Little Mermaid*. It was the sort of job that customarily fell to Renata, on her days off from work. Sitting through such an experience really did represent, in Paul's own mind, a major sacrifice; but he knew enough, if only from the look on Renata's face, not to fish for any special thanks.

They decided on Tuesday that Saturday would be the day, whispering about it in their bedroom; they had to wait until Friday to tell the boys about it, because otherwise they would have gotten overexcited. As it was, they all got very little sleep Friday night. At breakfast, Peter, with the timid voice and the sidelong glance of a child who knows he's risking his parents' temper but can't help himself, began asking how long before they could go.

"How long? How long?" Leo shouted, and Peter made a threatening face at him.

"Well, let's see," Paul said. "The movie's at eleventhirty. It takes us about fifteen minutes to walk to the theater. And it's seven-fifteen now. So. When do you think we should go?"

"Now," Leo said.

Renata, whose back was to them as she cut up an apple for Leo, laughed in spite of herself. "Close," Paul said, "but no. The correct answer is eleven-ten, or less than four hours from now."

"Four *hours!*"

"Well, you'd better leave more time than that," Renata said, sitting at the table. "There'll be a big line for tickets."

"There will?" Paul said.

She looked at him in amazement. "This is a very popular movie, you know. Some of Peter's friends from school will be there seeing it for the third or fourth time."

"Mortifying," Paul said.

"And this is the most popular show time. There's going to be a mob. Of *kids.* You better be ready."

"And popcorn," Peter said helpfully. "What if they run out?"

Leo's mouth fell open at the mention of popcorn.

"Okay, all right," Paul said. "Ten forty-five."

But that wasn't a lot better as far as the boys were concerned; each minute of the morning was a vast canyon of boredom, a desert in the traversal of which no toy could distract them from their martyrdom. Peter broke one of Leo's plastic cars, which led to tears, so Paul and Renata decided to let them watch a little extra TV to help the time go by for them. But a few minutes later Leo's earsplitting scream rose again, as a fight broke out over the remote control. At twenty past ten Paul gave in and told the boys to go get their shoes on. They sprinted down the hall to their room like dogs after a tennis ball.

"What are you going to do?" Paul asked Renata, while Peter, squinting like a diamond cutter, slowly tied his own shoes. Leo tugged at Paul's fingers.

"Me?" She smiled. "I don't know where to start. Maybe first I'll use the bathroom without anyone pushing the door open. Then I could see if I still have the ability to read a whole magazine article all the way through." Scrupulously not crediting him for doing something that she did routinely, she did touch him fondly on the cheek. "Have fun," she said.

He knew he could walk the eight blocks to the Metro without the cane; if he had to stand in line for a while, that might be discomfiting, but he had developed a certain stubbornness about it, a dislike of being helped, along with a desire to return life to normal by sheer force of will. Leo wanted to walk, but Paul knew the boy would tire on the way and want to be carried, so he insisted on the stroller. A light breeze gave them a tailwind as they turned down Broadway. Paul looked up and saw it was a beautiful spring day, though, as always, he had the sensation that this beautiful day was in fact located hundreds of feet above them, where no people lived—that they were like fish at the bottom of a river, able to see the sky but with no real relation to it. A beautiful spring day, he thought, which they would spend lined up in a dark, artificially cooled theater watching a story about a girl who lived in the sea. There was nothing strange about it to the boys, and probably never would be; the roots of their disenfranchisement in nature, of course, were in him, and the roots of his own severance were in the suburban life of his own childhood. This, he thought, was something he could use in the novel. He hadn't written a word since coming home from the hospital, and that sense of arrest, as well as the pressures that were causing it, weighed heavily on him. He thought more about it as they walked; as for the boys, their own thoughts were like blank screens, receptive to wonder, greatly excited by the movie about which they knew almost nothing except that they were sure to love it. Conscientiously, the three of them stopped at every light, even when there were no cars in sight. "Don't walk," Leo cautioned imperiously from the stroller.

When they reached 100th Street, Paul could see, before the boys could, that Renata had, if anything, underestimated the popular demand. Two lines already formed around the old theater—one, under the shade of the marquee, waited to buy tickets, and another, much longer ticket holders' line snaked around the block. "Here we are," Paul said, pulling in behind a father and daughter in front of the ticket window. His heart began to race with the fear that the show would be sold out. It would send them all back home again, for a grueling two hours until the next show time, and a knowing, exasperated glare from Renata. He didn't dare mention this dark prospect to the boys, who were darting in and out of line, jumping up to try to get a look inside the booth where a sullen Latina girl dispensed tickets and change, tickets and change, as if it might hold something of interest for them.

When Paul caught the eye of the father in front of him, he couldn't help asking, in a low tone, as if in a frequency only fathers could pick up, "Think it'll sell out?"

The father, a man in his forties who looked friendly and tired, scanned the other line. "Must be pretty close now," he said.

"What'll we do if we can't get tickets?"

The man shrugged and looked at Paul with the blankness brought on by great fatigue. What looked like patience had crossed over into fatalism. "There's a bar up the street," he said.

Paul smiled. He began to hear the distinctive sound made by a large group of small, excited children—a kind of steady, rolling noise, like the bubbling of a cauldron, high voices which had not yet grown easy to distinguish. It was odd to hear that sound away from a playground or a school. The line moved quickly. "Come on, come on," Paul mumbled as they advanced toward the teenage girl in her booth. The father and daughter in front of them got tickets and departed. The girl in the ticket booth looked at Paul with a kind of hibernating hatred.

"One adult, two children," Paul said.

Wordlessly, she slid him the tickets, and he finally relaxed. Stuffing change in his pocket with one hand, carrying the folded stroller in the other, he shepherded the boys around the corner of 99th Street to the back of the line.

"When can we go in?" Peter asked.

Paul checked his watch. "Half an hour or so," he said, trying to hide the disappointment in his own voice.

The boys, though, seemed to have at least as much patience as their father. In fact, the children as a group were, though loud, otherwise very well disciplined. It was a city thing, Paul decided; city kids were used to waiting in line for almost everything. He looked down at them; they stood patiently on either side of him, their faces open. "Nobody has to go to the bathroom or anything?" he asked.

They gazed up at him and shook their heads no. Neither was in the mood to speak, apparently. What, Paul wondered, does a little boy think about when he is trying to make time go by?

He heard an adult voice above the babble and looked up to see a homeless man making his way slowly down the line, his hand out discreetly, a black stroke against the all-white faces. The adults tried to avoid his eyes, while the children stared at him with great candor. In the spring sun and cool wind that carried the atmosphere of a baseball game, the man wore a greasy hooded jacket with a fake fur collar, no shirt, and industrial blue pants of the kind that city workers were issued. He was getting quite close to the faces of the parents whom he asked for money, and speaking in a soft, almost intimate voice. No one was giving him anything. They would shake their heads firmly before he could even get his plea out; knowing, though, that they were all trapped in place, he would linger for another few seconds, silently but not exactly unthreateningly, in case they weakened perhaps, before moving down the stationary line.

Begging was an honest human transaction, Paul thought, and he didn't see why deceit or intimidation needed to be brought into it. Still, it disturbed him that no one—at least no one he'd seen—had parted with a dollar for this unfortunate. Paul knew he was down to very little money, so he took out his wallet to see what he could spare. The answer was nothing; he had four dollars and change left, and the boys had already made their sense of entitlement to popcorn and soda quite plain. But the homeless man's eye, though he was still six or eight people away, had not missed Paul's wallet. When he arrived and mumbled in Paul's face his unintelligible plea—worn into abstraction by constant repetition—he was shaking slightly with anticipation.

"I'm sorry," Paul said to him. "I thought I had more money."

The man's eyebrow went up quizzically, as if to say, More money than who?

"I'm sorry," Paul repeated. "I can't spare anything. Really." Leo grabbed onto Paul's leg.

The man's disbelief was palpable. He thinks, Paul realized, that I've played a joke on him, to humiliate him. Nothing will convince him otherwise. Just then, the line began to move, followed by a high-pitched "Yay!" from those children closest to the entrance. The homeless man did not even bother with the three people behind Paul, the last three to get tickets. He stood still, wavering a bit, staring up the empty block toward Amsterdam Avenue.

As they slowly moved forward, around the corner, Paul was too upset even to think to conceal from the boys how upset he was. God damn it, he said to himself, God damn it, I *can't* spare any money, it's not like it's because I haven't been to the *cash* machine lately, it's because I'm fucking *broke*, my kid's pants are too short for him and yet here I am spending about two days' meal money on a motherfucking *Disney* movie, I'm not one of these people, I'm . . . He didn't know how to finish. He didn't know whom he was angry at. His mood was lightened somewhat, though, as they marched slowly past a newsstand next door to the theater, one of those upper Broadway businesses no bigger than a walk-in closet that stayed alive by selling pornography, with triple-X videocassette boxes filling the window; a young boy ten feet or so in front of them loudly asked his mother, "What's 'Super Wet Action'?" The mother opted not to hear him. Paul smiled as he thought of the natural appeal that phrase would have for any small boy. A few moments later they were inside.

Paul rushed them past the long refreshment and bathroom lines to find some good seats. He hadn't forgotten a principal difference between kids' and adults' movies, which was that, at a kids' movie, the theater filled up from the first row backward; so he was able to find them three great seats almost smack in the middle. Folding up the stroller, he told Peter to save those seats while he and Leo went for snacks. This was just the sort of instruction the overdramatic Peter loved; small enough to squeeze between the seats and the armrests, he stretched out flat like a diver, and glanced back up at his father for approval. "Perfect," Paul said.

He hadn't been to the movies in a while and so was floored by the price of the refreshments. Very clever of them, he thought, to schedule the show to run right through lunchtime. He could afford just two Cokes and two small tubs of popcorn covered with viscous butter substitute ("Buttery Topping," in their legally sound if linguistically appalling scheme); one large tub for the two boys to share would have been cheaper, but that was just asking for trouble. The whole lot was served up to them by miserable-looking teenagers; if there was any low-wage job that afforded some satisfaction, Paul would have thought it was serving sweets to children, but evidently he was wrong.

Once they were in their seats and the kids were eating, Paul could relax a bit, even in the anticipatory din. The theater was filled with a curiosity and a restlessness that seemed to feed off its own volume. Paul turned from side to side in his seat and saw mothers trying to settle their kids down, handing out napkins, grabbing wrists, wearing expressions of tested patience as they waited for the lights to go down. Something about the whole scene was depressing him, he realized. He hadn't been to see a movie that could fairly be characterized as popular in quite a long time. It wasn't the insultingly filthy aspect of the theater itself, with its missing armrests and its generations of sugary soda coating the unpainted floor. It wasn't the ugliness of the way the handsome old theater had been cynically chopped into two theaters, so that there was no more balcony, and the original moldings disappeared halfway up the wall. It wasn't the consistently hateful looks of the young ushers, or the sheer, noisy, inconsiderate democracy of the place.

It was the power of the crowd—or, more specifically, the power over the crowd of the moving image—that Paul was feeling, a power with which all the centuries had not had to contend, until Paul's own century. He had a sense of how thoroughly he had marginalized himself by choosing the life he had; but there was a difficult distinction between being marginalized and being irrelevant, between an elite and a nonentity. In his home, at his typewriter, he so rarely felt the touch of this kind of mass authority. Here among his fellow parents, fellow citizens, he felt decidedly out of place—not simply because no one here knew him or cared what he thought, but because he had no point of entry anymore into what they were experiencing. Even the attention of his sons, he could see, as they munched robotically, did not have any space for him right now.

The lights went down, to another monosyllable of celebration from the children, and the moldy red curtain parted loudly.

After a Coca-Cola commercial, *The Little Mermaid* began, and within ten minutes Paul was glad they were all in darkness so the rapt boys could not see the twitches of discomfort on his face. The movie turned out to concern a mermaid named Ariel—going out of its way to mention that she was sixteen—who, on a forbidden trip to the surface of the ocean where she lives, sees and falls in love with a human man. The Disney m.o., twenty-odd years after the death of Uncle Walt himself, seemed to have changed little since Paul's own childhood: the bastardization of some of Europe's oldest and most treasured fairy tales, the looting of the great heritage of folk storytelling, the effacing of all the ambiguities that were what made the tales enduring in the first place, the destruction of context, the relentless, antihistorical updating of every detail. All done because of the accountants' knowledge that these priceless plots were in the public domain—and, too, to be fair, because of some dim, barely conscious apprehension of the magic of myth. Though, to the Disney people, the real magic of myth was its ability to put fannies in the seats.

"Daddy, they're *not* barbarians," Ariel said hotly to her father, King Triton, who was forbidding her to revisit the surface world to search for her human love, Prince Eric. "I just don't see how a world that makes such wonderful things could be so bad."

"Spineless, savage, harpooning fish-eaters!" railed King Triton.

Paul's life seemed to him full of lost battles, his hours taken up by things he swore he would never do. Writing picture captions for a brochure for fur coats was one such thing; another was sitting in an expensive, run-down theater with his children, paying to expose them to a Walt Disney movie. With no interest in what was on the screen, he looked down at his sons on either side of him. They were frozen at attention; Peter continued to eat with his eyes on the screen, while Leo had a handful of popcorn suspended halfway between the bucket and his mouth. The rich colors played off their white-looking skin. Paul turned around in his seat to look behind him; one mother glared at him, but no one else seemed to notice. While it was easy to distinguish between the quality of the slack-jawed children's attention and that of the adults—the former looked as though they wouldn't notice if you poked them with a stick, while the latter were more distantly engaged, simply more experienced perhaps—everyone was watching intently, with no sense of the other strangers gathered there, with no sense that moviegoing was a communal experience. Which, in some ways, it was not.

Ariel was being spied on by a crab named Sebastian who spoke in a sort of Caribbean patois. How old a device was this—the "people" (which included the mermaids) spoke like white Midwesterners while the animals had foreign accents? Still, in a catchy ballad called "Part of Your World," Ariel sang mournfully of all she would gladly sacrifice just to join the human race.

Paul's ambiguous discomfort brought to mind an idea he had often heard debated (and had sometimes tried to resolve himself in a kind of daydreaming self-interview): what did it mean to say that movies were the enemy of literature? Alone in his home it had looked one way to him; now, in the belly of the beast, as it were, he had a new insight. While it was always contemporary writers who complained they were being abused by the movies, Hollywood was most demonstrably the enemy of *dead* writers. Certainly it was the enemy of Hans Christian Andersen. Movies did routinely what no previous form could do—they appropriated and reinvented the work of dead artists. This had been done in music for two hundred

sons? How long will they stay buried in memory? He looked again at the crowd around him, all staring, some even smiling, with interest, all of them as muted as Ariel herself.

Then he remembered something he had read about this movie, inadvertently as it were, in the arts pages of the *Times*. The man who had written the lyrics to these catchy, tuneful, often insipid songs—Paul didn't remember his name—was dead now. He had succumbed, most likely as horribly and as painfully as most of his fellow victims, to AIDS. What did this mean? This lyricist had had to live, as a gay man, in the very best scenario, a life of caution and fear, a life circumscribed by the prejudices of others, prejudices which could bloom into violence at virtually any moment of your life outside the four walls of your home. How could this kind of life not reap its own anger? And if the unthinking hatred of others weren't cause enough for despair, there was the plague itself, which Paul thought may just have been the single most absurd occurrence of the entire exasperating century: a virus—the very essence of meaninglessness—that attacked those marginalized social groups whose welfare the rest of society cared least about. The overbearing ridiculousness of it! And yet how had this man, whom Paul struggled to imagine, spent the days of his death sentence, days, perhaps, of grotesque physical discomforts?

Evidently, putting words in the mouth of Sebastian the minstrel crab, with which to lead the creatures of the deep in a Busby Berkeley number. This was not, say, Milton, or even Terence Rattigan, where those in the know could find in the carefully crafted words a second, forbidden story of the author's misfortune and pain. It seemed that Paul lived in a world where everyone, even the artists, accepted the divorce of experience and meaning—not only accepted but embraced it. How could you fight it? Just look, he said to himself as if there were someone beside him to whom the new world needed to be explained—a visitor from a past century, perhaps—just look at the faces of my children. Open, blank, riveted, dear to me perhaps but otherwise indistinguishable from the faces around them. Don De-Lillo said the future belongs to crowds. Don DeLillo, Paul now saw, was a fucking genius—too bad, because all his genius enabled him to see was his own archaism, his own obsolescence. For the crowd was deeply inimical to privacy, and thus was not to be entertained by contemplative, private forms. Maybe the novel, belief in which Paul had predicated his life upon, belonged to another world. Maybe this was a world into which new forms, forms which rejected private life as a kind of heretical insult, were struggling to be born. Maybe not. In any case, Paul could now at least give a name to his fear, which made it no less vivid and no more rational. He felt that he was in danger of disappearing.

Thus it was that the outcome of the story of *The Little Mermaid* came to be vitally important to him. And thus it was that he felt himself overwhelmed by the inevitable happy ending: wherein the sea witch, regardless of her apparent immortality and magical powers, was spectacularly vanquished, and Ariel was relieved of the burden of choosing; her father relented, sending her with his blessings onto the land, where, her voice miraculously restored, she turned her back remorselessly on the undersea kingdom to live as the wife of a prince. A happy ending, with no lesson; or, rather, that *was* the lesson. Paul thought of Goethe, in his old age, pacing the floor of his room, trying to figure out how to get Faust out of his contract with Mephistopheles. He didn't know exactly what a panic attack felt like, but he thought he might be having one now.

"It's like I always say," the crab said. "Children got to be free to live deir own lives."

Out in the lobby, there was a line out the door for the men's room; Paul leaned the stroller against the wall and stood absently with one reassuring hand on each son's shoulder, while Leo, full of Coke, grabbed himself with childish frankness. The lobby was swirling with voices, excited children and pleased adults. Outside, another throng stood gazing impatiently at them through the glass, waiting to be admitted for the one-thirty show. Lost in thought as he was, Paul gradually became aware of two adult, female voices, detached from the general noise somehow by his subconscious attention.

"It's that guy," one voice said. "That guy. What's his name?"

"What the hell are you talking about?"

"The one who got kidnaped." Paul's heart jumped, but he did not look over. "I recognize him from TV."

"Seriously?"

"I'm telling you. Look, there's his two kids, they kept saying on TV about how he had two sons."

Three sets of fathers and sons exited the bathroom; Paul fairly pushed the boys forward, but there was not quite room for them inside yet.

"Oh, you're right," the second woman said excitedly. "Look, he's even still got that limp."

Paul finally turned his head and saw the two young mothers, their children waiting impatiently beside them. Far from embarrassed, the women appeared thrilled he was looking right at them. One of them lifted her hand and shyly waved. Four more people came through the rest room door, and Paul, in the glare of his own celebrity, anxiously herded Peter and Leo inside.

Five minutes later, out on the sidewalk, they started north up Broadway toward home. Leo, worn out by excitement, was back in the stroller and was nearly asleep before they had gone two blocks. Peter, though, had not yet come down. His head was full of images, and with a touching faith in his father's omniscience he was peppering him with questions.

"Dad?" he said. "Why did Ariel's father smash all her stuff?"

Paul couldn't even remember this particular scene. "I

don't know why," he said, "but they made up at the end, so he wasn't mad anymore."

That kind of thing would end, he thought—still shaken by the two women in the lobby who imagined his privacy to have been gladly forfeited—and it would end sooner rather than later. He was not Rodney King. He was not Mary Jo Buttafuoco. Of course, in a sense, he was: another life annexed by a fame brought about not by distinction but by accident. But it was in the nature of such things that it would taper off.

"Was the sea witch dead at the end?" Peter asked.

Paul thought this over. "Yeah, I'm pretty sure she was," he said.

To what extent did an artist benefit by withdrawing from the world? Yet the more Paul felt he understood the time he had been born into, the less easily he could reconcile it with his faith in his art. The two had to be reconciled somehow, though, or he had nothing valuable, nothing personal, to live for. Maybe some sort of compromise could be reached.

"Did Ariel's father go back underwater in the end?"

"Yes." Maybe some sort of compromise could be reached. Maybe some sort of balance could be struck, while he worked to reason all this out. It was probably a good thing, he thought, that he was no longer so sure of himself. All of a sudden, as if he had broken through some sort of veil, he had a vision of the money. He couldn't think of anything he would want to use it for, other than to buy a few books; but Renata could have it, the boys could have it. They deserved it, after all. Or, rather, no one deserved it; but such fortunes existed under the sun, and so why shouldn't they have one?

"Dad? Why did Ariel have to get kissed by the prince?"

"She was afraid of losing her voice," he said.

They went home, the children had a nap, and Paul spent the rest of the weekend talking to Renata, taking occa-

school and petrified of black people, not some PD dressed like a Salvation Army bum who wasn't sharp enough to get a job at some high-paying firm. Victor, and subsequently the court, had granted the lawyer's request. They were meeting for the first time today.

He strode in, only five minutes late, chatting amiably with the sergeant, who was not chatting back. He had a kind of natural tonsure of white hair, with little half-glasses hung on a chain around his neck. Beneath his expensive-looking gray suit emerged a pair of pointy cowboy boots that looked as though they could kick through a car door. Without meaning to, Hartley stood up from his chair to greet him.

"Mr. Boggs," he said.

Boggs turned to look him over, and his life-of-the-party expression instantly changed into a scowl. Hartley froze with worry. Then Boggs looked over Hartley's shoulder at the guard.

"Officer," he said, "will you please take those goddamn handcuffs off my client?"

Hartley looked behind him; the guard, red-faced, was looking off to one side like a little boy. Then he reached for his keys, stepped forward, and drew off the cuffs.

Hartley felt as if he had witnessed a feat of strength. He turned back to Boggs, his eyes wide. Boggs, who loved nothing better than worship, gave him a small, confident smile.

"Would you leave us alone, please?" he said. The guard withdrew.

They were alone. Boggs put out his hand, and Hartley shook it.

"So," Boggs said.

Hartley was so excited now, he would have believed that this guy could spring him by the end of the day. Desperate, after months of stewing in his blank cell, to make some sort of progress at long last, he tried to get everything out at once.

"So I've been thinking about my testimony," he said, and Boggs smiled broadly. "I mean I know it's way off, but I was thinking about how I didn't have a lawyer present when I was first brought in, and maybe there's some technicality there, in my arrest, that would make all the other evidence unusable. Fruits of the poison tree, I think it's called, or something like that. And I don't know if any of the others rolled over on me, if they're using any evidence like that. It would be a lot easier to get some word on that if I was out on bail, but my old lawyer told me no way."

"Your old lawyer was a putz," Boggs said. "You let me worry about bail."

Hartley's hopes leaped. "You can get the judge to reduce it?" he said. "Because I can only get together about—"

"The judge will reduce it maybe fifty thousand." Hartley looked confused. "That's not the answer. The answer is getting you some more money to work with."

"Money?" Hartley said.

"And you can forget about your testimony in court for a good long while. That's many months down the road, if it ever happens at all. But that doesn't mean your trial hasn't begun yet. It began the day you were arrested, and you have some catching up to do. The thing is," he said, leaning forward and staring right into Victor's eyes, the same eyes his old lawyer was always trying to avoid, "most lawyers make the mistake of preparing only for the courtroom. Old as I am, I seem like one of the only guys around who recognizes how the law has changed, how the world has changed. It's a whole new system. You got to know how to work it. The fight's not in the courtroom anymore, it's outside it. It makes no sense to mount your defense in a place where nothing's going on. You have to go where the trial is."

He looked at his client, who was struggling to remember every mystifying word of this oracular speech, to try to make sense of it later in retrospect.

"And right now, the trial of Victor Hartley is being conducted in the media. Print journalism, tabloid TV, TV news, TV movies maybe, feature movies maybe. These are the things that make the world where juries come from. While your old lawyer was playing with himself in court, this Soloway guy has had the floor, uninterrupted. Well, the world has heard his side long enough. We've got to get your story out there. I've already made a few phone calls." He reached into his inner breast pocket with one hand, and with the other he balanced the reading glasses on his nose.

"My story?" Hartley said.

"I don't know why I didn't think of it before," Garland said. He sat in the leather chair in front of Andy Bayley's desk, in Andy Bayley's corner office. She smiled at him. It was five-thirty; the hazy sunshine burnished the tops of the old midtown office buildings visible through the windows behind her. Garland's coworkers also stood around the office, ill at ease, near the door, trying to look happy. They all held paper cups full of champagne—champagne Andy herself had ordered to be delivered.

"The novel was the key to the whole deal," he went on. The others had already heard this story but he couldn't have cared less about that. "The novel's what's always mattered most to Paul. So he calls me himself this morning to suggest the two-book deal. I practically had to put him on hold so I could smack myself for not thinking of it in the first place."

"Beautiful," Andy said, beaming maternally. She was dressed for a subsequent party. "I love it."

"So of course Spain goes for it right away, I mean what does he care. But he tries to make the novel a throw-in. I said, Come on, I don't think you want to begin this very important project by delivering an insult like that to the writer."

He waited for one of his bitter colleagues to ask again what the final deal was. Stubbornly, they refused.

"Three hundred and eighty-five thousand," he said anyway, "world English, hard-soft."

Ten blocks downtown, Spain spent the afternoon accepting congratulations of his own. He briefed the publicity department on what to leak to the press; then he took a cab home to celebrate in the same way he celebrated every six-figure acquisition, with a bottle of thirty-year-old Scotch and a bucket of ice on the terrace of his Sutton Place apartment.

Paul and Renata sent the kids upstairs to Mrs. Perez and went out for Cuban food at La Rosita. Though it seemed an absurdly modest kind of celebration, it was all they could afford—since the first check, for one hundred and sixty-two thousand dollars, wouldn't come for another eight weeks or so, Garland had said. They came home, put the boys to bed, and made quiet love, perhaps only because they thought they should; it was strangely tender, Renata thought, even a little sad, as if they were saying goodbye. But, exhausted by the emotions of the day, she didn't reflect for long; she passed into a sound sleep, like Ned, like Spain, like Martin, like Bayley, all of them newly sanguine now that the book, despite its author, was finally under way.

PART TWO

LATENESS

THEY PAID THE PHONE BILL, AND THE CON ED BILL, AND OF course the past-due rent. They paid off their remaining student loans, loans they had deferred and deferred and finally just evaded about four years earlier; the financial aid officers at Columbia were as simultaneously delighted and angry as if Paul and Renata had been long-lost children who had come home on a holiday unannounced. They paid a three-year-old credit card debt which had been a scarlet stain on their secret financial histories every time they had subsequently tried to obtain other credit; they figured out what the taxes would be on their new income and they put that in a CD for next April. They even paid back every dollar (at Renata's insistence they had kept scrupulous track) they had borrowed over the years from Paul's mother, Gail. When the family took the train out to Wethersfield for a visit, Paul and Renata waited until the boys were asleep and then surprised Gail with the check. "Now, I don't want to hear anything about it," Renata said—but, to her embarrassment, before the sentence was even out of her mouth Gail was folding the check in half and slipping it comically inside her bra, with a look of pride and festivity. They had tried, in the past, to pay her back in tiny increments, but she had always refused, with the awkward curtness of a parent who thought it gauche to discuss money with the children. This, though, was different; this was not money so much as an emblem, at long last, of her only child's success. Paul was offended but un-surprised that she interpreted events in this way; she was a woman steeped more deeply than her son in the culture of their times. She even went so far as to suggest that, when the canceled check had gone through, they ask if Paul could have it back so she could put it in a frame.

Though there was, to be sure, something awesome and totemic about that check when it came in the mail. (Ned Garland had originally asked Paul to come to the office to pick it up, ostensibly for security reasons but just as much for the pleasure and triumph it would afford him; Paul begged off, saying his leg was acting up again. In truth, he thought that the moment he and the check encountered each other was best passed in private, where he wouldn't feel obligated to act overjoyed. He had the vague idea that, if he went to the Bayley office, someone there would want to take a picture of him.) It arrived on a Monday; Renata, for whom a Monday without obligations was still an uncomfortable novelty, was the one who found it, on one of her frequent trips downstairs to the mailbox. Together they opened it, while Leo and Peter, home from school, napped in the next room. They slid it out of the envelope and stared at it—a perfectly normal business check—as if it were covered in hieroglyphs that spoke of how they were to live the new life it represented.

He even wondered how they would react at the bank when he brought it in to deposit in the account which, that morning, had a balance of fifty-nine dollars and eleven cents. Would they call the police? But no, of course not, they hadn't the faintest memory of Paul's identity or his niggardly banking habits; the only reaction this fairy-tale fortune elicited from the teller was a scowl owing to the fact that, for a check of this amount, he would have to go fetch a supervisor for approval. When Paul got home, Renata was already sitting at the kitchen table, writing checks to the collection agencies with a shaking hand.

But even after all the bill-paying, they hadn't made a significant dent in the money. And when Paul finished the book—he hadn't yet begun it—another check was going to come for exactly the same amount.

What did people do with such fortunes? In point of fact, Paul, who was not writing, and Renata, who was not working, had nothing else to do with themselves but spend the

money; it turned out, though, not to be so natural an effort. They could have bought a car, but Paul had to admit
to a heightened fear of cars now; besides, they almost
never had occasion to drive anywhere, so a new car would
sit in a garage at larcenous expense for three hundred and
fifty days of the year, and that kind of immoderation with
money, after a lifetime of frugality, wasn't quickly learned.
They thought about putting Peter in private school, but it
was already too late to apply for next year; besides, several
of his best friends were going into the local P.S. in the fall,
so he was bound to resist with panic if they told him they
were pulling him out of it just because they could afford
to. Similarly, they had a big, cheap, rent-controlled apartment they saw no need to move out of, though they did
look forward to refurnishing it entirely. Paul wanted to
travel—to London, to Vienna, to Florence—but they
agreed they would wait until Leo was a bit older and more
suited to it. In the end, all he could really motivate himself
to purchase, other than books, was a CD player and a personal computer he deeply mistrusted from the moment
Renata pulled it out of the box. So they were left with a
savings account containing about a hundred and thirty
thousand dollars, from which Renata would each week,
conscious of the absurdity of it, withdraw grocery money.
It was a confounding, though by no means painful, state of
affairs.

Interestingly, the boys had no such problem. They
caught on rather quickly, in their uncanny way—a moment's hesitation in their parents' voices was enough to do
it—to the notion that the old basis on which they were
accustomed to having their luxurious wants turned down
("We can't afford it") had been overthrown. Once they
grasped this, the world—or, more specifically, the television—became a toy chest, and all that stood between them
and the plastic treasures of their imaginings was their parents' new inventiveness in coming up with reasons to say
no, or, conversely, their willfulness in refusing to give a

reason at all ("Because I said so!"). Every petition for Transformers or a Magna Doodle Deluxe or a Game Boy took on, more and more, the air of a challenge, a direct confrontation with Paul and Renata's newly weakened resources of denial. In this way they came into possession of a good many toys, large and small; but their crowning achievement—a VCR—came about only when their mother temporarily joined their side and the three of them overwhelmed a skeptical Paul, who predicted dire intellectual consequences when that machine was introduced into their home.

Paul's mood in general, as even he recognized, should have been better than it was. Not only were his money worries erased for the first time in his adult life; he could also contemplate the idea—newly carried into the realm of certainty—that *Son of Mind* was going to be published. It, and he, were under contract. His dream had come true, he had to admit, even if he had never previously liked to acknowledge it to be anything so flimsy as a dream. And he didn't even need to look two years, or three or four or whenever the novel would appear, into the distance to see how his life had been improved; in fact, on an everyday basis, Renata's new unemployment had also given him something he had longed for—an extra two hours a day, at a minimum, in which to write. With little else to do—they hadn't discussed how long she would stay out of work, since there was no practical need to discuss it—she took the kids to school, and brought them back at the end of the day, and took them to the park or to friends' houses, or the barber or the doctor or wherever they needed to go. He rejoiced to see her at last in possession of some control over what to do with her own time—less harried than he had seen her since college, and, not coincidentally, more beautiful. She would smile slyly at him, conspiratorially even, on the way out the door, knowing as no one else could know the greatness of the gift she was giving him. Together with the new freedom from having to write book reviews or catalogue copy—and with the fact that his visits to the orthopedist were down now to once every two weeks—he had more time to write than he had had since Peter was born.

And not only that. An application for a residence at Pennyfield, the prestigious artists' colony in upstate New York, which he had anxiously filed back in January under the more pressing circumstances of his old life, had been accepted; in a gorgeous concurrence, his stay at the colony was scheduled for that October, just weeks after the due date on his contract—an ideal opportunity to get back to work on the novel. Time, like money, was suddenly in perfect overabundance.

So why, he asked himself, should he feel so panicked?

Sitting there in the apartment, with his unflattering glasses on, Paul tried earnestly to find a point of entry into the story of his own kidnaping, beating, liberation, and recovery, the story that now stood between him and his novel, between his family and the next check for a hundred and sixty-two thousand dollars. But nothing substantial got done—all that really developed in those solitary hours were bad habits of the kind he had never really suffered from before. In his decade of working on the novel, he had naturally had good days and bad ones, weeks of inspiration and weeks of hard work on what would ultimately be revealed as a blind alley. But he was always *working*. Now he started to play games of the most juvenile and privately embarrassing sort: he tried to guess from their weight the number of sheets of typing paper left in the box and then counted them to see how close he came; he found an old superball of Peter's and tried to see how many times in a row he could bounce it off the floor, against the wall, and right back to where he sat in his chair at the desk; he got up to see if there was anything new inside the refrigerator since the last time he had looked. So scared was he of being found out in this ridiculous behavior that he reacted to his family's return home each afternoon not with the cheerfulness he felt but with a kind of feigned sullenness, as if he were sorry to be interrupted, a sullenness which Renata contentedly took for the real thing.

"Begin at the beginning," Spain had said to him, as if that kind of advice had any benefit, any meaning whatsoever, to anyone but a total nitwit. The two of them had met the same week the contract was signed, in Spain's office about half a mile, or so it seemed, above Sixth Avenue. Garland had set it up, though he did not come along. Paul waited while the guard in the lobby phoned upstairs to confirm his appointment; he waited in a small crowd, heads constantly turning, for one of the twelve elevators; then he waited at the thirty-eighth-floor reception area for Spain's assistant to come and fetch him. Her name was Olivia, and her youth, her considerable beauty, and her look of being moments away from bursting into tears of fatigue told Paul something interesting about her boss before he had even laid eyes on him. "So nice to meet you," she said, shaking his hand delicately. "We're so excited to have the book. Books." She gestured to him, and he walked behind her through the familiar corporate maze of work stations separated by five-foot partitions. It was a vast operation, he could see, and this was only one of three floors Copeland Simonds occupied. What did these people do all day? He was cheered, actually, by such evidence of large-scale industry and opulence all connected with the production of books. He couldn't look around him for too long, though; if he missed one turn behind Olivia, he was done for, he would have to stand still and wait for her to retrace her steps and find him, like a child in a department store.

The layout of the thirty-eighth floor was frank; on its perimeter were the only actual offices, large ones with panoramic views and doors that closed, while the dozens of subordinates were virtually huddled together in the middle of the floor, with nothing to look at but the computer screens and the temporary walls of their cubicles.

Cartons of books were stacked everywhere. Most of them
—he could only make out a few titles, like *Cooking With
Less Oil* and *Marilyn: The Family Album*—were probably
books he would have disapproved of in another context;
but books themselves still held some fetishistic magic for
Paul, and he thrilled to think that his own work would
soon be part of this multinational enterprise. Craning his
neck to record every aspect of the place, he ran right into
the shapely back of Olivia, who had stopped outside
Spain's closed office door.

She laughed at his awkwardness, neither giving nor taking offense, with the wonderful unself-consciousness of
the very young. "Wait here a second," she said, "I'll let
him know you're here." She knocked on the door, slipped
inside, and closed it behind her again.

Paul stood with his back to the office, staring out at the
mysterious divisions of labor under the pallid fluorescent
lighting. Phones chirped constantly, at different pitches,
and he wondered if the pitches meant anything specific.
The junior employees were all seemingly about Olivia's
age, maybe a year or two older, and the nature of their
work, he saw, gave them very little opportunity to talk to
one another. He had waited years for the day when he
would arrive inside a publishing house as one of its authors
—heads turning, lips whispering his name as he passed, on
his way to meet with his editor—but now that he was here,
he had to admit that he didn't feel quite that sort of connection to it. He felt instead a bit like a diplomat, as if his
purpose here were only to report back to some other
country. Perhaps it was just a matter of time.

He was wrapped in these thoughts, and just when he
realized that four or five minutes had now gone by, Olivia
opened Spain's door. She looked different—with her back
to Spain, her smile was gone, and her face was colored in
two or three spots. "He'll see you now," she said in a subdued voice. She tried to smile as she passed by him on the
way to her desk. He hadn't heard any yelling, or anything

at all. He stood in the open doorway for a moment, looking behind him in bemusement at the young woman. Then he turned back again, and the editor was standing right in front of him.

"Come in, come in," Spain said brightly. "So sorry to make you wait like that."

He took Paul's arm—a surprisingly intimate gesture, Paul thought—and led him to a comfortable Eames chair; he then went and sat down behind his own broad desk, an antique flat-top with no drawers. Spain was a man in his fifties (or a little older, Paul guessed—he had the pampered aspect of someone who is a little older than he looks) with thinning, graying hair, and blue eyes which, despite his smile, held Paul in a gaze that was so direct as to seem almost impolite. He had a tan. His blue suit jacket hung on the back of his desk chair; his shirt had a wide, colorful Jermyn Street sort of stripe, and his tie was a solid red. He sat forward, with his hands folded on the desk. He made it clear that the generous fullness of his attention was now given to Paul.

"Coffee?" he said, reaching for his intercom. "Mineral water?"

"No," Paul said quickly; though he was a bit thirsty, he was thinking of Olivia. "Thank you." He felt oddly oppressed by the elegant surroundings and by the force of Spain's courteousness. Of course he had imagined that he would be received courteously, even respectfully, but there was something unsettling about receiving this treatment in so practiced a fashion—from a man, in short, who knew about politesse. Paul crossed his legs; he had to slip forward a bit in the Eames chair in order for his right foot to touch the floor. He didn't know what to think, other than that Spain didn't seem at all like the somewhat professorial type he had expected.

"We're so thrilled," Spain said, "to have the book. Really. Everyone here is very excited about it. And knowing that you're a novelist as well. A stroke of luck, in a way, no? It should give an already great story just that little added dimension. Of course, to some extent, a story like this should just about write itself."

Paul smiled wanly. He could tell already, somehow, that he wasn't going to be doing a lot of the talking in this initial meeting. The wall behind Spain had built-in bookshelves from floor to ceiling; it seemed to grow up from behind him, from his chair perhaps, like some massive carved medieval throne. The odd thing about the shelves, Paul noticed after a minute, was that they contained not one copy of a given book but usually four or five. The wall perpendicular to the shelves was all glass, and looked west across the plain rooftops, all the way to New Jersey.

"So how are you feeling now?" Spain asked him. "How's the leg?"

"Much better, thanks," Paul said.

"And your family? You have two sons, is it? How are they bearing up?"

Paul was confused by the question. Bearing up? he thought. "They're fine, thanks. Glad to have things close to normal again."

"I'll bet."

"Actually, they didn't seem to mind the reporters and all that. They thought it was fun. I don't think they actually connected it with what had—what had happened to me. It was mostly Renata who was put out by it. Once a reporter actually snuck into my older son's school—"

"It's astounding, isn't it? They're so competitive with one another that they don't stop to think about what they're doing, the *nature* of it. It's like privacy is some romantic notion, like dueling or something." He leaned further forward. "Don't you think?"

Paul sat mute.

Spain rubbed gently at something invisible on the surface of the antique desk. He was a man who knew value. "Anyway," he said, "you'll have to bring the kids in sometime. And your wife. We'll all have dinner."

He smiled broadly, but the smile had a finality to it, like a curtain call; it signaled, even to Paul who had only intuitive knowledge of the mores of business, that the small-talk portion of the meeting might now be dispensed with. The furniture, the view, Spain's clothes, the air-conditioned silence, all combined to make him ill at ease, which didn't bother Paul so much: what bothered him was not knowing whether these things were *intended* to put him off his guard, or in fact just the opposite. He wanted the meeting to be over so he could go away and think about it. His misgivings, which earlier in the day had tempered his excitement as he anticipated his first glimpse of the future publisher of *Son of Mind,* had now taken over completely. He watched the irregular flashing of the small green lights on Spain's phone.

"So," Spain said. "The book."

He reached down to the carpet near his feet and picked up a skinny file folder; sticking out either end of it, Paul recognized, was the oversized legal paper of his contract.

"Now, you'll have noticed," Spain said, "that the due date for the manuscript is October 1st. Your agent—a terrific young man, by the way—may have explained to you that, in most cases, these due dates are essentially written in pencil. That is, we pretty much expect, authors being authors, that they're going to miss that date from time to time. Am I right?"

Every time he asked one of these bantering, semi-rhetorical questions, Paul's head would actually pull back slightly in surprise. Spain pressed on.

"Well, while there is some truth to that—particularly where novels are concerned, I mean, how can a novel be late, really?—this, as you've probably figured out for yourself, is a slightly different kind of animal. We're all poised here to go into overdrive the minute the manuscript arrives—myself, publicity, all the way down the line to the sales force and the printers up in New Hampshire—so that we can turn the book around in maybe three months, instead of the usual eight or nine. Books in the stores by February—by the anniversary of the attack on you, ideally, if that isn't too ghoulish. Anyway, all this is a roundabout way of saying that, while the October 1st date isn't set in stone, it is something to which we should sincerely aspire." He opened the file and glanced over something Paul couldn't see.

"Why—" Paul started to say, but his voice caught, and he had to clear his throat.

Spain, looking up without lifting his head, said, "Sorry?"

"I was going to say, why does it matter?" Paul said. "I mean, not that I have any intention of turning it in late. But why go to so much trouble on your end to get the book out a few months earlier? If it's such a good story, won't it still be a good story in May?"

Spain was not thrown so easily; he put down the folder and politely cocked his head as if considering the question, when in fact it seemed to him about as worthy of consideration as the question of whether, if the rooster didn't crow, the sun would still come up. "Well," he said, "but who can judge what will last and what won't? Maybe the story of the abduction of Paul Soloway will become a modern legend, like Doc Holliday or, I don't know, Amelia Earhart. Or maybe it will fade away. Some of that, of course, depends on the book we ultimately make out of it. But mostly it depends on chance—or, if not chance exactly, then forces we don't understand and have no control over. But the one thing we do know, that our work can be informed by, is that the story is of pressing interest to the reading public right now. In fact," he said, "we even have polls, if you can believe it, that—"

"Polls?" Paul said. "About me?"

Spain lifted his hands in mock self-defense. "I know," he said, "but nobody's going to let me spend almost half a million dollars of this company's money without a little market research to back me up. I don't like it any better than you. In the old days— Anyway, yes, we had some research done, just name recognition, basically. And the results were terrific. But let's face it, a lot will happen between now and next March—floods, fires, earthquakes, violent crimes. People's memories are short. And no one ever went broke underestimating that. So, yes, it's certainly in our interest to strike while the iron is hot."

Designed to flatter Paul by pretending to take seriously the theoretical nature of his question, this response actually couldn't have disappointed him more. Catering to others' presumed short attention spans was not something he was eager to accept, even in the short term, as a guiding principle for his work. But, for once, he was more anxious to leave than to argue. Something was starting to take shape between them that he didn't think augured well; and he had a real stake now in not thinking ill of this man. It isn't so important that we agree on these things anyway, he thought; no point in picking a fight. Besides, the author always has the last word. He smiled gamely.

"So," Spain said gently. "By the nature of these queries, then, I take it you haven't started writing yet?"

"Actually," Paul said, "no."

"That's fine, that's fine," Spain said quickly. "Maybe it's for the best, actually, since we hadn't had a chance to talk about it yet. Let me see, what sort of advice might I give you?"

"Advice?" Paul said.

Spain looked at him. "Naturally, I don't mean to seem high-handed about it. It's just that I've edited a few of these books before, and they do tend to follow, quite profitably, a certain formula. Of course, usually, the authors of those books have never written anything longer than a letter in their whole lives, so with them I'm really starting from scratch. The worst are the movie-star autobiographies, let me tell you, those golden-age memoirs, I-remember-fucking-Monty-Clift and on and on. These people couldn't write a proper English sentence, most of them, but you can't tell them that; they've been worshiped all their lives, and they've forgotten what it's like to be criticized. But anyway." He smiled. "This is a rare treat for me, because, even though you are a first-time author, I know what extraordinary gifts you bring to the project, and I plan to take full advantage of them. Still, there are a few hints I'll give you that might be helpful, since I've been down this road before. One is, begin at— Maybe you want to write this down?"

"No," Paul said, "I'll remember it."

"Good enough. One: begin at the beginning. Any sort of fancy flashback method, crosscutting between you with Victor Hartley and his gang and your wife and kids at home, anything like that is fine—but we'll deal with it later. We can do that with a pair of scissors and a stapler, so to speak; the important thing for right now is to get the raw material, to get the whole thing out of your head and onto the page. I've found that that's easiest to do if you just think through it exactly as it happened. Then we can worry about fotzing around with the shape of it later. Make sense?"

Paul's eyes were cast down, with a peculiar look of revulsion on his face, as if there were a bug crawling on his lapel.

"Another thing," Spain said, his brows knitting but his voice still brisk and optimistic. The intercom buzzed on his desk, but he ignored it. "Remember the reader. What the reader is interested in is the personal. They want your thoughts, your feelings, your emotions, at all times as you're going through your ordeal. Now that may sound obvious to you, but in fact a lot of writers tend not to do that, either out of general shyness or because it's actually too painful to relive events in that way. But it has to be done. Remember that the reader is focused on you, and wants to know your particular experience in this crucible, and how you survived it. Third—"

The intercom buzzed again; a scowl broke over Spain's

face for just a moment, then disappeared. He held up one apologetic finger and picked up the phone. Astonishingly, Paul thought, he didn't say anything, not "Hello?" or even a gruff "What?"; he simply waited to be spoken to. Olivia said something in his ear that made him wince. "What time is it now?" he said to her, though he wore, as Paul could see, an expensive watch. "Okay. Two minutes, tell him." By the time he hung up, Paul was already rising from his seat. Spain, pulling his suit jacket off the back of his chair, did the same.

"I'm sorry about this," Spain said, walking to the door. "It's just one meeting after another around here. You get backed up in the morning and you're paying for it all day."

He placed one hand on Paul's shoulder and held the door open for him. Olivia stood waiting nervously outside, holding a thick brown folder for her boss.

"So I'm just thrilled we're finally under way here," Spain said, taking the folder from Olivia without looking at her. "It's so wonderful to meet you at last. You call me if you're having any trouble, any questions at all. Even just to check in once in a while. I'll do the same."

They shook hands.

"You can find your way back to reception?"

"Yes," Paul said, though he doubted he could.

"All right then."

He smiled again at Spain, then at Olivia, then started off in what he was pretty sure was the right direction.

"Oh," Spain called. "Be thinking about titles!"

Without meaning to, Paul absurdly gave his editor the thumbs-up sign, as if trying to find the idiom of the place. When he was out of their sight, he leaned over one of the partitions and asked a startled young man for directions to the elevators.

That had been three weeks ago. Now Paul's condescension toward the project was partially supplanted by a kind of frustration. He was annoyed by his inability even to begin writing something that should have been offensively simple. He felt like an adult who couldn't open a child-proof cap. In his lifetime he had completed, however reluctantly, all kinds of anonymous literary gruntwork; he had once written the jacket copy for a book about UFOs, for Christ's sake. What was so hard about this?

The more he tortured himself with this line of self-interrogation, the further he got, he noticed, from the specifics of the nascent book itself. So, eventually, Spain's dictum to begin at the beginning started to seem less off the point to him, and to resemble something like a key. In order to hunt the fox, supposedly, one had to think like a fox; similarly, Paul thought with a rueful smile, if one wanted to write a book for ninnies, one might try thinking like a ninny, in which case "Begin at the beginning" had all the force of a revelation. Of course, locating that beginning was still a subjective matter. Only when he had joined the idea of following Spain's advice to the prospective, subversive joy of imagining Spain's reaction did he feel the special kind of agitation that always impelled him to sit down and begin writing.

On a winter night, he typed, *in the late 1970s, a few months shy of my graduation from Columbia University, I took an evening off from my studies to attend a reading by the South African novelist J. M. Coetzee at the 92nd Street YMHA in Manhattan. I went alone: my friends at the time, even the most literary-minded among them, were caught up either with their senior theses or with drinking beer in order to ward off their fear of their senior theses; my girlfriend Renata wanted to go with me, but she had not been sleeping much that week owing to midterm exams, and at the last minute she decided that spending an evening in a warm auditorium, in a comfortable chair, being read to, carried too great a risk of embarrassment. (Renata tends to snore.) So, alone, I rode the two buses to 92nd and Lexington Avenue. I purchased my ticket and walked into the wonderfully somber auditorium, with its gold roster of the ancients—Plato, Homer, Herodotus—circling the eaves. I was early, but even by eight o'clock the auditorium was not more than two-thirds filled.*

A few minutes later, following someone's short, barely adequate introduction, Coetzee himself emerged from the wings. Thin and serious, he wore a blazer and a black turtleneck; his hair was still dark, but his beard showed flowerings of gray. He had traveled all the way from Cape Town to spend an hour on that stage, where perhaps he felt the presence of the ghosts of some of his own heroes, men and women who meant to him something like what he meant to me.

He read from his novel-in-progress, Waiting for the Barbarians. *Those who know this monumental book, an allegorical exposition of the heart of South Africa which time has only made more prophetic, should need no further explanation of the excitement that had taken possession of me by the end of that hour. In fact, as satisfyingly brilliant as the finished novel proved to be (when I was able to buy it, a year or two later), it failed, in some fashion, to match the thrill of encountering the novel half done; for on that cold evening there was something indescribably heartening, almost martial, about knowing, after the applause faded and the auditorium was abandoned, that somewhere well out of our sight, halfway around the world, this great, solitary labor would continue.*

It was announced that there would be a meet-the-author reception afterward, but the prospect of it made me uneasy. Despite (or because of) my great admiration for the man, the notion of being part of a line of anonymous fans lamely shaking his hand and thanking him seemed pathetically inadequate. Far more respectful, I thought, to leave him be. It was true, too, that for all my worship of him I simultaneously entertained a dream that someday I would find myself his peer—and that introductions were best put off until then.

But I still had a store of joyous energy from hearing him, an energy generated by the power of the written word, by the demonstration that there were things still left to be accomplished this late in the annals of the novel. I was twenty-two years old. I didn't want to go home right away; I told myself it would be inconsiderate to disturb Renata's sleep. So I decided to take a little walk through the unfamiliar side streets of the Upper East Side—to invent a circuitous route back to 96th Street, where I could catch the bus back across town. Ambling past the breath-fogged windows of the neighborhood restaurants and bars— places with cloying names like Mumbles or Mingles or Shenani-gans—it occurred to me that the overall sense of anticipation and dizzy longing in which I felt shrouded had another, less spiritual, more prosaic source: I hadn't eaten since lunch. But the Upper East Side was then, as it is now, a virtual game preserve of people with whom I do my best not to associate: the young and the bootless; young bankers, young lawyers, young speculators, young power. Fuddruckers and Beachcombers were not intended for the likes of me, nor I for the likes of them. On top of which I only had bus fare plus four dollars.

Then, rounding the corner onto Second Avenue, I caught an incongruous but still deeply familiar smell. It was the odor of bread—and a few feet in front of me was a tiny bakery, about the size of a city ice-cream parlor. The name on the door was an odd one, too: St. Famous. There were no customers inside, but a fortyish woman could be seen busying herself behind the counter. She seemed so startled when I stepped through the door that I halted and asked if they were still open. Blowing at the hair which had fallen over her face, she nodded and waved me in. She waited patiently while, near swooning from the warmth and odors of the place, I took two or three minutes before decid-ing on a large cinnamon bun. I ate it, along with a small carton of milk, standing in near-silence (there was the solid hum of machinery emitting from the back of the bakery—a strangely industrial buzz, I thought, to be juxtaposed with the smells of bread) while the woman returned to her work without a glance at me.

Between bites, I asked her where the name St. Famous came from. She said, somewhat contritely, that she had no idea.

Of such small pleasures—a night out, the flush of hero-wor-ship, the ordinary joys of smell and taste and warmth against

the cold—are our fondest and most persistent memories con-
structed. Those ten unexpected minutes in that bakery, between
the youthful hour in the presence of a master and the return
home to the nearness and comfort of the woman whom, as it
turned out, I would soon marry, stayed with me—or, to say it
more precisely, submerged themselves, to lie in wait for me, for
close to a decade.

There we go, Paul thought, peeling the sheet out of the typewriter. Now we're getting somewhere. On some level, he knew—had known even as he was writing it—that he was both following and mocking his editor's instructions, that this went well beyond Spain's notion of a beginning. Probably, he thought with some surprise, that had been the key; he needed to be writing in opposition to something, even in the narrowest, pettiest sense, in order to get himself to write at all. The novel came so easily compared to this; what was he in opposition to then? He was both miffed and secretly unburdened when these thoughts were interrupted by the sound of Renata's key in the front door.

The television started blaring in the lounge area at about eight in the morning, as soon as breakfast was over, and it went on all day long, until an hour before lockdown at nine at night. At some point each day the volume was turned all the way up, and stayed that way, because the prisoners were too lazy to get up and adjust it (you had to stand on a chair to reach the set) and there was no remote control. This last fact made perfect sense to Victor; you couldn't have a remote in this environment and expect an hour to go by without some brawl that ended up with somebody stabbed or dead. There were fights enough as it was. In fact, that's how the volume usually got turned up in the first place; while two or three inmates rolled on the linoleum screaming and punching, and the guards ran down the hall yelling and reaching excitedly for their batons, somebody would calmly get up, stand on the chair, and turn the sound up full blast, so as not to miss a word.

There was a lounge culture built up around the TV, an etiquette, whose rules were never spoken because knowledge of them served to distinguish the regulars from the interlopers. (The regulars were men who spent as much time as possible in the lounge, seven or eight hours a day typically, who would pile up good-behavior points not with an eye toward early release but toward maintaining and increasing their TV privileges. Maybe they did this because, of all the dimly lit, savage, unpredictable corners of prison life, this was the safest—always crowded, always supervised; or maybe it was done simply to make their time inside resemble as nearly as possible a life outside.) Custom dictated, for instance, that any time a good-looking woman appeared on the screen, the first few seconds of whatever she had to say would be obscured by loud demands for her sexual compliance. Any channel-changing was to be done by one of the regulars, by Dino or Jamal if they were there (which they almost always were), otherwise by one of their designated lieutenants. But the most inviolable rule of the place was the rule of nature when it came to which programs to watch—that is, nature as opposed to democracy. Programming decisions were enforced by strength. There was a schedule determined by the lounge hierarchy; voting had no place in it. The only way to change the evening's lineup was to beat up your adversary before the guards could get there to drag you both away, or, as happened more often, to face him down without violence but only the future promise of it. Dino and Jamal took these confrontations in stride, watching as objectively as if they were watching the screen, and then, when the outcome was certain, standing on the chair to enforce the decision.

It was this aspect of the TV lounge that had Victor worried; in fact, he had spent the whole day, and much of the night before, worrying about it. On the one hand, he felt sure that once he had made clear the extraordinary reason for his request, the one-time-only nature of it, they would certainly understand, just this one day; on the other, he knew instinctively that the very idea that this day was different somehow from every other day went against the grain of prison life in general. There was no question of trying to get there early and stake a claim that way; first of all, there was always somebody there, and even if he somehow contrived to get there a few seconds ahead of the others at eight o'clock, and sit guarding his seniority for nine hours, someone would simply take him out to regain control. He was not the hardest guy in this block, not by a very long shot.

He decided that his best angle was to appeal directly to Dino or Jamal, whichever one was there, and to ask in as humble and flattering a manner as possible for their intervention on his behalf. To allow himself some time, he arrived in the lounge at around four-thirty.

Dino was there, in his usual chair—the one with the even legs—watching Geraldo Rivera. Dino was bald, with a fiercely downward-tending goatee. A bluish teardrop was tattooed below the corner of his left eye. He was in this time for assaulting a police officer; that and his deadly calm at all times made him a local legend, frightening to approach. Geraldo was talking to women whose husbands had stopped having sex with them because they were too fat. Victor waited for a commercial, then went as quietly as possible to squat down beside Dino's chair.

"Dino, man, how you doing?" he said softly.

Dino didn't turn his head, nor did his expression change. Victor decided to assume he was listening.

"Dino, I got to ask you a favor, a big favor," he went on. Dino's somewhat bumpy skull still didn't move, but Victor noticed other men beginning to glare curiously at him, suspicious of his obsequious posture. It could be a disaster if anyone overheard. He shifted a little, to try to get as close as he could to Dino without breathing on him.

"At five o'clock," he said, "at five o'clock, I got to watch something. It's important, man, it's—I can't miss it."

Dino raised his eyebrows; easy, Victor told himself, ruing the impatient tone of his last sentence. Geraldo was back from commercial.

"What is it?" Dino asked dispassionately.

"The news. The five o'clock news. On Channel 4."

Dino's eyes closed, and he sighed.

"I know, I know—"

"You think these guys are gonna go for that?" Dino said.

"I know—"

"What you want to watch that for today, man? What happened?" The news was turned on in the prisoners' lounge customarily only when something of major and undeniable interest to them was taking place—the Fisk riots, for instance—and, as often as not, on the few occasions when this happened, the guards would come in and switch off the set under orders from the warden.

"Nothing—well, here it is. It's me, man. I'm on it."

Now Dino turned to look at him, though not in the friendliest regard. His quizzical, possibly threatening gaze indicated that such a claim was most probably a lie, and that he was having trouble believing that a relatively new prisoner would risk lying to him like that.

"What you mean," he said, "you *on* it?"

"Well, a story about me. My lawyer, my new lawyer, he had a big press conference today. On the steps of the precinct house where I was arrested, man. He told me last night to look for it on the news."

Dino considered this. Victor, his legs tightening up, got down onto one knee. Other inmates, he was increasingly aware, had taken notice of his conversation with Dino and were staring over at the two of them with unhappy concern.

"Just your lawyer?" Dino said. "And some reporters?"

"I don't know," Victor said nervously. "He didn't really tell me. Maybe more. He told me it was going to be big."

Even this last was a slight exaggeration. When Boggs

called yesterday afternoon to leave a message for Victor to call him back, he had been told it was past the time when prisoners were permitted access to the phone; he had added to the legend of his persuasive abilities by talking one of the guards into actually writing down a message to pass to Victor. The message, in the guard's own sausage-fingered handwriting, read, "Press conference tomorrow noon on the steps of the 25th. Full coverage on that night's TV news. Don't miss it." There may have been more in the way of explanatory adjectives which the guard had spitefully not recorded; or it may have been that Boggs, not knowing in detail the sociology of prisons, thought Victor could simply walk in here and turn on the news and therefore no explanation was necessary. Victor had been first in line for the phone today, but by the time he could call Boggs's office the attorney was already gone.

All through Geraldo, a lazy barrage of insults had been directed at the screen, mostly ruminations on every conceivable inconvenience a man would suffer in attempting to have sex with one of the obese women on the show. But now, through these obscene musings, broke a voice in a slightly less relaxed tone. "Dino, man," one of the prisoners said. "What's going on over there?"

A few heads turned. Dino stretched his muscled arms and laced his fingers behind his head. "Seems—" He turned to look at Victor.

"Victor," Victor said.

"Seems Victor here has a programming request. He wants to watch the five o'clock news."

A few catcalls followed, throwing into question the manhood of anyone who wanted to watch the news.

"No, no," Dino said in a tone of mild reproach. He relished his Solomonic role in here. "There's a special circumstance. There's supposed to be a story on the news about my man here, about his case. His lawyer had a big press conference today."

"His lawyer!" someone yelled. "Who wants to look at a fucking lawyer on TV!"

Another inmate, a large man in the center of the loose group of chairs, mumbled something.

"What's that?" Dino said sharply. "I didn't get that."

The fat man, with a very dark glance at Victor, said in a slightly louder voice, "Montel Williams is on at five."

"Yes, I know that, thank you," Dino said sarcastically.

"What time is it on?" another voice asked.

"What?" Dino said.

"What *time* is the story on? The news goes on for like an hour and a half."

"Good question," Dino said.

Victor licked his lips. The credits were rolling on Geraldo, which meant it must have been just two or three minutes before five. "I don't know," he said.

The others threw up their hands and groaned dismissively, turning back to the screen as if the issue had been decided. Dino looked at him resignedly as if to say, The people have spoken.

"Yo," Victor said, his eyes darting. "Yo, here's an idea." He took a deep breath. It seemed so ridiculous that he could end up in the prison infirmary for trying to dissuade a bunch of roughnecks from watching the Montel Williams show, but the absurdity of it did nothing to mitigate the danger he felt he was in. "I'll get up there and change the channel. Every couple of minutes I'll flip back to the news to see if they're doing my story. If they're not, I'll flip right back to Montel. You won't miss but two seconds at a time."

"Fuck that!" they yelled. "See ya!"

But something in the plan—Victor's audacity in proposing it, the potential for interesting violence if it fell through—appealed to Dino. Since his power, he felt, was unquestioned, he took a Magus-like interest and pleasure in fidgeting with his own laws, to see what the different outcomes might be. He held up his hand for silence, then spoke to Victor.

"You said this was a major story, right? Major news?"

Victor had a sudden premonition that this whole episode would turn out badly, and that Dino was raising the stakes out of mere cruelty. But there was no losing sight of his goal now. He nodded confidently.

Dino raised his eyebrows, then leaned back comfortably in his chair.

"Done," he said.

Victor bounded up and onto the chair beneath the TV, ignoring the cacophony that followed him. He turned the dial to Channel 4, since that was just one channel away from Montel Williams.

Synthesized trumpets blared, over the simulated sound of rushing wind. An offscreen announcer said, "And now, from the News 4 studios in New York, 'Live at Five.'" The anchorwoman appeared on screen and opened her mouth to speak.

"On your knees, bitch!" the men yelled perfunctorily. "*Show* me that ass!" Yelling at the television was perfect freedom, in its way.

Victor had to put his ear almost flat against the set to hear over the noise. The first story was a follow-up on a dog on Staten Island that had bitten a neighbor child. Victor quickly switched to Channel 5.

It could have been worse; Montel had on the family of a murder victim speaking via satellite to the imprisoned murderer. To the prisoners, this was something of a busman's holiday, not nearly as sensational as the idea of sex with fat women, and so perhaps their resentment of Victor would be softened. He waited for what he thought was about ninety seconds. He didn't want to switch back while one of Montel's guests was in mid-sentence, but there was no way not to—they yelled continuously at one another. He waited as long as he could stand, then switched back.

"God *damn!*" they yelled behind him.

The news was doing a story on someone's Senate confirmation hearings. Victor quickly switched back.

This went on for ten minutes, the most nerve-wracking ten minutes of Victor's life, he thought. The bent metal chair was not the easiest place to stand for long periods. The threats against him grew louder every time a news story began that had nothing to do with him or with anything they gave a damn about. Then, just as suddenly as if he had not been waiting for it, the anchorwoman started speaking, it seemed, directly to him.

"At the 25th Precinct today," she said, "an extraordinary—"

"Quiet!" Victor shouted in spite of himself; he winced, regretting it immediately, but nothing happened. He gazed up at the screen from about twelve inches away.

"—the lawyer for Victor Hartley, the man accused of kidnaping and assaulting Paul Soloway during the Fisk riots in February, held a press conference in which he maintained that his client, previously reported to be close to a plea bargain, would now plead not guilty to all charges. Our Magee Hickey was there."

Victor felt like a ghost, like a figure in a tale permitted to watch, in wonder, his own funeral. A picture of Boggs flickered above him—the white hair, the glasses on a chain, the heat of authority that seemed to transform the air around him, to transform the stale air here in the prisoners' lounge.

"Ladies and gentlemen," he said, "as we stand here today, my client, Victor Hartley, sits in that famous American warehouse for young black males known as Rikers Island. At the same moment, Mr. Wendell Fisk of Ozone Park is probably out tending his lawn, the same lawn he cared so much for that he would sooner shoot a black child in the back than have it sullied by his footprint.

"How many of us dare to say that we understand what it

means to be a young black man in this city, in this society? And yet the media have persisted in portraying Victor Hartley as a savage, a beast, a mindless sociopath. He is none of those things. He is a hard-working, decent father of two small children and a devoted son who has held his family together in the face of obstacles most of us here today will never comprehend."

Now Victor noticed, standing behind and to the left of Boggs, his two daughters Tanya and Renee, held in the arms of his younger sister Wanda. The children's mothers were not present, although, since his sister had not been identified, the press would probably take her to be the mother. The kids themselves were on display, and yet Keisha and Angeline had somehow been prevailed upon to stay at home. Of the tens of thousands watching this broadcast, Victor was the only one in a position to appreciate that this was perhaps Boggs's smoothest, most super-human feat to date.

The lawyer had a prepared text in front of him, but he did not look at it. The breeze blew, and the cameras flashed. "The press has made a fetish of the videotape that supposedly catches my client's co-defendants in the act of abducting Mr. Soloway. It is a sad day indeed when we are willing to toss away our judgment, our reason, our sense of history and context, simply because of our awe before a mechanical image. That image has been seized upon to tell a story—a story that feeds our basest, foulest, most racist fears—and, up till now, since Victor has been deprived of the opportunity to speak for himself, that story has been accepted as truth. Well, it is not the truth. The real story of what happened that day in February has not yet been told.

"I've asked you here today to announce that, when Victor Hartley is brought to his pretrial hearing on June first, he will plead not guilty to all charges against him. Earlier reports that he would plead guilty in order to lessen his jail time were totally false. A plea bargain, which takes place entirely out of the public eye, is exactly what District Attorney Harriman would like. Well, we're not getting out of the public eye, because we have absolute faith in the public's ability to understand and to judge fairly. We will go to trial, and when we do, the world will learn the real story of Victor Hartley. The world will learn something it's past time it learned—what it means to try to keep yourself alive in a society that would just as soon you were dead, that suspects you for no reason, that calls you nigger. The jury will come to know Victor as I have come to know him, and when they do, they will be able to feel what he felt during those years of abuse, during that day when Wendell Fisk was excused with the thanks of the court for shooting a black boy in the back. The jury will see that Victor's actions, while perhaps not saintly, were, under the circumstances, fully justified; and then, with all the media hype cleared away, you will know, once and for all, the answer to the question:

"Who is the *real* victim here?"

The news anchor went on to another story; Victor's hands had dropped to his sides, but no one shouted at him. Slowly he remembered where he was, and he turned to look, from his rickety height, down at his fellow inmates, all of whom were staring at him—not with respect, really, but with a curiosity that was rare enough in that closed society.

"Man," one of them finally said, "my lawyer sucks."

Years later, on a February morning warm as spring but with slush and jammed drainage catches at every corner more treacherous than the deepest winter, I rode that same bus, the M96, across still, neglected Central Park. The playgrounds were empty; the tennis courts netless and blank-faced. I sat in my customary seat, the one I always race for if the bus is not already too crowded: against the window in the last row of seats, the one perpendicular to the two long rows along the sides. There one can lean against something other than a suspicious fellow-passenger, and, more important, there is the top of the wheel-well on which to rest one's feet. The most comfortable seat on any city bus, if also the closest to the engine and hence the noisiest.

I was traveling to 85th and First, to the location of what my wife and I had discovered, in our researches, to be the cheapest car-rental agency in all of Manhattan. With our two sons, Peter and Leo, we would be driving to Pennsylvania, once Renata got out of work, to visit my father-in-law for the long weekend. Like many men, I have a wary relationship with my father-in-law. His own marriage decomposed, and though he later remarried and divorced again, the one consistent love of a woman in his long, pathologically unexamined life has been for his daughter. Scott, as I am encouraged to call him (the notion of "Dad" was never introduced), always looks at me as if for the first time, with a mixture of surprise and genteelly contained malevolence. Scott urges us to come visit him on his property—it was formerly a farm, but it would be inexact to call it that now—as often as possible. We would be there every weekend if he had his fondest wish. He pretends that this is because of his love for his grandchildren. And he does love them—as they adore him—but it is Renata who receives the real heat of his attention. Though she is still in her early thirties, and quite beautiful (with her long legs, her long, near-blond hair which escapes barrettes and pony tails with wild ease to fall over her face), he seems to wonder what has happened to her, and to blame me for it. The expression of this blame is typically oblique; he is friendlier to me than to anyone else in the family.

Renata and I were then leading a somewhat impoverished life, though; and a two- or three-day car rental in Manhattan could come (with gas) to nearly two hundred dollars, or as much as I sometimes made in a month. We tried to restrict our visits to Pennsylvania on that ground. Still, loophole-minded, Scott insisted ("offered" would be wrong) on paying us back for the rental when we came. In turn, Renata insisted that we keep that fee for our visits as low as possible. The mysterious fetishes made of money in a middle-class American family! Trying to argue the childishness, let alone the sexual nature, of all this, though, won me only her steeliest not-in-front-of-the-children glare. And so, on that Friday before Presidents' Day, I was dispatched miles across town, where the smirking recidivists would rent me a car for eight dollars a day less than the National branch four blocks from my home.

At 96th and Second I transferred to the downtown local bus (aboard which two savvy teenagers had nabbed my favorite seats). I rode wedged between a substantial middle-aged Indian woman and another young man who appeared to be a messenger: he wore tiny headphones which emitted what sounded like blasts of static and carried across his lap a gigantic manila envelope, the dimensions of a cabinet door. I sat facing west; I was half-watching the antic sidewalk, thinking about the work I had done that morning, thinking what the messenger might possibly have in an envelope that size, when, across the body of the bus, a sign scrolled past me through the window: St. Famous.

Paul got up from the desk—pushing off hard with his right hand to protect his right leg—and went to nuke himself another cup of coffee. He disliked instant, but in the past, if he made real coffee a pot at a time, it would get cold before he got halfway through it and he would wind up pouring it down the sink. In her search for things to spend money on, Renata had seized on an expensive solution to this tiny inconvenience—a microwave oven—and so it sat, gleaming and imposing, taking up half the counter space in the already claustrophobic kitchen. They hadn't yet figured out what else to use it for.

As he stared at the digital timer counting down thirty seconds, he thought about the nature of his discomfort. He had to admit it; the deeper he got into it, the more he was troubled by the fact that he wasn't more troubled by the actual labor of writing this book-for-hire. It had its small satisfactions, and to the extent he lost himself in those, he was okay. A sentence was a sentence, after all; it had its provincial laws. And even in a more general sense, he could see that perhaps he had been wrong; perhaps he *was* able to make this story his own, simply through the prism of his intellect and the stamp of his own style. If Edmund Wilson could write about the Ziegfeld Follies . . . Writing was the art first of cultivating and then of finding expression for a particular sensibility, a way of seeing the world in which the world has not seen itself before. That same sensibility could be brought to bear on lesser material—if, inevitably, with lesser results. It only proved, in a way, one of his own private aesthetic tenets, namely that plot was overrated, and functioned mostly as a pretext for what was really valuable in art—the artist's own voice.

But as he returned to the desk with the mug of thermo-regulated coffee—the spring breeze blowing warmly through the dead potted plants on the radiator by the window—he was concerned with a more immediate problem. Should he talk about the driving thing? It was odd that he should hesitate over it. He had already written at some length about cars and the American worship of them in his novel—Walter Havens, its narrator, had a contempt for driving which sometimes (mostly in his adolescence) butted up against fear and the pressures to conform. Paul's whole program in *Son of Mind*—which was what might be fairly, if somewhat reductively, called an autobiographical novel—was based on the idea that to conceal nothing about yourself, to explore every nuance of what it means to be a fully conscious individual and not to efface or ameliorate with the tricks of art, was the only way left to transgress the bounds of art. Now, though, when there were no such boundaries against which he might define himself, he found himself hesitating, calculating, subtly fictionalizing, as a kind of insulating measure, the "I" who was actually named Paul Soloway. But this seemed to him an impure motive. He decided, at least for now, to put it all down, and to attend to the larger questions at a later date, when it was time for revision. He went on.

*The fellows at Super Budget Rent-a-Car were their custom-
ary uningratiating selves. What license it gives them to know
they are the cheapest purveyor of their particular vital service on
the whole island! Not that the place has an actual policy which
dictates surliness to customers; it's just that their somewhat Sa-
tanic position as the lords of the low end enables them to give free
rein to their moods during the hours when most people in the
service economy must bring their feelings up to code. And, like
most New Yorkers, on any given day there is roughly a three-in-
four chance that the mood of the employees at Super Budget will
be lousy and confrontational.*

*They were listening to the radio when I walked in. They
glanced at me for a moment without saying anything, as if we
were in a gym locker room and I simply a stranger with as much
right to the place as themselves; then they turned back to what
they were doing, which is to say nothing. I moved timidly up to
the counter, just two or three feet from where they sat.*

"I'm here to pick up a car," I said.

Nothing.

"I have a reservation.

"My name is Soloway.

"It's a mid-size.

"I called last Wednesday."

*Finally, I reached into my wallet and found a scrap of old
typing paper. "The confirmation number," I said, "is 3606,"
and with that the penny dropped; one of them, with a brand-
new fade haircut he kept unconsciously touching, stood and
slipped through the employees-only door behind the counter, presumably to fetch the car. Or perhaps it was only because the song
on the radio had ended.*

*I went back outside and stood by the garage door, as an ex-
pression of faith that the car would soon arrive. The guy with
the fade drove up a few minutes later, hopped out of the car with
a form for me to sign, and left me there, the car door open and
the engine running. Not a word had passed between us. In retrospect, it seems to me it must then have been exactly eleven*

o'clock, because the old office radio, which I could still hear, had switched over to news. I mention it because, just as the kid with the fade opened the office door on his way inside, I heard his partner apostrophizing loudly in Spanish (which I don't understand); and then, quite clearly, "No fucking way!"

Unsettled, I got in the car, closed the door, and checked again to be sure it was an automatic. I should mention here that I hate to drive. Always have. I've never been able to connect with the whole car culture, even as a teenage boy—adolescence being the locus of all the phallic anxieties and revenge fantasies upon which the car culture is founded. I cannot become one with the machine, as I am urged to; I never lose sight of the central nature of this relationship, which is that a car is many times more powerful than I and weighs two thousand pounds. I do not feel I can be relied on not to make a mistake which would casually kill or maim me or, worse, some randomly-chosen stranger. I continue, in fact, to have nightmares about driving cars. In the most frequent one, I am in my living room with a steering wheel in front of me—a steering wheel which corresponds to a real, unoccupied car on the crowded West Side Highway. I must drive this car from my remote position, even though I cannot see it or the road. Of course, the cymbal-clash which awakens me is the dream-sound of my driverless car hitting a wall or another car or a group of pedestrians.

I am not so inured to bourgeois notions of manliness that I don't feel a little embarrassed about all this.

In any event, it was this apprehensiveness toward even a short drive across Manhattan (the most dangerous place to drive in the country, incidentally), as much as my reawakened memories of an optimistic night, that convinced me to break up the twenty-minute trip by stopping in front of the St. Famous bakery.

There was a college kid working behind the counter; once again, I was the only customer there. He, too, had the radio on, turned to the all-news station. I asked him for a cinnamon roll and a cup of coffee; he supplied it, in a not unfriendly but still rather brisk way, and went back to his stool by the radio. I sat at one of the store's two tables.

It wasn't exactly a Proustian experience, that cinnamon bun and coffee. I don't know what I was expecting. I tried to remember that evening at the Y a few blocks away; I could remember Coetzee's noble face, of course, and, in a wordless sort of way, his great voice; but that's nothing like resummoning the feelings I had, a feeling like terrorists must have, of secrecy and righteousness and belief in the ultimate upholding of one's own vision of the future. Feelings like that were easily overtaken now by anxiety over my responsibility for the car, which I had parked illegally, and worry about the time (I had to pick up Peter from school in less than an hour). And a sudden realization that the counter guy's head was really quite close to the radio.

"What's going on?" I called to him.

He lifted his face, full of worry without lines. "The Fisk trial," he said. "Did you hear? The verdict came in this morning. Not guilty."

The Wendell Fisk case will be familiar to everyone. I don't need to recount it, or to say anything other than that I was as flabbergasted and dismayed as everyone else.

"They're saying on the radio that some businesses are closing down," the kid said. "'Cause of rioting, expected rioting. I don't even know how to lock up here. I've never had to do it. I can't get my boss on the phone."

This seemed to contain the seed of a plea that I stay right there with him. Rioting on Second Avenue seemed a deeply unlikely occurrence; still, under different circumstances, I might indeed have hung out with him for a while, just to talk, and eat, and maybe to draw out from him this latent fear of the black male that seemed now to be pushing toward the surface. But I couldn't spare the time. I threw my trash away and put my coat back on. To loosen him up a little, I asked him a question I had wanted to ask, one that I'd asked all those years ago after the Coetzee reading.

"How did this place get its name?"

Wide-eyed, he said, "I haven't the slightest idea."
I waved goodbye, got back in the clean, strange car, and drove
uptown. At 110th Street I took a left turn.

The freedom from wage-earning, and the restoration of
the hours previously devoted to it, gave Renata the opportunity to relax a bit for the first time since Peter was born.
In the matter of relaxation, though, it had to be said that
opportunity was not everything; the ability, regardless of
one's circumstances, to get through a day without moments of sourceless anxiety and restlessness was something
that had to be relearned. She would never have thought of
herself, even six months ago, as one of those overtaxed,
drum-tight, solipsistic New York natives, with that look of
always falling behind schedule that only the grave would
efface. If someone had ever asked her (no one ever had,
except her mother, and questions like that from one's
mother have a diminished relevance) if she didn't seem a
little wound up lately, she would have answered simply
that things were just a little rough right at that moment,
what with one of the boys sick and a deadline at work and
Paul brooding over a difficult revision. At some point,
though, these external matters seeped into one's very
framework. Or that was the conclusion that Renata was
forced to, when more than four weeks of wealthy unemployment had gone by and she still was not cured of certain physical habits, like bouncing her leg when she sat, or
holding the arm of a chair so tightly that the skin under
her fingernails turned a bright red.

One of the new luxuries she possessed, though she
might not have identified it as such, was the leisure to explore these previously unanalyzed states of mind, both past
and present. For instance, there was her relationship to
Peter and Leo, which was, it had to be acknowledged, a
new one. Or at any rate a changed one. She was with them
all day long now, apart from the classroom—walking to
and from their schools, at the playground, at meal and bed

times, up at Mrs. Perez's. (The boys—and Mrs. Perez—had balked at the idea that their relationship was to be severed merely by the Soloways' financial windfall; so they still went upstairs for an hour or two every weekday, and Renata, even though she often went up there with them, still paid Mrs. Perez at the end of every week, knowing how she needed it.) She had wondered sometimes, when she was working, how she felt about missing out on just this sort of traditional maternal watchfulness. One of the blessings, she supposed, of her former life of work, pressure, and fatigue was that it left few such pauses in the day in which the tide of one's anxieties could slowly gain ground.

What she felt, she now remembered, in those rare, usually involuntary moments of introspection, was a guilt that pulled in two directions. First was the torturous thought that her only children's unrecoverable toddlerhood was passing by while she filed old photographs; she took for granted that she would regret this later in life and was more bound up in the fear that Peter and Leo would remember her, later in their own lives, as an infrequent visitor, an ill-tempered disciplinarian whose sleep one was always being warned not to disturb. The second guilt was a kind of reaction to the first; for she was a woman of her time, and she was harried by the incorrectness, the meagerness of those retrograde longings for domestic life and for the daily society not of colleagues but of small children. The desire for sex which had led her to take advantage of the existence of Brian did not cause her the same sort of inward reprobation; *that* desire, she felt, was natural, corporeal, ineradicable. But the longing for motherhood struck her in much grander, even historical terms, as a cowardly retreat. Paul's acceptance of the book deal had lifted her out of her dilemma regarding Brian and his urgencies, but it was an equally brilliant solution, she saw now, to this question of her conflicting responsibilities and desires as a modern mother; it brought about the outcome she had most longed for at the same time as it had taken the decision itself out of her hands.

Now there was no shortage of time to spend with Peter and Leo, time that was, at least so far, every bit as gratifying as she had fantasized. But in those few hours of the day when they were not together, when the boys were upstairs or in preschool and she and her husband had the apartment to themselves, it was brought home to her that the great change since March was not just in her own daily routine but in Paul's. In those quiet hours, she was, she recognized, a kind of ghost haunting his working day. Pleasantly tired, relishing the silence, she wanted to roam through her own apartment, she wanted to go to the living room and look through the shelves for one of the many books she had never had the chance to finish, or listen to music, or even turn on some execrable daytime TV. Or talk to Paul. But when she did any of these things, he would immediately stop working; he would look up at her, and turn off the typewriter, and smile inquisitively. Never once did he scold her, even indirectly, or ask her to keep it down, or betray any sort of impatience at all. True, in those days he was naturally much more prone to distraction (even eager for it on some level) than he might have been had he been working on his novel. But that wasn't the problem. The problem, she knew, was her presence. It didn't matter how quiet she was. It didn't even matter, apparently, if she went into the bedroom to read all morning and shut the door behind her. His notion of solitude had simply become, by virtue of the nature of his career, somewhat overrefined.

Four or five weeks into their new life of leisure, walking down the hall toward their front door after dropping off the boys for lunch and videos at Mrs. Perez's, Renata could hear the unbroken hammering of Paul's old Olivetti even before she put the key in the lock. As quietly as if she were burgling her own home, she slipped through the door, eased it shut, and literally tiptoed to their bedroom; but she barely had her coat off before she heard the typewriter's geriatric humming expire, and Paul walking down the hall, barefoot, his hands in his pockets.

"How's it going?" he said, smiling.

"Fine," she said uneasily. "Been working?"

He seemed surprised. "Oh, no," he said. "Not really." There was a pause, while he looked around their bedroom as if he had never visited it before. "So," he said, and smiled again. "Can I get you anything? Have you had lunch?"

"I'm fine, thanks, honey," she said.

"Have you seen the paper? I'm finished with it if you want to see it. I'll go get it if—"

"That's okay." She still had her jacket in her arms, meaning to hang it in the hall closet. Paul still stood looking at her; she marveled sometimes at how little he seemed to understand himself. "In fact," she said, "I was thinking what I'd do this afternoon is go out and catch a movie."

"Oh?" he said. He seemed almost shocked.

"Why not? Going to a weekday matinee is certainly up there on the list of ordinary things I haven't done in years. You never have to worry about the show you want selling out, either, like on weekends."

She watched him; he seemed to be struggling with something. "Well," he said finally. "If, you know, if that's what you want. I mean if you're sure."

He was searching for words which would suit the situation, which would convey his support for this idea of her leaving without seeming in any way to encourage or be pleased by it.

"I'm sure," she said, laughing. She put her jacket back on. "In fact, I'd better get going if I'm—"

"I, um . . ." She waited for him, patiently. "I probably shouldn't go," he said. "I should probably stay here."

His fecklessness was enough to make her want to cry

sometimes. "Oh, okay, fine. You probably should work instead. I'll just go by myself, then." They kissed, and she left him standing there in the doorway to the bedroom, still looking confused about something.

In another month or so, Renata realized as she stopped on the corner to buy a paper to try to find a movie to see, when school let out for summer, she would be with the boys, she supposed, every hour of the day.

"Bob Spain's office."

"Olivia?"

Olivia looked quickly over her shoulder at Spain's closed office door, then leaned back in her desk chair and ran her hand through her hair. "Hey, girlfriend," she said. "What's up? You're not in New York, are you?"

"I wish," Amy said. "No, I'm home." She walked slowly, as she talked, through all the three rooms of her apartment, the white living room, the white bedroom, the peach kitchen. There was little furniture to obstruct her as she circled with the cordless phone. "Which is where you should be. What is it, eight o'clock there? What are you still doing at work? I tried you at home and got that weird roommate. I left a message with her, but I—"

"The woman's never written down a phone message in her life," Olivia said.

"I didn't really trust her to give it to you, so I thought I'd just call here and leave something on your voice mail. And I find you at your desk. What the hell are you doing there?"

"What the hell do you think I'm doing here? You don't think the Inquisitor is going to pay me two-eighty a week just to work nine to five, do you?" She peeked at Spain's door again. "I'm typing up some letters, that's all. A much better question is what you're doing at home already at five o'clock on the dot?"

"I know, it's bad, but Frank had a premiere to go to tonight, so as soon as he was gone we all split. Listen, if you're working, you probably want to get out of there, maybe I should—"

"No, are you kidding? The only reason I even picked up the phone this late is because I knew it was probably something personal."

"Something personal?"

"Something personal, yes."

"Uh-huh," Amy said. "I see. So what's his name?"

Olivia grinned. "His name? I don't think it's anyone you'd know."

"Obviously, but names are still very important. Come on. I live in California now. I've bought into all this shit big time."

Olivia laughed. She could hear two or three other voices seeping over the walls of her cubicle, so she knew she wasn't the only assistant still in the office. Still, it was depressingly quiet; the silence and the late hour made the overhead lights seem excessively bright and invasive. She turned off her typewriter with her stockinged heel.

"It's Jason," she said.

"Jason, Jason. Any guy named Jason, dump him before he dumps you, that's what I say."

"Now, now. He's very devoted."

"What's he do?"

Olivia swallowed. "He— I can't believe I'm saying this. To you of all people. He plays in a band."

Amy stopped pacing in her kitchen and screamed. "Not the guitar?" she said. "Say it isn't the guitar?"

"Oh yes," Olivia said, "it's the guitar."

"Girl, have you lost all your self-esteem? Did Susan B. Anthony get on the silver dollar so smart women like you could date guitarists?"

"I know, I know," Olivia said. "It's so degrading. I never thought I'd be one of those pathetic chicks standing offstage pretending not to watch while their boyfriend gyrates in front of other women and sings about being doomed and misunderstood. And he's totally forgetful and never has any money and has a group of guy friends that he—well, it's the whole package. But still. It's been like six weeks. It's been a lot of fun. He has his qualities."

"I'll bet he does," Amy said. "What is he, like an Evan Dando?"

"More like a Dave Pirner."

"Nice. And so the band, what's the band's name—"

Spain could open his office door the way a sheriff unholstered his gun; he was standing in the doorway before Olivia could get her feet off the typewriter and swing around in her chair. He looked bemusedly at the receiver in her hand. His coat was on.

"Are those letters done yet?" he said quietly.

"All but one," Olivia said. "I'll mail them when I leave."

"Yes, but you see I'm leaving now. And if I'm not here, I can't sign them. So I guess they won't go out until tomorrow now."

"No," Olivia said. "I suppose not. Unless you want to wait a couple minutes."

"That call's not for me, is it?"

Olivia almost rolled her eyes, but recovered herself. "No, it's for me," she said. "A personal call. Incoming."

One of the things she most loathed about her boss was the way he seemed to grow bored with her answers to his questions even before they were finished. Almost before she had stopped speaking, he said, "Did you try Paul Soloway again?"

She nodded.

"How many times?"

"Four."

"You didn't leave more than one message, did you?"

"No, just the one, like you asked me to."

Spain shook his head. "What's going on with that guy?" he said. "Is he trying to give me high blood pressure? What kind of person doesn't return phone calls? What is he, out of town?"

He addressed these questions to her, though none of them seemed to require an answer. Olivia sometimes had the distinct impression (maybe because he so seldom addressed her by her name) that when he looked at her, he was seeing some assistant he had had fifteen years ago. She remained sitting, staring at him with the phone still in her hand, waiting for some signal that they were disengaged.

"Did you try calling his wife at work?" he said.

"She doesn't work there anymore."

"Send a letter?"

"Sent it."

"Well, then," he said in his most reasonable tone, "if there comes a time when you have a few moments between personal phone calls, do you think you might give some thought to why it is you can't find a way to contact one of our most important authors?" Olivia began to turn red. "It does seem like one of the more basic aspects of your job here. Is it your impression that other assistants have this problem?"

Spain had a special talent for asking these questions that were not really questions at all—that couldn't be answered, though nothing in his manner suggested that he meant them rhetorically. All Olivia could do at moments like this was refuse to meet his eyes. The appropriate responses, and the nerve to deliver them, always came only after he was gone; which made her angrier.

"The letters will be ready for signature when I come in in the morning?"

She nodded petulantly. He picked up his briefcase full of manuscripts and, without any actual farewell, walked off toward the elevators. Olivia brought the phone back to her ear and said, "Sorry."

"Man! Was that him?" Amy said.

"That was himself."

"Wow! What an asshole! He and Frank should get together sometime."

"Maybe go to a cockfight or something," Olivia said.

"And that was the Paul Soloway book he was yelling about, right?"

"Yup."

"Jeez, there's an awful lot of testosterone being spilled about that one book! Frank has been in my face about that since March. What's going on with it?"

"Maybe something," Olivia said, slowly relaxing again, "maybe nothing. Bob wants to see the pages as they're written, literally, and so far Soloway hasn't turned anything in. Which doesn't mean he's not writing. But he is ducking us, I'm sure. I think he just wants to be left alone —he came in here for a meeting about a month ago, and I don't think the two of them hit it off real well. So Bob is just stroking out about it, as you heard."

"I guess so. Men. Well, hey, I should let you go."

"I guess, but listen, I'll call you back soon. I haven't even asked about your love life, or your career. Have they made you a producer yet?"

"Oh, yeah," Amy said. "In fact, I'm already working on my memoirs. All right, sweetie. Hang in there."

"I will. Thanks for calling."

Amy turned the phone off and dropped it on the couch. She was just three or four miles from the coast, but she might as well have been back in Illinois; outside her window all she could see was a kind of slapdash suburban development, strategic trees, and the supposed bucolicism of streets that didn't run straight. Groups of UCLA students passed by on the block. She lived in a student neighborhood because it was what she could afford, but the sight of those students, just two or three years younger than she but living a life she was cut off from, increased her sense of limbo. She was depressed by this bit of news about the Soloway book because now she would have to decide whether or not to tell Pickert what she had learned. It was one thing to be asked to make hard decisions, even to compromise one's integrity; but she had never imagined that the major decisions would involve such comically minor affairs. If she did tell him—if he found out there were no pages yet—he would fly into a panic and make her life miserable. But not to tell him such a thing would be an outright act of sabotage; and if she were capable of such contempt for her job, then why did she continue with it at all? What was it she was really learning?

Listlessly, she turned on the TV. She remembered that at some point before she went to sleep she would need to eat some dinner.

On 110th Street, somewhere around Morningside, it became apparent to me as I sat in the rental car that something was wrong. One's eye, after years in the city, becomes acclimated to a certain type of street life, a certain character of public activity. Whatever it is that signals that this activity has crossed over into something heightened or threatening operates below the cognitive level: a kind of environmental instinct. When I was a boy, I had a dog who could tell from the tone of your voice, no matter how you strove to disguise it, when he was about to be given a bath. Sometimes my

The telephone rang; and since Paul was not enamored of the path of that paragraph anyway, he switched off the typewriter, removed his thick glasses to rub his eyes, and waited for the machine to pick up. It was around lunchtime, and the days were beginning to feel like the onset of true summer.

"Hi, Paul, it's Olivia in Bob Spain's office. I don't know if you got my earlier message—of course, if you didn't, then you probably won't get this one either—but Bob is very anxious to talk to you. Nothing important, he just wants to check in, see how things are going. But call us as soon as you can, okay? Bye."

He remembered Olivia in vivid counterpoint to the polite yet faintly corrupt Spain. She seemed so despoiled in those surroundings, like a beauty from a fairy tale, locked in a glass tower until she would submit to the king. Oh well, Paul thought; they are both genuine, in their way. He turned on the typewriter and hit the return button, consigning to oblivion any further thoughts about the mind of a dog.

The light ahead of me changed to green, but nothing moved—I was still locked in the intersection. Cars began honking furiously, from the block in front of me and the block behind me; and also, I noticed, from what seemed like a great distance away. Since I am such a poor driver, my instinct is always to believe that any audible car horn is directed at me. So even though the Dodge in front of me

Paul had no idea if that car had been a Dodge—had no idea, in fact, what a Dodge looked like as distinct from other automobiles; but he felt that such details gave a liveliness to any account which outweighed accuracy.

had its brake lights on, I tried to pull around it, just to maneuver myself out of the box. Of course it was impossible. Cars were parked on both sides of the street, leaving a lane for westbound traffic about one and a half cars wide. So I was forced almost immediately to come to a stop again, having gained about ten feet and a wild, angry, disbelieving stare from the man in the Dodge. The back end of my rental car now stuck out about six feet into the intersection. The horns were louder than ever—in fact, they seemed to have changed their character somehow; no longer could one misinterpret them as being directed toward a goal, such as warning a fellow driver or prompting him to notice that the light had changed to green. They had become a howl, a public panic, noise for the sake of noise: inspirited, somehow, by danger.

Then I saw the first of many things I would see that day which, even at the moment they were happening, I was conscious that I would never forget: the first, the most oblique, and so perhaps the most interesting. About four cars ahead of me in line—or rather in the line which I, in my impatience, had squeezed myself out of—I saw a man get out of his car and run. He ran east, back the way he had come, toward me. He looked like a salesman—fortyish, blue suit pants, black shoes, white shirt, a

conservative tie, top button undone. A little bald on top. He did
not look like he was from the city—perhaps that's why I think of
him as a salesman. He held a briefcase which he had not forgot-
ten and which swung awkwardly; and he had, I saw, thought to
close the car door behind him. The look in his eyes, similarly, was
not senseless panic: more like grim, Yankee determination. But
he was running. I could not see what he saw; I couldn't even see
if he had turned his car off before abandoning it. He quickly
disappeared among the idling cars.

What is it about that image of the man abandoning his auto-
mobile? Why do I associate it so strongly with images of apoca-
lypse, particularly of nuclear war? It's much easier, for some
reason, to be reconciled with even the imagined vision of people
fleeing their homes to get out of the path of some disaster than to
picture people shucking off the armor of their cars and just run-
ning for it. The car itself, only a century old, should be unavail-
able to our deep fantasies. Perhaps that's it—maybe what strikes
me about that fearsome tableau is not the running man, but the
alien car itself, sitting where it was never meant to sit, an ob-
struction, an anomaly, a ghost. A home abandoned is still a
home, living in abeyance until someone comes back to reclaim it,
but a car left in the middle of the road is so violated, so un-
manned, so subverted that you would swear it was impossible for
anyone to come along and drive it away again.

There was more to be wrung from the subject, but for
the last fifteen minutes Paul had been listening to his
stomach growl, so he took a break for lunch. Preparing
and eating a ham and cheese sandwich would take him less
than five minutes, though, and he wanted more of an opportunity to clear his head; so he went over to the new CD
player and put on some Schubert, the fifteenth and final
string quartet. He sat in the recliner in the living room,
chewing and listening. There were passages in that long
first movement that made Paul's breath seem to come with
more difficulty—in particular the secondary theme, fourteen minor-key notes that were sad beyond tears. Schubert
wrote them just about two years before his death at the age

of thirty-one. Paul was thirty-four; a few months ago, he had almost died. Say that ethereal "almost" had not been, at the last minute as it were, added to the record: what accomplishment would Paul have managed to leave behind, in that short life? What evidence that it had been lived at all? He put his plate on the floor and rested his head on his hand. When the CD was over, rather than go back to work, he played it again.

The press conference on the precinct steps was only the first volley in Boggs's media campaign. His shiny, noble head was a fixture on local television and in the tabloid press, passionately effacing the popular image of Victor Hartley as the stereotypical young black thug, and building, inch by column inch, a new construction to take its place. His success was measured in small, sometimes oblique ways; on one visit to Rikers, Boggs asked Victor if his mother or his girlfriends might have any snapshots of him, something family-oriented, with one of his daughters, maybe, or at a picnic, something like that.

"My mom," Victor said, somewhat confused. (Boggs still enjoyed the relationship with his client that a magician enjoyed with his audience, never explaining, never condescending, always one step ahead for maximum effect.) "Ask my mom. She's the one with the pictures. Every time I bring one of her grandchildren over there, I'm worried we'll all go blind from the flash."

Boggs went off to charm Mrs. Hartley, and within a few weeks, in with the newspaper clippings and transcripts Boggs regularly dropped off with him, appeared some of these old photos—Victor with Tanya on his shoulders, Victor hugging his mother, even Victor's high school graduation picture—shockingly familiar even in this grainy, black-and-white form. Of course Victor saw what his lawyer had done. Until now, the papers had had to run the same grim photo of him from the original perp-walk, in chains, head down, in an orange Department of Corrections jumpsuit, over and over again, because it was the only image of him they owned. Now that Boggs had parceled out this private archive to the *Post*, the *News*, and *Newsday*, not only did they have new pictures, but each of them had exclusives the others had not been given access to. The decision to run these much more sympathetic snapshots was not an ethical but a commercial, even an aesthetic one; still, their impact, as Victor himself could see, was revelatory.

One thing, though, disturbed him as he read through the clippings file in the relative privacy of his cell; and that was the frequent, astounding blasts of vitriol the newspapers directed at Boggs himself. He was called a bloodsucker, a pimp, a soulless publicity hound, crooked, immoral, greedy, hellbound. The next time they met in the sky-blue conference room, he asked the lawyer about it.

"Mr. Boggs—"

"Arthur," Boggs said, not for the first time—though he had a way of saying it that seemed to indicate he didn't really mean it.

"Arthur, how can you stand this? I mean, your friends see this, your family. The papers all hate you. And you haven't done anything wrong. How can you take it?"

Boggs laughed with pleasure, as if one of his children had asked him if it was true that when he grew up there was no television. If the broad table hadn't been between them, he would have clapped his client on the shoulder. "The first among many things I didn't learn in law school," he said. "The only bad publicity is no publicity. Besides, I don't take it personally; it's just their way of working off their own self-hatred. Anything—and this is important—anything we can do to make the media's job easier ultimately serves our interest."

One matter the journalists and editorial writers doggedly conjectured about was the exact nature of the financial arrangement between attorney and client. This was known only to the two men; but outsiders seemed so positive that it had to be unfair that Victor did allow himself to worry, belatedly, that he had signed something he shouldn't have. The agreement was that Boggs took no percentage of any money raised from any source toward bail—unless Hartley were to be acquitted at his trial, in which case bail would be refunded, and a third of it would then go to Boggs. Similarly, a third of any money raised above and beyond the one-hundred-and-fifty-thousand-dollar bail—as unlikely as that seemed—went to the lawyer. Victor looked at this from every angle, so worried was he that the newspapers knew something he didn't, that he had been taken. But the feeling remained that Boggs continually performed feats that bordered on the supernatural and it would be foolish to risk losing his services over questions of as yet unmaterialized money. Anyway, Victor had no desire to profit from this whole sad affair—no interest in money except insofar as it meant making bail and seeing his family, his children, in the relatively near future.

In fact, Boggs had managed to get a bail-reduction hearing scheduled for two weeks hence. Privately, he had told Victor that they should expect nothing to go their way in this hearing—that, in fact, he fully expected to be chewed out mercilessly by the judge—but the publicity would be more than worth it. Cameras would be there and would show an irascible white woman with a robe denying a young black man a chance to go home and be with his family in his, and their, hour of need. In the meantime, Boggs was off trying to gather new evidence, not so much for use in the courtroom, but as a carrot for reporters, who were growing tired of his constant imprecations and were wary of being used. But new evidence was always news, and if you didn't snatch at it, you had to worry that your competitors would. Of course, there was virtually no new evidence to exonerate Victor, so Boggs turned instead to what was just as good—evidence to impugn Paul Soloway. He didn't discover a whole lot here either—the guy appeared to be some kind of Ivy League egghead, no job, supported by his wife, until recently when he accepted a fat check to write a book about the whole affair—but that was probably plenty, Boggs thought. Facts were facts, and one was rarely better than another on the face of it; the whole trick was the use to which you could put it.

Victor's transformed celebrity was a factor not only in the outside world but within the closed, quite different society of the prison itself. His emerging status as a symbol, if not as a kind of mute spokesman, for black rage did not go unnoticed. But the effects of this were mixed. For every fellow inmate who now (even if they were strangers) nodded knowingly, intensely to him or passed him with a quietly respectful "My brother," there would be one who saw it all as the merest uppityness, an attempt on Victor's part to distinguish himself from his fellows which carried no coin in here, and who would gladly have beaten him simply to reestablish that the world's sense of hierarchy was not the prison's. Victor had known plenty of roughnecks in his time, growing up where he did, but not in this kind of concentration. Unlike back in East Harlem, avoiding these characters when you were in jail with them required considerable strategizing. He managed, with the help of some supporters, to stay safe.

One day, when Boggs was not scheduled to come by, Victor was surprised to be told he had a visitor. He followed the guard and took his seat at the table halved by bulletproof glass. It was like looking into a mirror in which everything was reflected but yourself. After a few moments the door on the other side of the glass opened, and his mother walked in. Involuntarily, Victor jumped up from his chair; the guard behind him took a protective step forward. Victor sat down again and picked up the telephone. His mother was smiling. In her hand he could see the inhaler that she used for her asthma.

"Mama," he said into the phone. "What are you doing here by yourself? Where's Jocelyn?"

"She don't know I'm here," his mother said. Hearing

her voice made raspy by the phone, while watching her lips move just two feet in front of him, was like watching a badly synched movie. "Your sisters told me not to come, that I wouldn't want to see you down here."

They had been acting, in fact, on Victor's own wishes— he couldn't bear to be confronted with the shame he had brought upon his mother by being imprisoned in the first place—but he let that go. "Are you all right? You made it out here okay?"

She smiled bravely and nodded, though he could see in her eyes that the trip had been longer than she was used to, and that she was a little frightened of this place. There was a pause then, while mother and son both came up against the difficulty of normal conversation as they had always known it in such extraordinary, even dreamlike surroundings.

"Tanya come over to the house," she said finally. "We had her for the whole day. We went over to that park, the new one over the river. Then we made some—"

"Mama," Victor said. "Mama, I'm so sorry. I'm so sorry for this."

She shook her head for a long time, in the mysterious, indeterminate way of the old, though she was only fifty-seven. Then she looked up at him.

"They saying you a hero," she said.

"Who's saying that? The TV?"

"The TV," she repeated. "And in the neighborhood. In the building. They come right up to me. They talk about it all the time."

"Mama," he said, "I'm not a hero. I let you down. I let you down by being in here." He touched the glass with his fingertips.

But at the same time, somewhere in the back of his mind, was the nagging, the confusing perception that this was just the sort of thing a hero would say.

Later, back in his cell, he looked again through the media file with which Boggs had supplied him. It was odd,

exceedingly new, not only to have the kind of public identity that he now appeared to have, but to be, in effect, a
spectator, a witness, to the construction and the operation
of this identity. So far, everything seemed to be happening
for the best. And it wasn't as if this media-double of his,
this alternate existence, was in any aspect objectionable to
him—a family man, a hard worker, a loving son, a young
black man with a consciousness of his obligation to uplift
the race. He was not insensitive, though, to the notion that
even this flattering portrayal of himself was completely in
the hands of a powerful, wealthy white man, that not just
his future but the very nature of his inmost identity was
being recast by a small cabal of white men and women
who did not really know him, while he himself idled in jail.
But to complain about this, he felt, was only to complain
that his defense was something less than completely ideal
—which, considering his circumstances, seemed like asking for the world.

*In unwisely jumping out of the one potential lane of traffic, I
had stalled myself behind a parked Jeep, or Range Rover, or
whatever those nonsensical urban playtoys are called, with the
result that, even as the uncertain, glowering noise on the block
ahead of me swelled, I could see no farther than the green behind
of this vehicle, with its vanity license plate above a bumper
sticker that read, "Easy Does It." The symbols of our addiction,
adhered to our cars—the modern prestige of the self-inflicted
wound. Frankly, I was still unable to devote full attention to
what was in front of me; I was much more consumed by the
problem of how to get the rear third of the car out of the intersection. The horns were sounding so continuously now that I
didn't really hear them anymore. I noticed that my whole body
was rigid, my fingers crooked painfully around the wheel, and
that was because I waited unconsciously for the impact of a crash.
I kept glancing behind me.*

*Then the car to my left—the one whose driver had glared so
disbelievingly at me when I pulled into my little dead end—did*

something that shocked me; looking over his shoulder, with his right arm draped over the empty passenger seat beside him, he zoomed in reverse right through the angry, snarled intersection. Just a moment after I lost sight of him, I heard him (or someone) crunch into another car. But a kind of vain clearheadedness had taken over me by now, and I quickly slipped into his spot in the line between the two rows of parked cars, which was in effect now a third row of parked cars, since the light ahead of us was green yet nothing moved, and in any case somewhere in front of me was the empty car abandoned by the terrified salesman. At least, I remember thinking, I'm safe now.

From my new vantage point, the first thing I noticed (of course, only in retrospection are perceptions obliged to form a line) was the open windows in the walls of buildings that rose up on either side of the street. It was an unseasonably warm day, but that couldn't have had anything to do with the fact that there was at least one body leaning out of every single window: some yelling, some silent with arms folded, some laughing, all of them gazing down at the theater of the narrow street like boxholders. I remember I saw one of them hurl a sneaker down into the motionless traffic. They made a vague, strange noise—passionate, virtually celebratory, yet riding along some dangerous borderline dividing mere headiness from real fever. Over the tops of the cars I could now make out some of the brown, barren trees of Riverside Park, just four or five blocks away.

A television came flying out of a window and exploded spectacularly on the hood of a parked car.

A gathering of men, mostly young, and exclusively black, now swarmed over this small block, throughout the narrow passage between the short tenements, empty-handed (it occurs to me now) with just two or three exceptions. They weren't doing anything menacing—they weren't doing anything at all, really, aside from milling restlessly in a way which defied or ignored the customary division between sidewalk and roadway, between pavement and the metal hoods and roofs of the empty parked cars. I saw no one screaming, and yet somehow a great deal of noise was in the air. And from whatever source, an authentic sense of menace was being generated, no doubt about it.

Anonymous solitaries in useless automobiles, black faces unified in expressions of anger. Nothing on the street was moving now except for those men. Thirty feet in front of me, men on either side began to rock one car back and forth, back and forth, until the great machine was bucking like a spooked horse and the driver's head repeatedly smacked against the roof. Indeed, the cars, for some reason, seemed the real object of the rage. Maybe they were not, in the fire of the moment, symbols of anything— merely large, noisy, flammable. To the left of me I heard the unique crunch of safety glass; I saw that a man had just spider-webbed the windshield of an occupied car with a golf club. I remember thinking to myself, A golf club? Farther away, another group was trying to flip over the car which the man with the briefcase had abandoned to them. From the windows above, men and women shouted rhythmic encouragement.

It dawned on me that what I was watching was a riot. With the twin consciousness that characterizes the life of every writer, I was perhaps insufficiently alive, in those moments, to the problem of my own presence there; the more I entered into the scene as an observer, the more absent, at least in my own mind, I became. There were no sirens—only human voices, considerably muffled by the technology that had gone into my unfamiliar car, and the endless, unharmonious din of a thousand horns, the soundtrack to chaos. Suddenly, out of nowhere, I was finally able to connect this awesome scene with the pale, blemished, anxious face of the boy working all alone at the bakery, the way he kept turning up the radio. It may seem exceptionally dim of me not to have connected all this rage and petty destruction with the Fisk trial more instantly. But there is a part of us all, particularly those of us who choose to live in cities, that secretly longs for the day when everything finally goes to hell; and in my fascination with every detail of this flowering of the urban subconscious, it was some time before I could begin to think so synthetically.

Somehow the thought of the nervous boy began the process

whereby my sense of myself was restored. I checked again that the doors were locked. Having weighed anew the relative risks of zooming in reverse back through the intersection, I even checked the rearview mirror; but the path was hopelessly clogged, cars pointing into the mirror's frame at every angle. At this point I wasn't sure what to do. I didn't know that I was any safer in the car than out of it, though my instinct was certainly to stay inside —even though I was, at that point, strange to say, just a few blocks from my home. I even thought for a moment about turning on the radio, to see if there was any news about the rioting, but the peculiarly modern absurdity of that idea struck me right away.

Then I noticed, motionless amid all the male fury, a lone black woman, my mother's age or a bit older, sitting on the front steps of one of the tenements. She wore a heavy brown coat over a thin dress. Her hands were on her knees, and on her face was an expression of granite impassivity. It was nearly impossible to read, but it was most certainly not anger. She watched as the men continued to shout, gesticulate, throw trash cans, assault cars, assert their ironic claim to the small neglected block. For the moment, all the action was up the street, at least thirty yards away from me. After a last look around, I rolled down my window.

The sound level quadrupled, and I flinched for a second, but still I stuck my face a few inches out of the car.

"Excuse me!" I yelled.

She didn't turn; I have no doubt she couldn't hear me.

"Hey!"

There was some sadness in her face, I thought I saw now, as she watched the activity up the street, and though there was no way to quickly determine the vintage of that sadness, I felt I had to reach her.

Cautiously I got out of the car. I ventured almost to the sidewalk, my hands resting uneasily on two parked cars.

"Excuse me!" I yelled again. This time she turned her head and noticed me. I was perhaps twelve feet away from where she sat.

"Can you call the police?" I said.

She did not respond. I may have detected a further, slight hardening in her expression as she faced me, though perhaps that was my imagination.

"Do you live nearby?" I said.

Her large brown eyes watched me with no curiosity. It was just as if I were on a TV screen, a kitschy image of a man in distress, unlikely perhaps but no more so than a lot of other things she might see.

"Don't you think we ought to call the police?" I said.

And before I could have sensed it, a group of eight or ten men had broken off from the general throng and were running toward me, pointing at me. I couldn't turn around quickly in the narrow space between the two cars. Still, I made it back into my car before they got to me, even managed to shut the door; but before I could lock it they yanked it ajar again and pulled me out into the open. Someone struck me on the back of the head and at that point, for a few seconds at least, I ceased to be able to see. The men shouted, as they hit me, in a manner which I could not understand. I lost my balance. Then, at last, I heard the sirens, it sounded like a thousand of them, coming from every direction, not the sound of deliverance but merely of a new level of engagement. The men surrounding me heard the sirens as well, and a tone of frantic uncertainty entered their own voices. A final muffling of sound indicated to me, just before I believe I passed out, that I had been taken indoors.

At this point Paul turned the typewriter off and put his hands behind his head, scowling slightly. Something was unsettling him; but he rejected the idea that that something was the dread reawakened by his beginning to live through, again, the most painful and dangerous hours of his life. Writing about an event was not reliving it; that was a canard favored by those who had no direct experience of writing's true nature. No, he decided; what galled him about these last few pages was the particular tyranny of the narrative itself, the tyranny that he strove to overcome in all his fiction but that for some reason seemed

particularly hard to disobey here. And he believed he had a
new insight into what had caused him to want to disown
these events in the first place; it was that very and-then-
and-then-and-then quality, the *futility* of it, that seemed to
mock him and his efforts. It was too much like a movie.
He himself was getting lost in it. Any idiot could connect
one line of dialogue to another; he was missing the real
story. Between every pair of these sentences, he thought as
he read over the day's work, were five or six unwritten
pages: on the face of that black woman on the stoop, on
the psychology of fear, on the individual and the mob, on
the world of missed connections that now existed between
himself and the man who had fled that scene on foot.
Well, he thought consolingly, he could always go back and
rewrite this material in a more interesting, complex manner; it was mere laziness to expect everything to come out
perfectly the first time.

It was ten minutes to four, and he decided to go until
the hour, just for closure's sake.

The image of the running man, the image of the lonely boy at
the bakery, these have become part of my private political vocab-
ulary. Reader, do you remember the day of the verdict in the
first trial of the policemen who beat Rodney King? So many
rumors exploded all across this city, three thousand miles from
the courthouse—a city bus had been overturned with people in it;
the LIE between Manhattan and LaGuardia airport was block-
aded by rioters; Macy's was on fire. Stores and businesses closed
early all over New York, just as they did on the day the Fisk
trial ended. Race is the fissure that runs through American life,
in all of its aspects. The day of the King verdict, there were no
riots in New York, and the day of the Fisk verdict there were
few to speak of. It doesn't matter. What's striking is the instan-
taneous, almost wordless spread of panic through white society. It
is clear now that, on some level of consciousness which our minds
have learned to simultaneously bury and nurture like an ember,
we expect *black rage and destruction, we* expect *our own pun-*
ishment, we live with the anticipation and the fear of the day it

arrives. We were more receptive to the idea that an assault trial in California would be the trigger for the final, apocalyptic confrontation with the black communities than those communities were themselves. We have judged ourselves to be oppressors, and we are too unsurprised by the notion of revenge ever to risk being caught by it unaware.

In the late, sunny days of June, the schools let out for the summer—first Leo's, then Peter's. Now, every morning, just as soon as they were dressed and the sleep was rubbed from their eyes, they looked frankly up at their mother, waiting to learn from her what new diversions this day would contain. It was a kind of escalation of the pressures of parenthood, but Renata was equal to it; the problem, instead, was that the apartment soon began to seem unusually crowded. She saw as she couldn't see before what importance his few daily hours of solitude had in Paul's emotional as well as his working life; if deprived of them, he was jumpy and distracted, though he would, out of consideration, never admit that that was what was bothering him. Perhaps, Renata thought, he didn't even recognize what was bothering him, at any rate not as clearly as she discerned it.

Seeing how he suffered—and not wanting to contribute to the forces that were blocking him from writing the book which had to be completed more rapidly than he had ever completed anything before—she racked her brain thinking of things for the easily bored kids to do that would get them all out of the house. They went to the Children's Museum on the West Side and the one in Brooklyn as well, to the Hayden Planetarium for a show about teddy bears traveling among the stars, to the American Museum of Natural History to see the dinosaurs, with which small children, for some atavistic reason, seemed to connect so intimately. But boys that age could show only so much patience with the hushed, crowded, imperious indoor atmosphere of museums, and there were very few she felt comfortable taking kids to anyway; so she was forced to get more inventive. (Or, sometimes, less inventive—there were always the playgrounds, and Toy Park on Columbus Avenue, and Kiddie City on 79th Street.) On a particularly warm day they went on the Circle Line, which the boys loved; Renata's enjoyment of it was compromised by her panic every time they would catch sight of something novel, like a drawbridge, and run headlong toward the railing. They went to Rumpelmayers, and South Street Seaport, and to Radio City Music Hall for a "Shining Time Station" show, even though it was rather too close to Renata's old office building for her comfort.

She even took them, bewildered but pliant, on a tour of Mommy's years up at Barnard, and it was there, just outside Bookforum on Broadway, that they ran into Paul's friend Martin. She surprised herself by feeling genuinely glad to see him. Part of it was that the kids were so obviously in love with him, running to hug his waist (even Peter, who was starting to develop a self-consciousness around most grownups) in a way that had to warm her heart toward him. But, beyond that, it made her realize, quite suddenly, how starved she had become for adult company, how she had missed simple things like swearing and longed for the relief of saying whatever came into her head without prescreening it for a child's suitability and comprehension.

It also revealed to her another desire she hadn't really articulated for herself, another simple thing which her current circumstances left her no opportunity to do, and that was to talk to someone about Paul. Martin, having lifted each boy up in the air in his customarily incautious way, mussed their hair, and generally whipped them into a frenzy, nodded a cordial goodbye and was about to continue down Broadway when Renata said, laughing, "Hang on a second. What's your hurry?"

He stopped, looking puzzled—as if he were indeed trying to remember what his hurry was. One of the things Renata recoiled from in him was the way his eccentric behavior seemed too much like Paul's taken to a kind of logical extreme. He seemed always to have just one foot in the here and now. No wonder nobody's ever married this guy, she thought; you'd never have a peaceful moment while he was out of your sight. At least, she thought, he served to prove that her own case could have been a lot worse than it was.

"No hurry," he said. "I was just out for a walk, really."

"Downtown?"

He looked all around him. "I suppose so," he said. "I mean I didn't have any real destination in mind."

"Well, we're heading down toward the playground," Renata said. "Why don't you walk with us awhile?"

Leo and Peter voiced their approval of this idea, and so Martin agreed. They walked a block or so in silence, Renata not really sure how to begin speaking with him. Social graces were so beneath his notice that she was unsure if he had ever felt her customary disapproval of him, as expressed in her reluctance to let Paul invite him over to the apartment. That was a slight, no question about it— if a necessary one, for the protection of her children's safety and her husband's already fragile ability to socialize normally—but if he had experienced it as such, he gave no hint of that now. He looked down as they walked, his lips moving occasionally.

"How have you been?" Renata said, reaching for something normal to talk about with him. "School must be finished for the year, right?"

He nodded. "Finals were back in May. The department made me give a final exam in poetry writing, can you believe that?"

"What did you do?"

"What was there to do? It was a joke, so I treated it as one. I had them define a sestina, a trochee, crap like that, and then for the other seventy-five percent of their grade they had to write a limerick. Just to make sure they weren't cheating, I gave them the first line: 'There once was a cunning young poet.' " He smiled.

Renata laughed. "But what if somebody in the English Department sees it?"

"Oh, they'll see it. I was required to hand it in."

"Won't they be furious?"

Martin shrugged.

Renata hadn't seen him in a long time—not since Paul went into the hospital, it occurred to her—and he looked more dissipated than she remembered him. It was hard to pinpoint. He had, if anything, put on a little weight, but he was sallow, and tired-looking. She had the idea that if she held a mirror in front of him he would be surprised by what he saw.

After they had walked about four blocks, Leo suddenly appeared in front of Martin, dancing backward, holding up his arms. "Do it, do it," he said. Martin smiled, reached down, and lifted the boy onto his shoulders. To Renata, this was like watching someone carry a tray of martini glasses down a flight of stairs. Her own hands kept flying outward as the two of them bobbed down the street, Leo's little fingers laced around Martin's forehead.

"So I haven't heard from Paul in a while," Martin said. "How's he doing? How's the book going?"

"Okay," Renata said. "There's scaffolding coming up here, Martin." He ducked so that Leo's head narrowly missed it. "All right," she went on. "He hasn't let me see any of it. I think he's struggling with it a little bit, actually."

"Struggling how?"

He had turned to look at her, without halting; involuntarily she reached out and grabbed his sleeve to pull him out of the way of a teenager on a bicycle coming up the sidewalk. "I'm not sure," she said. "He's upset, but I don't know if he's upset because he's not getting enough work done or because the work he's getting done is so distasteful to him. I try to give him as much room as I can, but it's pretty clear he's unhappy."

"Well, he has a pretty powerful ego, Paul," Martin said; Renata looked at him quickly to see if this was meant insultingly. But Martin's face made it clear that this was a simple statement of fact. "That sometimes makes it hard for him to live the way he wants to live. He wants to be Byron, you know? He wants to turn his back on society, but that only really works if society's looking. I can see how this would be agonizing for him."

"Did you try to talk him out of it?" Renata asked. She surprised herself with her boldness. They had reached 101st Street and the park entrance, so they paused on the corner; Leo still gazed in triumph at the world from above Martin's head.

"No, I tried to talk him into it, actually," Martin said.

Renata's eyes widened.

"But maybe it wasn't so wise," he went on. "I mean, the world in its relation to its artists has changed fundamentally in the last fifty or sixty years, I think. It's not the world of Hugo anymore, you know? No one wants to be led. Art has been democratized, experience has been democratized. There's no reason why this book has to be an embarrassment. All I was thinking was, it's got to be easier to drag Paul into the world than it would be for Paul to drag the world back to himself. But now," he said, smiling, "I'm not so sure that's the case."

He looked at Renata. "Just for the sake of truth in advertising," he said, "you do know Paul lent me some of the money."

Renata nodded. "Of course I know," she said. "He told me beforehand. I don't have any problem with it."

Martin lifted Leo off his shoulders and set him gently beside his brother. The boy's fingers had left a red imprint in the center of Martin's forehead, to which he was oblivious. Renata started to point it out to him, but restrained herself, without really knowing why.

"What about you, Martin?" she said. "Are you writing?"

It was as if she had asked him if he was eating right; he took it as a well-meaning but unnecessary question. "Sure," he said. "Well, have a ball." He looked at the boys, then back at Renata. "I love that playground. It's nice running into you. Say hi to Paul. Tell him to call me." He turned and walked back the way they had come.

Sitting on a bench in the playground while Peter and Leo took their turns on the slides, Renata checked her watch; if the boys could entertain themselves here for a little more than an hour, she thought, then it would probably be late enough to return home without interrupting Paul. Only three weeks into the summer, the long days were already starting to seem like a joke she had played on herself. Over the course of their dozen years together, she had maintained her faith in Paul's vocation in part because that faith had become, in the most practical sense, a vocation of its own; now that their needs had been magically relieved, what would take its place? This daily, unfunny, Odyssean attenuation of her return to her own home?

She looked around her at the other mothers. Some spoke animatedly to one another; some, like Renata, preferred solitude. One was reading a book. Some, perhaps only because they were overprotective, didn't like the sidelines and ventured right into the children's play, squatting uselessly in the sandbox, pushing the swings. Some of them, no doubt, had homes and pasts and feelings that made them much more like Renata than she knew; still, she felt no special kinship with any of them. Bizarrely, what she felt at that moment, distracted in the sunshine, was more like a sense of fellowship with Martin and with Paul—their attitude of shipwreck, of not figuring, despite

their protests, in any tally. It was a fellowship, though, that
didn't serve to bring them any closer together.

Of course, there were important differences. She had
never had a career she really felt devoted to for its own
sake. Now she had no career at all. What was a career,
though, exactly? She looked again at the other mothers,
sitting beside the playground in the middle of a sunny afternoon, and wondered if it wasn't a naive indulgence to
think that there had to be a reason why you were brought
into this world.

Good behavior consisted in large measure of having a
talent for not being noticed. The guards didn't care from
the outset who you were, and resented having to learn,
since the only way they did learn was if you repeatedly
complained or demanded fair treatment or otherwise got
out of line. There were things you could do to make their
jobs easier; but that wasn't wise either, since such traitor-
ous currying only brought you to the notice of the admin-
istrators of the inmates' own justice—and you didn't want
any more to be noticed by them. Any benefits accrued by
such toadying were far outweighed by the anonymous mis-
eries that hovered in wait for you, watching for the guard
to turn his face away.

Victor was proving a master at this tightrope walk of
self-effacement; but his increasing notoriety off Rikers Island made the truest sort of invisibility, enjoyed by many,
if not most, of his fellow prisoners, an impossibility for
him. He behaved at all times as modestly as he could, but
that only seemed to make some people angrier. The
guards, though they liked him all right, were increasingly
reluctant to show it, acting as if they were worried that if
they smiled in his presence someone was going to materi-
alize out of nowhere and snap their picture.

This had its corollary at the jail's highest levels—where
people could, indeed, have their pictures fugitively taken.

So Boggs's Herculean public relations efforts had a flip side: whereas Victor might normally have been considered for a transfer to a medium-security facility because of his stellar behavior, the lengthening delays in fixing his trial date, and general overcrowding, the deputy warden made it clear that, given the case's high profile, there was no way he was going to put his own career on the line and risk getting noticed by some bureaucratic higher-up.

Miffed, Boggs continued to push for other special privileges. He lobbied unsuccessfully to have Victor moved to a private cell, claiming that, as a celebrity, his life was in constant danger. He tried to have Victor's visitation rights expanded, as they would have been in a medium-security jail; the deputy warden said that if and when the other inmates got wind of it, then Boggs's client really would be in jeopardy. All this legal jockeying was not being done for publicity's sake (on the contrary: if any of these privileges were granted, Boggs would take steps to make sure there were no leaks to the media), but because he liked and cared for his client, and because any game—even a private, low-stakes face-off with some prison functionary wearing a light blue suit in a fake-wood-paneled office—was only worth playing to win.

He felt he had his best case when he came in and demanded that Victor be allowed a radio in his cell. Boggs had landed an interview on WABC in four days' time. Hearing it, he argued, was essential to his client's ability to assist in his own defense.

"How the hell do you figure that?" said the deputy warden, whose name was Vanderschaff.

"These programs are the voice of the people," Boggs said. "They take call-in questions from all over the city. They make it their business to have their fingers on the pulse of the sentiments of the average New York citizen. The questions I'm asked will be a critical insight into the potential pool for jury selection. Only by hearing it can Mr. Hartley and I know what questions to ask prospective jurors for his trial, in order to ferret out any prejudices they may have."

Vanderschaff absently stuck his little finger in his ear. "You want me to throw a radio—one radio—into a cell block? People get stabbed over stuff like that, you know."

"Issue it to him overnight," Boggs said reasonably. "Collect it from him first thing Friday morning."

"The show's on at night?" he said. "Even worse. We can't protect him."

"You can and you will protect him," Boggs said. "But, if you like, I can have an associate of mine tape-record the broadcast, so you can give it to him during union hours."

"Oh, a tape recorder," Vanderschaff said sarcastically. "That's a dandy idea. Why not just give him a few hundred dollars walking-around money? I'm sure none of his fellow inmates will trouble him for it."

Boggs, though he longed to crush this pathetic bureaucrat like a roach, decided the time was not right for going into his thundering, declamatory, William Jennings Bryan mode. All you had to do was hit him where he lived. Guys like this were about as hard to read as a billboard.

"Fine," Boggs said pleasantly. "Then the other option is to provide Mr. Hartley with a full transcript of the hourlong interview. My office will be happy to type it up, at the usual fee of two hundred and forty-five dollars an hour. I'll just send the bill to the Department of Corrections and say you approved it."

He closed his briefcase.

"Hang on," Vanderschaff said.

And so it was that Victor was provided, in secret in the warden's own office, with a tiny transistor radio. He walked back to the cell with the instrument held against his body by the elastic waistband of his prison pants. For the rest of the evening he sweated so profusely, he was worried when the time came that he would have shorted it out somehow; but a surreptitious check, in the cell after lockdown, showed that it still worked.

He had decided that the prudent course of action was to let his two cellmates, C-Dog and Michael, in on the secret right away; it seemed extremely unlikely, even with the volume low and the radio pressed between his ear and the bed, that they wouldn't hear something, and if they did, there would be no avoiding recrimination of some sort. When he showed it to them, they were ecstatic; Victor needed it between midnight and one, so they worked it out that C-Dog would listen between one and three-thirty, and Michael from three-thirty to six. Victor forbade any of them to turn it on before midnight, lest any sound of it reach a neighboring cell, sparking a protest which would cost them the radio and him his chance to hear his case debated by strangers in an ethereal public forum.

At a quarter to midnight, Victor disobeyed his own dictum, thinking a little music (how long it seemed since he'd heard good music!) might calm him down. But the little transistor could pick up only AM stations through the thick cement walls, and those stations apparently had forsaken music, having given themselves over entirely to their listeners' preference for hearing their own voices. At last, midnight came.

Lying in the half-darkness, in the eerie, frequently punctured silence of night on the cell block, Victor lay with the little radio flat against his ear and listened to the whispered story of his life.

"Now come on, Mr. Boggs. I mean let's get serious here. Let's put things in the plainest possible terms. Victor Hartley willingly took part in a riot, a riot that caused, city-wide, more than three million dollars' worth of damage. At one point in this riot, he and three friends of his decided to drag a random white guy out of his car, beat the crap out of him, and then hold him hostage for two days. Made a bunch of cockamamie demands. But instead, the cops find him, kick his door down, and drag his ass to jail, where he may stay until he's a middle-aged man. Now you tell me where in that whole sequence of events an injustice has been done to your client."

"The injustice"—Boggs's age-mellowed tone, as fault-less as his interviewer's was shrill, was perfect for radio, and it showed off his experience in the medium—"the injustice, here as elsewhere, is not so much in the events as in your recounting of them. What's wonderful about the media—and you understand I'm not singling you out here, Bob, I know that you're only representing a point of view—is their feeling of absolute dominion over the question of context, absolute control over it. Let's take that version of events that you gave us. At one moment you feel free to expand Victor's deeds, to enlarge upon what he actually saw and did, so as to, in effect, blame him personally for three million dollars in damage. Patently ridiculous. And in the very next sentence you feel equally free to deny his actions of any context—to deny him his life, his feelings, his experience as a young black man in a society that hates him—and reduce it all to two anonymous men in a room, one of whom beats up the other one."

"So you'd have us believe that Hartley beat Paul Solo-way nearly to death because he'd had a rough time of it by virtue of being born black?"

"No. I'm saying that that unique brand of experience, which is real, Bob, no matter how you make fun of it, as I'm sure a lot of your listeners can confirm, that it has to be taken into account. Which the media and the police and the DA would love it if we didn't."

"Okay, well, here's your chance. Here's your forum. Talk us through the day in question, the day of the Fisk verdict and the rioting."

"I don't want to talk about that. Instead of focusing on that day, as if Victor were some sort of monster created by all the anger rising out of that disgusting injustice, let's talk about the man himself. Let's remember that he lived for twenty-four years before that one day. Victor, at the time of his arrest, was working two jobs to support his two young daughters, Tanya and Renee. He had recently moved back home to look after his mother, who suffers from several serious ailments including asthma, and his sisters—three women living alone in East Harlem. Fifteenth in his class in high school; he even managed to pick up a couple of credits at CCNY, until the demands on his time as the sole support of his family made it impossible for him to continue his education. He is a regular churchgoer; in fact, his mother told me that around the time he was confirmed the pastor tried to talk him into studying for the priesthood, that's how highly they thought of him. About a year ago, Victor lost his job as a mailroom supervisor when the company that hired him went bankrupt. He was eligible for unemployment, of course, which would have paid him just about exactly what the mailroom job had paid, but he refused—he went out and found another job the next week. He was saving some money to enroll in a computer-training course, money that is long gone now, since without him his family is struggling just to pay the rent. And Victor made this kind of man of himself, I should add, against amazing odds; his own father abandoned the family when Victor was two years old."

"Very impressive. So where did he go wrong?"

"Where did he go wrong?" Boggs said, his voice rising. "Where did he go wrong? I'll tell you—he went wrong in thinking that hard work and a strong spirit were any insulation against racism and its effects. He was naive enough to think, for instance, that if a man shoots a young boy in the back and kills him it doesn't matter which one was black and which one was white. He went wrong in buying the myth that if he led a good and honorable life society, white society, would have to accept him as an equal. And when he found out how wrong he'd been, how little his life and the lives of his people were really valued, did he get mad? Was he susceptible to the well-documented phenomenon of mob psychology? Did he go out and shout and yell and maybe bust a windshield? You bet he did! Who the hell wouldn't?"

"Okay, well, let's go to the phones here before they melt. Ricky from Astoria, go ahead."

"Hi, I just wanted to say I think this Hartley guy should fry. I mean, the Fisk thing was wack, sure, but that's no excuse for kidnaping some random guy who had nothing to do with it."

"Thanks, Ricky. Mr. Boggs?"

"Well, first of all, Ricky, I take issue with the word 'kidnaping.' Victor's friends saw Soloway standing on the sidewalk, yelling at an old woman they knew, in a threatening manner. They went over to confront him. At this point, the police arrived. Ricky from Astoria, I'm guessing that you're a white man."

"Me? Yeah."

"Then you can't really know how fundamentally different is a black person's relationship with and attitude toward the police. Maybe you could say they panicked—although it's our position that, given what they could expect at the hands of the NYPD under those circumstances, they acted completely rationally—but in any case the idea that they kidnaped anyone is nonsense. It's just the DA following the old prosecutor's rule: if you have a weak case, slap as many charges on the indictment as possible. That way the odds are good that the jury will find him guilty of something or other."

"Silvio from Brooklyn."

"Uh, yeah, Bob, love the show. I have a comment and a question. First, I just want to say that Gandhi said if a law is unjust, then you are morally obligated to disobey it."

"Uh-huh. Okay."

"And second, why haven't we heard yet from Hartley himself? You always see these jailhouse interviews with killers on '60 Minutes' and stuff, so I know it's possible. Mr. Boggs, how come you don't let your client speak to the public directly?"

"Good question."

"The time will come for that, Silvio," Boggs said. "The time for that is when it counts, which means in a court of law. Meantime, I am in close touch with Victor every day, I talk to his family, and when I speak, I speak only on his behalf. It's true, too, I admit, that I take on the role as Victor's mouthpiece because I'm naturally a lot more experienced than he is with the media, with the tricks they pull, with the traps they lay for you to try to get you to trip yourself up. When Victor speaks, it will be on our terms."

"Which means money, doesn't it?" the host said. "Isn't it true that you're trying to whip up demand here, so you can get a bidding war going for *The Victor Hartley Story*?"

"Look," Boggs said. "First of all, I don't have to get any bidding war going—it starts up all by itself, whether I think the time is right for it or not. You know that. I get calls from Hollywood a couple of times a day, and they're a pain in the neck, quite frankly, because I'm concentrating right now on getting my client acquitted. But I will tell you one thing. If we ever do offer any movie rights or anything of that sort, it will be for one reason and one reason only: to raise the absurdly high hundred and fifty thousand dollars bail necessary to get Victor Hartley off Rikers Island and back to the family that depends on him. Which is a hell of a lot more than I can say for this Paul Soloway, by the way, who's capitalizing on this whole thing to the tune of almost half a million dollars for a book deal. He goes back to his normal life, the only difference being that he's rich now, while my client rots in jail."

"Well, I agree with you there. Everybody's in it to make a buck these days. A guy's dog bites you, you take him to court for emotional damages and then sell the movie rights and you're a millionaire. It's disgraceful. Alice, from Sheepshead Bay."

Victor listened raptly to the universe of thin voices feeding into his ear. The extraordinary thing about it, he thought, was that out of all these people, with all their disagreements and their variety of perspectives, no one was saying anything about him that wasn't true. He was a criminal, he was a role model, he was violent, he was kind, he was a responsible son and father, he was buffeted by societal forces he couldn't influence but only react to. It all contributed to a sense that, in the end, you had to decide for yourself who you were, you had to decide on the true narrative of your own life, and that the choices here were far more diverse than you might have previously suspected.

The sound of late-night talk radio was unfamiliar to Victor. It was slower, with more silences—more natural somehow; even though voices were raised in anger sometimes, that anger was recognizably sincere. It was after one in the morning by now, but the calls, to his amazement, continued to come in. Joey from Brownsville, Doris from Staten Island, Mohammed from the Bronx, William from Cobble Hill. All of them held by the same thin filament that held Victor to the radio. They all called up, and even though it was his fate they were discussing, even though some of them hated him, Victor felt a sense of connection to all of them that he never could have imagined before.

That summer was the first that Peter, now five years old, began to give his parents the sense that his imaginative landscape encompassed more than just school, the apartment, and the playground. He was reading more now, for one thing, and his conversation was sprinkled with arcane references to various kinds of bugs, or construction equipment, or even to fictional characters from the books he picked out himself now on trips to Eeyore's downtown. He was old enough to want to read these books on his own, even to insist on it, but still not bereft of the impression that there was no such thing as a book which his parents had not read; his look of disbelief, when Paul or Renata would ask him to explain who Nate the Great was, was both comic and profoundly sad.

What presented more of a practical problem, though, were Peter's occasional, shocking expressions of dissatisfaction with their home as a wellspring of entertainment. He had picked up on boredom as a concept and as a distinct feeling; more and more frequently he would go up to his mother and pronounce himself bored, a feeling that was momentarily allayed by his awe at the effect this produced on her. For Renata's part, she felt that each of these incidents constituted some sort of pop quiz on her skills as a parent, for which she had been given no time to prepare. She wished she knew some of the other mothers well enough to call up and ask if their kids ever exhibited this kind of advanced dissatisfaction, or whether it was only Renata who was not sufficiently resourceful.

Then again, Peter sometimes became withdrawn now from his parents and his brother, retreating to his bed with a Maurice Sendak or a giant volume of Peanuts cartoons, somberly flipping the pages and declining any invitation to join them in the living room or to have them join him. This may have been perfectly normal. But Renata and Paul looked on it with a mixture of pride in his precocity, nostalgia for his infancy, and fear. Renata's worry was not lessened by the intuition that what Peter was really doing was imitating his father. Paul dismissed this notion as ridiculous and overdetermined.

True, she had never felt so responsible for her children's minute-by-minute entertainment quotient before, and perhaps part of the reason it got to her now was only that she had so little else to worry about. Or maybe it was that any sign of imperfection in their new style of life could so easily look to her like a portent. In any event, on one hot Wednesday in August she trumped the boys' highest hopes by offering to take them to the Bronx Zoo. They implored

Paul to go; and he would have, for their sake, if he had not been so far behind on the book. Either Spain or Olivia would call him every day now. He wrote for a few hours to the Zenlike hum of the new air conditioner. They came home late. Peter and Leo dashed over to his chair to shout their competing, disjointed narratives of the day's many wonders, from the monkey house to the monorail to the cotton candy whose buzz had evidently not yet worn off. Paul listened and nodded and watched over their heads as Renata, sunburned, her hands hanging straight down, plodded directly into the bedroom.

He let her sleep for an hour or two while he changed their clothes and got them some dinner, constantly putting a finger gently to his lips to quiet them. Even in clean clothes, they still smelled of the monkey house, and so he told them at the dinner table that there would be baths before bedtime, even though their regularly scheduled bath had been just yesterday. This met with vocal resistance; and by the time the negotiating was over he had agreed, in exchange for their cooperation, to let them watch the Raffi videotape again. He knew Renata would never have given in so easily. Luckily for him, she came sleepily into the kitchen just moments after the painful concession had been extracted from him. She waited until they were all out of the room and she heard the sound of water filling the tub before pouring herself a large glass of white wine.

They were too old now to bathe together without getting into some sort of kicking fight over space. Peter perched on the toilet in his underwear while Leo sat amid bobbing toys, squirming beneath the washcloth.

"Daddy, you know what?" Peter said.

"Leo, I can see the dirt in here," Paul said, referring to his son's ear. "Just hold still for one second."

"Daddy, you know what?" Peter said.

"What, sweetie?"

"Bats can't see."

"Is that right?" Paul said absently, sneaking up on Leo with a palmful of shampoo. "Can't see? I'll be darned."

"Ow!" Leo shouted.

"Ow? What do you mean, ow? It's shampoo, for God's sake!"

"You know how they know where to fly?" Peter said.

Amid all this, Paul didn't hear the ringing of the phone; or if he did, it just seemed part of the natural evening chaos, as crickets might have if the Soloways lived a hundred miles north of there. Renata stuck her head around the bathroom door.

"Honey?" she said. "Phone's for you. It's Bob Spain."

Paul looked at her, then at his watch where it lay on the edge of the sink. It was after eight o'clock.

"Did you tell him I was here?" he said.

Renata's eyebrows rose in confusion. "Afraid so," she said. "Shouldn't I have?"

"That's all right." He straightened and dried off his hands. "Can you take over here for a minute?"

Paul was not a skilled liar, which was why he had been ducking Spain's phone calls in the first place. Nor was he especially good at picking up on falsity in others; so he was both relieved and baffled by the jollity in Spain's voice.

"Well, well! A rare sighting! We were beginning to worry you'd absconded with the advance, gone off to Tahiti or something."

"No, no, nothing like that. Listen, I'm sorry I haven't returned—"

"Never mind about that. No need to say anything on the subject. Look, I've worked with writers my whole life, right? I understand solitude, the need for solitude. I understand writers about as well as anyone who's not a writer himself can do. Don't worry," he said, laughing, "there's not a lot you can show me that I haven't seen before."

Paul laughed back uncertainly.

"So listen," Spain said, "I just wanted to check in, make

sure everything's going okay, that we're still on track. You're writing away?"

"Oh, yeah. Everything's fine. I'm maybe a little bit behind where I ought to be. But it'll come. It takes as long as it takes; it's no good trying to rush yourself."

Spain—who was sitting at Olivia's desk in the empty office, where he had gone to look through her Rolodex for Soloway's number—bit his lip. "Quite right," he said. "Well, a little lateness goes with the territory. I don't think in thirty-odd years I've ever worked with a writer who said he was ahead of schedule." He laughed. "Of course, we do have something of a special circumstance here."

"I appreciate that," Paul said, "and I—"

"But there are little tricks of the trade, you know, things we can do to jump-start the editorial process. If I can save time on my end, you understand, then that extra time is in effect passed on to you. Do you follow me?"

"No," Paul said.

"Do you remember we spoke about your sending me some pages, as they were completed? Just to look them over, give me a head start on editing, give me some idea the direction you're going in?"

Paul swallowed. "I remember that," he said, "but I really don't think anything I have right now is in good enough shape—"

"Oh, don't worry about what kind of *shape* it's in," Spain said in a tone of mock reproach. "I understand what a rough draft is. I don't expect this to be polished. Don't worry—no one will ever see it but you and me."

"That's not the point," Paul said. "It's just that I'm really not used to showing my work to anybody before it's done. I'm—"

He was interrupted this time by Leo who, naked, soaking wet, a big grin on his face, ran through the kitchen and rounded the corner into the living room.

"Really, it's nothing," Spain said. "I'm not going to be judging it. It will just give me some idea of structure, make sure you aren't going down any cul de sacs. I could wind up saving you a lot of time and effort—"

"I don't think there's any question of my going down any cul de sacs," Paul said. "I mean, I know my own—"

"Of course, of course. I didn't mean to— You're absolutely right. It's just that, you know, this is a big book. I'm under some pressure here, and when some big poobah comes into my office and asks me how the Soloway book is coming, it would be great to be able to give some knowledgeable answer. So at the very least—and I'm not admitting I can't be helpful with the writing itself, that is my job after all—but say for the sake of argument that I can offer you absolutely no worthwhile advice about anything. The bottom line in that case is that you'd be doing me a big favor."

Paul scowled.

"So what do you say? I'll read it, and afterward we'll have an excuse to go out and have an obscenely expensive lunch on the company."

"There's not a lot I could show you right now," Paul said, weakening. "There's only maybe thirty-five pages."

Spain leaned forward over Olivia's desk. He was worried he might pass out. "Well, no, that's not a lot, but that doesn't matter," he said calmly. "Just a taste. Just to give me an idea. I'll send a messenger over first thing in the morning."

"No," Paul said. "Make it afternoon. I'll have to go around the corner and get copies made."

"No problem. I'll make it for around lunchtime then. I can't wait to see it."

When he hung up the phone, Renata was waiting in the doorway for him. Her wet hands were on her hips, and she looked at him disconsolately.

"Did you tell them they could watch Raffi again?" she said.

"Afraid so. It was my only bargaining chip. They didn't

want to take a bath; they said they liked the way they smelled."

From the living room came the overfamiliar sounds of the voice of Raffi, insidious beguiler of millions of small children. Peter had recently learned to load the tapes into the VCR by himself. Renata and Paul both flinched.

"Do you know," Renata said, "that sometimes, if I'm shopping or on the toilet or something, I actually catch myself singing those songs?"

"The evil of banality," Paul said.

"I mean it. My brain is actually beginning to putrefy."

"Well, you're off the hook tonight. I'll go watch it with them. I'm the one that caved in, I deserve to suffer."

"See if you can get them to turn it down a bit at least," she said. "Oh, one more thing. I talked to my father a while ago, and he—"

"I can't possibly go out there," Paul said, shaking his head. "That was just my editor on the phone."

"Yes, I know who it was," she said, a little crossly. "You didn't let me finish. I know how busy you are, and the weather's beautiful, and the boys are running out of things to do, so if it's all right with you I thought instead of all of us going out for a weekend the kids and I could spend the whole week before Labor Day out there, and you could stay here and work."

"That's a great idea," he said.

A little disarmed—she had half expected him to object— Renata smiled, said, "Okay, then," and went back to the bedroom to read, away from Raffi. It was a great idea—it would work out for the benefit of all of them, and especially the kids—and so she wondered if it wasn't just a vestige of superstition to worry that a threshold had just been blithely crossed.

Paul sat dutifully in his chair in the living room and watched Raffi, the beard, the receding hairline, the Hawaiian shirt, the enervating, alien voice. The boys sat on the floor in front of the set. On the mantel was a small but growing collection of videos for children, not just Raffi but *Thomas the Tank Engine* and *Barney and Friends* and *Beauty and the Beast.* All that money they now had, which he had presumed would perform a kind of insulating function for the family, had in some respects had just the opposite effect; with the VCR and the new color set the world of pop culture had gained a firmer foothold in their home, and at times it seemed to Paul that there was literally no controlling his own borders, no hindering the access of these mercenary strangers to the hearts and minds of his children—no strategy other than poverty, ironically, which they had left behind.

> The more we get together, together, together,
> The more we get together,
> The happier we'll be;
> 'Cause your friends are my friends,
> And my friends are your friends . . .

The boys, he noticed, often sang these songs at other times, in other places, but they never sang along with Raffi when the tape was playing, except sometimes when Raffi himself instructed them to. Their fascination with the tape was undimmed by repetition. Of course, this was true, and always had been, of any tape, or any song, or any book or story they particularly liked. When, Paul wondered, did one lose this ability to hear the same stories over and over without any hint of restlessness or loss of suspense? Or did one lose it—was it simply, in adulthood, channeled in some hidden way that allowed you to feel that what you wanted from stories had undergone a fundamental change?

It developed that the impassive old woman I'd been urging to call the police was the grandmother of one of my abductors; just at that moment, though, the logic of cause and effect was not available to me. Consciousness itself was a kind of endlessly flipping coin; and even at my most lucid I was only able to watch and record what was happening to me, not form any sort of response to it. My feet, for instance, were useless. From the original splinter group of eight or ten, only two men had remained, or been stuck, with me (the others, I suppose, were able to disperse at the first sound of the sirens); now they were attempting to drag me up the stairs of the dingy building they had fled into when the police were heralded. I remember mostly the surprising darkness of the place even at noontime, and of course their panic, their rage which, at that stage, was directed less at me than at each other.

"Move your fucking legs, man!" one of them shouted at me— then, to his partner, "God damn, what's wrong with you? Why'd you have to hit him so hard?"

"I didn't! I don't know what the fuck his problem is!"

I do remember distinctly the sound of doors shutting up and down the halls as we approached. No one wanted anything to do with us.

"Why'd you go off on him like that?"

"What you mean, me? You did it too!"

"Because I thought you were after the car!"

"No, man, I don't do that! Who the fuck told you I was jacking cars? I ain't never—"

This argument took place in the space just before my unfocused eyes. I could already feel a great swelling that seemed to be not on but actually inside my head.

"Well, now we're fucked. Now we're stuck with him, cause of you!"

"Cause of— Hey, fuck you, all right?"

"Shut up. What floor is Victor on, man?"

"Four."

"Four?"

Each of them held me under one of my arms, accusing each other with myself as the barrier between them. I was trying my hardest—not out of fear, I think, nor out of courtesy, but simply out of an urgent desire to relearn what I knew I should know— to coordinate my legs and walk up the stairs without their having to drag me.

But by the time I could manage it, the one on the left of me was pounding on a black, heavy, scarred door with four locks on it.

"Victor!" he was shouting. "Come on! It's us, man! Let us in!"

A shadow passed across the

What the hell was that properly called, Paul wondered, the part of the door that you looked through? There had to be a better word than "peephole," which was all he could think of. He left it blank for now—

and not immediately, but only after, apparently, some deliberation, came the varied sounds of the different locks being unbolted. Then the door opened slowly, reluctantly; I did my best to raise my throbbing head, and I came face to face for the first time with Victor Hartley. It wasn't the best circumstance for a first look at either of us; I can only imagine how I looked, and his face was an unflattering stew of confusion and anger. He was shorter than the other two; he had the sort of pugnacious alertness often associated with shorter men. It seems to me in hindsight that his ire had to do with a feeling of being ambushed by his own amazement; he was a man who liked to be in control. Victor looked me over once, then looked back over my shoulder at the empty hallway; then he grabbed my shirt front and pulled me, not roughly but hastily, into the apartment. The two men supporting me were pulled along. Victor shut the door, and the screaming began again.

"What the fuck is this?" he said, pointing to me. "Felipe?"

Felipe suddenly looked hard pressed to explain any of it. "We were out on the street," he said, "and we saw this guy get out of his car and start yelling at Jimmy's grandmother. So we went over there." A long pause.

"And you bring him here?"

"Please, man, we're sorry, we didn't have nowhere else to go, Jimmy cracked him in the head, and the cops were coming—"

"Why didn't you leave him out there?"

Jimmy and Felipe looked at each other. The answer didn't readily come to them, though it seems clear enough to me. They were simply trying to protect themselves by removing any trace of any crime that might have been committed, and that trace was me. I must have wobbled on my feet at that point; Jimmy and Felipe grabbed me again.

"Does he need to go to the hospital?" Victor said.

Felipe said nothing. Jimmy said, "No, man, he's all right."

Victor looked me over. He took a step toward me. He reached around behind me and pulled my wallet out of my back pocket. He scowled as he flipped through it. When he found my driver's license, he stopped.

"Paul," he said. "Do you need to go to the hospital?"

I cleared my throat. "Yes," I said.

Victor laughed. "He's all right," he said. And then he did something I hadn't expected. He folded my wallet, reached around me, and stuffed it back in my pocket where he'd found it. It was clear to me from then on that I was nothing more substantial than a nuisance to Victor—not an opportunity of any sort. I had nothing that he wanted.

"Let the man sit on the couch, at least," he said, and Felipe and Jimmy led me over and dropped me there.

At that point there was a knock at Paul's front door. He turned and glared at it. Had the sound been the buzzer from the lobby, or the phone, he would have ignored it (two more personal-injury lawyers urging suits against the city had come to the building in just the last week); but a knock meant it was someone from inside the building, most likely either the super or Mrs. Perez. Yet when he opened it there was a young stranger standing there, smiling, but glancing nervously every few seconds to either side of him. He held a yellow plastic shopping bag which Paul recognized as coming from the bodega around the corner on Amsterdam. Thinking, instinctively, that there had to be a camera in the bag, he flinched and almost closed the door; but the stranger made no move for it. He just went on smiling politely, though it was clear something unseen was making him jumpy.

"What is it?" he said evenly.

"Mr. Soloway? My name is Douglas Spelman. I'm here representing QuadraStar Productions in Los Angeles. I hope you'll forgive my dropping by like this unannounced, but I—"

"Dropping by?"

"But I had called a few times and there was no answer." Clearly nothing would induce young Spelman—he looked to Paul to be just one or two years out of college—to depart from the remarks that he had prepared, or that someone had prepared for him. "I know you've been besieged by offers from film and TV studios, and I can understand your reticence. But QuadraStar has a long and unusually distinguished track record as a—"

"Douglas, was it?"

He licked his lips. "Yes?"

Paul looked again at his new windbreaker, his chinos, and his Air Jordans, and he realized that the young man, who had probably never been north of 96th Street in his whole life, imagined himself to be working under cover, to be in native disguise. Perhaps he had stopped at the bodega for the same reason—just to obtain the flimsy yellow plastic bag and thus to look like he lived in the neighborhood. Paul marveled at the fact that the young man had made it all the way to his door without having the shit kicked out of him. "Douglas," he said, "I have an agent who handles this stuff."

In an involuntary display of exasperation, Spelman blew out a mouthful of air and rolled his eyes. "You mean who refuses to handle this stuff," he said. You could see, Paul thought, that he wasn't as sinister as some of them, if you could just get him off the script. "Last time I called him, he threatened to call the FBI. He called me a brainless sack of shit. An *agent!*" Spelman recovered himself. "That's why we felt it was important that we reach you directly—"

"Listen, Doug, you showed real ingenuity in getting

into the building, but I work during the day, and I don't
have time for this."

"Of course, absolutely, it will only take a minute."

"Goodbye." Paul started to close the door.

"No, wait!" Spelman immediately cringed with fear at
having spoken so loudly. All at once Paul realized what it
was the young man was afraid of—the super. Paul waited,
holding the door. Spelman then reached down and fum-
bled through the plastic bag—it wasn't just a prop after all
—pulled out a small black box, and handed it to Paul.

"This is a videocassette of one of our most recent productions, *Uneasy Lies the Head: The Charles and Di Story*.
We wanted you to see that what sets us apart is that we
treat our stories with respect, we don't sensationalize. You
would never have to worry about being taken advantage
of, being portrayed—well, I think the film speaks for itself.
TV Guide called it 'a rare sparkle of class among all the
tabloid titillation.' Maybe you saw it?"

Paul laughed merrily; Spelman jerked his head back in
surprise.

"Forty-seven million people watched it," he said, a trifle
defensively. "It was in the top ten."

"Charles and Di, Doug? Charles and Di? You're a
young man. Isn't there anything else you can think of that
you want to do with your life?"

He was unsure whether Paul was genuinely taking an
interest in him or whether he was merely being teased; but
he knew what his bosses at QuadraStar had told him—
maintain interpersonal contact for as long as possible.
"Well, sure," he said. "Nobody really wants to spend their
lives in television production. Ultimately I plan to go into
movies."

Paul pinched the bridge of his nose as if in pain. "Well,
I'm confident that you'll go far," he said.

At that moment they both heard heavy footsteps on the
landing above them, and they looked up. Paul could see

Douglas swallow. He wondered if the young man had had some previous run-in with the super in his efforts to get to Paul's front door, or whether—and this would account for his exaggerated fear—he knew him only by reputation, only through the war stories of his fellow drummers in the rights trade. Paul wondered what the super would make of the idea that his natural propensity for violence had somehow made him a kind of folk legend in Hollywood.

"Well, I guess I'd better leave you alone now," young Spelman said softly. "Our phone number is on the label of the video. But I'll be calling you again in any case."

"Please don't," Paul said. But Spelman was already down the hall, jabbing at the elevator button.

Paul closed the door. He looked at the Charles and Di videotape in his hand; he went to the mantel above the bricked-up fireplace, inserted it among the boys' tapes, and went back to his desk.

Whenever you worked on one sentence, there were three or four or five subsequent or ancillary sentences that floated just on the perimeter of your consciousness. The drive to remember them, to deal with them one at a time fast enough so that they had no chance to disassemble themselves, was, as much as narrative itself, what gave momentum to a writer's working day, what propelled the work forward. Interruptions like Douglas Spelman cut through that process like scissors through a tape; this was something that non-writers never understood, and it was the reason Paul never answered the phone. He spent a few minutes reading through his morning's work, and resumed.

A key turned in the front door lock. Jimmy and Felipe jumped and spun toward the sound, their empty hands stretched out almost as if for balance. Victor, though, didn't react.

A young woman pushed the door open. She held a baby girl against one hip, and at the sight of the four of us, particularly of me, her mouth fell open in an expression of unparalleled exasperation. Finally her gaze locked onto Victor's.

"Excuse me?" she said. "Excuse me?"

Victor jumped up and took the baby from her. "Shut up," he said, heading toward the back room of the apartment. "I'm handling it."

The woman now regarded Felipe and Jimmy with narrowed eyes and a hard-set jaw which conveyed that she knew every single sorry thing about them.

"Excuse me?" she said again.

"We ain't staying," Felipe said.

"Well, I don't know where you think you going, not with that under your arm." She was pointing at me. "Cops all over the block."

Jimmy and Felipe looked at each other. Felipe was the bigger of the two of them—strong in an unmaintained way, the type of bulk that in fifteen or twenty years would have turned into indolence and the memory of power. Jimmy was strong too, but closer to Victor's size, with three earrings and wide, almost Asian eyes. The apartment we were in, which I now realized belonged to the woman (my faculties were slowly reconnecting, and I noticed the curtains, the small pillows on the couch, the particular magazines), had no window facing onto the street.

"Jimmy, man," Felipe said. "You got to go back downstairs and see what's going on outside. See if they're looking for this guy."

"Oh yeah," Jimmy said sarcastically. "Be right back. Pick up a bag of chips while I'm out there."

"Yo," said the woman, "there's a window on the fifth-floor landing you can still see out of. Go on have a look."

They stood still.

"Both of you, God damn it, sorry-ass niggers think they best friend gonna flip on 'em if they turn around—"

With that summary accompaniment, she hustled them out and closed the door behind them. I waited to see if she would lock it and was somewhat surprised when she did not. Back in what I took to be the bedroom, the baby started to cry. Then the woman began looking at me in a way I had never been looked at before. She was still dressed for work, in a very attractive red suit, and she seemed to tower above me as I sat in the too-soft couch, obsessively touching the tender back of my head, still a little too disoriented and shocked to be appropriately frightened. Her hands, with their painted nails, were on her hips. She stared at me with great ferocity; but it was too impersonal, really, to be mistaken for hatred. Her gaze said she did not want to be troubled with knowing the first thing about me. She did not want to know how I had come to be there; she did not want to know if anything set me apart, in terms of urban stupidity and incautiousness, from my white fellows who would never dream of passing through this neighborhood under any circumstances, least of all on the day of a riot; she was not the least bit interested in any feelings I might be experiencing, not just fear but anger and thoughts of revenge, thoughts which, if I ever got out of there, it would be possible to follow up on. But I had no such thoughts at that moment in any case. I felt myself incinerating like an ant under a magnifying glass as she turned on me the most detached sort of contempt. It was exactly as if I were an ancient stain on that old couch where I sat, a sight which called up circumstances she would just as soon not think about.

I started to apologize to her—after all, she had had nothing to do with bringing me there—but as soon as my mouth was open, before I had even found a suitable word to begin with (which would have been difficult), she turned and looked through the peephole; then, apparently satisfied, she opened the door and showed me the vacant, dark hallway.

"Get out," she said.

She did not know that, though I was starting to concentrate again, I could not have risen from my seat, much less walked down four flights of stairs, without her help. But beyond that, staring into the dim hall, with its broken moldings, its pockmarked tile floor, and the blank door opposite, I was frightened for some reason; I wanted, at least for now, to stay right where I was.

But I could communicate none of this.

"Go on!" she said impatiently.

At that point Victor re-entered, with the baby still crying in his arms. "Can't you feed this child?" he said; then, seeing her standing beside the open door, he said, "Keisha, what the fuck are you doing?"

He strode toward her, and she stiffened her grip on the doorknob.

"I can't have this," she said furiously. "I can't have this. Cops going in and out of every building, and those pathetic fucks think they can just dump some white—"

"Where are they?" he said.

"They split," Keisha said; but we could hear their arguing voices now as they came down the stairs.

Keisha looked pleadingly at Victor. "Your daughter lives in this apartment," she said. "What were you thinking? Why did you let them in?"

"I know," he said, irritated but conciliatory. "I didn't know what to do. But I didn't know what they were running from. Look, baby, they can't send this guy out in the street now. All he's got to do is fall on a cop, and we all go to jail. They just got to sit it out for a few hours. Then they can straighten it out, let him go on home when everybody's cooled down."

All this anger and emotion attributable directly to my presence; and yet it seemed to me that I had never been as invisible, as insubstantial, as I was right then. I was reduced (or perhaps elevated) to the ideal observer. They paid no attention to me at all.

Felipe and Jimmy burst back into the room and shut the door behind them. They were panting and excited; and Felipe, curiously, had a small, nervous smile on his face, which he seemed to be making an effort to control.

"They're everywhere, man," Jimmy said. "There must be twenty cop cars on the block. They've cleared the whole street."

But Felipe's smile had not escaped Victor's attention either. "What's with you?" he said.

Felipe pointed at me. "His car, right? It's already gone. It had the keys still in it, and somebody came along and boosted it even before the cops got the street blocked off." I realized then that he was controlling his smile—his pleasure, his relief—for my sake. "*So we're golden, man. That car's in the Bronx by now. Nobody knows this guy's here.*"

Olivia had been in emotional agony ever since opening her eyes, alone in bed, sometime before dawn. Nothing all day would be as bad as that moment she woke up (at least until she lay in bed that night, trying to go to sleep again); still, that feeling of grief bordering on nausea had abated only slightly, and, like nausea, it had a way of rolling back over her with the least provocation. She had started crying again as she stood in the shower. Only the unthinking, routine aspect of getting to work on the uptown subway had gotten her there at all; and now that she was there, sitting at her desk staring at a large coffee and a dry, un-touched muffin, she felt something new had been added to her list of woes, some other feelings of uncertain but not benign character were acting as a kind of coagent to make her emotional state even harder to bear than it had been all night. She wished she had had the presence of mind to call in sick.

Bad enough was the feeling of vulnerability produced by her little work station, a characteristic she had never no-ticed so clearly before but that seemed now indisputably to have been part of a cruel design. Where she sat, she could see no further than the creepy gray fibers of her cubicle walls—in other words, no more than six feet in any direc-tion; but since the walls themselves were only about five feet high, anyone could surprise her at any moment from any direction with a question or a demand or even just a bit of friendly chatter like neighbors over a fence. It would take a type of strength she did not possess to deal with any such surprises now. In her apartment, small though it was, it was a simple matter to go into her room, close the door, and be assured at least of the comfort of perfect solitude, of not having to worry about putting on a good face for anyone. Certainly she didn't have to worry about any solicitous intrusions from her roommate, Astrid.

Olivia could have sat in front of her tying a noose in a length of rope and black-clad Astrid wouldn't have reacted —unless it was to ask if she could maybe borrow a bit of leftover rope to use in one of the imitation Cornell boxes she was always working on, for purposes Olivia couldn't even guess at.

And then there was the unusual suspense over whether Spain would come in to work that day. It would be so much more feasible to make it to five o'clock if he wasn't around. He had been home sick yesterday; he suffered from terrible allergies, and this (he had informed her) was the worst year for the pollen count on the East Coast since 1973. Illness—or maybe what he perceived as the embarrassing puniness of this particular illness—made him even harder to take than usual; and yesterday had been a tense day even without his presence, since the Soloway pages were coming in. Spain had called her three times to ask if they were there yet, and then twice more to ask if the messenger had left yet to bring a copy of the manuscript to his apartment. Still, no matter how curt or demanding he was, it was a breeze dealing with him on the phone, as opposed to having him listening like a tiger (as she imagined it) behind his office door. Yesterday had been the least stressful workday in ages. She should have known that things were going too well; she should have recognized that the easy day had been given to her not as a gift but as a preparation for the humiliating night. She had even looked forward, like an idiot, to seeing Jason, the guitarist, at The World after work.

Suddenly she heard a monstrous sneeze explode from the direction of the elevators, and she knew that her hopes for some leniency this day were naive. A moment later Spain came into view, and he looked worse than she had anticipated. It wasn't his attire, which was as self-consciously natty as it always was; and it went beyond his horribly inflamed and swollen nose and his teary, red-rimmed eyes. Something else was working on him.

He looked at her impatiently. "Calls?" he said.

"Nothing yet this morning. Yesterday's messages are typed up and on your desk. Are you feeling any better?"

He fairly glared at her. Being sick could not fail to compromise his self-image, and he did not like to be reminded of how he looked, or of his inability to control it. He looked critically at her untouched breakfast on her desk. "Do you think I can trouble you," he said, "to make a phone call?"

She made no answer, but picked up a pen and message pad and waited, stoically.

"Get Paul Soloway," he said, "and set up a lunch for us at Gare St. Lazare. As soon as possible. Today would be fine."

"Today you've got lunch with Mort Janklow."

He scowled. "Tomorrow, then. I don't care. Just as soon as humanly possible."

Still writing, Olivia said, "You want to talk to him if I get him?"

"No," Spain said, and she looked up at him curiously. "Just set it up. If you can't get him, call up that agent of his, what's his name, and put me on with him. Before you do that, will you bring me a big glass of water? I'm supposed to take a bunch of pills."

When she took it to his desk a minute later, he was holding a handkerchief over his tender nose. He was the only man she knew who carried a handkerchief; she considered it disgusting, though forgivable perhaps as a generational thing. He was staring morosely at a small stack of paper in front of him which she recognized, from the heavy, uneven print of a typewriter rather than the word-processed manuscript they were used to seeing, as the Soloway pages. Spain took his eyes off the stack just for a second to stare at her as if he had forgotten who she was, as if this glass of water were not something he had requested of her moments before. Sensing his mood, she shut the door behind her as she left.

She called Paul Soloway, who, of course, didn't pick up the phone; she had known he wouldn't but had also known better than to suggest this to Spain, who did not like others, particularly underlings, to run ahead of his own thoughts in any way. She left him the message regarding lunch, in a self-consciously casual tone, lest any of her boss's urgency seep through. Then she started to do some of the typing she was behind on; but before long her fingers were resting on the keyboard, and she was staring into the foreshortened space.

Jason's band had played a short set at The World, an East Village club the size of a museum, the night before. Though they hadn't spoken that day, the gig had been scheduled for weeks, and she had mentioned several times that she would be there. She went home and made herself a salad for dinner. Then she watched some TV before heading over to the club, since nothing would be happening there much before eleven. The band came on about midnight, on the stage at the end of the huge dance floor; Olivia watched from the other end, near the bar, because she wanted to maintain, for the benefit of imagined observers, a literal as well as a psychic distance from the band's few groupies in the impromptu mosh pit, simultaneously staring and dancing, like teenagers. She wanted to project the confident air of someone who knew these guys well, knew all the music, who was a part of them, in a way.

They played about a twenty-minute set, which was optimum, since at that point they only had about twenty minutes of decent original material. As they left the stage, and the thudding, entrancing techno music the DJs favored took over again, Olivia turned around to get a drink before going to find Jason; but apparently there was some sort of promotion taking place at the club that night, because about two hundred people were in front of her waving free-drink chits. After a few minutes of waiting she went upstairs to the third-floor bar, but the same situation obtained there.

Then she had what she thought was a brainstorm. Jason had played so well, and she knew he would be in an expansive, celebratory mood. She had a little extra money. She thought the occasion called for her buying her lover a little present.

Buying coke for your boyfriend, she thought now. Incredible. What had become of the vigilance that should have kept her from turning into someone so pathetic?

She crossed the balcony to the third-floor bathroom. It was technically a men's room, but such distinctions tended to break down in clubs, and it was well known anyway that you could almost always pick up drugs in small quantities there. She pushed open the door.

The drummer and bass player, to her surprise, were in there. "Hey," she said cheerfully, "great set," though the music which followed her through the open door was so loud she couldn't even hear herself. They didn't respond at all; they looked at her, it struck her in retrospect, with a great but essentially dispassionate curiosity. They were both holding beers. She looked around her for a likely face, for eyes that would inquiringly, surreptitiously lock onto hers. She didn't see that; but what she did see, though it took her a second to realize it, was a familiar pair of boots under a half-closed stall door, pointed at a right angle that indicated that the toilet itself was not in use. What was more, they were not the only shoes in the stall.

As if in a dream, she took a step forward, and gently pushed the stall door open. She was spared nothing; there was no other instant in which she might, theoretically, have opened that door and seen anything more explicit, more horrifying. The jeans Jason always wore onstage had been pushed—with difficulty, Olivia knew from experience —down to the tops of his boots. Had the whole tableau allowed for any ambiguity of interpretation, he might have been more upset, but as it was, the look of slack-jawed fear that flashed over his face when he saw her lasted only a second or two; understanding that this was an occasion that it would be ridiculous to attempt to explain, he only smiled sadly, and gave a kind of apologetic, pitying shrug. Much harder to take was the look Olivia got from the girl, who, even though she was on her knees, was only supremely annoyed at this tactless invasion of what she imagined, somehow, to be a private moment. She showed no awareness that Olivia was in any way different from herself, or from the other women who might happen through the bathroom, who watched the band onstage, who were strangers but fancied themselves something more than that. And she was right.

With the money she had been going to use to get him high, Olivia took a cab all the way home, sobbing noiselessly in the sprung back seat. It was one-thirty in the morning, on a Thursday; there was no one she could call for help or sympathy. Astrid, perfectly useless in such matters anyway, was asleep in her room. Then by some inspiration Olivia remembered the time difference in L.A., and she called her friend Amy Rubinstein. But Amy wasn't home. Olivia, not wanting to alarm her, tried to speak in her normal voice when she left her short message. Then she went in and lay on her bed.

The incident's effect on her was, she had to admit, way out of proportion to any love she felt for this Jason, whom she had been dating for less than three months. But the whole thing was, in terms of embarrassment, so far beyond anything that had ever happened to her or even to anyone she knew—so deep into heretofore unfamiliar regions of humiliation and shame—that she wasn't even sure that, when the time came, she would be able to tell any of her friends about it without holding back a little or resorting to vague euphemisms. And if she did that, if she kept the starkest details to herself, she knew that, no matter how earnest their attempts to comfort her, she was not going to get any relief.

The humming typewriter and chirping telephones had long since woven themselves into the general silence; and when Olivia finally snapped out of it, it was twenty past twelve, and Spain was due at lunch in ten minutes. With an oath, she jumped up and burst into his office, catching him in the act of blowing his nose.

"Bob, it's twelve-twenty," she said. "Mort's in ten minutes."

He glared at her. "Where?"

"Perigord." It was across town.

"God damn it!" He began trying to rush out the door, but he was only slowed down by his futile attempts to do too many simple things simultaneously—rolling his sleeves down, pulling his suit jacket on, opening and slamming drawers, checking his wallet, flipping through the contents of his briefcase, all the while directing a stream of much harsher than usual invective at his assistant without once looking up at her. "I'll be twenty minutes late, thanks to you. Call his office and see if they can warn him. I don't know why I have the only assistant in town who can't tell time. Did you type up the Simmons contract yet?"

"No, not yet."

"No, huh? How about the stuff for Frankfurt?"

"No, but it'll go out before the end of the day."

"Did you get ahold of Soloway?"

"Left a message. He never—"

"How many times did you try him?"

"Twice," she lied.

"Well, did it ever occur to you that maybe the man takes a break for lunch? Did it occur to you that maybe the best time to try him is right now?"

She said nothing.

"Is it necessary that I do your job for you?" he said. "Oh, by the way—did you make any copies of the Soloway pages yet?"

"No," she said, "you were in such a hurry yesterday, I just had the messenger go directly—"

"Good. While normally that would be an idiotic thing to do, in this case you've lucked out. Listen to me." He closed his briefcase and came over to the door where she stood, uncomfortably close. "I don't want you," he said in a lower voice, "to make any copies of it. Not one. Not even for in-house. Understand? And if anyone comes by asking to see it, you just tell them I'm working on it at home."

Olivia nodded; and she sniffled.

Spain looked at her sharply, cocking his head, as if suddenly recognizing her. "Have you got it now too?" he said. He was talking about his hay fever.

She looked at him. "No," she said pointedly. "I've just been crying."

Immediately she regretted having been so daringly sarcastic; but with Spain there was no danger of that. He was not interested in her suffering unless he could compare it somehow with his own. He glanced at his watch again and frowned. He started for the elevators, but he turned around after a step.

"When I get back," he said to her, "I think the two of us need to have a little talk in my office. I'm beginning to wonder how well this is working out." Then he was gone.

Olivia sat down at her desk, trembling even more than she usually did after one of these encounters. She had never seen Spain so mad. But within a few minutes her own mood had turned to anger as well. It was all just variations on a theme. Her life, it appeared, was all about trying to please some man, in whatever capacity, and then being degraded by him. True, Spain was in an unusually bad temper that day—a mood apparently attributable, in some way, to the Soloway book—but didn't occasions for such emotional abuse seem to come up practically every week? Why should she find excuses for his demeaning her? Here it was less than twelve hours after a completely different male, in completely different circumstances, had brought her as low as she had ever been. Was there no sort of experience, she asked herself, from which she could be expected to learn?

Instead of typing or making phone calls, she went into
Spain's office, gathered up the Soloway pages, and sat
down in his leather Eames chair to read. After just a page
or two, she was smiling, and in a few more minutes she
was actually laughing out loud. It wasn't so much the writing that amused her as her certain knowledge of the apo-
plexy such a style would induce in her boss. He had started
going over it closely with a red pen but had evidently
given up after just ten pages, writing large Xs through entire long paragraphs. Olivia got about twenty pages into it
before she heard her own line chirping out at her desk.
She picked it up on Spain's phone.

"Bob Spain's office."

"Sweetie! Are you okay?" It was Amy. "What's the matter?"

"Hi, Ames."

"Your message sounded awful. And it must have been
like 2 A.M. when you called. I'm sorry I didn't call you
back, but I was—I was out last night. So what happened?"

"No big deal. Jason dumped me, is all."

"Oh," Amy said. "Oh. Oh, I'm so sorry, Livvie. I know
you were really in deep with him. God, no wonder you
sounded so upset last night."

"Yeah," sighed Olivia, "well, at least I'm feeling a little
better now. And it's nice of you not to say I told you so.
But listen, forget that for a second. You're at work, right?"

"Yeah, I'm sorry I didn't call you first thing, but it's just
if I waited till I came into the office, it's a free call—"

"No, that's okay, that's good actually. We haven't got a
lot of time here. I want you to hang up, and go wait by the
fax."

"What for?"

"Because you're a great friend and I love you, and I
want to do something for you. Okay? Just do it. I'll call
you when I get home tonight, and we can talk longer."

She gathered up the pages and went to the fax machine
at the opposite end of the thirty-eighth floor. Since it was

lunchtime, there was no crowd around it; only one guy from publicity was there using it, and Olivia hid behind one of the gray partitions until he was gone. Then she punched in the number for Frank Pickert Productions in Hollywood, and, sheet by sheet, looking nervously all around her but at the same time feeling protected somehow, began feeding the Paul Soloway manuscript into the machine.

In a handsome old stroller, wearing a purple jacket and matching knit mittens and hat, the baby sailed through the open door, followed by her tight-lipped mother. Keisha and Victor did not exchange any sort of tender, apprehensive farewell, nor, indeed, did they so much as look at each other as they parted; with so much rancor still in the air, they had no energy, I suppose, for any resolution more tender than Victor's giving Keisha money for cab fare to her mother's. For an hour they had shouted, and though it was understandable in one way because the stakes were so high (owing mostly to the presence of the baby—who had been gradually stunned into silence by the volume of her parents' tirade), still, the unflagging hostility of their argument was exceptional. Victor argued, sensibly enough, that the street was still saturated with police, and thus, even if they weren't actively looking for me, the sight of a white man with a head wound coming out of a run-down tenement supported by two young blacks was going to get them all arrested on the spot anyway. And Victor was not going to roll over on his friends, no matter what, especially not just because one of his women (I could see how bitterly he stung her with that formulation) was screaming that they had to get out. They would just have to sit tight for now until things outside cooled down, which would be maybe six or eight hours and probably less; the fact that the other apartment buildings on the block weren't being searched was a very good sign.

Keisha argued, with similar force of logic but much greater heat, that there was a baby in this apartment where a man was effectively being held hostage—Victor's own daughter, she re-

minded him—and that he was endangering her life ("You know," she said, "that when they come in here, they coming in shooting anything black") simply out of a misguided and useless loyalty to a couple of shiftless, pimping, unwashed deadbeat Negroes who just happened to have gone to the same school as him on the days when they weren't breaking into cars. And what was more, she said, he was making her—it was, after all, her apartment, rented in her name—an accomplice to their crime, which would mean, even if she ultimately beat it, that the little girl would go straight to Social Services, maybe just long enough to screw her head up for life, or maybe forever. ("We ain't committed no crime," Felipe mumbled shyly, sullenly, from the couch. "We ain't done nothing.") It happened like that all the time, she said. She started listing women's names, counting on her fingers.

Eventually Victor prevailed; Keisha would take the baby to her mother's place, claiming that the plumbing had stopped working again (the landlord, I gathered, tended to hold off on repairs of any kind until the court order came), and saying nothing about what was really happening. In return, if the worst-case scenario came to pass, Victor, Jimmy, and Felipe swore to say that Keisha had never been there, never seen them, that Victor had been staying there by himself. They did not include me, even a mention of me, in any part of this negotiation. No one asked for my promise, but, thinking of the baby and essentially wanting to go along, I gave it silently anyway.

No effort was made by the couple to conceal their discussion from Felipe and Jimmy either. Their various shortcomings, their misdeeds from childhood to the present, were loudly recapitulated just five feet away. The two of them sat across from me, looking very glum indeed. Every few minutes one of them would leave—gratefully, I was sure—to check out the window on the fifth-floor landing to see if the situation on the street had changed.

I felt a kinship with them in those first few hours—and not simply the sort of identification with one's captors that popular psychology has rendered so familiar. Though they struggled to maintain faces of defensive, even belligerent unconcern, their own fates, their own futures, were being decided in that room just as surely as mine was—even more so, in fact. Equal imperatives of pride and shame, I suppose, prevented them from stepping in to defend their own characters. Though worried, they were willing to trust Victor to argue their case—a trust that, one could see, was rooted in the years. The only times their glances fell on me were by accident. I can understand their bristling at the idea that we were now in similarly tenuous and dependent positions.

Our situations diverged again, though, once Keisha had left, pushing that stroller before her without a word or a backward glance. I felt a renewed sense of danger, not so much from the presence of the three young men as from a fresh absence, the absence of the shrill but mitigating influence of the maternal, the practical, the cautious. That absence was palpable to me, and it occurred to me that it had created a vacuum where calamity might eventually rush in. Felipe and Jimmy, on the other hand, made no effort to conceal their relief once Keisha was gone. Brotherhood had won out, they felt, over weaker loyalties, and after hearing themselves abused for so long, they dared to rouse themselves to dignity.

"Man," Jimmy said. "What a bitch. Any bitch of mine read me like that all the time, man, I'd—"

Victor pointed a finger at him. "You shut up," he said.

And that was that.

Four hours later, the sun was down, but nothing was different out on the street except for the grinding noises of a small fleet of tow trucks, hauling away the cars that had been damaged or abandoned. By that time the minutes were beginning to bear out the truism that the most salient characteristic of any hostage situation is boredom. Felipe had turned on the television across from the couch where I sat, ostensibly to see news of the city-wide rioting (all the local stations were covering it live, like a sporting event), but after a repetitive and unenlightening thirty minutes or so, he started flipping to other channels, finally settling on a rerun of a sitcom called "Taxi." Felipe actually pulled up a chair and sat behind me, looking dully over the backrest of the couch;

evidently sitting on the couch alongside me was not something he
thought proper, for the sake of the preservation of

Of what? It bore thinking about. Paul stood, wincing—
it was raining outside, and though he could scarcely believe it, his leg hurt more now when it rained, as if some
grotesque cliché had been surgically grafted onto him—
got a can of Coke, and sat on the windowsill for a minute,
thinking. He looked out at the sad darkness of the air in
the minutes just before an afternoon thundershower, the
little explosions on the dusty awnings, the handful of
luckless pedestrians (those without umbrellas moving with
an extra urgency), the garbage already dampening in the
wire-mesh garbage cans, the lone tree standing in the
heavy stillness. The children were upstairs, and Renata was
out—he wasn't sure where, but he hoped tristfully she
would be back soon enough to beat the storm. After a
minute or two, he went back to the typewriter.

some curious solicitousness toward me which had begun, in the
course of the afternoon, to manifest itself; or maybe our circum-
stances had nothing to do with it, maybe he would never have
sat on any couch where I was sitting, as a reminder to me of the
vast distance between us, which he could never afford to forget
about, even if I could.

There was something to attract our attention when the regu-
larly scheduled news came on TV at five. Victor and Jimmy
came and stood behind me, leaning on the couch. It was the first
real summary of events, after hours spent simply chasing after
things with a camera as they happened, and for the first time I
was actually impressed with the scope of the rioting, which was
spread not only over all five boroughs but even, quite sporadi-
cally, to black communities in other cities. They replayed the Fisk
verdict of that morning (it seemed days ago by now), the shocked
reaction inside the courtroom, then outside, then spreading faster
than it could be tracked. Concentrating hard, not talking, my
captors watched the news from beginning to end; and when it
ended, and there had been no reference at all to me or to my at-

large status, they all three looked at one another in silent relief, as if learning that certain things had never taken place at all.

But another quick check from the fifth-floor landing revealed that the police were still patrolling the block, on foot and in cruisers; so it was back to waiting, though the atmosphere was moderately less tense now that we knew that no one was looking too hard for me. I asked for some aspirin, and Victor got it for me; Felipe kept watching TV. Then Jimmy said what all of us were thinking, afraid of censure: "Anything to eat in here?" At first Victor scowled at him as if this were an inappropriate request; but as the hours dragged by, such prosaic concerns began to assert themselves. Already it had occurred to me to wonder what we would all do about sleeping when the time came. I remembered reading somewhere in the forest of cheap advice that sleepiness in a person with a head injury is a danger sign. Still, I asked at one point if I could go back into the vacant bedroom to lie down; and, anxious, I suppose, to start showing some good will, they let me. Small as the apartment was, there was a second television back there, which I did not turn on.

What made the boredom particularly terrible was that it left nothing for any of us to do except think about things we would have greatly preferred not to think about. In my case, this was not my own immediate fate but instead what must have been going on at that very moment in my home and in the minds of my wife and two sons. It seemed—and still seems, I guess—oddly selfish of me not to have been thinking of them all along; but pain serves to narrow one's focus with remarkable, natural efficiency. I hadn't picked up Peter at school, I realized; surely they would have called Renata at work in that case. And when she got home and found I had not returned with the car—and that Leo was still upstairs with the babysitter—what would she have done? Called the police? What would I have done in those same circumstances? Probably, I thought, out of timidity and an instinctive refusal to consider the worst, I would have exhausted every possibility, called every friend, every acquaintance, gone through every scenario, before making the commitment to disaster implicit in reporting her missing. I would even have wondered, it occurred to me, if she had simply run off and left me, as "missing" people in news accounts so often turn out to have done. So perhaps she had not yet called the police at all (recognizing that they had their hands full, today of all days); perhaps she was sitting nervously in our living room, a short distance away, listening to every sound, concentrating primarily on not doing anything to frighten the children.

As for the others, it didn't take a great deal of imagination to know what they were forced to contemplate. It was plain from their faces that, now that the street was calming down and I was regaining my wits and the end to this standoff was in sight, they were wondering about me—about my memory for faces and names, my capacity for revenge. I had heard no last names, but surely I would be able to lead police back to this building; Keisha's freedom to return to her own home, whether she realized it or not, depended in large measure on my own capacity for forgiveness. And people had seen Felipe and Jimmy out on the street. Where would they have to go now, and for how long, in order to wait out the eventuality that I would want them punished?

This, it struck me all at once, was the reason I was still being held; not for mercenary or strategic reasons, and not because they were genuinely concerned about my health, but because of the strange, manufactured, galling yet all-important need to obtain my mercy. How were they even to set about this? Could, or should, the subject be broached directly with me? All these calculations, springing from an uncalculated instant of anger, a moment of violence and misunderstanding and bad timing. I held the key to all their fortunes now, and they knew nothing about me. The only alternative to this state of affairs would have been to murder me—and none of these men was capable of such an act. We all knew it. I held the key, and I could feel them surreptitiously sizing me up, trying to extrapolate, on no evidence, what I would do once they let me go. The balance of power in that apartment shifted, as the night wore on, from my captors onto me; and I cannot say this was a welcome phenomenon.

Victor couldn't find much in the cupboards besides baby food; he finally wound up making eight grape jelly sandwiches, two for each of us, and when he brought mine to me, he surprised me by taking a seat on the far end of the bed.

"Yo, look," he said to me, staring at the brown print bedspread. He found himself in the role of emissary to a total stranger, defending his own friends, at whom he was himself plainly angry; thus he spoke, understandably, with great difficulty. "I, look, I have to apologize for those guys. This whole thing was maybe kind of a misunderstanding, you know? I mean, it's not important now maybe, but they said they saw you yelling at Felipe's grandma—"

"I just wanted her to call the police. I didn't know whose grandma she might be. I was only yelling because it was so loud, and she didn't seem to hear me."

"Yeah, she's maybe a little deaf, I think, but anyway, I'm sorry Felipe had to go off on you like that. Maybe, if you have any doctor bills or something, we—but I don't know how we would set it up—"

"I've got insurance," I said. "Money's not really the issue here. If I do have to go to the hospital, it won't cost me much of anything."

"That's good, man, that's good. Those things are expensive. You feeling better now, though, right?"

I nodded.

There was a long, agonizing pause.

"I can't think," I said finally, "of any reason why anybody ever needs to know about this."

Victor looked me in the eyes, but he didn't smile or nod. There was an implicit understanding between us that my beneficence in this matter must not be made a show of. "Nothing to be gained," he said warily.

"The problem," I said wistfully, "is the car. I have to report it stolen. I don't see any way around that. And I don't know what sort of questions that would lead to."

He continued fingering the bedspread. His agony was obvious; he didn't seem to know how to go about asking me what he needed to ask me. Then suddenly he scowled. "Well, you gonna do whatever you gotta do," he said. Abruptly he stood up and left the room.

By ten o'clock it was agreed that the coast was now clear; they would take me out onto the street, abandon me there, and split up for a while. At least this was what I assumed their plan to be; they discussed it amongst themselves in the living room in tones too low for me to overhear. Victor went upstairs to satisfy himself with one last look outside; Jimmy checked to see that the hallway and stairs were clear; and Felipe stood guard over me. He switched on the bedroom TV just as the ten o'clock news commenced.

"Oh, my motherfucking God," Felipe said quietly.

From Heraclitus to Dostoevsky, men have put forth the theory that each of us has a double who stalks us through this world. What Felipe and I were watching—he with a jelly sandwich in his hand, I still touching obsessively the growing knot on the back of my skull, both of us seated together on a strange woman's bed—felt something like the introduction to each other of our two doubles, our phantoms, in the netherworld of the TV screen. In a strange way it brought us closer together—it sealed more convincingly the notion that our two destinies were now accidentally interdependent—than anything else which one might have thought more genuine or substantial that had happened previously that day. On the TV, leading the newscast, was a grainy image, an amateur videotape, of Felipe, Jimmy, and the unknown, scattered others setting upon me in the now departed rental car, dragging me out into the daylight, and beating me, before the action moved out of camera range.

"Jesus Christ," Felipe kept mumbling, awestruck, "holy Mother of God son of a bitch motherfucker—"

One of the remarkable things about it was how short it was; the whole violent episode had taken just eight or nine seconds. (Like all video cameras, it had that annoying date-and-time superimposition in the lower left corner.) Another was that, in spite of what one takes to be an innate tendency to exaggerate one's own misfortunes after the fact, this actually looked far more menacing—and the blow to my head more severe—than I remembered. The videotape—which, because of the imbalance between its brevity and the significance accorded to it, was played in an endless loop, like the Zapruder film, in an apparent faith that such crushing repetition would yield up some clue, some explanation, some inner narrative—had the flavor of a recovered memory for me. In fact, it does to this day, since the blow to the back of my head seems to have erased a few seconds on either side of it from my recollection. Over and over, the man who now sat beside me in a state of near catatonia dragged me from my car in broad daylight and struck me with some sort of stone or brick; over and over, my knees gave that effeminate little buckle, as if I were fainting, and I disappeared for a moment beneath a sea of anonymous, angry heads and hands.

Imagine the impulse to videotape such a scene! I think from time to time, even now, about the anonymous camera operator, the recording angel; was he taping the rioting on the street with the thought that he would want to view it again in years to come? Was he concerned that television news coverage of violence is not sufficiently ubiquitous?

Felipe had seemingly become unhinged by terror. He was famous now. He looked directly at me. He said, "What am I gonna do?"

Then Victor and Jimmy re-entered through the front door, and that snapped him out of it; he began calling for them frantically. They came into the bedroom, and together the four of us watched the tape a few more times. Now the news anchor was identifying me by name; now she was saying that my car (its license plate was visible in a few frames) had been found abandoned in the East Tremont section of the Bronx. Now she explained that the Manhattan man who had videotaped this shocking kidnapping had brought the tape to the station just minutes before, so that the police were seeing the tape for the first time on the news, along with everyone else. They were describing what had taken place as a kidnapping; and, indeed, *the absence of sound on the amateur videotape, the nonexistence of the sirens that had frightened my attackers away from the street, made it look quite authentically like an abduction.*

Felipe and Jimmy were staring at each other, struck dumb with panic, or perhaps with awe at the forces that had convened that day to entrap them into sin and ruin their lives. Victor, though, was thinking clearly, perhaps because he alone among the four of us was not watching himself on the TV screen. He switched off the set and cuffed both his friends in the chest so hard they took a step backward.

"Grab him," he said evenly.

Somewhat uncertainly, even gingerly, they took me by the arms.

"Where are we going?" Jimmy said nervously, taking the words out of my mouth.

"I know a place," Victor said. His jaw was trembling as he looked through the drawers of Keisha's dresser. "Just get to my car. It's two blocks away. I'll drive it around. We got to hurry." Then, as we watched, he found what he was looking for amid his lover's bras and old T-shirts: a handgun.

"Another white wine," Pickert said to the stewardess, with the ease and inoffensiveness of a man not uncomfortable giving orders. "Amy? You?"

Amy looked bewildered, as if it were an unrelated, more direct question.

"Sure, why not," Pickert said, "bring her another as well. You look like you need it. You look nervous."

She was indeed nervous, though not, as Pickert seemed to think, about flying. Once, three or four months ago, some now-forgotten date had taken her to a trendy restaurant out in Venice. As they were leaving—it was about nine-thirty, and Amy, having ascertained that this was not someone, in spite of his lavishness, she would be seeing again, was already thinking with dread of the inevitable awkwardness when he dropped her off at home—they ran into Frank Pickert and three or four of his Hollywood

cronies, just arriving for dinner. He said hello in a genuinely friendly way. And yet afterward Amy was so shaken
by this mini-encounter that she didn't say a word the
whole trip back; the baffled date had let her go without
even offering to walk her to her door. It was the one and
only time she had ever seen her boss outside the office,
and there was something deeply unsettling about it, silly as
it seemed. Pickert was, or at any rate represented, a con-
catenation of forces with which Amy had trouble dealing—
emotional cruelty, material lust, anger, competitiveness,
male aggression, relentless compromise, the love of the
deal. It was one thing to visit, as it were, Pickert's habitat,
from eight-thirty to five, five days a week, an arrangement
that was fundamentally voluntary and fixed in one location, like a zoo. It was quite another, though, to think that
these were forces, even as represented by Pickert, that
were loose in the world. And now here she was, sitting
next to him, in a setting—an airplane, forty thousand feet
somewhere over the vague Midwest, at night—so weirdly
intimate that it carried the sense of a self-devised trial
which Amy associated with dreams.

The stewardess brought their new drinks with startling
promptness. Pickert took a sip and smiled happily.

"Actually," he said, "you're not supposed to drink on
airplanes." He looked at Amy. "Jet lag. Makes it harder to
overcome. But I can never resist. There's just something
about first-class air travel. One of the last real corrupting
influences."

Oh, God, Amy thought briefly, I hope he's not going to
get drunk. If there was anything more frightening than the
Frank she knew, odds were it was the scarcely imaginable,
hidden, private, regretful Frank. She had no desire for a
glimpse of it. But she calmed herself and reflected that the
prospect of Pickert's putting away six or seven glasses of
wine and starting to get confessional was quite remote. It
was true that he was, in her limited experience, one of the
very few upper-echelon Hollywood people who still drank

at all, but his nonconformism took him only so far. He could tell you exactly how many calories were in each glass of that wine.

And she probably would have agreed with him about the dissipations of flying first class—which she had never in her life done before tonight—had she been able to relax and enjoy it a little more. The seats reminded her of her father's chair in the TV room at home, and the food was several degrees better than usual airplane fare, though there was still no mistaking it for the food served back on the earth. Instead, all she could really be grateful for was that the two of them weren't back in coach, where their thighs would be touching every time one of them took a deep breath.

It was just that sexual element, in fact, that was the chief contributor to her anxiety—not because she felt helpless against it, by any means, but because Frank's abnormality was so hard to fathom that she could not decide just how attentively on her guard she needed to be. She was not unmindful of the general situation, which was menacing even if in a somewhat trite way: a powerful executive, on a major business trip to New York, orders along with him an untested, attractive young assistant—a perk, others in the office might suggest, wholly out of proportion to her duties or her tenure. If at the hotel, say, he was going to make some overbearing pass at her, Amy felt capable of fending that off by any means required. But Frank was much harder to read than that. It wasn't that he was not a sexual being—on the contrary, he exuded a sense of the rapine that would have made him at home on Olympus. But all that sexual energy, she realized, all that predatory urge, was channeled directly into business; he never looked and sounded so lustful as when he was on the verge of closing out a deal. (She could remember her shock when, in her first month on the job, he returned, looking like a lion who had just eaten, from a breakfast meeting with a Paramount production executive and, when she asked him

how it went, told her that he had fucked the guy senseless.)
Amy had serious doubts that actual sex could come close
enough, for Frank, to this kind of animal satisfaction to
make it seriously worth his while.

And there was also the fact that, despite any office back-
biting the two of them might have left in their wake, she
had been instrumental in setting up this meeting, even if
her role had taken shape primarily by accident. She remembered how she had felt herself flush with guilt and
excitement when the first of the thirty-four pages of the
Paul Soloway manuscript slid out of the office fax machine. Olivia, she knew, was risking her own job to do her
this favor. She sat at her desk and read them quickly, fear-
ing that Pickert would catch her and berate her for not
carrying them to him straight out of the fax. It was a puz-
zling fragment—there were some nice sentences (nice,
though, in a somewhat self-conscious way, she thought),
but it was as if Soloway didn't understand what kind of
book he was writing. It was all so slow and internal, a kind
of endless mitosis of his own perceptions and feelings, like
something out of Henry James. At any rate, whatever its
other merits, it seemed destined to be the worst true-crime
book she'd ever seen. And, unquestionably, all wrong for
the movies. She took it in to Pickert, who sat talking on
his headset phone and shooting rubber bands against the
window. When he saw the name on the title page, he
stopped in mid-sentence and said, "Look, call you back."
He took off the headset, looked at Amy, and said, "Get
out."

He had never said anything, actually, to praise her for
this coup, but by now she knew him well enough not to
hold her breath waiting for that. She knew that whether
the book itself was good or bad was of no import to him—
what made him happier than anything was being the only
one in the whole town who *knew* whether it was good or
bad. And when he asked her to come with him to New
York the next day, to be part of a hastily arranged meeting

with Victor Hartley and his lawyer, she understood that she was being obliquely, materially, congratulated.

She finished off her wine. All around her, the passengers were silent; many were asleep. The only sound was the unwavering, breathy note of the engines. It was too dark now to see anything in the tiny window but her own reflection. Airplanes were a kind of magical suspension of everything, of gravity, of time, of responsibility, human interaction, the idea of travel itself. Even Frank seemed softened, somehow, by this unrushable hiatus in his pursuit of movie property.

"So tell me again," she said, "what happens tomorrow."

He smiled, thinking of the agenda, of the unique perversity to it; he expected it would become legend before long among his industry peers. "So we land tonight," he said, "and the car service takes us to the Westbury Hotel, where we relax, take a shower maybe, get a little room service. Then we get a good night's sleep. In the morning, we go downstairs to the Polo, they do a nice breakfast there. Then the car service picks us up and takes us to New York's famous Rikers Island Correctional Facility. There we ask for Sergeant Ongley. And as for what waits for us beyond that, I have as much curiosity as you."

Frank turned to her. He seemed unusually sleepy; perhaps he was simply conserving energy for the morning. "I have no idea what this Hartley is like. But I think you'll get a kick out of his lawyer, Arthur Boggs. He's an original."

"You know him?"

"He and I have tried to do some business before, talked on the phone a lot, but I've never actually met him. Seen pictures, of course, in the paper and on TV. Guy's been a criminal lawyer for like thirty-five years, and for the first twenty of those, he's got a solid practice in New York, successful, good reputation, but nothing special."

The stewardess stopped beside Amy again, this time carrying a basket of headphones wrapped in plastic bags.

Pickert held up two fingers; she gave a bag to each of them. "What's the movie?" he asked.

"*The Man Without a Face,*" the stewardess said. "With Mel Gibson?"

He smiled his thanks, and she moved down the aisle. "So," he resumed, "about fifteen years ago, some crazy woman in the Bronx or somewhere goes nuts and starts threatening everyone in her building with a knife. Just goes off her medication or something, I think. The cops are called. So they tell her to come out with her hands up, but of course she's nuts, she's not going to do that. She starts waddling toward the cops, babbling, waving the knife. Fat, middle-aged woman with a carving knife, right? The cops shot her twenty-eight times. You never heard of this case?"

Amy shook her head. "I would have been about eight," she said.

"So the media has an absolute field day with this, and in another month or so four of the officers are indicted for murder. They hire Boggs to defend them, 'cause he's done some business with the PBA before or something. These are now the four most loathed guys in New York, and I tell you, by the time Boggs got finished with that jury, they would have *adopted* these cops. Four young men under intense pressure, their lives being directly threatened by a lunatic, and anyway no conclusive proof of which bullets came from which gun, et cetera. All four of them found not guilty."

A light flickered in front of them on the tiny projection screen. A short travelogue came on, as a prelude to the movie.

"But that's half the story," Frank said. "The dead woman's relatives aren't satisfied. They decide to try a civil court, and they file a lawsuit against the city. And who comes forward to offer to represent them? Boggs. The four cops aren't named in the suit, so there's no conflict. The family obviously doesn't need to be convinced how talented Boggs is. He goes to court, tells *that* jury about the police brutality endemic to black communities, about the lack of departmental training and supervision. The jury awards the family eleven million dollars." Pickert shook his head in apparent admiration. "One case, two victories. I tell you, love him or hate him, no question it made the guy famous overnight. My boss at the time at Fox tried like hell to buy the story, but he got beaten out. He was mighty pissed off about it, too."

The movie was starting. Amy took her headphones out of the plastic bag. A movie on an airplane: remove within remove, a chance to forget about everything, even about her boss in the seat next to her, for a full ninety minutes.

"You gonna watch?" Pickert said.

Amy nodded. "I never saw it," she said.

"Me neither." He put his headphones on, but he also lifted the small pillow up to the wall between his seat and the window, and he leaned his head against it. "Listen," he said, "do me a favor. If I fall asleep, wake me up for the credits, will you?"

All the vandalized cars had been towed, and the blue police barricades just recently removed, to reopen the path for traffic. Still, there was no mistaking the block for a place in which an ordinary day had just closed. Powdery broken glass drifted over the sidewalks like sawdust on a barroom floor. A pair of shoes lay in the middle of the street, side by side, as if someone had just stepped out of them. And strangest of all, as Jimmy, Felipe, and I cautiously peeked out the doorway on the ground floor, was the nearly complete darkness—something one never encounters in the city; something, one might say, that the city was built to ward off. The streetlights were all out, smashed by rocks or by target shooters; and evidently many of the neighborhood residents who had fled the morning's violence had not yet returned (or perhaps some had been arrested) because, for ten-fifteen on a Friday night, there were very few lights visible in the windows

—almost none, in fact. Were it not for the half-moon and the clear night, it would have been difficult to see anything at all.

We heard an approaching car. The noise of the engine, in the unsettling stillness, grew louder and louder; but we saw nothing. Then all at once a battered red Ford drew up to the door, just ten feet from us. The headlights were off. With a wave and a frantic whisper, Victor beckoned us, and Felipe and Jimmy grabbed my arms and hustled me across the sidewalk. There was some animated disagreement over whether Jimmy should ride in the back, to help Felipe keep an eye on me, or whether it would look too suspicious to leave Victor alone in the front seat, like a parent or a chauffeur. Jimmy settled it by hurdling the seat and planting himself up front. Victor drove through the intersection and then turned his headlights on.

"What do we do now, man?" Felipe said nervously. He felt exposed; he kept glancing out all the windows. "Where are we going?"

"Think," Victor said calmly. "Just think. We'll come up with something. The thing is, we're safe now, we're away from that apartment. So long as we keep driving, we're fine." This surprised me; apparently his remark in the bedroom—that he knew a place to go—had been a savvy, timely lie, just to get us all focused.

The rest of their minimal conversation—and the next two hours in the car—were attended by me from an awkward position: lying on the floor between the front and back seats, with the long hump of the transmission under my stomach and Felipe's feet resting—gently, more out of awkwardness than authority— on my back. I didn't feel I could complain about it, particularly since it was the position I had requested. They had at first planned to put me in the trunk.

Paul was a few minutes early for lunch. Not that he was overeager for it, in any respect. He felt out of place in fancy restaurants; and this Gare St. Lazare (as if it weren't crystal clear from the name alone) was the very latest, he could see at a glance, in insufferability. In the distant, noisy dining room he could see nothing but suits; he was woefully underdressed, even without his customary sneakers, and as much as he wanted to be insensitive to the maître d's look of strained, almost ironic civility, he was not. The absurdly fashionable man, who was Paul's age or even a bit younger, raised his eyebrows interrogatively.

"I have," Paul said, "or I'm here for, a twelve-thirty reservation. It's in the name Spain. Like the country. Robert—"

But the connection was made with the first mention of the name, as if it had produced the man himself; and the maître d' snapped into action. He wrote something in his oversize book, picked up two oversize menus, and gestured to a nearby waiter—all while Paul was still speaking.

"Cedric, Mr. Spain's table," he told the waiter.

Paul followed this new, even younger guide into the crowded dining room. It had the conversational low boil of a train station, accompanied by the high-pitched clicks of silver and china. Cedric led him toward a table for two which offered no privacy whatsoever—he could have reached out from his seat and taken the salt from the tables on either side—and which was, to his consternation, empty.

"Mr. Spain's not here?" he said to Cedric.

With the equilibrium that had helped him to the top of his profession, Cedric ignored the seeming obviousness of the answer. "No, not yet, sir," he said. "He called to say he'd be a few minutes late."

"Well, I could have waited at the bar if I'd—"

"Not at all, sir, that's fine. I'm sure he'll be right along. Can I get you anything to drink?"

Paul shook his head morosely and sat down. He felt like a child, for some reason. He felt at once uncomfortably scrutinized and completely invisible. In the briskness and clamor of the dining room, his own silence seemed absurdly damning. It was a struggle not to listen to the conversations taking place at arm's length on either side of him; his solitude, he felt, made him appear so suspect, he labored not even to look up. He opened the menu and tried to lose himself in apparent study of it. Roasted quail. Rabbit with couscous. Dandelions and chevre. Though not a gourmet himself—when he ate, he liked to take the opportunity to think of other things—he had nothing against those who took an expert's pleasure in food, who made an art of it. But to do so at lunch, for some reason he couldn't quite put his finger on, seemed nothing more than profligate. This was not France or Italy, where a midday meal was a kind of observance, a centerpiece; these were American businessmen, more often than not continuing their business even as they ate, and in that case putting away a plate of venison or artichoke risotto cakes seemed to Paul to be a form of aggression, a kind of steamrolling of cultivation and taste, a display of barbarism of great if subconscious import. At home, when he was working well, Paul sometimes forgot about lunch entirely.

He heard Spain's jovial voice approaching through the din and looked over the top of the menu just in time to see his editor sitting down. He wore a seersucker suit, and his nose was red; give him a straw hat, Paul thought, and he could play a Tennessee Williams character.

"Thank you, Cedric," Spain said, accepting a menu and laying it down without looking at it. "Paul, how are you? It's wonderful to see you. It's been too long. I'm very sorry to be late. My assistant lost track of the time."

"A glass of wine, Mr. Spain?" Cedric asked. Spain certainly had the home-court advantage here, Paul thought.

"Regrettably, no," Spain said. "I'm taking all these damn allergy pills, and if I have any alcohol on top of it I'll pass out right in my soup." He smiled. "But Paul, please feel free. The house Bordeaux here is always fine. Or have you ordered something?"

"Just a Coke, thanks," Paul said.

"You sure?" Spain said distrustfully.

"I have to go home and work after this," Paul said. "Drinks at lunch knock me right out."

"So you do, so you do. Well, that's fine then." He dismissed Cedric with a kind smile. Then he gazed, almost adoringly, it seemed, at his author.

"Well," he said. "What a pleasure. It's great to see you. You're well?"

Aside from his first meeting with Ned Garland—who had been almost as awkward as he was—Paul had never before been to a meal at which business was meant to be conducted, and he wasn't sure how such things progressed. He would just as soon have started right in; he was not particularly looking forward to eating anyway. But his was a reactive role, and he had no choice but to let Spain determine the pace.

"Just fine, thanks," he said.

"You look good, You look healthy."

"Thanks. I'm pretty much recovered." Then Paul was struck by something: Spain had come to the table empty-handed. The manuscript which he thought he had been summoned to discuss was nowhere in sight. In his confusion, he forgot his manners. "So, what did you think about those pages I sent you?" he said.

He thought he saw Spain frown just briefly, as if at an ignorance of etiquette. "I tell you what," he said. "Let's order first. The soft-shell crabs and fig cole slaw are wonderful, by the way."

Paul had a broiled chicken breast and some steamed vegetables; it was conceived as a diet plate, but Paul chose it as the least Dionysian item on the menu. Without meaning to, he ate ravenously, anxious to get to the editorial discussion, anxious to get it all over with, this perverse search for approval from a man he didn't understand about a project he felt contaminated by. But Spain was not to be hurried. He ordered melon soup and a grand bowl of pasta with shellfish, which he continually exclaimed over and tried to foist on Paul. He doubled the time it took him to consume all this by talking continuously to the mute Paul about publishing gossip, movie gossip, and the social foibles of other such people whose lives were as effectively remote from Paul's as if they had lived on a different planet. After almost an hour the plates were cleared. Spain took two more pills and ordered coffee. Finally he looked at Paul in a way which at least acknowledged the latter's anxiety and impatience.

"So," Spain said.

"Was I supposed to bring my copy of the manuscript?" Paul said. "I'm sorry I didn't think of it. Maybe the author is supposed to bring it."

"No," Spain said, smiling amusedly, "don't worry about that. It's a little early for any sort of line editing, and besides, that's not the kind of thing we can do here. I thought we could just talk about it in a more general way for now."

Paul nodded uneasily.

"I love what you've done so far," Spain said. "You're obviously a marvelous writer. There's some really brilliant language in there. Before I go any further, maybe I should ask how much more you've written since the section you showed me?"

"A bit more," Paul said.

"A bit more?"

"I've gotten," Paul said tentatively, "somewhat further along."

Spain cocked his head. After a few seconds he said, "Well, I won't belabor the obvious. You've got a calendar, I'm sure, same as I do. So let's talk about what we do have."

He leaned back in his chair as Cedric put a cup of coffee in front of him.

"I admit I'm slightly concerned," he said, "that you may have, in just one or two respects, taken something of a wrong tack. It feels—I'm not sure if this is the clearest way to put it—it feels as if you're shying away from your subject. It seems you're having difficulty getting through the events themselves—difficulty in reliving them. Do you see what I mean?"

"Not really," Paul said.

"If it were a different sort of book, I might say that you're having trouble getting to the point. But that would be awfully reductive in this case. I mean, any fool could see how writing about the events, living through them again, would be painful for you. I mean," he said, smiling slightly and pointing at Paul's face, "you could say that the whole thing has changed the way you see the world. Literally."

Paul realized Spain was talking about his glasses, which he had put on to read the menu and then forgotten about. He grimaced and took them off.

"Still, I wonder if you might try looking at it in the opposite way, if this kind of re-creation might not have some kind of beneficial, liberating, I don't know, *therapeutic* value for you as well. If it's not presumptuous of me to say so. I mean, that's part of how I've envisioned this book all along, as part of a healing process for you, finally getting to set the record straight, put it all to rest. Don't you think?"

"Well, no. It's just . . . no. I think we look at it a little differently. I'm not reliving anything. And I'm not sure what you mean by my having trouble dealing with the subject matter. To the extent that I am, it's a purely aesthetic trouble—I'm having a hard time making anything interesting out of it. It's far removed from any sort of healing—the farther the better, in fact. I've always hated the idea that writing is therapeutic somehow. Writing isn't therapy, it's art."

"Ah. Well, fair enough. As I said, I can only try to imagine what it's like to be in your position. What I was getting at, then, in a more technical sense, was that, even in the pages you've given me, we don't get beyond the threshold, really, of the story itself, which is to say of your own specific actions and feelings. Instead, we have long sections—

and extremely well written, mind you—dealing with, for one example, your admiration of J. M. Coetzee, a reference I think will be lost on a lot of—"

"Well, here's what I was thinking there. I know it may seem a bit off the point when I've only given you the beginning section. But when I reach the conclusion, I plan to bring *Waiting for the Barbarians* in again, because there's a passage in one of the climactic moments of that novel that's—that's—" Paul stared at the salt shaker, his hands moving excitedly in front of his face, as he remembered it. "The narrator is introduced to his torturers, representatives of the government he has devoted his whole life to serving, and he says, 'They were interested only in demonstrating to me what it meant to live in a body, as a body, a body which can entertain notions of justice only as long as it is whole and well. . . . They came to my cell to show me the meaning of humanity, and in the space of an hour they showed me a great deal.' " He paused. "I mean, you can see how that would connect."

"Ah," Spain said. Meditatively, he had a sip of coffee to stall for time. "Now, I'm not sure I understand. This is something that occurred to you at the time?"

"At what time?"

"At the time you were, when Hartley—"

"Oh. Well, no, naturally I can't say I was thinking much of anything right then." He seemed slightly miffed, as if worried he was being made fun of.

"So this quote is introduced how?"

Paul was perplexed. "How? Well, by the narrator. I mean as distinct from the character. It's just part of an effort to maintain some kind of perspective, to recollect in tranquillity, I guess, to give the whole thing some kind of interesting form."

"Now, that's the second time you've mentioned that," Spain said, "and I'm not sure I know what you mean. Whatever else this is or is not, it's a great story. A suspenseful, gripping story. Maybe it's easier for someone who's not quite so close to events to see that. That's why there's such massive public interest in it, after all. That's why we paid all that money for it," he said, laughing. "I think if you just put your trust in plot, you'll be surprised how the formal questions take care of themselves."

"Plot?" Paul said, disturbed. "But that's just it. There is no plot here. It's false to pretend that there is. Plot is a construct. Plot is a superimposition. It's a device, and if you look at the work of Forster or Dickens or someone like that it can be an exalted device, but it does not occur in nature, and it's not what's happening here. It's the media that makes a fetish out of plot, pretending that they're finding it and not making it, that it's some kind of natural phenomenon. A, I don't see what purpose it serves, and B, it happens not to be what I'm really interested in as a writer anyway. So yes, I am trying to impose other forms on it."

Cedric appeared at Spain's left hand, with a coffeepot.

"No, thank you," Spain said, not looking at him. When he was gone, Spain said, "Well, this is interesting. I'm very glad we're having this discussion before I give you back the edited manuscript, because it's giving me a much better insight into what I think are some of the book's potential problems. Again, I have to go back to this feeling I have that you have insufficient confidence, insufficient trust, in your material. Leaving plot and its definition aside. What the reader wants, the reader who already knows this story in its broad outlines but who picks up the book in a bookstore and buys it anyway, what he or she wants to see, to understand, is you. You personally. The unvarnished you, who one day found himself in extraordinary circumstances. Do you agree with me there?"

"Fine," Paul said. "I have no problem with that idea."

Increasingly present at the table was a shared sense, though the reasons for it differed considerably, of the importance of cordial relations between them, and a shared apprehension of risk now that those relations seemed in danger of disintegrating. Paul, though he might have known from the first that he had not found his particular Maxwell Perkins, hadn't anticipated before now that the atmosphere between editor and author could ever begin to seem so distinctly adversarial; but there was no disengaging from him, and so he tried to listen to the advice he knew Renata would give him were she there.

"And what I'm worried about here is, one side effect of your efforts to make the portrait of yourself more interesting by gussying it up with meditations on the car culture or on race relations is that you—forgive me for saying this —but you don't come off, in your own self-portrait, as a very likable guy."

"But I have no interest in coming off as likable," Paul said. "Or as unlikable, for that matter. Besides, I thought you said you wanted a true account."

"But that's just it," Spain said. "You *are* likable. I mean, I know you a little bit. You're a smart, funny guy, a family man. I want to see a little of that in the writing. No purpose is served by your obscuring it. It only makes you come off as self-centered."

"See, I just don't get that," Paul said intemperately. "When it comes to writing, I could not be less concerned with how I come off as a *character*. Only as a writer. And besides, on the one hand you tell me I'm self-centered, and on the other you say all the reader wants is to see me."

"Yes, but what I meant is more a point-of-view matter," Spain said. "The reader wants to see what you saw, to hear what you heard. When you leave that here-and-now, and begin exploring the various mechanisms of your own consciousness, you're chasing that reader away. As I said, just give us your experience. There's no need to dress it up."

"But that *is* me," Paul said. "Why must anything with any sort of intellectual bent be assumed to be pretentious or false? The—what did you say—the mechanisms of my own consciousness are of great, of *vital* interest to me. Why do you think I must be lying about that? This business with Hartley and his friends, it could have happened to anyone, but it happened to me, and I am not going to dumb myself down in order to maximize sales, to increase the number of people who can identify with me. All along, everyone has been telling me that all they were interested in was my story, giving me an opportunity to tell my story. And now that I'm finally doing that, I find out that I'm not what was wanted, that I'm not sufficiently typical. That anything that might be distinctive about me, about my own way of seeing the world, is not only not interesting— it actually chases readers away. Well, I don't know what to do about that. That's a problem for someone else. I can only be faithful to myself."

He had spoken a bit too loudly, though the dining room was nearly empty by now. Spain looked very worried all of a sudden. Cedric came along and discreetly placed the brown leather folder containing the check by Spain's elbow. Without taking his eyes off his author, he reached into his wallet, tossed his American Express card inside the folder, and shut it again.

"Well," he said quietly. "I believe that the impasse we've arrived at here may be more serious than I thought." He paused for a few moments. "Let me ask you this, Paul," he said. "Clearly you believe that you should be looked to as a man well beyond the pale of the ordinary, as an unusual mind, as a *leader*, at least in an intellectual sense. On what do you base that belief?"

"I'm sorry?" Paul said.

"What evidence do you cite—to a prospective reader, or even just to yourself—to demonstrate your extraordinariness of mind? I take it that it is in no way linked to your extraordinary experience. You offer, for instance, in the book, your opinion on black rage and white guilt in American society as a whole. A black man beat you with a pipe. This makes you an expert on race?"

Paul was taken aback by this quiet offensive. Suddenly he could see, as if through a kind of superimposition, that

Spain, though still civil, was quite annoyed. He was not a man accustomed to having his own counsel thrown over.

"If you had written novels, or *a* novel, which made manifest your genius, that would be one thing. And that's not to say you never will. But you have to concede, I think, that, having lived for almost thirty-five years, by any objective criteria, there is only one thing that marks your life as out of the ordinary. Am I wrong?"

Paul didn't answer.

"And you want to deny that one thing," Spain said. "You want to reverse the equation: everything about you is remarkable *except* your violent kidnaping, which you hold to be contemptibly ordinary." He pursed his lips. "You know, to me, this has always been of interest primarily as a kind of urban legend of innocence lost; but it's becoming clear to me that you haven't really lost yours yet."

Innocence lost? Paul thought. Innocence lost? The lines of philosophical opposition between the two men had hardened into something more daunting, more real. Looking into the face of this man who was about the same age Paul's father would have been now—a face made florid by allergies and by a kind of reluctant instinct of protection against Paul and his mandarin squeamishness—Paul had a sudden nightmare vision, an eviscerating realization that this was the man in legal custody of Paul's novel, his life's work. Spain was the monster, the Cerberus who would have to be appeased if Paul's true connection to his own world and time were ever going to be realized.

"I can't do it," Paul said softly. Spain leaned forward. "I can't write the kind of book you want me to write. I can't write the kind of book most readers might want me to write. Absurd as that sounds. I don't know why, really. Certainly it would be easier for me. But you do see, I hope, that I'm not just trying to give you a hard time. I believe in my future as a serious artist very strongly. As for your question why others should share this belief, well, there's no reason they should, I suppose. But that doesn't change what I think. And that belief is all I have in the world. All I have in the world. If I sacrifice it to you, what then?"

Spain's expression seemed to relax. He began to fiddle with the pink packets in the sugar bowl. "We both know," he said gently, "that I cannot make you do anything. I can urge, I can plead, and I can scold. But if you lay down your pen and say that's it, then I'm helpless. I'm out of resources. I can respect your position, I suppose, though I think it's misguided, I think it's a young man's mistake. In a way, it would be nice if we could just shake hands and part company. But we both know there's something standing in the way of that now."

Paul stared at the embroidery on the edge of the tablecloth. He nodded his head. "The money," he said.

"The money. My own job is on the line here. It's now about four weeks before the due date on your contract. If, within some reasonable time after that, I don't have a completed, usable manuscript, or the very real promise of one, the expensive suits at Copeland Simonds are going to invoke that contract to get the money back from you."

It didn't take much thinking to discern the impossibility of this. Renata had no job now. To repay the advance would mean, in theory, calling up Con Ed and the Columbia student loan office and their landlord and even his own mother and asking them to return the money with which the Soloways had erased their outstanding debts just three or four months ago. They had him. He didn't care about money, really, any more than he ever had, and still they had him. Paul saw Spain in a new light; the editor had known all along that he held the winning card, but he had been reluctant to play it, out of sympathy or pity or merely a more personal distaste for unpleasantness.

" 'The leap that was to settle him,' " Paul said softly, with a small grin.

"What?" Spain said, an odd, surprised tone in his voice.

"Nothing," Paul said lightly. He was feeling the touch

of gallows humor. His life was over. "Well, I'll be going up to Pennyfield for a few weeks next month. I was hoping to work on the novel there, but I guess I'll be finishing up this book instead. It'll be easier to work there. No telephone, no kids . . . I've never been before. Well, in the meantime, I thank you for this lunch, but I suppose I'd better get right back to work, don't you think?"

He tossed his napkin on the table; but when he looked up he was startled to see a very unbusinesslike expression of anger darkening Spain's face. His brow was knitted, and he was staring at Paul very closely.

"What?" Paul said, unnerved.

Calmly, not taking his eyes off him, Spain touched his own napkin to his lips one last time. He shook his head. Avoiding his eyes, Paul saw Cedric across the dining room, waiting patiently to break down their table.

" 'He saw the Jungle of his life,' " Spain said to Paul's astonishment, " 'and saw the lurking Beast; then, while he looked, perceived it, as by a stir of the air, rise, huge and hideous, for the leap that was to settle him.' Look, son," he said. "You and I have our differences. And I can tell that in some way you actually see me as the enemy. And that's fine too. You and I don't have to be pals. But if you think that I'm just some illiterate barbarian, some corporate philistine, and that that's just a piece of bad luck from which all your troubles have grown, then you're missing the point. You're missing the point."

Spain stood up and left without waiting.

By the time they came to the last door, the one the sergeant had to open with a key, Amy's nerves were so shot, she felt that if someone were to rap her on the forehead she would shatter like a figurine. Nothing had prepared her for the simultaneous vastness and claustrophobia of the Bantum Center. None of the doors through which the fat sergeant (who was slow, but only as a bull was slow) led her and Frank looked like doors; they were two feet thick with small panes of chicken-wired bulletproof glass and electronic bolts. At each one, Sergeant Ongley would stop and bellow something that echoed too loudly for Amy to make it out; whereupon someone somewhere would throw a switch or press a button that enabled him to open the door with a grunt like a man rolling a stone away from the mouth of a cave. There were six such doors to pass through, once their credentials were checked, and after three of them Amy no longer had any idea where they were in relation to the outside world. She tried to remember the name of that mythical figure who descended into the underworld, but in her nervousness she couldn't remember the name or even if the girl had made it back out again; all that came to her with any readiness, in terms of something with which to compare this morbid journey, was the credit sequence of the TV show "Get Smart."

Pickert, on the other hand, showed no sign of terror. Indeed, he had been in high spirits at breakfast at the Polo, and once their limo had crossed the bridge to Rikers, a small half-smile had stolen over his face and was playing there still. Walking behind the guard, he looked as if he were following the headwaiter at Mortons. Several explanations for this casual attitude suggested themselves—the subordination of all feelings, including fear, to the tracking of the scent of business that lay inside these walls; the feeling of invulnerability Frank carried with him whenever there was a deal to be struck; even a simple, appreciative foresight into the way these moments would swell his reputation among his bitter rivals back in L.A.—but, under the circumstances, Amy had little of her usual interest in her boss's rich pathology. She could only be grateful right now for his air of invincibility; it was all she could do to avoid taking his arm. As the guard searched unhurriedly for the right key, Frank put his briefcase down and fastidiously shot his cuffs.

Beyond the final door was a small, windowless room, painted sky blue, with another door opposite, which presumably led back to the cells. In the middle of the room was a long table made of pine and darkly weathered. Sitting side by side on the far edge of that table were Victor Hartley and his lawyer. Arthur Boggs, who was sitting calmly with his hands behind his head, his open briefcase on the table beside him, rose to greet Frank as he entered; Hartley, though, stayed seated, leaning forward, not out of any calculated malice but only because his interest in the scene was so great, so consuming, so focused, that he had in effect forgotten his own presence in it. He had looked forward to this meeting for so long that he was having trouble believing it was actually taking place. It was plain to Amy, as Hartley stared at her with an urgent curiosity that made her weak for just an instant, that she was as exotic to him as he was to her, even though, she happened to know, the two of them were just a year apart in age. It was similarly clear that there was no anger or minatory defensiveness in his stiff, unsettling attitude—only an interest so overwhelming, he could not be troubled to make any effort to contain it.

"Mr. Pickert," Boggs said in the burnished tone he used for professional speech. "So nice to be able to match the face to the voice, at last."

"Well, I can't say the same," Pickert said, smiling, "because I would have recognized you anywhere."

"Mm. Well, yes, one does tend to get photographed, even against one's will. Sit down, please. It's extraordinary of you to consent to meet with us here. But, of course, I didn't want any sort of negotiation taking place without my client present."

"Naturally," Frank said.

All this bonhomie, in itself and as a prelude to business, excluded both Amy and Victor, who sat across from each other now, apparently in the roles of amanuenses. Amy couldn't take her eyes off Victor; his intensity in the midst of this foreign banter caused him to shine, it seemed, to burn with light in the featureless room. His eyes roamed over all three of them, taking in everything, scrutinizing every look, every phrase, for something beyond the emptiness they seemed to contain. Amy put her bag down on the floor beside her chair.

It was clear that Pickert was enjoying himself hugely. He had taken instantly to Boggs, who was old enough to be his father. It was always most fun to negotiate with people you loathed, but a close second was the pleasure of bargaining with someone you liked and respected, someone you had no trouble identifying as a worthy adversary. Those two categories, though, accounted for only about ten percent of the people in the business world; the rest of the time, you were across the table from the lifeless, the functionary, the meek and unimaginative, whose greatest weapon was precisely their ability to bore you out of your native vigilance. "So is this the room, then, where the two of you normally meet?"

"Oh, yes," Boggs said. "Lavish, isn't it? In fact, apart from one brief court appearance, Victor and I have never even seen each other outside this room. We've gotten to know this place pretty well, haven't we, Victor?"

"That's right," Victor said hoarsely.

"Which brings me to something else," Boggs said. He pointed over Pickert's and Amy's heads; they turned and saw that the sergeant who had opened the door for them was still there, somewhat bored, it seemed, but watchful. "Would you mind if we dismissed this kind officer here? There must be some more important duty he's—"

"Not at all," Frank said, and Amy couldn't stop herself from glancing at him in shock. "We feel very safe here, don't we, Amy? Oh, my God, I've forgotten to introduce you properly. My associate, Amy Rubinstein."

Swallowing, Amy shook first Boggs's hand, then Hartley's, as she heard the departing guard pull the heavy door shut behind him.

"Better we should be alone anyway," Boggs said more

softly after the sergeant was gone. "Or next time you see that guy's face, it's on 'A Current Affair.' "

"There's slime everywhere," Frank said absently, opening his briefcase. "Well, I understand, Victor—may I call you Victor?—that your time with us here is limited, so maybe we should get right to it."

"Fair enough," Boggs said. "Well, I think from our perspective, discussions about money should come last. Should we even get to that point. What we're looking for here, first and foremost, is a dramatic opportunity to show the world what Victor is really all about, and consequently what the prosecution case against him is really all about. A chance to set the record straight, to offer a true portrait. That is, we want the focus to be on Victor's whole life, and not just on the specific days in question in the allegations against him"

"I understand that," Pickert said, "but of course you know that what I'm trying to do here is assemble a package which I can then turn around and sell to the networks. And they are going to want to build around that, that confrontation between you, Victor, and Mr. Soloway. A straight bio would be an impossible sell, as I'm sure you know."

"Well, of course," Boggs said. "We're going into this with our eyes open. What we're looking for is some insurance that the final form will be—what's the right word?—*expansive* enough to make room for some meaningful background, some context, from Victor's life."

"Specifically?"

"We were thinking of four hours, over two nights."

Pickert looked at Amy, who stared back blankly, unsure if she was merely part of a strategy. "I think we can sell that," he said finally. "No provision, though, that the nights are consecutive. That kind of decision is out of our hands."

"Understood," Boggs said.

"Now, just so there are no serious misunderstandings, why don't we talk a bit about this portrait that you want to emerge. How do you see Victor Hartley's role in this drama?"

Boggs leaned back and looked thoughtfully down at the glasses that hung against his chest.

"A somewhat ironic one," he said. "A man who is caught up in events, then, when the smoke clears, is publicly vilified as the author of those events. A man whose everyday struggle against poverty and racism, just when it shows every sign of succeeding on a personal level, is undone in one stroke by a circumstance so bizarre that no one, not even someone as conscientious as he, could possibly have foreseen it. A classic story, really: one man victimized by the turning wheels of society, and even, if you like, by fate, his fate as a black man. It's easy to see why it should have mass appeal, if it's done well."

Frank folded his hands thoughtfully. "He's an ordinary man, a virtuous man. And then, through a bizarre chain of events—I suppose you could even play it comic if you wanted to—an unwelcome guest is tossed into his home. Asked to choose between loyalty to his friends and personal risk to himself, he chooses loyalty. And he's subsequently accused of being some sort of mastermind. Of course," he said, raising an eyebrow, "the ending presents a problem."

"By no means," Boggs said, "an insurmountable one."

Frank nodded; then turned his head. "And what about you, Victor?" he said; Amy, surprised, cringed a bit at what she took to be a slightly condescending note in his voice. "What is it that you want the American people to learn about you? It's your life, after all, that will be up on that screen. Other than money, of course, which is a part of the reason all of us are here, what is it you want to come out of this project?"

Amy thought Frank had included Victor in this conversation mostly as a technique for unnerving Boggs, but if so, it hadn't worked; the lawyer looked very calmly at his client and waited with full faith for the answer. Clearly he had no misgivings about letting the young man, agitated though he looked, speak for himself.

"How does this whole story play itself out," Frank prompted, "from your point of view?"

"My point of view," Victor said.

"Well, that's what we're here to acquire," Frank said in a tone of gay self-deprecation, "your point of view."

Amy watched Victor thinking and it struck her that he was the only one in the room who really took these matters seriously—understandably, she thought, considering the stakes involved. "It's hard to say," Victor said finally. "I mean, I know what I did, I know what I saw. But as for judging all of it, maybe it's not for me to judge, because I was too caught up in it, you know what I'm saying? I can tell you what happened. But as far as point of view, maybe that's best left to other people. Anyway, it changes, is the strange thing. Every day, the further I get from it, the more different it seems to me than what I thought it was."

"That's right," Boggs said. "I can tell you, when I first met this man, he had no concern for himself whatever—all he was worried about was the family that depended on him, how they would manage now that he had been thrown in jail. He didn't set out to be any kind of a hero, but let me tell you, his family and friends and neighbors, his whole community—Victor has a tremendous constituency now, people who see him as a martyr to white society, to the idea that justice for blacks and whites in this country is grossly unequal."

"Well," Pickert said, "as far as that angle, we can't play it up too much. There's good controversy and there's bad controversy, you understand. What all of us want, I think, is to maximize the audience for Victor's story, and the way to do that is to focus in on the personal."

"That's all we want," Boggs said in a conciliatory manner. "That's all we've ever asked for. The more personal, the better. Now, as our time is running short here, let me put forward two more questions. One is contract language regarding script approval."

"I don't think we'll have a problem there. We'll show you working scripts as we go. But as far as legal recourse, all I can offer is that if for some reason we can't agree, as long as shooting isn't under way yet, the contract will be voided and the money has to be returned."

"The second question," Boggs said, "which is really part of the first, has to do with the book on this same subject which Mr. Soloway has contracted to write. If you're considering buying rights to that, and producing some amalgam of the two stories, we are vehemently opposed to that idea. We're mindful of how attractive Soloway's side of the story might seem, given his background, given the sympathy he's received in the media."

"That's not going to be a problem," Pickert said.

"How do we know it's not going to be a problem? In addition, even if we have your guarantee that you won't obtain those rights, we would like some kind of assurance that your production will air before any competing production which does make use of Soloway's book, and if this is not the case, we would like an additional payment built in."

Pickert hesitated. "Soloway," he said, "is not a factor at this point."

"Really? And what's your basis for this?"

Pickert pursed his lips. Finally, he turned to Amy. "You have those pages with you, don't you?" he said.

Grateful for the opportunity to do something, Amy reached down into her bag and withdrew her copy of the Soloway manuscript. She placed the small pile on the table where they could all see it.

"It goes without saying," Pickert said, "that this matter stays in this room. We are in possession of what we know for a certainty to be the only copy, outside of Copeland Simonds, of the existing portion of the manuscript of Soloway's upcoming book. No other producer has seen it. As you probably know, Soloway and his agent have made it clear that the book, when completed, is to be the sole foundation for movie offers based on Soloway's side of the case."

Deliberately, Boggs leaned forward and picked up the manuscript. He put his glasses on. The heavy editorial marks were visible on it, in black now instead of the original red. After reading a few sentences, he flipped through the next four or five pages; then he looked up at Pickert, who nodded.

"It's useless," Pickert said. "He's trying to turn this material into something it's not. No one will want to touch it. The difference is, we know it now, instead of a few months from now or whenever he finishes the thing, and we're prepared to act on that knowledge today. If you want to wait, then eventually there will be other bidders, but the case might go to trial between now and then, and in the meantime, Mr. Hartley, you'd have to stay here in jail."

Boggs nodded. He took his glasses off again. "I think," he said, "we've reached the point in our discussion where the subject of money might be fruitfully introduced."

While Pickert set about getting the lawyer down to two hundred thousand dollars, Amy couldn't help but notice that Victor Hartley's attention was now divided. He heard everything that was said, she knew, but he looked only at the Soloway manuscript, which he appeared to be trying surreptitiously to read upside down. There was nothing threatening in his character, Amy saw now, unless you counted her impression that he seemed to feel things more deeply than the rest of them; what unsettled her was how apparently bizarre they were—*she* was—in his eyes, an agent of deliverance, a frivolous pirate of other people's histories, with, in his own life, all the power and the carelessness of a god.

Pickert had pulled a preliminary agreement out of his briefcase which Boggs was quickly scanning.

"You may be amused to hear, though," Pickert said, "as far as rights go, that I did have an interesting phone conversation with the gentleman who took the videotape. He asked me for fifty thousand dollars. My counteroffer was for him to get lost."

After a minute or two Boggs looked up, untroubled. "Any questions, Victor?" he said.

"Who'll play me?"

They all looked at Pickert. "Oh, it's a bit early in the game for those decisions," he said, speaking as if to a foreigner. "But you always start at the top of your list, and I was thinking maybe Will Smith. You know Will Smith, right?"

"Sure," Victor said. He seemed astonished.

A distant but approaching series of shouts and electronic clicks began to sound; Pickert cocked his head. "Well, that's our cue, I bet, Amy," he said. "Mr. Boggs, we'll be in touch very soon. Mr. Hartley, I'm very gratified that you and I could help each other out."

"And the check?" Boggs said.

"Of course I can't cut it until I get back to L.A., and anyway I need to overnight you the complete contract. But I should think by end of business Thursday."

Boggs smiled and laid his hand on his client's shoulder. "You'll be home for the weekend, my friend," he said. For the first time, Victor smiled broadly.

The guards entered the room, one through each door. Amy stood and gathered up the various papers to put back in her bag; as she reached for the copy of the Soloway manuscript, Victor's hand started to shoot out, obviously an involuntary movement, since he stopped it right away, but sudden enough to frighten her, and then to leave her embarrassed by her own reaction.

"Would it be all right," he said politely to her, disconcerted by her fear, "if I could see that?"

Amy looked at her boss, who waited by the door.

"We have a copy at the office, right?" he said. She nodded.

"No harm in it now," Pickert said. "Sure, why not. Take it. You'll probably get a kick out of it."

It must have been past midnight when Victor finally stopped driving and told us to get out of the car. From the landscape it was obvious that we were still in the city; but beyond that, I had no idea at all where we were.

The street was silent. Victor, Jimmy, and Felipe surrounded me like bodyguards the moment my feet hit the pavement, and they hustled me into the shadows of a ravaged old building whose windows, from the second floor up, were covered with old, warped, weather-stained plywood. The first-floor plywood had been punched out. The front door was missing. Never, except perhaps in wartime photographs, had I seen a human structure with such an overwhelming air of abandonment; in spite of which, as we approached the entrance, human voices could be heard. Evidently it was some sort of squat. The building, which was seven or eight stories tall, gave off not one ray of light.

The voices in the hallway were emanating from the level of our feet. Though it was too dark for me to see anyone, my captors were more concerned that none of those eyes so accustomed to the dark should see me. They surrounded me tightly, and one of them put his damp hand on the back of my head and forced it down. Perhaps they were worried that my pale skin would give off a sort of moonlight glow. Perhaps they were right to worry about that. Whoever lay in the darkness of the squat could be relied on not to know the particulars of our flight, but they would surely take note of the presence here of a disoriented white man, which could only mean trouble of the sort that might be best avoided, or else profited from. I'm sure that Victor would have preferred to take us to a place where no human gaze could find us, if such a thing were still possible.

Low voices could be heard as well behind some of the apartment doors; we walked all the way up to the fourth floor, to

*make ourselves as isolated as we could, before picking an aban-
doned apartment to enter. The door stood wide open, though it
had a working lock on it. There were two rooms, both furnished
only with mattresses and trash; in the back was a narrow,
rusted, mildewed bathroom, but the water, like the power, had
been turned off here long ago. On an old orange crate in the
front room was a disconnected phone. Very little moonlight made
its way around the wooden windows. Felipe did not want to lose
sight of me, and so we sat on one mattress in the darkness,
wondering what would happen next. Victor went back outside to
find someplace to stash his car. I never really doubted that he
would return. Mercifully, there was no wind to come through
the gaps in the warped plywood; but it was still quite cold.*

*Nothing much happened until dawn; and even then, all that
took place, really, was that our faces and the changes the night
had wrought in them became gradually visible to one another.
The three of them were now quite transformed; past fear, really,
for there was no longer much hope, in their minds, of a reasonable, peaceful break in this chain of hazardous events. A little
room left to maneuver, perhaps—maybe they wouldn't have to
kill or die—but mostly they appeared to be waiting. And even
though the ostensible source of this whole disaster was me, the
more their bunker mentality took hold, the less they seemed conscious of any need to attend to my presence at all, to woo or
intimidate me or even to guard against my bolting.*

*The hours back in Keisha's apartment had been characterized
by extreme nervousness, confrontation, and mistrust; and now
something else had been thrown into that mix that ratcheted the
tension to another, unfamiliar level. To my mind it was the gun
that did it, and I will dare to say that that was part of the
dilemma for them as well. It was an unseen, fifth identity in the
filthy room, which changed our alliances, changed the permuta-
tions that the next event, whatever that turned out to be, might
bring.*

*Their fear was such that the notion of obtaining my forgive-
ness was totally forgotten. By them, that is; I was not prepared*

yet to discard it as a strategy for getting out of the whole senseless situation. What had brought us to this incredible and life-threatening pass had been a series of accidents, and not particularly ill-intentioned ones at that. I remembered this as well as they. Why not, then, simply give ourselves up, come out of hiding? Why did they keep me? Of course, they had no way of knowing if I saw the day's events in such a generous light—and even if they had asked me, my answer could not have been trusted under such duress. Nevertheless: why not just let me go, take a chance on my good will, and try to go back to their lives? But they had grasped, I suppose, that it was all no longer just between the four of us—that even if they stayed out of jail today, they no longer had recognizeable lives to go back to; they were fugitives from the law. And the law, of course, was to them nothing like the fantasy of even-tempered ratiocination I was capable of indulging in. They had no delusions about finding mercy now. In fact, they seemed to accept me, by this time, as a sort of metaphor made flesh—and my troublesome, awkward existence as the natural and even in some way inevitable burden of their lives.

No one could sleep. Jimmy rather listlessly mentioned that he was starving. But no one volunteered to go out for food. They felt they could not show themselves; they felt they bore a visible mark now, a fame laid upon them by the anonymous owner of the video camera; and, like so much in this sordid tale, it was both ridiculous and gallingly true.

Renata's father's house had a broad porch in the back, from which she could drink a glass of wine while watching the kids play near the borders of the vast, sloping lawn. The view of the Alleghenies above their heads was so inspiring that she had to remind herself to be vigilant about watching the boys; every once in a while Peter would forget all her stern dicta and slip off the edge of the mown rectangle into the tall wheatgrass and toward the woods beyond. Whenever this happened, a shout from her was enough to bring him sheepishly back into sight. Now she was sitting in the Adirondack chair, reflecting that it wouldn't be too many more years—three or four—before she would lose that power over his curiosity. Her father sat a few feet away, an ashtray full of spent cigarettes beside him, shaking from his fingers the condensation from a tall gin and tonic, a drink Renata had been taught how to make for him when she was ten years old.

"They love it here so much," she said to him.

The house, set against a small hill, was surrounded by trails, with a brook forming one side of the property and even an old stone wall deep in the woods in back. But Leo was still too young for Renata to feel safe about their walking into the woods unless she was accompanying them. It was just as well, for they had come nowhere near exhausting their interest in the lawn itself. It was too large, and the grade too steep, for Mr. Hayes to mow it himself anymore, so that afternoon a local teenager had come by to do it; the boys watched from the porch with impatience and awe as the high-schooler rode jauntily back and forth on a riding mower, a vehicle the machinery-crazed boys had never encountered before. Nearly an hour ago, when the awful engine had finally gone silent, she gave permission and they sprinted out there. This was not the house Renata had grown up in—her father had bought it about twelve years ago, after taking a bonus for early retirement —but that only heightened the sense of dreamy comfort she enjoyed here; the place had no associations which were not pleasant ones.

"Sure they love it," Mr. Hayes said. "Manhattan is no place to bring up a child." He said this in a needling tone, as a kind of acknowledgment that he had said it many times before.

"Oh, now, come on. They're very happy. There are things for kids to do in New York, you know, that they're deprived of out here."

"Just look at them. A simple patch of grass, and they're

in ecstasy. Probably never seen any green grass before where they live."

"We're right near two huge parks, Dad. They see fields this size every day." Yet there was something to what he said, something that jibed with a phenomenon she'd been wondering about all week. The truth was they did play differently, more ecstatically (it wasn't a bad word for it), at their grandfather's, and the size or the greenness of the grass had nothing to do with it. They seemed to be exercising an innate sense of the joys of ownership; they weren't going to have to share this spot with anyone, and some capacity for fantasy in them was freed by that.

"Well, anyway, now that you're a woman of leisure, you and the kids can spend as much time out here as you want."

"I guess that's true," she said. Then, something in the scene pushed her a little further, and she said, "I mean, I haven't really got any plans to go back to work or anything."

"No reason why you should," her father said quickly. "I don't think anyone in his right mind would begrudge you a little leisure, after what you've been through. Besides, you've been working hard for more than ten years. You deserve a break." Speaking into his glass as he raised it to his mouth, he said, "Let him support the family for a little while."

"Hey," she said sharply.

Her father shrugged, unwilling to hurt her feelings but equally disinclined to apologize.

"He's the one who's been through the ordeal," she said, "not me."

"It's a shame he couldn't come out," he said, somewhat unconvincingly.

The sun was going down behind the mountains. It got cold early in the valley. Peter and Leo were suddenly running up the lawn toward them, Leo holding his finger out in front of him and staring at it; Renata stood up, thinking he must have cut himself somehow, but it turned out he had captured a short, fat, brown-and-black caterpillar.

"A woolly bear," Renata said, amazed at how readily the word came back to her even though she had not held a woolly bear in at least twenty years.

They found an old peanut butter jar to put it in (Mr. Hayes punched holes in the top with a screwdriver), though Renata would not let Leo keep the jar on the table in front of him during dinner. Afterward she read to them in the living room, while Mr. Hayes watched "Jeopardy" in the den beneath the stairs. Then she took them upstairs to change into pajamas and make their good-night call to their father. Before long Leo's eyes were closing, and she put them both to bed easily. Four days had already passed in much the same way.

As she came down the carpeted wooden staircase, a portrait was gradually revealed to her of her father, who had turned off the television but still sat in the same recliner; the cast of his face told his daughter that he was looking at something that was not there in the room with him. Whether he was looking forward or backward in time she could not guess. He was only sixty-eight, and his health was fine; but that calm, unfocused, unnerving gaze, more than any physical aspect of him, brought it to Renata's attention that he was getting old now and, what was still more amazing, that she would not have him forever. She paused on the steps, to avoid disturbing him; and when she paused, he noticed her, and smiled, and just like that seemed vital and present again.

"Everyone asleep?" he said.

"No problem. It's so easy to let them wear themselves out when they're here."

"Did I hear you on the phone up there?"

"Yeah," Renata said, "we called Paul, and the kids had to tell him everything that went on today."

Mr. Hayes nodded.

"He's so good with them," she said, as if in answer to

something. "He's very patient. He's never too busy for them."

Mr. Hayes wiped at the ancient stain that his glass had left on the arm of his chair.

"What?" Renata said.

"I didn't say anything. I just—I haven't figured out why he's not here. It seems to me that this would be a much better place to write, out here where it's peaceful, than in some apartment practically in Harlem."

An old defensiveness rose in Renata's heart. "It's not the place, Daddy," she said. "It's the solitude. That's the thing he needs. If he were out here, the kids would be all over him, and he'd want to do things with us, and he wouldn't be able to get any work done."

But Paul and his father-in-law had very different understandings of the character of solitude.

Renata went into the kitchen to pour herself another glass of wine, then came back and sat down expectantly on the ottoman right in front of him, as she used to do as a girl. He looked at her with mild surprise.

"I don't care to question Paul's working habits," he said after a moment, "and I don't want to have the argument again about the great American novel he's writing. I know he's been through a lot. I wouldn't bring any of it up if it weren't for the fact that you don't seem very happy to me right now. I'm just trying to figure out if that's because he's not here or because of the way things go when you *are* together."

Her father's great quality as a parent, Renata thought, was that, although he loved her and would do anything for her, he didn't feel the need to exercise an imaginary power to rescue or protect her the way so many fathers did. If she had a problem, he might want to know what she planned to do about it, but he wouldn't feel compelled to step in.

"I'm not all that happy, I suppose," Renata said. "But I don't blame him for that, and you shouldn't either." She swirled her wine in the glass. Maybe this was why she had come out here, she thought—not just for the kids' sake, but to feel goaded into mounting a defense of all the things in her life she had begun to doubt. "Life was easier, in a way, when we were struggling financially, because I had to work, I had a role, I had to take whatever decent job I could get, because that's what held the whole family together. There wasn't any time to think about—well, actually, there wasn't anything *to* think about, because I was accomplishing something. But now that need is gone. So I have too much time on my hands to think about the ridiculous questions, like, who am I, exactly? What do I want to do? What am I equipped to do? Why was I put on the earth?"

"Not for some job, surely," her father said. "You've never, thank God, been one of those people whose whole identity was wrapped up in their job."

"Well, maybe those people are happier than we give them credit for. Anyway, it's not about a job, it's about a forward motion, a sense of direction, an end. I don't know if I'm losing my sense of myself, or if I'm just learning that I never really had one."

Mr. Hayes scowled. "Do you talk about this with Paul at all?" he said.

Renata winced. "Not really. He's—he's been very unhappy lately himself, is the thing, and yes, I guess it is a little hard to talk to him when he's like that."

Mr. Hayes smiled ruefully. "You know," he said, "if I had a dollar for every time you've told me that Paul's been a little depressed lately, I could buy you kids a house just like this one. Besides, you shouldn't even have to bring it up. He's a writer—I thought he was supposed to notice things."

Renata thought about this. "He notices a certain class of thing," she said. "And anyway, it's true that he's having a particularly hard time writing this book about what happened to him. He feels under a lot of pressure."

"Well, I can understand that. Naturally. He's reliving a horrible, frightening time in *his* life. Of course that's hard."

Renata decided to let that go uncorrected.

"And I'm not saying he's faking anything," he continued, "and I'm not saying you're covering up for him. My impression is certainly that he is depressed most of the time. And now that you're a parent, I hope you'll understand when I say that my only real concern about *his* unhappiness is how it affects you."

"Of course it affects me. He's my husband."

"I'm talking about something else. His work is more important than yours. His problems are more important than yours. His unhappiness has to take precedence over yours. You know, even when you were little you had this tendency. Your mother and I were fighting all the time, and dragging you into it. And you were very unhappy for a while there, and your marks went way down in school. You remember all that? And any time I asked you about it, you insisted it was all your fault, that it was because you weren't trying hard enough, or you just weren't smart enough anymore. Remember?"

Renata nodded. It wasn't the memory of this time in her life that made her so emotional; it was the dramatic novelty of hearing her father discuss it in an unironic manner.

"I tell you," he said, "it very nearly broke my heart. All this is very close to me, because I was in a bad marriage, and for too long, because when you get too deeply into something you lose your perspective on it. I'm not saying that's the situation you're in."

Renata looked away.

"What I'm saying, sweetheart, is here you are again, blaming yourself for your unhappiness, when to the more objective eye, there are other factors involved. Maybe it's got to do with your not working, maybe not. But you can't change your nature, or not very much. If your life is making you unhappy, you can do things to change that life."

She laughed, a little too loudly, perhaps, given her emotional state. She didn't want to start crying in front of her father; she had enough of a sense of regression, sitting here at his feet, as it was. The most shameful thing in her heart—that she was not looking forward to going home—was not something she could bring herself to say out loud.

"And do what, Daddy?" she said. "Move out here and live with you?"

He didn't respond. When she looked up, she saw in his face that she had touched some pride in him, that she had mocked him in a way he couldn't immediately conceal. It wasn't that he had been leading up to that suggestion, or indeed even that he thought it was possible that such a thing could ever happen. But she had stumbled upon something he would never have articulated even to himself; and he was not used to having his inmost desires ridiculed, or even discerned so clearly at all.

In the movie, thought Victor—who had begun, with a certain detachment, to compare both his memories and his life as he was living it to their eventual, improved fictionalizations—the car trip from Rikers to the lower Manhattan court building for his bail hearing would have given him his first glimpse of city, water, and sky since he had been thrown inside seven months before. But in reality this was his fourth pretrial court appearance, and thus his fourth trip in leg irons through the security points, to the transport bay where the prisoners' bus idled, and all the way through Queens and Brooklyn on the BQE (stared at and taunted by the people in their cars) to the special prisoners' entrance at 111 Centre Street. There, after a two-hour wait, a bailiff finally summoned him to one of the conference rooms, where Boggs stood waiting for him, smiling proudly. His glasses hung on their chain against an especially natty gray pinstripe suit; resting beside his briefcase

discretion or tact. And, Victor noticed as the knot of people waiting for the slow elevators gradually thickened, the law enforcement people were not the only ones; others, people with no connection whatever to him, were staring at him openly. He knew he wasn't making this up. They all knew just who he was.

When they approached the glass doors of the lobby and the screaming and the flashbulbs started up, Victor decided instinctively that the best way to keep his cool was to watch Boggs and imitate his air of calm aloofness as nearly as possible, even if he didn't feel the slightest bit aloof himself. He could tell that questions were being asked of him just from the inflection of the voices; but everyone was shouting at once, so that he couldn't make out a word. He heard Boggs ask somebody something about a podium, and when it was pointed out—standing on the plaza, topped with a thick growth of microphones like a lush, neglected potted plant—again the lawyer gently took Victor's arm and steered him up the steps.

The cameras were already set up; the reporters quickly jockeyed for their places. On the benches along the borders of the plaza, old men feeding the pigeons stared quizzically. Boggs held up his hand, and the horde quieted down somewhat. He looked around for a moment, to make sure everyone he had wanted to be there was present. "We have just a brief statement," he said, "because Mr. Hartley has been kept away from his loved ones long enough." His statement, as it developed, was not so brief, but Victor, standing to his right and just an instinctive half step behind him, didn't really hear it. He did hear more clearly the sound of car traffic, and the maddening flutter of the fat pigeons, and the rustle of the thin trees in the sporadic autumn wind. This, finally, unexpectedly, was his first apprehension of real freedom—which had to do not just with being outside of the prison itself but with an uncircumscribed moment in the day, and a view of pedestrian things not compromised or muted by the safety glass of a courthouse window or a Department of Corrections bus. He was finally out of danger. He was not grateful, at that moment, not even to Boggs—just amazed, in thrall to the surprising, revivifying powers of the ordinary. Then Boggs, in mid-sentence, nudged Victor below the level of the podium; and, refocused, he looked ahead of him again and finally noticed the crowd of faces and cameras, all come to see him, all trained right at him. He felt brand new.

"And now," Boggs was saying, "we have time for maybe one or two questions."

The shouting began again, and then seemed magically to hush as one woman in the first row behind the cameras called out, "Victor, how do you feel?"

With a glance at Boggs, Victor stepped forward and leaned down slightly in the way of one inexperienced with microphones. "I feel happy," he said. "I feel relieved. It's good to be going home."

Another man beckoned to him, and Victor was startled to see that it was someone whose face he recognized from television. "Victor," the man said, his tie blown over his shoulder by the wind, "can you say something about how you feel about everyone casting you, for better or for worse, as a kind of symbol of the racial strife in this city?"

Victor looked again at his lawyer, who, just perceptibly, and with a feeling of some cockiness, nodded. He turned back to the reporter.

"Who is everyone?" he said.

The crowd of reporters laughed savvily, save for the man who had asked the question.

"What about the movie deal?" a woman shouted. "How much did you get?"

"I'm afraid that's all we have time for," Boggs said, smiling. "Thank you all for coming." More questions trailed them as they descended the steps of the plaza; the

cops, Victor was delighted to see, kept a path clear for
them. "Ah, there we go," Boggs said, and steered Victor to
a town car that idled illegally by the entrance to the courthouse. The two men climbed into the back seat, and the
uniformed driver swung the car down to Chambers Street
and over to the West Side Highway.

"Well," Boggs said pleasantly. He was jocular, flushed;
he seemed reluctant to concede that the afternoon's mile-
stone was passed. "I think that all went just fine. We can
catch it again on the news in a few hours."

Victor was still taking in the car itself. There were dials
controlling the radio in the back seat, something he'd
never seen before; just behind his head, under the sloping
rear window, was a box of Kleenex.

"This is nice," he said.

Boggs smiled, gratified. "Just a little something I hired
to mark the occasion," he said. "Style counts, you know."

Everything he saw along his way was charged with life,
with the significance of itself. The limo, the quietest car
Victor had ever been in, curved serenely up the highway.
The Hudson River, which at some hours could look as still
as a lagoon, was running strongly south out to sea; a Circle
Line ferry traveled with the current, equidistant from the
highway and from the Jersey side, the lone craft on the
river. Rollerbladers and stubborn sun worshipers haunted
the margins of pavement between the traffic and the crum-
bling piers. They passed the transparent Javits Center and
the hulking ocean liners in their docks. When they got as
far north as 72nd Street, Riverside Park appeared, the surprising boat basin and the playgrounds, and for a while
everything was green, with lightlike flashes of the red and
gold of full autumn, as if they were somewhere else entirely. Victor wondered how long he could expect this feeling of vibrancy, this somewhat burdensome consciousness
of his freedom, to last. It was like the effects of a drug—
not unrelievedly pleasant, but all the same extremely hard

to let go of. Soon enough, he supposed, everything would be back to normal. He had not forgotten where he had woken up that morning.

"I thought you handled those questions just fine," Boggs said softly; his mind was still running over the events of the afternoon. "It may be a little different scene when we get to your mother's house. There won't be any podium there, or any courthouse demeanor. They'll get right up in your face. Just remember, try not to lose your temper, because that's just exactly what they're trying to make you do. Don't answer any question that makes you mad. If you do get mad, just remind yourself that the best way to hurt them, the best way, is not to answer the question at all. That really kills them."

Smoothly the limo found the exit ramp at 125th Street, and as the blocks became more familiar, Victor was surprised to feel himself growing more rather than less nervous. He heard good music beating faintly through the car's soundproofed windows, and he saw the familiar way the neighborhood life was magnetized by the street, in storefronts and on stoops, but none of it made him feel especially comfortable or at home. Something marked him, he felt. It certainly wasn't his having been to prison; he knew plenty of characters for whom Rikers was like a finishing school.

"For instance," Boggs said, "bet you five dollars one of them asks you this: Mr. Hartley, do you have anything to say to Paul Soloway? Do you apologize to him for having kidnaped and savagely beaten him?"

A dark look passed quickly over Victor's face at the mention of the name. A portion of his last days at Rikers had been spent studying that mysterious document by which Soloway planned to profit from their mutual misfortune—a misfortune which had ended for Soloway when his bones healed but which might not be over for Victor for another twenty years. The arrogance of it, the frankly colonial approach this white stranger had taken with

Victor's own mind and motivations, with Victor's own life, had left him shocked and finally inarticulate with anger. He was as yet unsure how such an old-fashioned act of disenfranchisement could best be dealt with.

"See, that's perfect," Boggs said, nodding with satisfaction. "If a question gets under your skin a little bit, just clam up. It never ceases to amaze me how people will ask questions that, if they didn't have a microphone in their hand, would be guaranteed to get them punched in the face. Oh boy, here we go."

Victor looked out the window and saw eight or ten white strangers camped out lazily on the stoop of his mother's building. At the same moment the reporters caught sight of the limo and, knowing it had to be him, jumped to their feet.

"Just go right in," Boggs said as they pulled up to the curb. "If we get separated, I'll call you tomorrow morning. There's some money matters we have to discuss."

They climbed quickly out of the car. It was difficult for Victor not to brush away with his hands the mikes, the pocket cassette recorders, and the cameras that were so heedlessly thrust near his face, but he knew somehow that that wouldn't look right, so he trudged forward. "Happy to be home," he mumbled, just before disappearing behind the door that led to his mother and sisters and the cramped rooms of his childhood, leaving his lawyer, who had stopped halfway up the steps, to answer questions.

Hopelessness, even such as one's life has never known before, is an unsustainable state of mind; time tends to blunt it. I'm not certain whether I slept at all that night, with the three men sitting vigilantly on the mattress beside me in turns. But with the cold sunrise came a renewal of my feeling that all of this was simply too inadvertent to be truly perilous, and thus that we were going to find our way out of it somehow. I was further encouraged when they shut me in the back room so that they might discuss what to do next; but they were still not sufficiently collected to keep this from turning into a shouting match, every word of which I could hear.

"He knows us!" Jimmy said. "He knows the address and he knows us! If we let him go, he goes straight to the cops and that's it!"

"Maybe," Felipe said, "maybe if we tie him up, and then by the time—"

"Aw man," Jimmy said, "we ought to just do him, straight up."

There was a long pause.

"Man," Victor said more softly, "you know you ain't made for that. You know it and I know it. Now the reason we're not thinking straight here is that we're all starving. Jimmy, you go out and find us some food."

"Okay," Jimmy said wanly, "and if I see a phone maybe I—"

"No. Don't call home, don't call nobody. If they figured out who you are from that tape, then they'll be sitting on that phone. Just pick up some stuff and come back."

"Got no money," Jimmy mumbled.

"I got it," Victor said. "And see what he wants"—meaning me.

A moment later, Jimmy came through the door; he was trying to look as tough as possible. Sitting against the wall, I reached into my pocket, took out my wallet, and threw it to him. He caught it, dumbfounded—insulted, actually. I think what he wanted at this point was for our relationship to conform to the circumstances we found ourselves in.

"Just get me some orange juice or something," I said. "And some aspirin for my head."

He went out, leaving the door open between the two rooms. It was already colder than Friday had been. There was now a breeze swirling through the apartment, but my gloves, which I had taken off to drive, were unfortunately still in the rental car. Outside, all was silence—the population of the squat declined precipitously, it seemed, in daylight hours. Before he left, Jimmy held out his hand to Victor; after looking at him for a long moment, Victor reached into his pocket, pulled out the gun, and gave it to him.

Jimmy closed the door softly behind him, and Felipe locked it. Victor looked in at me from where he sat. His black down jacket was zipped up to his chin. "You all right?" he asked me.

I shrugged. "I want to go home," I said, as matter-of-factly as I could.

He looked at me steadily. "You'll come out of this just fine," he said. He was more relaxed, or maybe only more resigned, than his old friends. Weary as he was, there was a glint in his eyes—something like contempt. "I ain't worried about you," he said.

An hour went by, and Jimmy did not return.

Victor and Felipe, by the end of that hour, had been trying for some time not to look at each other. Finally Felipe couldn't stand it; he stood up and went to the boarded window. I saw his Adam's apple rise and fall.

"Five-oh," he said softly, in amazement.

Victor and I got up and stood beside him. Through a gap where sun and rain had warped the wood, we could see more than a dozen police cars in position, having approached without lights or sirens. A crowd had started to gather behind temporary barricades. There were men in riot gear everywhere.

"One of them fucking junkies in the lobby probably gave us up for five dollars," Felipe said.

Whereupon, ten feet or so away, the phone rang.

We all practically jumped into one another's arms. It did not ring in the way we were accustomed to hearing; each individual ring lasted at least five seconds, and was followed by a one- or two-second pause. Showy as it was on the part of the cops, it had its effect on us; it was a type of magic, designed to instill awe, I suppose, about whoever was on the other end of the line.

Felipe and I both looked at Victor. There was such an edge of terror in the air now that I caught myself wishing along with them that the police would just go away. I wondered if Jimmy was dead.

"Don't answer it," Victor said. "No, wait, we— No, wait."

He stepped over the mattress beside the orange crate and picked up the phone. He said nothing; he listened in shocked silence for a few moments, then put his hand over the mouthpiece and said, "They don't know our names." This seemed like good news. I remembered the news broadcast and realized he was not talking about me.

"Listen here," Victor said suddenly in a deep but shaky voice. "We got a gun to his head right now. No, you can't talk to him, motherfucker. You move them cops away from here or I swear to God I'll cap him." Deliberately, I noticed, he kept his back turned to me as he spoke. He started to hang up, but something the voice on the other end was saying made him bring back the receiver to his ear. "What?" He sounded confused. "Hold on a second." He held the phone to his chest and said to Felipe, "He wants to know if we want something to eat."

His mother had always been proud of him—not the kind of pride that flowers from self-satisfaction, as if the child were only the logical end of the parent's methods and expectations, but more like an awe, a faith. She had had a hard life, Victor knew, one that didn't allow her much of the luxury of taking in the vast world outside her own mean circumstances; and, though it seemed in some ways unnatural, it was nevertheless incontestible that she was neither as smart nor as bold as her three children had turned out to be. Much of what they knew about life they had had to learn somewhere outside of home, but they did not hold that against her—on the contrary, it made them more protective of her. In her turn, she trusted them to explain the world to her. Even before she had begun to be really ill, about five or six years earlier, she had greeted every worldly accomplishment of Victor's in particular—graduating from high school, getting a job, standing for the baptism of his two daughters, even just buying her a new stereo and hooking it up himself—with a sort of hushed respect, as much as admitting that he was her better. At the bottom of these feelings, of course, though she never said it, was the fear that one day the spell would be broken and he would be killed somehow, as so many of her friends' sons had been.

But now, after he had been back at home two or three days—days spent seeing a few friends, but mostly eating joyously, sleeping uninterruptedly, and reflecting on his life, old and new—he realized that his mother's feelings toward him had undergone a change. When he sat in the living room, thinking or even just watching TV, she would not come in and sit with him, even though he knew she was nearby, usually just beyond the doorway. Always a soft-spoken woman, she now became positively spectral. If he asked her for a sandwich, she would make it hurriedly, as if afraid of being scolded. It dawned on him that she was now, in some measure, afraid of him. For a few hours he wondered if this was because of the capacity for violence he had shown so briefly those seven long months ago. Could this inadvertently public explosion really have changed her image of her child? But instinctively Victor knew that couldn't be right—others might be willing to change their opinion of him based on that one day out of his life, but certainly no mother would, certainly not *his* mother.

She hovered uncomfortably in her own house, waiting to see if he needed anything, not daring to ask.

Then it struck him what she was really intimidated by. It was his celebrity. She had seen him on TV and in the newspapers; not only friends but strangers stopped her even now, to congratulate her on having mothered him, a man looked up to by his people. She would not accept such congratulations, though she was polite about it. For celebrity was a power beyond her making and certainly outside her control; with the somewhat arrogant random-ness of the divine, it had visited her home. Her son Victor, as he sat in the easy chair thinking about God only knew what, was the living testament to that power. The distinc-tion between celebrity and heroism was too fine for her anyway to be useful. She felt that, in merely doing nothing to displease him in his new station, fate had given her perhaps a greater task than she was equal to.

It was true that there was a general air of unreality in the Hartley home in those few days, even when nothing was happening at all. Meals strove to seem like normal meals, but they were not; visits from neighbors of Mrs. Hartley lost somehow the simultaneous airs of spontaneity and routine which they had acquired over twenty years. In fact, there was only one incorruptibly real presence in the apartment that week, and that was the money. It remained the weight at the still center of shadows, even after Victor had signed the check over to his mother and she had nervously escorted it to the bank. It was more money than they were used to, but Victor knew, and took pleasure in the knowledge, that it would only be used to make the household run a little more smoothly for the next few years, to relieve, for that interval, the customary, constant worries about the rent versus the gas bill, the gas bill versus new shoes. Maybe he could coerce his mother into using the money for some kind of short vacation; probably not. But the fact that the money would not go toward some luxury made it seem that much more substantial to Victor. In some odd, indirect, yet very measurable way, he had provided for his family; and this fact cast a new light back onto exactly what he had done to provide for them.

It's the most natural thing in the world for the ramifications of an event—in this case, the money, the media exposure, the respect from strangers, the prospective enshrinement in a movie—to alter that event's outlines; and this was part of the general reordering taking place within Victor as he sat in the easy chair in his mother's living room. His sister had given him a scrapbook she had put together on his case. Much of the material he had not seen before. There was an editorial in the *Amsterdam News* hailing his courage in resolving to obtain justice for young Khalid Wheeler (Fisk's victim) by any means necessary, even if it meant sacrificing his own personal freedom and bright future. There was even a flyer asking for contributions to the Victor Hartley Defense Fund which his sister had torn off a bus shelter; it referred to Victor as "a brother who dared to speak out against the policy of urban genocide" and was bordered with pictures of Nelson Mandela, Malcolm X, Louis Farrakhan, and Martin Luther King. Victor had never heard of any Victor Hartley Defense Fund and had certainly never received any money from it; the flyer was a scam, but the mere fact that a scam might be built around his name and likeness had a gravity of its own.

Whose keen sense of his own guilt could survive both time and an environment which insisted that one was guilty of nothing? The more Victor pondered the scenario of last Presidents' Day weekend, replaying it over and over in his restless mind, the more authentic and vital it seemed to him, and if he could not, even through the burnishings of memory, quite efface Paul Soloway's presence in it, he could at least sharpen his not untruthful sense of Soloway's role in the drama, which was that of a walk-on, an accident, a stooge, a nobody—in point of fact, a plot device.

Soloway intruded on his memories just as he had intruded in the first place on what was, up until then, a solid, respectable, unremarkable yet promising life. Victor sometimes became so absorbed in his retrospective self-assessment that Soloway disappeared from the picture entirely. But when after a few days he came out the other side, as it were, of his meditations, there was Soloway again, encroaching on the present. It incensed Victor to think that, perhaps at the very moment he was searching his soul, just across town this accidental hostage, his bank account already bulging, was adding to his fake, competing version of those same events, a version which, with typical white arrogance, put himself at the center of everything. Even though he had done nothing. Even though the story, finally, was in no way about him.

His daughters came over to the apartment—one at a time, as always, since their mothers could not be expected to acknowledge each other—and in his tearful happiness at being reunited with them, in their uncomplicated pleasure in having him restored to them, in a resurgence of pride at being able to buy them toys and clothes he hadn't previously been able to afford, he forgot his troubles for a while. But it wasn't long after they were gone that his thoughts returned to Paul Soloway. He wondered if it was possible to talk to him reasonably, to make him see the unfairness of what he was doing in profiting off Victor's life story. Probably not, he thought; Soloway hadn't seemed, in their brief acquaintance, like an especially unreasonable guy, but hundreds of thousands of dollars were in play now, and that kind of money wrought strange changes in people. Still, Victor couldn't shake the feeling that it was important to let Soloway know that there was considerable injustice in what he was doing. It would be best, of course, if some kind of understanding could be reached without voices being raised or tempers growing short.

He went back to page one of his sister's scrapbook and scrutinized the news accounts for any clue as to where in the city Soloway might live. There were none. Then he remembered that this man, just like himself, had in the very recent past been living the life of a perfectly normal citizen. Victor got out the Manhattan phone book, found Soloway's number and address easily enough, and, without anything specific in mind just yet, wrote them down. Then he went to the movies.

Renata and the boys came back from Pennsylvania and the family was reunited, but only briefly; for it was just four weeks later that Paul's sojourn at Pennyfield was set to commence. The children were not happy about this; it meant, among other things, that Paul would miss Halloween. Peter's silence on the subject was even more ominous than Leo's insistent whining; he seemed to intuit enough (more than his parents, really) about their variously maintained separations not to want to come too near to the matter.

Indeed, Paul would have changed the date if he could, for the kids' sake and also for his own—since the whole attraction of the trip had been as a kind of private celebration of his return to his personal aesthetic foundation, the novel, a return which was not as yet possible. The nonfiction book, still unfinished, was now officially late. He would have to spend the time in upstate Canahonta, time he had so looked forward to, finishing up the hackneyed popular tale of his own severe beating, while those in the rooms around him no doubt worked on their first symphony or retranslated *Les Fleurs du mal*. But when one applied for a residence at Pennyfield, the venerable artists' colony that had housed John Cheever, Aaron Copland, Robert Penn Warren, one was admitted, if at all, for very specific dates, and Paul knew decisively without even inquiring that last-minute reschedulings were traditionally not permitted.

Their month together, though, was a pleasant one. Paul, to assuage his guilt about leaving, spent almost all his time with the children, hardly writing a word, pleased to be out of the house and thus honestly unavailable for the frequent phone calls from Spain, Olivia, and now Ned Garland, whose voice, even on the machine, contained an ill-disguised tremble. Cooking was beyond the scope of his domestic talents, but he did occasionally take the three of them out for dinner or offer to go pick up a pizza. He bought the boys a miniature football to bring to Riverside Park, and he took them to Lamston's for school supplies— Power Ranger lunchboxes, scratch paper, colored pens. Renata watched all this attentive parenting with ambivalence—she knew that guilt was at its source, yet she felt it would be the merest perversity to interfere on those grounds. On the rare occasions when they were alone together, they didn't say much; they smiled and spoke in the abrupt yet friendly shorthand of people who have been married for fifty years.

As a rule, they didn't watch a lot of TV, but it did not escape their notice that Victor Hartley had been released on bail. It was reported, though his lawyer would not confirm it, that the money had been raised through a movie deal. "What a world," was all Renata said. Paul was about to deliver a short sermon on the American cult of victimization and the new perception of the hero not as one who acts but as one who is unjustly acted upon, when videotape of Hartley himself, at his press conference outside the downtown courthouse, began to roll. The months in prison, unsurprisingly, seemed to have changed him; he was calm, thinner, his piercing eyes, which had moved so restlessly, lingering now on the objects of his curiosity. Or so it seemed. Paul had to remind himself that he had only seen that face before under the most exigent circumstances.

He tried several times before leaving to call Martin, to say goodbye, though that was really just a pretext for checking to see that his friend was not in any serious need. The poet had been fired from his teaching job. Paul worried when none of his messages was returned, but with Martin you never really knew how to interpret such things. For him, friendship was like travel—pleasant, sometimes exacting, sometimes edifying, but always valuable in direct proportion to its foreignness, to the contrast it presented to his more authentic life in solitude.

Renata offered to drive him to Canahonta, thinking she might make it into an outing for herself and the kids; but Paul insisted on riding the train. Nine straight hours in a car with the boys was an impossible test of one's patience; anyway, he loved the train, and particularly loved the long slow rocking trip alongside the Hudson, which seemed little more than a polluted canal in Manhattan but upstate achieved a substantial, noble force. The foliage unrolled like an action painting, while in the foreground ran the gravel roadbed, just a few feet from the water. Once in a while the train would slow down to pass hardhatted men obscurely patrolling the thin median between the track and the river, there and gone before Paul could ascertain what they were repairing.

It turned out there was at least one other passenger on that train heading to the colony; for when Paul told the taxi dispatcher he was headed for Pennyfield, the old man promptly and wordlessly paired him off with a mousy young woman whose luggage consisted of an overnight bag and a large instrument case. A bassoon, Paul thought, or a horn of some sort. Her name was Adrienne. The two of them put their luggage in the trunk and sat shyly in the back seat of the cab, which was really just an old Chevy with a meter bracketed to the dashboard. The driver, a wiry older man with a white brush cut and copies of that day's *Post* and *Daily News* folded on the dashboard, kept looking, Paul noticed, in the rearview mirror as he drove.

"I'm guessing," Adrienne said loudly, startling him, as they started to pass through the old town, "that you're a writer. Since you have the typewriter case."

Paul smiled.

"Your first time here?" she said.

"First, yes. And you?"

"Christ, no. I'm here every year, just about."

"You're a composer, then?"

He thought he saw her stiffen a bit; he knew about such defensive social reflexes. "That's right," she said, rather noncommittally. "And I suppose you're working on a novel?"

"What else?" he said.

He had not decided in advance to lie about this. But when confronted with artistic seriousness in the person of this drab, pretentious, but unmistakably dedicated musician with whom he was to live for the next three weeks, he had felt a desire to belong, a desire not to cut himself off from the possibility at least of a community of people like himself—the opposite of the desire he customarily felt. His spontaneous untruth, though, had just the opposite effect, at least in his own mind. As they rolled along the road that formed the seam of the manicured estates—great verdant flattened lawns, as if the land bore the footprints of ancient giants of wealth—Paul had ignited in himself a slow-burning feeling of fraudulence that was to turn him into even more of a hermit while at Pennyfield than Pennyfield's founder intended.

As he pulled their luggage out of the trunk, the white-haired cab driver looked critically at Paul.

"Hey, can I ask you something?" he said finally. "Are you that guy Paul Soloway?"

Paul grimaced and nodded dismissively; he had to relax, though, when he saw the comical look of bemusement on the face of poor Adrienne, who could only imagine that she had committed some gaffe in not recognizing this novelist whose fame apparently extended even to cabbies.

It was hard to countenance that, even in the days of the robber barons, the vast, spiky mansion they had driven up to had been built for a single family; even harder to imagine the chutzpah required to build it in what was then, essentially, deep forest, an ostentatious demonstration of money's power over society's locus. The porter greeted Adrienne warmly and Paul with an unforced politeness. He was shown to his room in the west wing, while she, without a parting word to him, went up the stairs toward the east. When he saw his room—a prototypical garret, with a ceiling that sloped down toward the small bed, a wooden desk, a pine dresser, and yellow wicker wastebasket—he wondered for a moment if the good rooms were given to those like Adrienne for whom the place was practically a time-share; but of course the division had more to do with segregating the writers, who coveted silence, from those who were apt to try out various themes on the clarinet all day. Unpacking took less than five minutes; on the desk he laid his portable typewriter and two typing-paper boxes, one containing the novel, the other containing the nonfiction book, which he had taken to calling *St. Famous*, even though he knew it was a title his editor would squelch on the grounds of excessive irony. He sat on the edge of the bed and thought about where he was.

At five o'clock in the downstairs ballroom there was a cocktail party to welcome the new arrivals. It was a shy and sullen affair. The doyenne of the colony, known as Mrs. Chase—who must, Paul thought with a kind of grim admiration, have presided over literally hundreds of these moribund get-togethers—chatted and introduced and moved on with a grace that spoke of past civilizations, of finishing schools and Edith Wharton and not eating dinner with your father until you were thirteen; but the colonists themselves, with the exception of one or two men who seemed to have come to the colony specifically for the opportunity to have a discreet affair under the cloak of art, were not feeling very sociable, it seemed, Paul himself not excepted. There were only four other writers there, none of whom copped to having heard of any of the others. There was a good deal of drinking, but it seemed like private drinking, even as one stood in a faded ballroom with eighteen other people and a white-jacketed bartender. Perhaps it was the ballroom itself that paradoxically dimmed the party spirit in everyone except Mrs. Chase; lurid, unnecessary, obsolete yet overpowering, it was so remote from the artists' real lives that some of them may have felt as though they were being mocked. In addition, many of them, having juggled schedules and angered families just to come here, were already, even before the first sunrise, feeling the overbearing pressure to work, to be productive and to justify their decision to come to this odd mansion in the woods in the first place. Guilt, and competitiveness, and fear of oneself and one's unfamiliar desk.

"Leaving so soon?" Mrs. Chase said. "Well, it's a great pleasure meeting you, Mr. Soloway, and I am so glad you have recovered from your injuries. I hope you will have an enjoyable stay here. We will see you at dinner?"

Paul smiled. As he trudged up the broad stairs (like a Bolshevik, he thought, in the Winter Palace), he looked forward joylessly to the work that awaited him in the morning. He had never mentioned his injuries, of course; he imagined Mrs. Chase watching "Hard Copy" in her private parlor with a pitcher of gin and tonics while the kitchen staff prepared dinner. This place was famous, a living temple to the idea, at least, of high artistic endeavor, yet so far he only felt as if he and these others had been sent off here to a kind of internal exile. He already missed his children. He wondered what this revealed about him.

The new teacher was treating him differently, Peter felt in his heart, though "different from what?" was not a question he could have answered. But then, since he did not tell his troubles to anyone anymore, he was not burdened with questions such as that, which, in his childish subjectivity, it would never occur to him to formulate. Still, he felt, with a child's accuracy of feeling, that there was something inauthentic in the way Ms. Stein-White—Peggy—spoke to him, squatting down on her thin legs to meet his eye, putting her hand on his near shoulder and smiling at him. It had been that way ever since his new school began, almost two months ago. He watched her, when he could, with the other children (some of whom were friendly to him and some of whom were profoundly indifferent); and while her smile, her gaze, her posture, did indeed look the same, nevertheless he felt that something different, something invisible, attached itself to their interactions, and he did not see how he could be mistaken about this. The question was, was he depressed because she was treating him so piteously or was she treating him solicitously because he was depressed?

"Depressed" was a new word he had gotten from his mother. Lying in his room one afternoon, bored but uninspired to play, surrounded by books but lacking even the energy to read, he became so self-conscious that he rolled off the bed and walked into the living room where Renata was reading a thick book of her own. She put the marker in it when she heard him coming.

"What is it, honey?" she said.

He tried to describe to her the way he had been feeling, sad but without reason, and how the very unfamiliarity of it had made him uneasy.

She smiled a mysterious grownup half-smile. "You're depressed," she said. "That's the name for that feeling. Everybody gets that sometimes. It's nothing to worry about, as long as it doesn't last too long."

"You feel this way too?"

"Well, not right now, but sometimes, sure. So does Daddy. So does pretty much everyone in the world. Leo doesn't, I suppose, because he's still too young."

"Why does it happen?"

"I don't know, it might be that you miss your dad and don't know it, or it might be something bad that happened at school. Or it might be that nothing caused it, it just sort of came over you. That happens too. But the big question when we get depressed is not what caused it, but what can we do to snap ourselves out of it. I know. We could go out to Häagen-Dazs. Want to do that?"

"No, thank you," he said. The strange truth was that he was not really sure he wanted to be snapped out of it.

She looked at him for a long time then. "All right," she said. "I'll come in to check on you in a while. Give me a kiss."

He did so gladly. As he leaned back from her, his fingers brushed the fat volume in her lap. "What book are you reading?" he said.

She raised her eyebrows, as if only now noticing the size of it. "It's the story of the life of a woman named George Sand," she said. "A woman named George. Isn't that silly?"

Now it was a week later, and an hour after school, and in brooding over the demeanor of his teacher Peter felt that he had—unwittingly, though it was not altogether unwelcome—called down on himself again this state named depression. It had the capacity, it seemed, to shore up one's sense of oneself, one's uniqueness, even when—as now—he was in the middle of a playground crowded with a hundred other kids. His problems at school were a burden to him; yet they did have this power to keep him somehow at the center of the world. His mother sat on a bench fifty yards away, talking with another mother; his father was away for a few weeks, to work, at some place called Pennyfield, a name which still, in spite of everything else, could make him giggle if he said it enough times in a row.

This business about his father's traveling far away from them to work—something he had always done at home before—was troubling, notwithstanding his mother's conspicuous efforts to treat it as a matter of course. Why did he want to leave home? He knew other five-year-olds whose fathers had left home and then never, or rarely, came back. He knew that if he asked his mother about this she would laugh, and hug him, and say reassuringly that that was not happening and indeed would never happen; yet, in spite of this, something kept him from asking.

Peter walked casually from the empty wading pool, where a soccer game of sorts was going on, to the sandbox. He was too old to play there now; he sat on the edge and watched the two-, three-, and four-year-olds playing in the cold sand with plastic buckets and shovels or simply with a sieve formed by their fingers. One little girl, with black skin and hair that her mother had painstakingly cornrowed into a pattern that held Peter's admiring attention, was trying to fence off one corner of the sandbox with her legs, in order to protect a series of castles she was building with a set of Dixie Cups. She was neither polite nor impolite about it, Peter saw; if some two-year-old inadvertently wandered over her borderline, she simply pushed him away, not hard, but without looking.

Without really knowing why, he had made the intuitive connection between his father and his own lack of ease with Peggy. "How is everything?" Peggy would say to him, squatting down, smoothing her skirt. She would put her hand on his shoulder and look into his eyes. "Did you have a good weekend?" Was he imagining all the freight of pity and earnestness in these words, the way her tone set him apart from his classmates and their presumably normal lives? The thorniest question of all, the one he had been trying and trying to resolve, was this: did Peggy's manner upset him because he knew it was wrong, unjust, a misreading of him and his situation, or because it was the first external evidence that really reached him (for he liked Peggy a great deal, though he couldn't feel close to her) that he was indeed a child marked by a special misfortune?

"Hey," he heard. He looked down; the black girl, who was probably Leo's age though she acted older, was tugging lightly on his pant leg. "Hey," she said, "watch your feet." While he had ruminated, her row of sand structures had expanded to the area just beneath him. She said it without rancor, which made him like her. There were three black kids in his class this year. He tried, unsuccessfully, to summon up an image of his mother patiently working his own hair into an exotic pattern like that.

Her miniature city had grown now to the point where her splayed legs couldn't quite encompass it; she had to rock back and forth to police it against the carelessness of the other kids. Still she kept building, with no real end in mind, only to see how long she could carry it off, how much of the sand pit she could annex before someone really resisted her. She caught Peter staring at her, and stopped working for a moment; then she picked up the biggest Dixie Cup and held it out to him.

"Get me some water?" she said.

Entranced, he took the cup from her. "What's your name?" he said.

"Tanya."

"Mine's Peter." He went toward the fountain at the end of the playground, passing near his mother, who stopped listening for a moment to the woman on the bench beside her in order to smile at him encouragingly. He wondered what his father was doing at that moment. Back in the winter (he often reviewed this for himself) his father had been beaten up by some bad man, and he had to stay in the hospital for a while until he got better. He *had* to stay there, his mother had emphasized; he wanted to come home and see them more than anything, but he wasn't allowed, because he was too sick. Peter had accepted this explanation. But others apparently saw things—saw Peter himself—differently. It wasn't just that everyone seemed to know about what had happened to his dad; he was still young enough not to be surprised by that or sensitive about it. But he was old enough, barely, to be confused by this discrepancy between the way the Soloways saw themselves and the way others saw them, and to wonder if these other interpretations—which implied that something truly terrible had happened, not just to Paul but to Peter himself, and in fact was not over yet—had any validity.

When he returned with the Dixie Cup full of water, he saw that Tanya's father had come over to the sandbox and was admiring aloud her miniature urban planning. He was short, and wore a baseball cap pulled down low over his eyes. Adults came to the edges of the sandbox all the time, if their kids were still in diapers or if they were just a little overprotective in general; still, Peter stopped a few steps away and waited until Tanya held out her hand, patiently, for the water, and her father looked at him and smiled.

"Have a seat," he said. Together they watched Tanya for a short while, as she used the water to firm up some already damp sand so she might make a tower out of two or even three Dixie Cup molds. Her first try was unsuccessful. Peter noticed that Tanya's father's eyes never stayed on the sand castles for very long; he would look to one side, then the other, then at Peter, then back to his daughter again. Peter thought perhaps he had another son or daughter at the playground to keep an eye on. At length the man turned to him and smiled warmly.

"So your name's Peter?" he said.

The boy nodded.

"And that's your mom on the bench over there?" The man didn't point or glance in that direction. Renata was chatting away and did not see them.

"In the blue coat," Peter said.

The man smiled. "This is a nice playground," he said, his eyes continuing to move. "Tanya and I have never been here before."

"Are you hiding?" Peter asked.

Victor actually started; but one look at the boy's open face convinced him that it was his own nervous demeanor, not his appearance, that had led to the question. There was no fooling kids that age. "Not hiding," he said. "Looking to see if I know anyone here. Like I said, it's our first time." In spite of the boy's unexpected question, Victor, who had been so nervous about being recognized —even though, he kept telling himself, he had just as much right to bring his child here as any other citizen— that he had actually considered some sort of disguise, was feeling more and more at ease. This playground was full of white people, and he was a young black man; they didn't look at him, ergo they didn't recognize him.

"Is your daddy here too?" he asked.

Peter was watching two boys playing with a Tonka truck right behind Tanya's back, making heedless circles and ominous gear-shifting noises; he wondered why Tanya's father didn't notice this too. "No," he said. "He's at Pennyfield."

The man pulled a comic expression, and a smile flickered across Peter's face. "Pennyfield?" the man said. "That's a silly name. What's a Pennyfield?"

"I don't know," Peter said, laughing a little now.

"Is it here in New York?"

"No. It's in Canahonta."

He looked at the boy. "Pennyfield in Canahonta," he repeated wonderingly. This was too much for Peter, who laughed at the solemn adult pronunciation of this fairy-tale-sounding name. Just then the Tonka truck flattened a whole block of carefully constructed sand homes. There was a silence as all five of them—Tanya, her father, Peter, and the two startled boys with the truck—regarded the destruction. Then, with the straight face of justice, Tanya reached out and punched the nearer boy in the chest with all her might.

Things happened very fast then. More out of shock than pain, the boy set up a howl; whereupon Tanya's father, making no effort either to scold or to console her, picked her up under his arm like a duffel bag and carried her off without a word, walking briskly all the way through the gates of the playground and out of sight. A few moments later the sobbing boy's mother came and collected him—not interested in an explanation, which her son was crying too hard in any case to supply—and they too left, along with the boy's stunned playmate, who at least had the presence of mind to grab the truck.

Peter was left there, extraneous, feeling somewhat jilted. After a minute or two he got up, walked automatically across the synthetic blacktop, and presented himself to his mother.

"There you are," Renata said brightly. "Perfect timing. We have to go get Leo about now. Did you have fun?"

Peter wasn't sure how to answer. "I met a girl named Tanya," he said instead.

"Did you now? Well, maybe we'll see her again tomorrow. I was thinking maybe pizza tonight. Okay with you?" She stood, adjusted her purse, and, smiling, took his hand;

together they walked through the gate, thinking their own thoughts.

At breakfast there was a place set aside, known as "the silent table," for those artists in residence who wanted to take care of the pesky business of nutrition and then get right to work without risk of some chance pleasantry—"Sleep well?"—puncturing the inspiration and resolve with which they had awakened. Certainly that was the implied reason for the existence of the silent table; but it must also have been understood, Paul thought, that there were those who took advantage of this tradition for reasons that had nothing to do with the elusive muse. Some people were simply bears first thing in the morning, whether at home or in a strange place; some had been thrown together with a group of colonists whom they disliked, or even with just one gregarious bore who drove others to refuge; some were just misanthropes. And some must have had Paul's own problem, though none, he felt sure, had ever come to it from quite his angle—they did not want to be asked any questions for fear of being found out as the impostors their short stay at Pennyfield had demonstrated to them that they were.

Paul knew the terror, in other contexts, of infecundity, of setting aside a block of time in which to create and then, when that perfect opportunity came, freezing up under the self-imposed pressure; he thought he recognized that panic of self-judgment in some of the faces that surrounded him at the silent table. It was seven-fifteen in the morning, on day sixteen of his stay. He could interpret in detail the fear he read on the face of the poet from Drew University, the pianist from Chelsea—upstairs in their private rooms were piles of blank pages, a full wastebasket, their most compromising secret, and they had come to the silent table in a vain effort to guard that secret, never knowing how it was written on their faces. I, too, am a fraud, Paul said to himself, though not the same sort of fraud as you; for Paul didn't doubt that he was producing more work in his little studio than anyone else in the mansion.

Absently he picked up on his fingertip the crumbs left by his corn muffin, drained the coffee from his blue and white china cup with its Pennyfield coat of arms, and rose to leave. Even after sixteen breakfasts, he felt an unconscious pang of bad manners at this moment—he had to remind himself that no one expected a word or even a glance from him, that in fact they dreaded it. He passed through the swinging door and back up the broad, polished stairs to his room. He was just ten or fifteen pages from finishing the book, which, at the rate he had been producing, meant he might well wrap it up today. Perhaps not, though, for the impending end of this project made his heart and head full, and left him in a contemplative mood.

This place was a willful anachronism, a generous refuge from the present and its demands, a church, in its way, dedicated to a certain ideal of living; and here he was secretly defiling it, scribbling away at the most commercial book imaginable. One or two of the colonists recognized his name from the papers, and so, by cocktails on the second day, everyone knew his recent history—indeed, some seemed to condescend to or draw back from him because of it, as if he had been complicit in his own transformation to pop-culture artifact, like LaToya Jackson or someone, he supposed. Still, no one knew the purposes to which he was putting his valuable residence here. The question was, was this perverse routine, this withdrawal from the culture in order to create just the sort of work that formed the base, as it were, of the cultural pyramid—was it to be considered a grimly ironic metaphor for what had happened to him in the last year, or as something more damningly concrete?

He sat on his bed and looked out the tiny window at the hills, bright with autumn color, the foliage as tightly woven as a rug. He thought about who he was, as opposed to who he dreamed he might become. The room was, fittingly, halfway between a Cape Cod summer house and a jail cell. His novel felt shockingly remote from him now, and not just because he hadn't worked on it in so long. The hard fact was that nobody in the world cared if he ever wrote it or not. The nonfiction book, on the other hand, meant a great deal to a great many people, and not just in a business sense. Where was the beauty in it? What did it signify? What hope did it have of lasting?

None. That was the point, somehow. Less than any other sort of artist could a novelist afford to cut himself off from his own time; yet cut off was how Paul felt himself to be, simply by virtue of wanting to *be* a novelist. He felt a much more authentic connection to what was an increasingly unreverenced past; he felt he was living out the deep twilight of the age of his loves, Balzac, Goethe, Flaubert, Tolstoy, Keats, Whitman, James, Forster, Yeats, Auden, Faulkner, an age he had never even known. He had thought he could refuse to live in his own time; punitively, that time had taken him up and made of him what it willed.

What was the will of his time?

It seemed to be that the occasions—and they did come up, they didn't need to be manufactured—when life imitated melodrama should be confirmed and examined and celebrated, until such time, perhaps, as the two notions themselves were hopelessly conflated. His life had been just such a nexus of the ordinary and the melodramatic, and there was little gainsaying that the world had seized upon this, upon him, and would not turn him loose until its desires were satisfied. He was simply intimidated, the more he thought of it, by the forces which had amassed not merely to witness his experiences but to turn them into bad art.

Martin and, to an extent, Spain had suggested that he was caught up in a kind of ultracontemporary process of mythology. That he had been chosen, as, say, Leda was chosen, to become a certain story, perhaps for all time, but more likely to abet the sensibility only of one's own age. All he had ever wanted was to be a creator; but still, if this were true—if his life was indeed passing into legend, if its effect was to make his experience, rather than his art, immortal—then there might be some attraction, even some ironic sense of duty, attached to it. But what was happening to him seemed destined to bring about just the opposite end—to render Paul, in the aftermath of his nominally extraordinary trial, disposable, inarticulate, ordinary, typical.

The only weapon against this process of commonality was genius—a genius which, since Paul had been manifestly unable to withstand the forces of kitsch, he was forced nearer to concluding he did not possess. This was, in the life of a young artist, the true abyss—confronting the notion, absurd as it might sound to an outsider, that one is not Tolstoy, or Shakespeare, or Picasso, or Beethoven. He had broached the subject once or twice with Renata, and she did not understand the bitter despair connected with the idea that one is merely good enough to be published and well reviewed. That sort of mediocrity, if it was his destiny, would strand the rest of his existence between two worlds. Not that a mean existence in this life was in itself scary to Paul; the lives of Emily Dickinson or Maupassant or Schubert were not cautionary examples to him, but rather like lives of the saints, to be cherished and aspired to in proportion to their very suffering. Deprivation and obscurity were easy to withstand if you knew that it would take the world a long time, longer than your life, to catch up to your genius. What it must feel like to know that!

Voices came through the wall behind his head—a pair of voices. The married sculptor who lived next door was having an affair with a woman who was writing a biography of Lee Krasner. Paul could go nowhere without the feeling that his face was pressed against the glass of some sort of genuine life, whether exalted or debased. To distance himself from their cooing, he went and sat at his desk and flipped through some of the books he had brought—far too much to read in two weeks, more like talismans to inspire him. Kundera, Yeats, Gogol, Camus, a biography of Dickens, the two volumes of Flaubert's letters. It was hard not to envy Dickens his fame. Well, not his fame, Paul corrected himself—I have that, at least as it's now understood. His centrality. His consequence.

Gogol was a hermit. Certainly it was easier then. But Solzhenitsyn, Pynchon, Salinger, they still managed the trick. Paul, anonymous and unpublished, had nevertheless failed even in his hermitage; he had allowed himself to be driven out of it. This culture hated hermits with the zeal of young Communists—hated seclusion, and hunted it where it hid.

"A novel," Kundera said, "is a meditation on existence in the form of a dialogue between imaginary characters. The form is boundless freedom. Throughout its history, it has never known how to take advantage of its endless possibilities. It missed its chance."

The silent breakfast table was easy to take advantage of, but there were other functions—cocktail hour at five, and especially the frequent evening readings in the main parlor—Paul found much harder to avoid. (He was not the only antisocial one; he could see how their absence bemused the dowager, who made the amateur's mistake of thinking of artists as a supportive community.) The idea was to read or otherwise perform the work in which one was engaged during the day. This took place in the shiny old parlor, with hors d'oeuvre and the inescapable drinks. The work was awful; but Paul shunned the company of these other writers for a different, private, more longstanding if less rational reason. He had a barely conscious superstition about not befriending other novelists, not wanting to be taken, however fleetingly, as part of a particular group or scene. For as long as he had been reading, he had had an undeniably silly but nonetheless powerful phobia about being remembered by posterity only as an incidental friend, or, worse, an acolyte, of someone of greater ultimate achievement. As much as he wanted his name to survive, better to be forgotten, he believed, than to live only as an obscure, vaguely pitiable name in someone else's biography, an Emil Weiss to someone else's Kafka, a Cosgrave to another James Joyce.

Paul thought of how he used to fantasize—at the end of a good day of writing, or even during something as ordinary as a trip to his in-laws, in order to invest it for himself with some significance—about his own posthumous biographer. What would he or she say about that particular day? What clues had Paul inadvertently left to work from? He smiled masochistically at this conceit. His biography was being written right now, he felt, by a committee of millions.

They decided on two large sausage pizzas and a six-pack of Coke; it was still about quarter to ten in the morning, but none of us had any real sense of that anymore. It was only my fear of provoking them into some further stupidity that kept me from pleading with them right then to give themselves up, so that no one was killed, and to then try our best to explain everything that had happened. The two of them, in that scenario, would still be culpable—and would go to jail—but that paled, at least in my mind, in comparison to the need to lower the ever-escalating stakes, to make it clear that all this was not what it looked like.

But that course of action never crossed their minds. They would have thought it contemptibly naive: and they were probably right. For while I persisted in dwelling on how we had gotten there, they were alive, wisely, to the present problem, which was that they were two black men with a white hostage, surrounded by police, in a city whose latent racial hostilities had just yester-

day broken the surface. They had no faith in argument, but rather in force and in symbol.

"We got to have some demands," Victor said.

A helicopter buzzed overhead; it might have belonged to the police or to a TV news department. The phone started to ring again, but Victor ignored it.

They knew that there was a politics of anger, and for the next five minutes they set about connecting themselves and their actions to it, retrospectively. They repeated and slightly honed the same sentences over and over to commit them to memory, because there was no pen to be found in the squat and because of the insistent long ringing of the telephone. I stood anxiously in the doorway between the two rooms. Finally Victor answered the phone.

"Listen up," he said in his normal voice. "These are our demands. One: that the killer of Khalid Wheeler, Wendell Fisk, be brought to justice by the government of New York City. Two: that the city pay full reparations to the family of Khalid Wheeler. Three: that a van, with a driver whom we will name, come to the front of this building—" he squinted, trying to remember—"Four, that the van contain one hundred thousand dollars in unmarked bills. We will get in, along with our hostage, and drive until we feel like stopping. If at any point, once we leave the city, we see a police car following us, we will shoot the hostage. That is all."

After he had hung up, Victor caught me staring at him. My own violent death was now very much on my mind.

"They won't do that, you know," I said, my voice shaking. I thought he must have been thinking of some movie he'd seen. "They won't agree to all that."

"Calm down," he said irritably, not looking at me. "I know that. I'm just giving myself some things I can bargain with later. Good negotiating strategy."

Within five minutes, though we hadn't heard a thing, the unmistakable smell of sausage pizza wafted under the door. We looked at each other, the same thought in mind.

"Who's gonna get it?" Felipe said.

The logical answer, of course, was me. I opened the door a crack, while Felipe stood behind it, with one hand around my belt. In those few seconds with my head outside the door, I looked around—down the damaged halls, in the dark stairwell; I saw no one, though that doesn't mean no one was there. I had to flip the pizza boxes on end to get them through the door.

We ate; and then another long period of waiting began, punctuated only by our taking turns using the non-functioning toilet. The sense of connection between the two friends seemed to me to be fading. Each of them sat alone with his as yet unlived life, contemplating either an end to that life or a radically new course for it. The contemplation of these things was evidently too private to be discussed.

When the sun went down again, all our fears were redoubled. Victor's deadline for an answer to his demands had passed an hour ago. I kept looking from one of them to the other, afraid to speak, searching their faces for any sort of clue as to the practical depth of their despair. I thanked God that the pistol was no longer in the squat—the first coincidence in almost two days for which it was possible to be grateful. As our faces started to disappear from view again in the darkness, Felipe began to show the strain; his large, bearish body appeared to me to be shaking a little, and the corners of his mouth were turned down. Victor was watching him too.

"Why haven't they called, man?" Felipe said.

"They waiting to see if we'll crack," Victor answered.

"Well, let's call them," he said. His tone of voice was childish. "Let's call them and find out what the fuck's up, tell them if we don't get our demands met we gonna ice this motherfucker . . ." He got up, as he was speaking, and walked toward the phone. Victor watched him carefully but made no effort to stop him. Felipe picked up the receiver, and his eyes became very wide.

"It's dead," he said.

"Okay," Victor said. "Take it easy. They're trying to sweat you."

"I'm gonna die right here," he said in an awestruck voice. He looked around the room. He laid his big hands upon his face. "This is the place." Suddenly he turned to me. "How old are you?"

"Thirty-four," I said in a scratchy voice.

He nodded. "I'm twenty-five. Twenty-five motherfucking years old." He turned and looked toward the door, and fell silent.

"What," Victor said. "You hear something?"

Felipe made no answer. But there was no sound in the hallway. He was hearing something else.

"They got to talk to us, at least," he said. "It ain't fair. What the fuck's the matter with them?"

"They will talk," Victor said angrily. Whatever he might have thought, his voice was not a calming influence. "Right now they just trying to sweat you."

Felipe started for the door.

"No!" Victor hissed, springing with difficulty from his mattress on the floor. Felipe unlocked the door and threw it wide open so that he could pass through with his hands up. Victor changed direction in mid-stride and dove out of the frame of the open door. But no shot came. Victor reached out and kicked the door closed.

"Hey!" we heard Felipe call out in the hall. "Hey! You got to talk to us! What the fuck is the matter with the phone? We can't see nothing in there!"

We heard his own tentative footsteps moving down the hall, but nothing else.

"Yo!" he said. "Police! You still here?"

The silence that followed this remark extended for several minutes. The light through the gaps in the windows was turning a deeper blue. At length Victor got up, locked the door, and began methodically piling the old mattresses in front of it. He wouldn't look at me.

"You think he's coming back?" I said—anxious to break the silence, to make some connection.

He didn't turn his head. "No, he ain't coming back," he said. "What do you care?"

"*What do you mean?*"

Now he turned his face to me; and I saw right away that something had changed. "Maybe he's dead," he said. "Would that make you sad or something?"

There was no one now for whose benefit he had to keep himself together. His instinct for loyalty had left him on the hook. Something had changed; and so everything had changed.

I swallowed. "I don't think he's dead," I said. "I mean we would have heard a shot—"

"What are you, trying to make friends with me now?" He came and squatted down in front of me. "Huh? Think that will work?"

His expression was volcanic. I tried to back up further against the wall. "I don't think he's dead," I repeated.

"You know who's dead, though?" He paused dramatically. "Me. My life is over." His voice was weary, intimate, as if he wanted me to lean forward to hear him. If it had been a little darker—if I hadn't been able to see his face—I might not even have been afraid.

"You could give yourself up. I'd walk out with you. They wouldn't shoot if—"

"I'm not talking about that. I mean my life is over. It's already ended. I'm talking about the life I had two days ago. I did have a life, you know, before this, before I let your sorry ass in my door. Do you care about that? Do you care to know about that at all?"

"Yes," I said hoarsely, not sure if it was a rhetorical question.

"Bullshit. You don't want to know. I'm just a young black criminal, and if they shot my head off through the window right now"—involuntarily I glanced over to the window—"you'd be glad."

I licked my lips. "What did you do," I said, "before this? I mean, what was your—"

"Shut up!" he screamed.

Then we heard a sound outside, like a door slamming. Victor's head went up; then he went into the ruined bathroom, whence I heard a kind of ringing noise and the sounds of great exertion. He came out again holding about a three-foot section of flaking iron pipe, which he had evidently torn out of the wall. He went to the front door and put his ear against it. He tried the dead phone again. At length he came back and stood between the door and me. Silence and darkness, I felt, were corrosive forces in our situation, so I spoke.

"It doesn't have to be like this," I said quietly. He started to walk toward me, to hear better, I thought. "I'll tell them it was all just a big—"

Victor hit me in the stomach with the pipe so that the air rushed out of me all at once and I fell forward onto my hands and knees.

"Don't talk," he said. "Get in the back room."

We heard the sound of heavy footfalls in the apartment directly above our heads. Victor grabbed me by the sleeve and we retreated into the bedroom and closed the door. There was no lock, but Victor pushed the two rank mattresses in front of it. He crouched down beside me as I struggled to take a deep breath.

"My life is over," he whispered, staring at the door. "My life is over. And it's because of you. You killed me."

Somehow, that first blow had served to loosen my inhibitions. My life to that point had managed not to include any really extreme physical pain. The thing I had most feared (apart from being shot) had happened—and so, in a way, the difficult part was over.

"Why are you so angry at me?" I said, quietly but still boldly. "What have I done?"

The end was near, now. The police had been waiting for night. There were running footsteps on the stairs that made no effort to be quiet.

"You don't get it, do you?" Victor said. "You see it from the center. You're the center, and that's how you see it."

"What did I do but get caught in traffic and beat up and get my car stolen?"

"What you intended," he said, "don't enter in. You're the fucking angel of my death. I work hard my whole life to stay—

and it is work, man, you can't imagine, you have no way of imagining. And then one day you blow in like some motherfucking bug or something, and that's it. It's all brought down. It's all nothing now."

We heard an amplified voice outside the squat. It might have been addressing us, but we couldn't understand a word.

"You have no idea," he went on, "about living in my world. In the old days, you had to keep your eyes down, because if you looked the wrong way at some white woman they had grounds to lynch you. Well, how different is this from that? What have I done to harm you?"

"That's just it. It's not too late to—"

"You and I came together just by chance. You saw my baby girl. I have another daughter, too."

"I have two sons," I said.

"And when this is over, you'll go back to your children. And if I ever see mine again, it'll be in prison. Is that fair?"

I shook my head no. I was very afraid of him now; at last I felt the longing I should have felt much earlier, for the police to arrive and deliver me.

"Why do you think it will happen, then?" he said. "You put it all down to accident?"

There was the sound of a crash in the outer room; Victor leaped to his feet. They were trying to break down the front door. It wouldn't take them long.

"They know I gave away the gun," Victor said.

"It isn't too late," I said. "You're looking at me in the wrong way. I didn't come here to kill you, or to do anything to you."

"A hundred cops. My life is over now. I'm a ghost. And it's because I tripped over some white man. Isn't it?" He looked at me with malevolence. "Why should some accident of yours cost me my life?"

"They're almost here," I whispered. I was crying now, I think. "You have to trust me."

"Trust you?" he said, venomously, incredulously. "Man, what city are you living in? Do you go through this life with your eyes

open? Do you see that there are other factors besides you? Trust
you? Who do you think you are, anyway?"

"Please," I said. The front door was starting to give way;
there was shouting in the halls. Victor raised the pipe over his
head.

"You think you different?" he shouted. "You think you differ-
ent?"

And, true to his philosophy, Victor set about, in the minute or
so we had left together, showing me the very concrete ways in
which I am, indeed, no different. I made myself into a shifting,
feral ball. Our voices were subsumed into the adrenalized voices
of the crowd trying to get to us, his strokes with the pipe fused
with the strokes against the door; and one of the loud, steady
blows I heard was the blow that ended our solitude and turned
me back in the direction of a permanently altered, incomplete,
but still familiar freedom.

Victor had some old friends out in New Jersey and central Long Island and even as far upstate as Wappingers
Falls; but he hadn't traveled outside the widening penumbra of suburbs since probably junior high. His mother was
seeing a man then who owned his own electronics store,
and he took the whole Hartley family to Cape Cod for
July Fourth weekend. They stayed in a wooden house near
the beach that looked deceptively like a stiff wind would
knock it over, and they swam, so tentatively, in the powerful Atlantic, each wave making them shout with fear and
delight. That turned out to be the last really good time
any of them had with the man from the electronics store,
who had passed into oblivion as completely as that store
itself.

Victor hadn't thought about that trip in many years, but
it all came back to him with surprising readiness once the
train had cleared Beacon and Poughkeepsie and he was
headed north into towns so small they lived outside any
sort of urban orbit. The Hudson was much broader here

than he had known it was capable of. Occasionally an actual island would rear up out of the water, seeming to stare with annoyance at the noisy passing train. Deep into autumn, the hills on the far bank were still a profuse riot of color; Victor tried to think what was so compelling about it—there were trees to be seen in New York, after all, and God knows there were colors—and he finally decided that it was the randomness of it all, as if the trees were doing it somehow for their own sake and didn't care if anyone watched or not. It was exceedingly pleasant to look at, and to think about, and he almost wished he might not have to get off that train at all.

It was fairly crowded for a Wednesday afternoon, particularly, he thought, if you took into account the places the train traveled to. I mean, he thought, I could understand it if we were going to Boston or Philadelphia, but what manner of business could all these people have in Croton or Saratoga or even Utica or Binghamton?

He was hungry, but he didn't dare stand for twenty minutes on the long line for overpriced, microwaved snacks in the club car; though it was proving remarkably easy to go unrecognized in this context, he didn't want to push his luck. In his own neighborhood, it had seemed at times that he was as recognizable as Jesse Jackson—people stopped him on the street, people he *knew* sometimes, to ask for his autograph—but his urgent quest for a conversation with Paul Soloway had led him to places where the society was mostly white; and those people, who would have been so scared had they identified him, were, paradoxically, too afraid of him to see him. No one on the train would even meet his gaze. In fact, he had noticed, back at Penn Station, a few other black men boarding the train—and it was they whom he was very careful to avoid. This got him thinking about the nature of his fame. Was it simply that, in this as in so many other spheres, there were two American cultures, and you existed only in one or the other? Or was it that his fame (or notoriety, to look at it through white eyes) was so outsized that it had become a kind of second identity, and people genuinely did not recognize his small, human face within, as it were, the larger, more famous one?

The train gradually slowed to a stop between stations. It was probably nothing, but Victor automatically put his hand lightly against his pocket, where the gun was. Out the window, between the roadbed and the water, were four or five railway workers, wearing hardhats and reflective vests and looking none too busy. That's a sweet job, Victor thought—looking at the hills and the river and the trains all day. In a moment the train was moving normally again.

The gun had come from an old friend who dealt near his mother's place; Victor had tentatively inquired about it during lunch at White Castle, and he had it in his hands by sundown. "No charge, man," said his friend, awed, imagining what new exploit might be in the making. It was a .45, bigger than he really wanted, though a deep pocket and an untucked shirt were enough to conceal it. A year or so ago, his sisters had bugged him about purchasing a little .22 for their mother to keep in the apartment after a break-in in the building—as Keisha had done the year before—and now he wished he had not refused. At the time, though, he had had a very sharp mental picture of his mother aiming that .22 but unable to bring herself to fire it, and of what would surely follow.

Victor didn't care for guns in general; in fact, they frightened him, and it was in that very capacity—to frighten, not to kill—that he considered them useful. They may have lost a lot of that capacity where he was from, but for this particular purpose he felt confident the gun would frighten Paul Soloway. Frighten him into what? Victor still wasn't really sure of the answer, and yet, typically, he had made the trip anyway, the trip that was now almost over.

After that trip to the 97th Street playground, he had dropped Tanya at her maternal grandmother's and gone home to look on the map for a town called Canahonta. The name was so unmelodious that he worried Soloway's boy had probably gotten it wrong somehow; but no, there it was, two hundred miles away but still in the state of New York, still, he reminded himself speculatively, within the travel parameters allowed him by the court while he was out on bail. At first he was infuriated that Soloway should have foiled him, maybe even on purpose, by decamping to such an obscure place to work on his cowardly book. But as he thought about it—looking out his mother's window, then down at the map, then out the window again—he began to wonder if this wasn't a helpful development after all, if there weren't some positive aspects to the idea of approaching Soloway at this cryptic, neutral site: away from his family; away from the crowds; away from the pressures bearing on both of them; man to man.

Maybe not frighten him into, Victor thought, so much as out of: out of the horrible egocentricity that enabled him to profit so obscenely from Victor's own and his family's enduring misery—or what was worse, to discount that misery, not even to notice it or consider the possibility of it. Out of the typically white conceit that put him at the center of everything, even a happening at which he was undeniably just a chance bystander. Out of the vulgar worship of his own feelings. Out of the complacency that would let him describe Victor's face to the world as an "unflattering stew of confusion and rage." That would let him describe Victor at all! *I* will tell the world who I am!

But here he was losing his temper again, reaching his crescendo before the scene had even started. He stood and walked up the aisle to the tiny bathroom to wash his hands and face. The metallic mirror showed him an image that was somehow both ghostly and harsh. He had a brainstorm: throw out the bullets and keep the gun. Then he thought about throwing out five of them and saving one. Then he decided that, even though he couldn't come up with a scenario in which he would have to shoot at someone, in the end you never really knew, and he put the fully loaded gun back in his pocket and returned to his seat.

Fifteen minutes later, when the train pulled away from Canahonta, leaving Victor standing on the platform, he felt as if he had traveled back in time. The train station looked more like a museum. The lush green of the lawns and the distant fields and even the waste area across the tracks was just beginning to turn a wintry brown. There were some places in the world where Victor still felt conspicuously black, and even though there were no other people around right now, this was one of them. He followed the sign and found a cab driver leaning against the hood of his car, reading a copy of the *Post*. Thin, old but spry, with brush-cut white hair, he looked a long time at Victor, not distrustfully, but with a candor that was demeaning even if not intended to be so.

"Pennyfield," Victor said, trying out the strange word.

The driver knew just what he was referring to, though. "No luggage?" he said, almost sweetly. Victor shook his head. They both climbed in.

It was a longer, more expensive trip than Victor had anticipated, past old estates of ancient excess, through an old-fashioned town, even past a racetrack, out here in the middle of nowhere. He took it all in with equanimity—the distracting novelty of it helped calm his nerves. He didn't notice the driver's frequent looks in the rearview mirror; or, if he did notice, was not unfamiliar with the phenomenon. The trip passed in silence.

When they turned up the long driveway to the mansion Victor, who still did not know anything about this place other than the name, wondered if it was all just some folly of Soloway's, to have rented himself a palace simply as an ostentatious way of disposing of some of his new wealth. But then why would he leave his family behind in Manhattan? Even after the cab parked, Victor sat there looking up at it, confused, and strangely irritated.

"Twelve-fifty," the cabby said, nervously.

Victor paid him and got out.

The cabby tried not to go too conspicuously fast back down the long driveway. When he was out on the main road again, behind the hedges, he had to pull over to calm himself down. He drummed his fingers on the wheel. "Holy cow," he tried saying. He said it a few times. Victor Hartley stalking Paul Soloway at Pennyfield. The guy probably had a gun. What should he do? Go back there and try to warn someone? Drive straight to the police station in town? Drive up to one of the other local mansions and try to get someone to let him use the phone? Stay out of it and pretend to know nothing?

He picked up the radio and called his dispatcher, instructing him to call the cops and have them meet him on the road; that was better than trying to explain everything to the dispatcher first, who was bound to get it wrong. Then he switched off the engine and waited. There were no other cars on the road. Though it was cold out, he rolled down his window and listened. His breathing still had not returned to normal. For another ten minutes he would sit like that, all alone with his excitement over having entered, by virtue of his own fascination with it, the famous story.

Renata put Peter and Leo, who were passing a cold back and forth between them, to bed a little earlier than usual, and poured herself a big glass of white wine. Before she could really settle down she had to fiddle with the living-room window—the heat in the old building was always either off or, as now, on full blast, in which case the sticky window had to be opened just a crack to keep them all from sweating. When this was calibrated, she sat down and turned on the TV, and had a first long sip of the wine, a '78 Tavel, the most expensive bottle she had ever bought. She had been unable to think of a reason not to buy it.

This single motherhood gig isn't so bad, she said to her-

self with a mischievous smile. No one to fight over the
remote. No one to share the wine with. Your word with
the kids was law without appeal. Of course, the trick was
to have a hundred and twenty thousand dollars in the
bank. Then it would be no sweat at all. She felt a little
freer to joke about it, since Paul was coming home from
Pennyfield in three days.

In less than five minutes she had gone twice through the
seventy-five cable channels without finding anything on
which her attention might snag. Muting the volume, she
went to the kitchen for the wine bottle. She was wide
awake—it was only just past eight—and didn't feel like
starting a new book; two pages into it, she knew, and the
whole pageant of George Sand would be driven from her
head, and she didn't want to let that happen quite yet. So
she went to the mantel, where the videocassettes were
shelved, in the casual hope that there would be something
there anyone over the age of six could bear to watch. And
there, strangely, in between Barney and Bop and the
Mighty Morphin Power Rangers Volume 4, was a title
she'd never seen before; *Charles and Di: Uneasy Lies the
Head.*

Charles and Di? she thought. She took it off the shelf
and looked inside the box, but there was no packaging at
all—the tape must have been made either professionally or
illegally. How the hell did this get in here? she wondered.

She popped it in the machine, and from the tacky pomp
of the opening credits, it was clear that the title referred,
of course, to the Charles and Di of the popular imagination, the Prince and Princess of Wales. It had to be some
sort of TV movie. She supposed that it was something sent
to Paul by one of the production companies that had been
after him, though why he had hung onto it she couldn't
guess. She reached for the remote again.

But by that time the movie had begun, with an American soap star—his handsomeness cut only by the fact that
he was apparently wearing prosthetic ears—engaged in a

dialogue with his mother. "Charles, you're thirty-seven," the queen said, as they sat in front of a roaring fire. "It's past time you found a suitable girl and got married. How hard can it be? This *is* 1979, you know."

"Oh, Mother," the prince said, "if only it were that easy. It's so hard to meet anyone, shut away in the palace all the time. And those you do meet, how can you be sure they're interested in you for who you really are?"

Renata put the remote down, smiling. TV dramas like this had, at certain times and in certain moods, a definite cheesy appeal that Paul never understood. He claimed to understand and reject this kind of lowbrow aesthetic, but Renata knew that that was inaccurate—it was more like he was missing a gene. Whatever the reason, his disapproval took all the fun out of it, which was why she never got to watch such things anymore.

She refilled her wineglass, trying not to giggle. "I'm in the mood for trash," she sang quietly.

On the tape, though there were no commercials, the commercial breaks themselves were marked and numbered, and before the first one had come, shy, awkward, but still dignified Charles had met Lady Diana Spencer, a tall, attractive teenager (or so the script took pains to point out; for the actress herself was closer to Renata's age) from one of the oldest, most aristocratic families in England.

"She's different from all the others," Charles said to his mother. "I think she bears herself like a princess already."

"A bit young," said the queen, playing with her Corgis. "But I think she's an excellent choice."

The condensation that went on in these two-hour TV biopics was really breathtaking, Renata thought. But condensed into what?

After the break came the famous wedding at Westminster Abbey, hundreds of thousands of dollars, Renata supposed, spent to simulate an event which was itself an expensive, universally watched TV show. A painstaking re-creation of certain images—the carriage, Diana's transposition at the altar of his middle names, the kiss on the balcony—already burned into the popular memory. Why? Of course, this version also threw in many close-up shots of the faces of bride and groom, the former teary and perhaps a little fearful but smiling, the latter struggling to maintain his royal poise though clearly bursting with love. Well, *that's* why they re-created it, Renata thought: to improve upon it in this one small way, and to have the improved version, by reason of its very subtlety, supplant the original, already dubiously real one. Twentieth-century culture is the culture of the face. Twentieth-century politics: the politics of the face. She remembered watching the original wedding on a summer morning in 1981, hung over without having slept, after an all-night royal wedding party in a friend's Yorkville apartment. She remembered the relative reserve of the long shots in the cathedral, the charming shouts of the crowd beneath that balcony: Kiss her! Kiss her! Charming because of that sense of having broken through a wall of privacy and reserve, that sense that there was a wall there to break through at all.

Renata was pretty drunk by the time the royal marriage began to hit the rocks. Diana began putting her fingers down her throat in the bathroom at state dinners. Sarah Ferguson joined the royal cast, a kind of sex-crazed fishwife in this telling of the story. Charles grew colder and more withdrawn, lighting up only around the older, more correct, but still faintly sluttish Camilla Parker-Bowles. Charles even suggested to his mother, frowning with her Corgis by the fire, that Camilla was the one he should have married, while a silently weeping Diana listened behind the door.

Then came the famous tapes, now acted out in full, of the miserable prince and princess, each cooing over the phone to a lover in what they then imagined were conditions of total privacy.

"Oh, you're just the sweetest person in the whole wide world," Diana said.

"What if I was your tampon?" Charles said. "Then we could always be together. I could live up there."

And, just like that, Renata thought of Shakespeare. Not as a way of demeaning the quality of the movie's script, which would of course have been unfair, and beside the point, for the script was perfectly appropriate to the very existence of such a TV biography. Rather, she found herself thinking of Shakespeare and the subject of kings. For centuries, really, the lives of kings had been considered worth condensing into two-hour dramas (with the occasional fudging of detail that necessitated) because they were exemplary in some way; their virtues were virtues to which we might aspire only in dreams, their flaws and demises outsize parables by which we might be gratefully cautioned. Also, the real lives of kings were then thoroughly remote, almost unimaginable; and so these dramas, customarily posthumous, took advantage of a genuine gap in the historical record.

Then what was this on the television before Renata? Something similar in form, if one discounted the quality of the writing (and it was only fair to do so: think of the hundreds of lesser Shakespeares whose royal dramas must have been swallowed up by time). But these similarities only made the differences more astounding. The drama no longer complemented the historical record, but supplanted it; the trash unrolling on the screen for Renata's diminishing amusement *was* the history—the history of kings.

The popular need had changed, and the drama along with it; the average was now the drama's ideal—an ideal for which no one had to strive. We wanted now to be taught not that those born to royalty were heroic or tragic but rather the opposite, that they were *just like us*. They think and speak and live in immediately and wholly familiar ways. The more banal their dialogue, the more melodramatic their acts, the larger that "us" becomes. They are just like us; and, to the extent that they are not, it is necessary to render them so. Hence *Charles and Di: Uneasy Lies the Head.*

Hence, she realized with a start, Paul's book. For the principle extended not simply to those born into unusual situations but to those who have distinction from the crowd thrust upon them. If democracy was the great leveler of the distinctions between people, this political evolution had its cultural correlative; the best way to democratize experience, in effect, was to commodify it. The process was awesomely refined: books into movies, movies into TV shows, symphonies into jingles, the restless material of art and of life itself moving impatiently toward its kitsch existence, the final and lasting stage. Indeed, the appetite for the TV movie was an appetite for *disposing* of experience, a way of laying something genuinely troubling to rest. Something out of the ordinary had happened to Paul, in a culture whose tidal pull was always toward the least common denominator. The book, or the TV movie that the book would lead to, was the culmination of a process, the terminal reclamation of Paul's own identity. Its purpose was to reassert the familiarity of Paul's experiences and thoughts and feelings against any evidence to the contrary. And by flattening these aspects of him into common property, this popular art was declaring its antagonism to his privacy, and thus to his uniqueness. She wondered if Paul understood all of this, or if he was too close to it.

Suddenly she felt a surge of protectiveness and pity for him. How could he be expected to get through this life without her? She emptied the bottle into her glass and watched the royal separation with tears in her eyes.

It was twenty minutes before the cocktail hour. Paul liked to get there right on time or even a little early, to have his requisite drink (tonight, maybe two or three) before everyone was there, and before those who were there could get too loquacious. He was sitting on his bed with his back against the wall, reading an old John Marquand novel he had found downstairs in the failing light from the window, when there came a soft, cautious, almost intimate knock on the door.

"Come in," he said, surprised.

Victor Hartley walked in and closed the door behind him. He looked, in evident confusion, around the tiny room with its sharply angled ceilings, its pine furniture, its threadbare rug, such a show of deprivation inside the walls of the mansion. His hands were at his sides, and the left one held the gun.

"Man, what *is* this place?" he said.

Paul had involuntarily dug his heels into the sheets to push his back harder against the wall. Every muscle in his body seemed to have gone into some kind of arrest. Screaming for help seemed out of the question. The oneiric abruptness and incongruence of this moment left him with a similarly dreamlike capacity for clear thought. The thing to do, he said to himself, is not to anger him; the way not to anger him is just to answer his questions.

"It's an artists' colony," he said thickly. "A rich woman who lived here left a trust so that the place could be used by writers or painters or musicians who needed someplace to work for a couple of weeks."

"That woman I met downstairs?" Victor said, gesturing behind him with the gun.

Paul swallowed. "Her ancestor. Her grandmother, I think."

"I told her you were expecting me."

"I wasn't," Paul said.

Victor nodded. He could see how his own calm was putting a scare into Paul. The sight of that fear, the condescension in that exaggerated patience, made him irritable again. "So you think you're an artist now, huh?" he said.

Paul looked at him blankly.

"Because of this book you're writing about me," Victor prompted.

"Oh," Paul said. "Oh. No. I was—I was an artist before. A writer. That's how I made my living."

"Is that a fact."

"So, then, you know about the book?" Paul said.

Victor scowled. "Yeah, goddamn skippy I know about it. I've read it. That's what I came here to see you about."

Paul was so shocked that it actually served to relax him, at least for a moment. "You've read it?" he said. "That's impossible!"

"It ain't impossible. It starts with some shit about going to a bakery."

Paul put his hand to his forehead. "It's not even finished," he said. "I don't even want to think about how you—"

"Well, I read the first part of it, then," Victor said impatiently. "What I want to know is, how could you even write a book like that?"

"What do you mean," Paul said, "you didn't like it?"

Victor pulled the desk chair across the oak floor and sat down across from him. "Hell no, I didn't like it," he said. "Did you expect that I would? Or I'm guessing that you never considered my opinion about it at all?"

The dream aspect of Victor's visitation was slowly wearing off. How did you find me? Paul kept silently asking. How did you get here? What do you want from me? "I thought I told the truth," Paul said. "It may not be a work of art, but it says what happened. Do you think there's something I got wrong?"

Victor shook his head wearily; his nostrils flared. "Now I'm starting to remember what it was about you made me so mad," he said. "Listen up: when you say 'truth,' you're talking about a truth that excludes me, that disregards me. You're talking about the 'truth' of your own feelings. Well, something greater than that was going on there. But you don't see it, because you don't want to see it. You just like the rest of them."

This is it? Paul was thinking. He's traveled all this way to force me at gunpoint into a debate on literary politics? "The rest of them," he said, a little less inclined to be conciliatory. "I'm not just like the rest of them, by which I assume you mean white people. How would you feel if I said something like that to you?"

"Look around you," Victor said, waving the gun in a circle around his head. "You think you're not part of something? Look at this place you're in!"

Paul nervously watched the mouth of the gun tracing a path through the air. Someone might have stopped by around now to ask if he was going down for cocktails, he thought, if only he'd been friendlier these past weeks. "And also," he said, "*they* came to *me*, they asked me to write this book. So what can I do but write it from my own perspective? Would you be any happier if I'd tried to write about what you were thinking, how you felt? Wouldn't that have been kind of presumptuous of me?"

"But you're not getting it!" Victor said, agitated. "Somebody waved a lot of money in your face, and you said Okay, I'll do it, I'll take that man's story away from him and turn it into my own. The story is about me! Without me, there'd be no book, there'd be no money, and you'd still be nobody. You didn't act—you did nothing! It's my life that was at risk, and it's still my life—I might be spending the next twenty years in jail, while you're getting rich off me!"

He was standing now, waving the gun again, unconsciously. But Paul sensed somehow, from Victor's attitude —from the appearance that he was consciously trying to make a display of his anger—that the only real danger in the room was the danger of an accident. "You know," he said, pointing to the gun, "if I could just get you to—"

"You're making money off me, but that's not even the

bad part. You're all trying to make me disappear. Well, I'm a hero to a lot of people now, believe it or not. I'm not going to kid you, I'm not going to say that I started out with that in mind—but that's what it *became*, you understand? It became heroic, it became inspirational, and you all are not going to take that away from me."

He lifted the gun and pointed it at Paul's chest.

"I want the story back," he said. "I want you to give it up. I want you to acknowledge it as mine."

"Fine," Paul said instantly. "It's yours. I never wanted it. Believe me. I never asked for it."

There was a pause. Victor had thought this was what he had come for—it felt right when he said it—but once it was done, and so easily, he wasn't sure at all what had happened, what had been exchanged. It was all so insubstantial. He felt Paul had answered too quickly, as if not understanding the gravity of the subject.

"It's because of this, isn't it?" he said angrily—meaning the gun. "Well, fuck that. I came here to talk to you man to man. This isn't what I'm about." And he tossed the gun into the full yellow wicker wastebasket beside the desk. Paul flinched, as if it might go off in there like a grenade.

"You understand now?" Victor said, more calmly. "It's not about money. I got some of that money myself. It's about respect."

Paul was waiting for his heart to start beating again.

It was growing dark outside, but Paul still didn't dare get up from the bed to turn on a lamp. One or two minutes went by in ambiguous silence. Victor was just sitting there in Paul's desk chair, thinking, head down; he appeared to be growing more depressed, which didn't seem like a good sign, and Paul wondered how this could all be brought to some end.

"So listen," he said softly. Victor looked up. "I can't stop the book. I'd give it up, give up the money, if it were just me, but a lot of it's spent. And I can't just take it away from my family. You have a family, you can understand that."

Victor nodded glumly. "I talked to your son," he said. "He seems like a smart kid."

Paul felt for a moment as if he'd been hit by lightning; he recalled, though, that he had talked to Renata and the boys on the phone just that morning, and nothing seemed amiss. "How did—"

But Victor had noticed something. He stood up and went to the desk; he picked up the sheaf of paper stacked neatly beside the old typewriter.

"This is it," he said softly, "isn't it?"

Paul was unsure what to do. "It's just a draft," he said. "There's time to change things."

Victor sat down again, with the manuscript in his lap. He looked at Paul. "I just wanted to be treated like a man. I'm not even saying what I did was right. But it happened. I have a right to be seen and heard. Why did it have to be all about you, about what's going on in your head? It's like there's a whole world out there you don't know anything about."

"Maybe you're right," Paul said. "It's not personal, though. I mean it wasn't intended as some slight to you. It's just that that's the way I'm used to writing."

Victor lifted his eyes. "You just write about yourself?"

"It's the only thing left to write about."

He laughed dryly. "Well, I hear that," he said. "If you don't make yourself an individual, no one else has an interest in it."

They were silent. The room continued to darken. The old house creaked slightly in the wind.

At length Victor stood up, with the manuscript in hand. Two or three pages fell to the floor. "I guess I better go," he said. "Going all the way back to New York. I'm taking this with me. I'm sorry."

Paul stood as well. His mouth was open. He had made

no photocopy of the manuscript. Racing wildly through his head was the renegade idea that here at last was his deliverance from the whole ordeal, in a form so fantastic he could never have dreamed of it—having his only copy of the finished manuscript, five months' work, stolen from him at gunpoint. He couldn't think clearly right now what the consequences of this might be. Whatever else it was, though, it certainly was not his fault.

"I guess I have no choice," he said finally.

Victor nodded. It was cold in the room. "Listen," he said—with some awkwardness—"you all right now, right? I mean you're better?"

Paul raised his eyebrows in confusion.

"Your leg, your head. That's all better."

"Oh," Paul said, oddly discomfited, just as Victor was, by this change in tone. "Yeah. Pretty much. I have these glasses I have to wear."

"Makes you look like an artist," Victor said. Then he ventured a mischievous smile. "So you could say," he said, "that everything's same as it was for you before, except now you're rich."

Paul regarded him without malice.

"You turned my life into a comedy," he said.

Victor looked down. After a few moments, he nodded. "I guess it would have been a lot better if we'd never met," he said.

He turned toward the door, then stopped; he reached down into the stuffed wastebasket and pulled the gun out by the butt. He looked at it in his hand, then at Paul.

"This isn't who I am," he said.

He put it in his pocket and left without another word. Paul sat on the bed and listened to the diminishing footsteps. Another wave of fear came then, and he waited for it to recede. The temporary thrill he had felt when Victor put the manuscript under his arm was gone now; in its place was a fresh sense of his own humiliation, the two of them alone in a room again. It had been childish, of course, to entertain, even for an instant, the idea that he could be so easily let off the hook; still, the only thing he could bring himself to regret about the loss of the manuscript was that it meant he wouldn't have the option of keeping this latest episode to himself.

Victor came again to the top of the grand staircase, each step so long two men could lie head to foot across it. He started down. At the bottom of the stairs was the parlor area where, normally at this hour, the colonists would have been gathered for cocktails. But no one was there now. It was all so grand and unfamiliar that he felt an urge to wave, as he descended, to an imaginary cheering throng, to acknowledge their imprecations to look at them, to gesture to them, like the Beatles or Michael Jackson or the Knicks stepping off an airplane. But Victor recovered himself. As he reached the last step, he thought, How am I going to get back to the damn train station? Across the polished floor was a small table with a telephone on it; he was reaching for it when the cops jumped on him.

EPILOGUE

PETER WAS STANDING AT THE LIVING ROOM WINDOW, FID-geting with his unfamiliar, clip-on tie, trying to turn his face with his forehead flat up against the glass, in order to see around the corner of 107th Street. It didn't really work, so he peeled his face from the window and directed his concentration instead toward the traffic light. "Red, red, red," he whispered hypnotically, until the light facing him changed to red and a new batch of cars would round the corner of Broadway in his direction.

But each batch consisted of hopelessly prosaic vehicles —station wagons, compacts, vans, a police cruiser, one battered pickup truck. Sporadically, they filed by under his nose for ten disappointing minutes. Their drabness only served to raise the flame of his glee when, finally, the magnificent, fantastically large, forbiddingly black limousine slowly turned the corner, seeming both to transform and to belittle their twilit block, as if the car itself were breathing fire. Peter's own breath had stopped. The limo rolled smoothly to the curb just beneath where he stood, and halted there. In the back seat, her own face against the glass, was his mother. She wore a black dress Peter had never seen before, and her hair was pinned up in the back. She was gazing out the window at the old apartment building, all her clouded feelings unexpectedly dispersed by the embarrassment she felt, the impatient desire for Paul and the boys to come downstairs so they could all get out of there before someone from the neighborhood recognized her in this unlikely situation.

But Peter wasn't really looking at Renata. He turned and ran down the hall, yelling, "The limo's here! It's here!" toward the bedroom where Paul was trying for the third time to get the ends of his tie to come out evenly. He had occasion to wear a necktie about once a year, and as he stared into the mirror he was wondering if the adult preju-dice against the clip-on variety wasn't misguided. Leo sat on his parents' bed, watching Paul's reflection intently. Peter burst through the door, his face flushed with excite-ment and awe.

"Great," Paul said. "Your mother's there?"

Peter nodded, grinning.

"Okay. I just need one more second." He tried again with the tie; this time the front end came all the way down to his fly. It was getting harder not to lose his temper. The boys sat there waiting, blank-faced, somehow impatient and patient at the same time like dogs taking a bath, will-ing to endure whatever it took to get them to the limou-sine ride. They had been talking about it for a week. Leo believed anything Peter told him about it, and where Peter got his own ornate ideas on the subject his father had no idea.

"Can we wait downstairs?" Peter said tentatively.

"No," Paul said. "There—got it." He buttoned his suit jacket, figuring that no one would know the difference.

It was a most generous arrangement: the driver had first gone all the way up to Putnam County to get Renata at the house, then swung back into the city for the rest of the family. The four of them had first seen that house in July, just before the opening of the Victor Hartley trial and just after the second half of the book money had come in; Renata had suggested escaping from the city for a while as a way of protecting themselves against the media, a way of not having to hear about the case every time they turned on the TV or looked at a paper or even just went to the store. "Not to your father's," Paul said nervously, and Renata replied testily that that was not what she had in mind. After a few solitary day trips, she announced that she had found them a reasonably secluded place to rent on two and a half wooded acres, set way back from the road and with a gate at the end of the driveway that actually locked. And it was close enough to the train that Paul wouldn't have to drive into Manhattan on the days he was scheduled to testify. It took Paul a while to come to terms with the idea that he was caving in to the press by letting them drive him out of his apartment; but on the day a photographer from the *Star* showed up in Leo's day camp, he agreed to it.

The trial went on until nearly Columbus Day. Paul had to be there for six full days of testimony, but he didn't really follow it after that; he had found it all too draining. It was hard just to sit on the witness stand and look at Hartley, who, depressed and abandoned, spent most of the trial with his head resting in his hands. Paul noticed that he didn't seem to have a good relationship with his new lawyer—the previous one, the famous one, had quit after Victor's second arrest, in Canahonta. Renata read in the paper that Victor's movie contract had been voided as well due to the bad publicity.

Even though, after Paul gave his statement to the Canahonta police, no legal residue of their Pennyfield encounter remained except a gun possession charge, that second arrest, and the resultant publicity, proved damning to Victor's case, in the eyes of the public and eventually in the hearts of his jury as well. He was found guilty on every count and sentenced to a minimum of sixteen years in prison. The length and the outcome of the trial both pleased Bob Spain exceedingly, as it all wrapped up the very month of the publication of Paul's book—the book he had once thought was finished, but whose theft and return necessitated the writing of an unexpected coda.

And then something happened which managed to take Paul by complete surprise. A week or so after the guilty verdict, he and Renata were silently packing clothes in their upstate bedroom, in preparation for their return to their normal life in the city, when he noticed that Renata had started, most uncharacteristically, to cry. Halfway between the dresser and the bed, still holding an armful of

T-shirts, he halted in confusion and waited until she could bring herself to look at him.

"I don't want to go back," she said. She laughed a little, through her tears, as if acknowledging that it was an amazing thing to say.

"What do you mean?" Paul said. "What does that mean, 'I don't want to go back'?"

"I don't know what it means. But I want to stay here. I know that was never the idea, but I like living out here; I like the quiet, I like it that if something goes wrong in the house we have to fix it, I like it that the kids don't have to play on asphalt all the time. I like the real weather. I just find myself thinking how much I would miss all this."

There was a long silence. Paul knew—and felt Renata must have known—that he could never live outside the city. They were fifteen miles from the nearest bookstore, the library in town had fewer volumes than the Soloways' living room, people had huge satellite dishes on their front lawns, you had to drive ten minutes just to get the *Times*.

"But it's a rental," was all he said. Then, when she didn't respond, he asked her, "You've already called about buying it, haven't you?" She nodded, not taking her eyes off him. The owner was willing to sell—in fact, she had never lived there; she had been renting the place out for four years, ever since her parents moved to Arizona.

A year and a half later, he still wasn't sure how much weight to give to her original explanation. For at the time, strange to say, they didn't even talk that much about it, because the whole thing was so much less frightening if they kept it simple: she was only asking that they buy something that she liked, something they were certainly in a position to buy. And no one was suggesting that they couldn't keep the apartment on 107th Street as well. After all, they were rich.

For, between Paul's completion of the book and the opening of the trial, Hollywood had come calling. The news that Paul's assailant had hunted him down a second time, with a gun, in order to protect his own film rights had introduced a dimly understood irony to the whole affair, which served to lift it out of the trashy realm of television and into the artier world of theatrical release. Rights went to United Artists, who quickly commissioned a screenplay and were subsequently proud to announce that Tom Hanks and Larry Fishburne had been attached to the project.

It was all one to Paul, who had to confess to himself, after the second round of publicity, that his name no longer bore any significant relation to him anyway—it now referred to something else, something not of his manufacture. Indeed, he had given up on it. In the idle months between delivery of the nonfiction manuscript and the trial, he had gone back to work in earnest on the novel. Something—some fresh perspective, some sense of reduced stakes, some awareness that he had only himself to please—had generated a delightful breakthrough, and within the year he was able to finish it, writing the final pages alone in the apartment one Sunday while Renata and the children were upstate.

But before turning in the novel manuscript, he extracted, with the help of Ned Garland, a new concession from Copeland Simonds. He wanted the novel to be published under a pseudonym. Spain was stupefied. Paul reasoned with him at great length, explaining that he couldn't let the novel, which had meant everything to him, be treated like a joke; the only way to allow it to be taken seriously was to, in effect, conceal his own involvement with it. All Spain could foresee in this scenario was lost revenue; but ultimately Paul was able to call on the reserve of good will he had built up when the nonfiction book— after heavy editing to which he put up no resistance— earned out its hefty advance in a matter of weeks, and Spain agreed to respect his wishes.

Son of Mind was published eleven months later. It was respectfully, if not prominently, reviewed; the *Village Voice*

called it "a worthy homage to the confessional art of Rous-
seau, Proust, Brodkey" and "the stirrings of an authentic
new voice in American fiction." It sold just under three
thousand copies, which was, Spain assured him, about average.

The Soloways had closed on their new house the pre-
ceding February, past the middle of the school year, so the
family stayed in Manhattan those first few months. They
traveled upstate for the odd weekend, more and more regularly as the weather warmed, and when summer vacation
arrived, they packed for a more extensive stay. Paul was
the only one with any occasional need or, it seemed to
him, desire to return to the city, whether for a book he
needed or heavier clothes or just for a revitalizing walk
down upper Broadway. He was surprised to learn, from his
semi-rural experience, just how accustomed he had become to the sensation of the multitude.

By autumn, the boys had come to think of the country
house as authentically home and, though nervous, were
nonetheless quite receptive when their mother told them
of the plan to enroll them in the local elementary school.
Much more pleasing, if also more shocking, to Paul was
Renata's announcement that she had simultaneously en-
rolled herself part time in the master's program in English
at Sarah Lawrence, a forty-minute drive away. She would
attend class in the mornings, while the boys were in
school; Paul would have the house to himself. Paul could
hardly disapprove of Renata's deciding to reroute herself
in this way, to spend her days and nights in the contemplation of some of the great books. His pleasure was alloyed
only by his utter surprise; for such an abrupt move (not
unlike the abrupt purchase of the house) had to be taken
to mean both that she was very unhappy and that the days
of this unhappiness, the meditations on it, had escaped his
notice. Sometimes, in the early years of their marriage
when she was working those unremarkable jobs, he had

felt that he was the only one in the world who knew how smart she really was. He truly wanted her to be realized.

Even on the autumn days when everyone in the family but him was in school, though, contractors the Soloways had hired to make various structural improvements sauntered all through and around the place; so Paul found himself commuting back to their apartment in the city to work on the novel. He was, he had to admit, more comfortable there anyway. Sometimes he would spend the night, rather than take the train two hours north only to arrive after the kids were in bed, and then face the same trip south again in the morning. Gradually this spontaneity turned into routine; Paul spent more and more nights on 107th Street, coming up to the country for three- or four-day weekends. Sometimes they would all come into Manhattan, for a shopping run or a museum trip or just a visit. Paul tried not to lobby too hard for these returns to the city; but it had gotten to the point where he actually felt some awkwardness about traveling by himself up to the house. He never felt as if it were really his home.

Then, about two months ago, Renata had called him in the city to say that she was coming in to see him, just for a short while, alone. He sat nervously in the living room until he heard her keys in the door. She had made the trip to tell him in person that she had become involved with another man, someone she had met at Sarah Lawrence. It had only been going on for a few weeks, and she didn't even consider it serious; but she didn't like the idea of deceiving him about it. She wanted him to know, and she said she would handle it in whatever way he thought was right.

He was silent for a long time.

"I don't want the kids to meet him," he said finally, just audibly. "I don't want them to know about him at all."

She swallowed, and agreed that that was a good idea. Then she went over and sat on his lap in the recliner, kissing his face, stroking his hair. She seemed as confused as he was.

"I'll do anything for you," she said to him. "Anything you need. That will always be true."

That the two of them were united now for something as unlikely as a film premiere was the boys' doing. They seemed able to absorb the new arrangement into which domestic life had gradually fallen—whereby all four of them were together, in the house or in the apartment, two or three nights a week—as a function of convenience, undesirable perhaps but not catastrophic; but to have their mother miss the big night in the limousine would have sent a signal to them that something had taken place between their parents that was both disastrous and final.

The limo glided across town and nosed its way aggressively onto the FDR. The driver hadn't said a word since greeting them as he held open the back door. Paul had exclaimed over how beautiful Renata looked, and she had kissed him gratefully; it was a show for the children, on some level, but it was still more than that as well. Peter and Leo, though a little itchy in their good clothes, behaved for the most part, acting only marginally disappointed that there was no microwave or TV or swimming pool in the back of the car, as had apparently been predicted by some of Peter's second-grade classmates. Paul only had to ask them twice to stop fiddling with the sun roof.

Just before the 79th Street exit ramp, traffic slowed drastically and then stopped. The driver said nothing, though the Soloways could see his neck turning red; when, after nearly fifteen minutes, they had inched as far as the exit, he pulled off and went lumbering down the busy expanse of Second Avenue. In one sense they were running late—the studio people had said more than once to be there by six-thirty—but the movie didn't start until seven-fifteen, and so Paul wondered what the hurry was. Once they came in sight of the theater, though, he thought he had it figured out.

A section of the sidewalk outside the Baronet had been cordoned off and the street cleared of parked cars. Up against the outside of the velvet ropes were assorted stargazers or perhaps just curious pedestrians. Between the ropes, from the outer edge of the sidewalk right up to the theater doors, ran a long red carpet. A formidable line of limos already waited to unload there, bending around the corner of 58th Street. Each took its turn disgorging its passengers just on the edge of the carpet. As they swung around the corner to take their place in the back of the line, Paul saw several couples making their way slowly up that red path to the theater, some in suits, some in tuxes. Flashbulbs went off in the twilight.

"We're going to get our pictures taken," he said.

As they inched closer (Paul didn't see why they couldn't all just get out now and walk half a block, but he supposed this would probably get the driver in some kind of trouble), and he got a better look at the highly orchestrated activity, he finally understood why such pains had been taken to get the Soloways to the theater early; the real movie stars were arriving now, closer to curtain time. Paul's face might be recognized, but he and his family would still be violating the hierarchy by arriving this late, instead of milling in the lobby for an hour with the studio people.

"Wow," Renata said. "There's Martin Scorsese."

"There's Bruce Willis and Demi Moore!" Peter said.

Paul noticed that, among the crowd behind the ropes—whose shouts they could now faintly hear—there was a small subsection cordoned off, maybe twenty feet from the curb, reserved for the professional photographers. These were all men, their necks and shoulders burdened with equipment, and the space seemed too small to fit them all comfortably, perhaps by design. Each time a well-known figure stepped out of a car they began jostling with one another—really quite roughly, it seemed to Paul—and, as they snapped, shouting at their subjects, six feet away, to turn and smile. Usually these demands went unheeded; both photographer and subject acted as if the space between them were a mile wide and a mile deep.

"Diane Sawyer and Mike Nichols," Renata said, laughing uneasily now.

The carpeted path looked more like a gauntlet the closer they drew to it. Paul happened to glance behind him and saw that the following limo was so enormous it made theirs look like a VW Bug. He turned to Renata, but she was staring out the other window. They moved forward slowly, a limousine length at a time. At last came their turn.

The noise that hit them when Renata opened the soundproof door was deafening, but only for a moment; it was a noise of expectation, and it died down once the four of them were standing uncertainly on the carpet, because no one in this crowd knew right away who they were. Or almost no one; Paul could hear his own name being passed quickly up and down the lines.

Renata took his hand; surprised, he smiled at her, but she was only trying helpfully to remind him to move. Unable to avoid it, he looked directly at the group of paparazzi as they passed; they stood slump-shouldered, even angry-looking, though one or two of them did take his picture. The faces of the onlookers, as they leaned forward over the flimsy ropes, took him in critically. Paul and his family were almost at the door to the theater when a great roar went up behind them.

He turned to look. Out of the enormous limo quickly stepped Tom Hanks and his wife. The paparazzi seemed to have come unhinged. "Tom!" they screamed. "Rita! Tom! Over here! Over *here!*" Paul saw one of them fall to the ground, on top of his cameras. He swore vociferously. Another photographer stepped on him. "Tom! *Tom!* God damn it! One fucking shot!" But Hanks gave just a quick wave to the rest of the crowd and a charmingly rueful smile, and he and his wife strode quickly past the pen of photographers without acknowledgment.

The actor passed right by Paul, within a foot of him, and through the door an usher was anxiously holding open. The two of them had never met, and so there was no good reason why Hanks should have recognized or spoken to him. Still, it was disquieting to Paul to be so thoroughly invisible, so ghostlike, to the figure whom, as far as this world was concerned, he had become.

"Asshole!" Paul heard a voice yell after them. "Fuck you too!"

He turned back toward the street and saw that, in the photographers' area, a shoving match had broken out. Yet most of them, he could see, were still looking after Hanks, and their livid curses, to Paul's amazement, were certainly directed at the star. At that moment, though, another limo door was opening, and the flashbulbs fired again, so many and so continuously that they formed one flickering light.

"Paul," Renata called. She was holding the door. "It's five of seven. There's a big line for the free popcorn."

"I'll meet you there," Paul said. He was starting to understand the popularity of movie stars, an intimate popularity without precedent in the history of the world. It went beyond their immanent glamor, and it went beyond their acting talents; movie stars could in fact be seen to live instructive lives. Forever being interviewed about the state of their marriages, about their childhoods, their addictions, their sins, being photographed every time they stepped out of the house—that is, when they weren't inviting the photographers *into* the house—they laid themselves open, sacrificing the possibility of a private life, but the beauty of it was that, all the while, they insisted, they *believed*, that they would tolerate no such sacrifice.

Yet apparently this practice was not without its conflicts, its opposing forces. What a perverse, impoverished vestige of private life it was, to arrive at a movie premiere in a limousine and then walk within a few feet of the army of photographers while refusing to look directly at them. But they hated you for it. They *hated* it. It was really only a kind of degraded relic of privacy the movie star was working to sustain at this point, but they would do anything to strip him even of that. Paul studied them. They were fighting more openly now, their shouts to the famous faces decidedly not seductive or even friendly, lit by the penumbra of their own constantly flashing cameras, shrieking and hopping, little spirits consumed in the eerie matchflame of celebrity.